THE CITY OF
BAAL

■ ■ ■

CHARLES BEADLE

THE CITY OF
BAAL

by Charles Beadle

INTRODUCTION

by John Locke

Off-Trail Publications

Elkhorn, California

With thanks to Norm Davis, who invariably answers "yes" to questions like "Would you happen to have a Swahili-English dictionary handy?"

Front cover satellite photograph courtesy of:
NASA's Earth Observatory
http://earthobservatory.nasa.gov/
Back cover illustration from "The Tree of Life,"
Adventure, August 3, 1919
Cover design by John Locke

OFF-TRAIL PUBLICATIONS
2036 Elkhorn Road
Castroville, CA 95012
offtrail@redshift.com

Printed in the United States of America
First Printing: January 2007

CONTENTS

Introduction
by John Locke

THE FOSSIL RECORD shows that mankind evolved in Africa over many millions of years. At some stage in this process, small numbers of people migrated out of the continent and eventually populated the world. While civilization emerged in Eurasia, long ancestral links between destinations and origins became lost. Africa—that is to say, sub-Saharan Africa, separated from the Mediterranean by the unfathomable immensity of the Sahara Desert—became a place of legend, myth, mystery. A place to be "discovered."

To early mariners, making tentative forays from the Mediterranean down the west coast of Africa, it seemed as if the desert continued forever; an endless expanse of nothingness in return for an arduous sea voyage. It fell to the great Portuguese mariners of the 15th Century to leapfrog each other down the coast until the Africa of legend was found. Vasco da Gama achieved the great prize at century's end, rounding the Cape of Good Hope and continuing to the southwest coast of India to establish a trading route with Europe.

With Africa discovered, African history begins. Prior to that, the sub-Saharan continent left a sparse written record. What is known of earlier times comes from the interpretation by anthropologists of fragments of physical evidence—bones, teeth, pottery, iron artifacts. What is known of the events and personages we generally think of as history comes in the last 500 years. The main authors of that history, the Europeans, framed the themes—exploration, slavery, colonization—the experiences of Europeans. They "discovered" Africa—for themselves; ventured into the interior which was "unexplored"—to them. And, as in other places, "discovering" and "exploring" foreshadowed "owning."

The Africa fiction we're familiar with naturally follows this Eurocentric tradition. H. Rider Haggard featured an hunter-explorer, Allan Quatermain; and, of course, Tarzan, the greatest of African characters, was an Englishman of noble birth. Charles Beadle, the author of this collection, is no exception. His African stories take place at the height of the colonial experience, the early 20th Century. His protagonists are usually English, like himself; policemen or adventurers, as he had been. Some, as he describes in "Gifts of Diamonds," are "of the breed blessed or cursed with a mania to wander the four corners of the earth wishing there were five"; which sounds suspiciously autobiographical.

What differentiates Beadle from Tarzan's creator, Edgar Rice Burroughs, is the authenticity of his Africa. His stories reflect extensive firsthand experience of the settings he writes about. He displays a wide-ranging familiarity with the geography, the flora and fauna, the political situation, and the general conditions of life in Africa; and, with a natural storyteller's touch, he steers clear of didacticism. His brief background details effectively bring the environment to life, as in this passage:

> . . . from the land side of the village was a vista of regiments of tree-stumps in native fields hewn out of the primeval forest, fields in which women—many with babies wrapped in skins upon their arched backs—worked diligently with the small native hoe preparing the ground for the annual sowing. ("The Tree of Life")

Such detail convincingly connects the story with the wider world.

In particular, Beadle demonstrates an impressive knowledge of local tribes and customs. The relationship between Europeans and native Africans—the gulf between the cultures—lies at the heart of the stories. Indeed, observation of these uneasy relations suggests that 500 years of friction hadn't done much to bridge the cultural divide.

The fundamental question that arises is why civilization advanced across Europe and Asia while in Africa time seems to have stood still. It's by no means simply answered but much can be explained by the harsh conditions of sub-Saharan Africa. It's not the coast-to-coast jungle of storybooks; in fact, the rainforest makes up a small percentage of the land mass, in a belt surrounding the Equator. The rest consists mostly of mixed savanna and woodland. The climate is generally hot, often punishingly so. Africa has more land mass around the Equator than any place on Earth. Only South Africa, as far south of the Equator as the Mediterranean is north, is blessed with moderate temperatures. The way of life that evolved in Africa is primarily pastoral and agricultural. But the odds against success run high. The poor soil over much of the continent leads to low yields at high cost in labor.

Africa has been subject to an ugly array of plagues and diseases, the most common of which is malaria, contracted by humans and domesticated animals through the bite of the tsetse fly. Untreated, malaria can be fatal, but native Africans have built-up resistance. For them, malaria weakens rather than kills. Beadle's stories reflect the breadth of the problem, as evidenced by his incessant references to malaria, fever and other afflictions, insects, quinine, etc.:

> The following day, I think it was, that I noticed that [the dog] Kopman was doomed—the fly had gotten him, in spite of Harry's arsenic preventative. The staring coat and a slight discharge from the nostrils were sure symptoms. I pumped some more arsenic into him—when I had him bound and chained—but that would only hold him together, I knew, until the first rains or he got wet. ("Gifts of Diamonds")

Beadle even names the villain of "The City of Baal" "the Matakini," after the chigger that lays eggs under the toenails.

Quinine, an alkaloid dissolved in water, was discovered as a treatment for malaria in the mid-19th Century. Prior to that, survival in Africa by outsiders was extremely problematic and impractical on a large scale. But even in Beadle's time, premature death by disease was taken as commonplace.

If the insects and diseases weren't enough for Africa to suffer, decades-long droughts destroyed agricultural societies, leading to migrations, and conflicts with invaded neighbors. Periodic locust swarms destroyed crops. And then there was the age-old "elephant problem." The behemoths dominated Africa, roaming in great numbers, respecting no fences or boundaries, with a fondness for the kind of food that people like to grow. They were considered a gigantic pest, killed without sentiment, hunted for ivory, sport, or simple elimination. Their numbers are severely diminished now, but in Beadle's time they were a major threat to farmers.

The abundance of wild animals forms much of our impression of Africa. The continent has teemed with hostile wildlife since time immemorial, but the condition was especially acute in Beadle's time. Starting in 1890, a rapidly-spreading plague wiped out a phenomenal 90% of sub-Saharan Africa's cattle. As a result, traditional grazing land overgrew and wild animal populations soared, allowing Beadle to describe, in "Buried Gods," the view of East Africa from the Mombasa-Kisumu express as "a country in which apparently the Bronx Zoo had cut loose."

There are, in sum, numerous reasons why life in Africa has been a challenge to humans. As a result, Africa has been historically underpopulated compared to most of the world. For example, the land mass of the (contiguous 48) United States is about 31% of the continent of Africa; yet, in 1900, the population of the U.S. was approximately 57%, nearly double the density. We may theorize that the harsh conditions which restrained the human population in Africa created an instability to society; and that subsistence living on a vast scale did not lead to the divisions of labor that aggregate populations into cities and promote the learning at the core of civilization; and that the geographical isolation of sub-Saharan Africa acted to keep the outside advances of civilization from entering in.

IN FACT, THOUGH THE AFRICA OF LEGEND abounds with lost civilizations and cities, the sub-Saharan continent has no great legacy of ruins and monuments. A notable exception is Great Zimbabwe, in the nation of Zimbabwe (which takes its name from the ruins), the former British colony of Southern Rhodesia. The stone ruins of Great Zimbabwe are scattered throughout a 200-square mile area. They became of great interest to scholars during the late-19th Century. The prevailing theory in Beadle's time was that since Africa lacked the requisite architectural legacy, Great Zimbabwe must have been built by outsiders. The leading candidate was the Phoenicians, an ancient maritime culture from the area of Lebanon. "The City of Baal," in effect, is Beadle's extrapolation of what an active Phoenician city in Africa would have been like. He placed his Baal—named for the ancient god worshipped by the Phoenicians, and represented as a bull—farther inland, in "unexplored" country, as the living embodiment of what Great Zimbabwe represented at the time. Ultimately, the Phoenician theory fell by the wayside. The perceived similarities between Phoenician and Great Zimbabwe architecture proved to be superficial; and Great Zimbabwe turned out to be too recently built, its construction spanning the 11th to the 15th Centuries, more than a thousand years after Phoenicia had been absorbed by the Greco-Macedonian Empire. Great Zimbabwe, in the 15th Century, came under the dominion of the indigenous Monomatapa Empire; incidentally, the lost race that ensnares the fortunehunters of "Gifts of Diamonds." The actual Monomatapa Empire morphed into other peoples of the region hundreds of years ago.

So, when European mariners "discovered" Africa, they found not alabaster cities and men in togas, but people significantly less advanced than themselves, dressed in little or nothing, with strange languages and beliefs. The mariners were not anthropologists, and intellectual curiosity not their ultimate purpose. Trade was the justification for travel; and the slave trade quickly became the main link between Europe and Africa. The practice of slavery predated the coming of the Europeans, making it easy for them to enter into and expand the commerce. During the trade, native Africans brought captives to the coast to be sold; the victims, spoils of battle or the plunder of raids.

Europeans traders didn't have to brave the interior to capture them. Slavery persisted in Africa after the trade to Europe and America had been abolished, which explains the frequent references in Beadle's stories. The lost races of "The City of Baal" and "Gifts of Diamonds" keep slaves, but it's also clear that contemporary peoples, so to speak, also keep slaves, such as the tribesmen of Basayaguru in "The Tree of Life."

Slaves represented cheap labor. They also represented the contempt of Europeans for different people—dark-skinned *and* non-Christian—without which they couldn't have justified depriving them, as a matter of law, of freedom. But even after moral outrage back home led to the abolition of the slave trade—after three centuries— functionaries in the field retained the contempt, clear from the language of Beadle's characters. Early in "The Cave," the first story here, a British police trooper describes a native as a "fool nigger." "Nigger" and similar racial epithets occur occasionally in the dialogue, a natural consequence of Beadle's authenticity. Most of Beadle's characters are Englishmen in the employ or ex-employ of the Empire, and the word "nigger" was common in the British Empire as a description of dark-skinned peoples. Of note, the epithets do not appear as verbal abuse from a white to a black. Instead, they are descriptions shared between whites, a seeming affirmation of their common understanding of racial superiority, as in this passage:

> "You must have," agreed Pete. "For that's rot. Can't work up a theory of a nigger using a battery, and anyhow he'd have to carry some powerful battery to kill a man so quick. ("White Magic")

Today, "nigger" is generally, and somewhat dramatically, regarded as the worst thing a white could ever say to a black. The word has attained a political status well-elevated above its weight at the time Beadle was published. Evidence of this is found in the editorial conventions of *Adventure*, the magazine where all but the last of these stories appeared. Beadle's characters curse incessantly, indicated by the long dashes used to censor oaths in the dialogue. It's clear from the context that the reader was being shielded from "damn," "hell," and like terms. "Nigger" is never censored, suggesting that religious-minded readers were considered worthy of being shielded from offense, but that African-Americans, in that era of Jim Crow, or whites sympathetic to African-American causes, were of no concern. The policy of *The Frontier*, which published the last of these stories, was a bit looser. In addition to "nigger," religious oaths are sprinkled throughout the text:

> "Sorry be damned! You've cost two men's lives. Sergeant-major, put that man under arrest." ("White Magic")

If nothing else, this tells us that the censorship in *Adventure* was the magazine's policy, and not Beadle's preference. Beadle's views on race are a little more complicated. We can't draw any conclusions from his minimalist biography; we're left to examine the tea leaves in his text. As we would expect from pulp stories, he betrays no agenda beyond the desire to tell a good story. He does portray acts of barbarism among the natives—dramatic high points—but as narrator he expresses no shock. He allows the experiences of the characters to guide the mood of the reader. Beadle's understanding of native beliefs and practices do not suggest the thoughts of an ignorant or jingoistic man; in educational temperament, he seems to split the difference between the sociologist-doctor of "The Tree of Life" and the adventurers and enlisted men who populate most of the stories. While the worst of the native practices provoke revulsion, Beadle doesn't portray the natives as inherently evil; rather, as servants to their own primitive mythologies. But even this is not absolute. Beadle exploits the situation in "The White Frog" for irony, blurring the line between "white rationality" and "black superstition."

In the most dispassionate interpretation, "nigger" is a simple measurement of the perceived gulf between the races. That gulf manifests itself in other forms. In "Buried Gods," the good-natured protagonist, Dorsay Beffert, communicates his intentions to a native guide by using what he believes is a correct word, but questions the result:

> "Good Lord," reflected Dorsay with misgiving, "I wonder whether he does understand, or whether he thinks the word is some sort of magic or a white man's greeting? Heaven knows the way these minds work."

The language barrier between races makes communication problematic, compounding fundamental differences in aims and philosophy. At times, white characters voice a need for racial loyalty:

> "What d'you mean by holding me up? You're white, aren't you?" . . . "You as a white owe me an explanation for taking the side of a native." ("The City of Baal")
> "It just gets my goat to see a darn gang of blacks put it over on a white." ("White Magic")

Some whites maintain face in the presence of native characters, to keep control of the situation. Part of that, undoubtedly, derives from their attitude of superiority. There is also a practical aspect. Typically, the whites are outnumbered by the natives and the air of misunderstanding creates a fragility, a sense that control can be lost in a moment if weakness is shown. The natives act according to their own beliefs and the failure of whites to understand the meaning of appearances could be fatal:

> The order of march was to leave about nine and march until four or five and camp again for the day, as the animals could make better going in the comparative cool of the night. After that, since they would be getting into an inhabited country, this would be inadvisable lest they provoke an attack by the natives, who might suppose them to be evil spirits of the night. ("Buried Gods")

MODERN AFRICAN HISTORY starts with the discovery of diamonds in South Africa in 1867. Diamonds are formed at great depths and forced to the surface by volcanic pipes, a rare formation. Most diamonds are mined from the mouth of the pipe; some will be found in nearby alluvial deposits. South Africa's pipe, by far the world's most prolific, is a site named Kimberley. The claims on the land were eventually consolidated into the De Beers mining company, under the control of Cecil Rhodes and others. (Though founded by the Dutch, the South African Cape Colony came under British control in the early 19th Century.) In 1885, gold was discovered elsewhere in South Africa. This mineral wealth, and the alluring possibility of discovering more is dramatized in "Gifts of Diamonds." The main character, Brandon Harvie, writes in his diary:

> With what little cash I had left I went off to South Africa, intending to find a second De Beers, arguing optimistically that if there was one there must be another. . . . I tried East Africa, still chasing stones. . . . I did find a likely pipe down German East. . . .

When he hears of a friend who has caught wind of a "second Kimberley," the story is off and running. The long-awaited confirmation of the rumor is appropriately dramatic:

> Honest to ——, at first I thought I had gone insane and then I nearly swooned—for there were seven stones as big as pigeon's eggs, diamonds beyond question!

But Beadle's story is as much about character as treasure:

> What insatiable greed a man has! It never even occurred to me to be content with that handful of kings' ransoms. I steadily set in to get more drunk on the possibilities that the river-bed would yield.

The issue is "Africa's greed," as the doctor in "Buried Gods" calls it. "Gifts of Diamonds" tells a story of foiled motives, and comeuppance; of Africa turning men's greed against them. One senses Beadle's approval of the retribution.

The events that sparked the "scramble" of European colonialism in Africa came at the instigation of King Leopold II of Belgium, who, with private financing, started developing the Congo basin. The public motive was altruistic, the desire to uplift Africans; the private reason, which Leopold concealed with great craft, was the untold riches that might be found. His actions led to dissension in Europe, eventually resolved in the 1884 Berlin Conference that led to major portions of sub-Saharan Africa being divided among European powers. At first, the major export from the Congo was ivory which, though lucrative, ultimately didn't cover the debt. Leopold's venture may eventually have gone broke but for fortuitous timing: the rise of the bicycle and motorcar, and the need for rubber, abundant in the Congo. Rubber, extracted from rubber trees and vines, is a sustainable resource if managed properly. In the Congo, it was not. Native workers, of all ages, taken by gunpoint and treated as disposable beasts of burden, were forced to harvest the region's rubber at ever increasing rates. The Congo became home to the worst of European exploitation, an African holocaust.

This was the backdrop for Conrad's *Heart of Darkness*; and the inspiration for the references to rubber that turn up in Beadle's stories.

Beadle frequently refers to Arabs and Arab-influence. In the period before the arrival of the Portuguese mariners, Arab traders established an Islamic presence down the east coast of Africa. Ivory, gold—and slaves—were taken to the Arabian Peninsula. In the colonial era, the scourge of "Arab" slave-trading was used to justify the "civilizing" intervention of Europeans; though, by then, the "Arab" slave-traders were actually

African Muslims. The most prominent was Tippu Tib who, for a time, ruled the eastern Congo. His slaves, though, were provided for the acquisition and transport of ivory and rubber, for Leopold's private empire. ". . . your confounded people ruined the vine rubber ages ago," the English doctor says to his Arab interpreter in "The Tree of Life," which takes place in the French Congo, north of the river from Leopold's domain; certainly, a reference to Tippu Tib and his ilk. It's a curiously narrow remark, in that it ignores the greater question of European complicity. A little later, the obsequious interpreter, making reference to their native hosts, sets the doctor straight:

> "These peoples have, as you know, Doctor, been much influenced by the incursions of my own people. They were at one remote period the storehouse of our slaves, although in these days of your exquisite civilization one is compelled to take tribute in the form of merchandise only."

These remarks accord with the post-1900 time period for the story, when Leopold's true nature had been uncovered and exposed, facts of which Beadle would have been very much aware.

BEADLE WROTE AUTHENTIC STORIES, of the sort the great pulp *Adventure* prided itself in publishing. But what is meant by "authentic" in Beadle's case? A rigorous fact-checking finds him obedient to his settings: the geography, the political and historical context, the nature and location of native tribes, the nationalities and attitudes of his assorted characters. He doesn't write of historical events, but his stories reveal things that history conveys imperfectly, the points of view of commoners. What he excels at is using his firsthand experience as a foundation for sensational, sometimes fantastic, stories.

Who then was Charles Beadle? *Adventure* routinely published letters from authors in a back-of-the-book column, "The Camp-Fire," often in the issues containing their stories. Dispatches from Beadle are uncommon, however he did supply brief biographical notes intended for publication with his first story for *Adventure*. His letter, delayed in the mail, appeared a month-and-a-half later, in the issue with his second story (July 3, 1918):

> My native heath is somewhere in mid-Atlantic. I was born rolling and have been ever since. No moss. My infancy was spent around Siam and the farther East: early memories, fire-flies, mosquitoes and ayahs. Educated at boarding-schools in England; hence no home life and consequent atrophy of the sentimentalities. Parental Government required me to become a consulting marine engineer; but a congenital dislike of work and a gaudy poster persuaded me to learn poker, to starve in Cape Town where I held down a waiter's job for four hours, and to join the British South African Police.
>
> Too late for big rebellion but kindly chief got up a small one to console me; saw Boer War in B.S.A.P., Morley's Scouts (unpaid Looting Corps) (if any of the Scouts should read this should be glad to hear from them) and Stock Recovery Dept. After Peace held various jobs from three days to a week—in a news office, a bar, hawker, insurance agent—and peddled cheap jewelry for three months (and made money!); served in Transvaal Customs and became Asst. Compound Manager to the Witwatersrand Native Labour Association.

Then I raised a syndicate to finance me for an exploring-trip on the headwaters of the Zambesi. Returned to London to promote a company; failed—of course. A head on a coin sent me to British East Africa and Uganda; native trading, running transport from Victoria Nyanza to the Kilo Mines, Congo; shooting and various ventures. England again, company promoting; and failed again.

Went to Dutch Borneo, rubber planting. Afterward returned to go to Morocco; penetrated into interior in disguise during rebellion; met Pretender Sultan, Mulai Hafid; instead of cutting my throat or crucifying me as predicted he gave me a palace and an escort and treated me as an Ambassador; eventually I failed and Hafid lost his throne. We both had a royal time, anyway.

Until I came to America last year I have lived in France.

The following Beadle comments, from the June 20, 1922 *Adventure* containing "Gifts of Diamonds," provide insight into how he folded his personal experiences into the stories:

The inner yarns on which the plot, if you like, is founded are historical, the strangulation of the priests by the Monomatapa, a chief who did reign over an empire as told in the story. The center of his kingdom was in ancient times in the Mazoc valley, Southern Rhodesia, and his lineal descendant is now called Mudojumbo and he lives on the Urania. I've met him in Police days and he it was who was responsible for nearly all the Mashona Rebellions.

The dogs Kopman and Oompie I had on an exploring trip with me. When passing the Zambesi I had to leave one behind because of the fly and regulations, and when I returned, I found the beast madder than ever, stuck on an island in the middle of the river because the Boer with whom I had left him was scared to death of him. Also the Wheeler in this story is drawn from the life of a man once on safari with me, the incident of Oompie following Kopman outside and the threat to shoot me and afterward the fantastic challenge to a duel at a hundred yards with elephant guns! Yet that chap was one of the best—in civilization. Afterward, off safari, we were great pals, but never again as a partner on the trail, thanks!

The "big rebellion" Beadle was too late for, a native uprising, occurred in Southern Rhodesia in 1896. The Boer War he participated in lasted from 1899-1902. These events define the window for his arrival in Africa. Overall, his Africa travels show a steady northward trend: South Africa, Southern Rhodesia, the Zambezi River, British East Africa, Morocco; with side-trips to England and Borneo. The Morocco rebellion he refers to occurred in 1908, when Mulai Hafid became Sultan. Abdelhafid abdicated on March 30, 1912 and Morocco became a French protectorate, which narrows down the window of Beadle's departure from Africa to those dates. Additionally, the Morocco experience suggests a linkage to France, which may have been his next port of call.

Though his backgrounds are solid, it's worth pointing out that Beadle is occasionally imprecise in his nomenclature. He refers, for example, to the Albert Lakes. Lake Albert is part of a complex called the Great Lakes, of which Lake Victoria is by far the largest. Whether "Albert Lakes" represents a shorthand usage, an incomplete knowledge of the geography, or a lapse on the part of a writer drawing upon aging memories, is hard to say. It's easier to conclude, though his stories are peppered with native African terms, he lacked fluency in the languages. For example, in "Buried Gods," he frequently refers to the Wakikuyu tribe. The Kikuyu is, in fact, a large tribe in Kenya (British East Africa), where the story takes place. In Swahili, prefixing "wa" to a word means "belonging to." So it's correct to say "Wakikuyu," meaning belonging to the Kikuyu tribe. But a phrase like "god of the Wakikuyu" is awkward in strict translation. In "The White Frog," Beadle uses the crudely phonetic "Sintabilli" in reference to the Sindebele language of the Ndebele people. These and other examples suggest that Beadle's knowledge of Africa didn't venture too far past the experiential, that some of his facts were garnered through oral communication. (In this collection, interpretive issues like "Wakikuyu" have been left as is in the text. Clarifications are made in the Glossary.)

Like Edgar Rice Burroughs, Beadle seems to have gotten a great deal of varied experience behind him before sitting down to write. He may have been weary of the "rolling" by then. It's likely, after his sub-Saharan days, he suffered from malaria; it would have been a small miracle if he didn't. Though treatable then, malaria was still a chronic affliction.

The first Beadle publication we're aware of is a novel, *The City of Shadows: A Romance of Morocco*, published in England in 1911. This was followed by *A Whiteman's Burden* in 1912 and *A Passionate Pilgrimage* in 1915. There were also English magazine appearances in the same period. We know of no publications between *A Passionate Pilgrimage* and his first appearance in *Adventure* in the May 15, 1918 issue, by which time he was living in America. It's reasonable to assume the conditions of World War I compelled him to flee France. He doesn't hint at involvement in the war, and since none of his work appears to be war-related, it's unlikely he served. One war, the Boer, may have been enough.

Beadle eventually contributed 26 stories to *Adventure*. Arthur Sullivant Hoffman, *Adventure's* renowned editor, must have thought highly of him since several of his longer works, "The City of Baal" and "Buried Gods" included, lead off the magazine. Two of the 26 stories were serials, the 4-part *Witch-Doctors* in 1919 and the 3-part *The Land of Ophir* in 1922. He also published a 3-part serial, *Through Rabat's Eyes*, in *Argosy* in 1919, one of several pulp stories he set in Morocco. In 1922, *Witch-Doctors* was issued in hardback in England and the U.S. It was widely reviewed in American newspapers. In general, Beadle received praise for his fascinating African lore, but reproof for his novelistic skills. The stories in this collection tend to confirm the assessment. Though he possesses great narrative gifts, his stories exhibit an occasional lack of polish in the plotting and a frequently awkward prose style marked by overlong sentences.

He may have had some disagreement with *Adventure* in late 1922 or early 1923, when his string of regular appearances came to an end. He appeared in *Adventure* only two more times. It probably wasn't due to decline in quality since "White Magic," from the March 1925 *The Frontier*, is every bit as good as the *Adventure* stories. Perhaps he was refused a word-rate increase and left in protest. After *Adventure*, Doubleday's *Short Stories* appeared to become his publisher of first resort. He appeared in the magazine as early as the June 10, 1924 issue and as late as October 10, 1933. He made a reappearance, as it were, in *Short Stories*, starting in the middle-'40s, but these were likely reprints. He all but vanishes from the pulps after his last *Adventure* appearance in the April 20, 1925 issue. This may be the time he returned to France.

It also presages a series of books that begin to appear: *The Blue Rib, etc.* (1927), *The Esquimau of Montparnasse* (1928), and *Expatriates at Large* (1930). *Expatriates*, an experimentally structured novel, revolved around the experiences of bohemians in postwar Paris. It was his second novel published in the U.S. and the second to receive weak reviews. (*Expatriates* may be an American retitling of *Esquimau* [i.e. Eskimo]. *Esquimau* was published in England, whereas *Expatriates* was published in the U.S., and they share the same setting.) The *New York Times* criticized *Expatriates'* "superficial technique." *The Saturday Review of Literature* wrote, "the work is formless, lacking in all trace of dramatic development, in coherency of situations, and sanity of characterization." It appears Beadle was attempting to make the heavenly ascent from pulp adventure to literature and failed; an outcome, according to his bio, he was accustomed to.

His next two books, *The White Gambit* (1933) and *Dark Refuge* (1938), were both issued by Paris publishers. The latter volume essentially provides the closing quote to his career as we know it—although a more fleshed-out bibliography might tell another tale. If we assume he was born about 1880, perhaps a few years earlier—which fits the circumstances—he would have been at least fifty-eight when *Dark Refuge* came out, not remarkably young, had he died about then.

"AFRICA SEEMED TO GET IN MY BLOOD," the explorer, Warren-Dukely, says in "The Tree of Life," and that may reflect Beadle's own feeling for the continent. These thoughts of Dorsay Beffert's from "Buried Gods" echo the voice of experience deepened, perhaps, at some drastic moment:

> He was conscious, too, that he had grown older; that if ever he escaped he would be a man, no longer merely a careless boy bent on seeing something of the world.

The 1985 film *Out of Africa* (based on the memoirs of Isak Dinesen) depicts Kenya from about 1914 through the early '30s, a period not long after the time of Beadle's Africa stories. The film is a lament for an Africa of vast, unspoiled beauty whose time is ending. As seen from a biplane near the end of the story, the plain is scarred with the tracks of a new kind of safari, conducted by automobiles bearing tourist-hunters. In short order, Africa passed from a place where man huddled for safety in fenced-in kraals to a place where rangers herded wildlife onto game reserves. Man, once the endangered species, switched roles with the beasts. "The wild, threatening voices of Africa"—in Beadle's words—were silenced.

Beadle is one of the last spokesmen for the Africa of legend, preserving the mystery of distant places in words. He portrays a world where a man could test himself against an unforgiving, unpredictable environment in pursuit of experience, knowledge or fortune; where the only law is native superstition; where survival carries little certainty. The very stuff of adventure.

Africa in the 1890's

Adventure, October 3, 1918

The Cave

THREE TROOPERS of the Rhodesian Mounted Police sat in a round hut facing three civilians.

"Well, we're mighty glad you're here," said the eldest, a tall man in worn khaki; "although"—he passed a lean hand over his beard—"although what in —— use you'll be without a machine gun, I don't know. I thought you had one at Motokos?"

"We had," assured the senior trooper, Blake, "but last year they commandeered it for the Mrewa affair and we've never got it back. I've had one on requisition ever since, but you know what the headquarters are. Is it going to be serious?"

"You'll probably know all about it by sun-rise tomorrow," asserted Newman Smith. "Did you notice that all the gully *kraals* are deserted? Munojumbo started it; but the loss of that fool nigger in No. 1 shaft fixed it—gave 'em the excuse the witch-doctors wanted. And since then the Uranya people have joined them. The drums have been going all night."

"Well," said Blake, lighting a cigaret, "there're six whites and eight Black Watch and they're Angonis, and'll fight like tigers. That's fourteen guns."

"Yes, but we haven't got a well on the top of this hillock."

Blake and Newman Smith walked to the door and stared over a line of sandbags down the flat gully, which had once been a river bed, where the heat sizzled upon the blackened maize fields and scrub.

"You see we can't cover the well without a gun, and the first thing they'll do will be to poison it."

"—— headquarters!" muttered Blake.

He gazed contemplatively over the boulder-strewn *kopjes* to the southwest where, about three miles away, rose a conical hill above its fellows.

"Do you happen to know the altitude of that chap over there?"

"Two thousand seven fifty," replied Newman Smith promptly.

"Good," commented Blake, reflectively. "I could pick up Mrewa from there with the hello."

"You'll never get through by daylight."

"I know. We'll make a night dash, and get the morning sun. Moon sets about three, don't it? We'd better start at the half-hour. They'll probably attack at dawn, and you can keep 'em amused and give us a chance to get through." He turned to the other troopers in the hut. "Charleton, you're the lighter, so you come with me. I'll leave you in charge, Carter. And if we don't get through you can tell headquarters to—but I guess you won't if we don't. And you'd better let Charleton have your mare. She's faster. It's a dash or nothing. Come on, let's have a drink!"

As the silver of the moon faded to the deep sapphire of starlight the horses were saddled, water-bottles were newly filled and heliograph stands strapped to the saddles. Carbines were left for the benefit of the besieged; revolvers were handier. At the half-hour the two men mounted; dim shadows in the gloom. Camel, who had been a water-cart horse of the Dragoons in the Rebellion of '96, towering above the ex-polo pony, Lady, for even a smart corps can not be particular where salted horses are necessary.

From the hillside came the distant throb of drums. A jackal yelped intermittently down the gully. A grip of the hands, a whispered "good luck," and they were gone down the farther side of the hillock.

Camel's great hoofs clattered alarmingly upon the granite outcrops; but once they had reached the soft soil of the river bed they plodded along quietly enough. Blake dared not enter the denser woods bordering the *kopje*-side for the ground was thickly strewn with boulders.

Twice they pulled up to listen. Still continued the drums and the chanting. A distant hyena yowled dismally. They gained the last of the maize fields and entered the light timber and scrub beyond. Blake sighed.

"I guess we're through!" he whispered. "Look, there's the dawn!" Then his keen eyes caught something which moved. "Quick! Left! Canter! Gallo-p!"

They drove home their spurs. Camel grunted and plunged away. A loud yell rang out. The bushes vomited figures. As Blake filed behind him other forms rose up in their path. Cries and yells sounded on all sides. Charleton fired. Came a terrific report and a flare of flame almost under Blake's horse. Both animals swerved violently.

"Run for it!" shouted Blake.

Spurs assisted fright in the speed of the two horses. Ponderous Camel, whose canter was like an earthquake, lay down to it like a hartebeeste. Lady shot ahead. Yells and another crash of a blunderbus came from behind them.

As Camel thundered across a piece of bare ground the dim form of Lady disappeared. A crash as of undergrowth was followed by an exclamation and a hearty curse. Blake pulled up.

"What's the matter?"

"Hole," came Charleton's voice. "——! My leg's caught. Go on!"

Turning 'round in his saddle Blake stared down the back trail.

"Try! For God's sake!" he shouted. "Quick! I'll hold 'em off."

The snorts of the pony and Charleton's curses mingled with an outburst of yells. Blake fired at a moving object. A scream followed and a renewed outburst of yells reverberated in the adjacent *kopje* as Charleton shouted:

"I'm free! I'm free!"

Blake fired again and heard Charleton's exclaiming—

"Oh, my God, Lady's done for!"

"Up, quick, you fool!" yelled Blake emptying his revolver, and kicking free his off stirrup. "Quick! Leave her!"

As he felt the weight and Charleton's hands around his waist, he drove home the spurs. Charleton opened fire. But Camel, terrified, pulled stupidly at his bit. Blake cursed and punched Camel's head to get him 'round. A form rose out of the grass almost beneath them as Camel jibbed. A spear glinted in the pale light. Charleton fired point-blank. Camel bounded forward as the warrior twirled and dropped into the grass.

"Game-trap!" gasped Charleton as they galloped. "Broke her back, I think. Oh, ——, I can't even get the cartridges in!"

"——!" Blake's legs were desperately drumming the flanks of the horse which was blowing heavily. "What the devil's the matter with the beast!"

The answer came as Camel crashed forward, throwing both riders over his head. Blake was on his feet first.

"My God!" he exclaimed, "he's done, too!"

In the flanks stuck a spear flaying violently as the beast struggled.

"We must run for it! Only chance!"

"But I've lost my gun!" ejaculated Charleton.

A yell close at hand echoed in the *kopje*. Charleton stared disconsolately around.

"Don't stand there like a ——— fool!" shouted Blake. "Make for the hills! Come on!"

They went off at a lope. The denser forest of the hillside was about a quarter of a mile away. On the fringe they paused to listen. The savages were hot on their trail, an easy trail made by their boots in the soil. Cries to one another sounded near at hand. Suddenly came a distant crackling of rifles.

"They're at it!" exclaimed Blake. "We must ha' run into a fresh party! ——! Come on!"

They ran on up the hill slope, their boots ringing on the granite outcrops.

"Ought to be—a scream—other side," panted Charleton. "Lose 'em."

"Never do it," gasped Blake. "Look out for a cave."

The roar of a musket, a yell and the smack of a pot-leg on an adjacent boulder drove them to racing speed. The yells were repeated close behind.

"God, I'm nearly done!" gasped Charleton.

Up, up they struggled, stumbling over loose stones, slipping on rock. Their lungs seemed to crackle like brown paper. The boulders grew thicker and bigger as they mounted. Again came the bang of a musket as they scrambled across an open ledge. A yell drew a hurried glance to the bronze form of a warrior leaping from boulder to boulder.

"Double!" panted Blake.

They dodged 'round a great conical boulder. Charleton's boots skated on rock. He sat down.

"I'm done!" he choked. "Go on!"

"No, no!" Then with a triumphant gasp: "God! Here!"

Immediately behind Charleton was a hole which appeared to be the entrance to one of the caves with which these *kopjes* are honeycombed. Charleton threw himself forward, and followed Blake on hands and knees into the darkness. They crawled hurriedly at first, very conscious of a possible shot into the cave; then more cautiously began to feel their way. The darkness was as dense as sepia; but the sounds of their movements echoed vastly. They lay still and listened, trying to control their breathing. The gray of the dawn was a pale smudge like the indefinite sense of light caused by pressure upon the eyeballs. There was no sound save a drip of water; each tiny splash magnified to a fantastic *clop* like the beat of a failing heart.

The labor of the lungs seemed like the panting of a great beast; other sound was there none.

"D'you think that they've missed the trail?" whispered Charleton.

"Crossing that ledge has put 'em off—probably. Listen!" Faint cries were just audible. "Perhaps they think the caves are haunted—got any matches?"

"Yes." Charleton fumbled. "Oh, ——, I've sprained my wrist or broken it. Funny I never noticed it—ow! Yes, here they are. Have you?"

"Yes, of course—I—oh, confound it! It's chocolates—and oh, my God, I've lost my cartridge pouch!"

"Doesn't matter. I've got plenty."

"Sh!"

A shout outside startled them. The grim glow of the mouth of the cave was obliterated.

"Quick! They've trailed us!" whispered Blake.

More shouts, the rattle of loose stones and the light blinked as they scuttled like crabs into the recesses of the cave. Some loose objects tinkled musically in their passage over the rough floor. A spurt of flame illuminated furrowed walls and a yard of curved roof as a lightning flash would do. Then a deafening concussion half-stunned them as they flattened their bodies on the ground.

The impact of a pot-leg or chopped wire against the cave walls showered them with splintered rock. The drip of the water pierced the roar in the ear-drums like a steel punch going through an iron plate. Blake screwed his head 'round from one side to the other seeking the glow of the entrance. The light blinked several times and remained open. The murmur of voices came.

"What's happened?" whispered Charleton.

Blake fumbled with his hand to silence him. He touched rough rock only. The light went out again; stones rattled; some one grunted. They were entering the cave.

Instinctively Blake scrambled on in the darkness. Voices reverberated. He plunged on again hurriedly. He bumped his head into a wall; felt with his hand and followed it. Again came a blinding flash and a terrific concussion. Only a vision of the rock in front of his eyes remained. As he listened intently the drip of the water sounded farther away. Voices mumbled. He peered to the right for the light; then to the left. Blackness.

"There must be a man in the entrance," he thought.

He lay rigid.

The murmur of voices died away; only the solemn *clop-p clop-p* remained. He stared anxiously. Blackness. Strange. What were they doing? Where was Charleton. He put out his hand. Nothing. He crawled on, fumbling cautiously; and on again. Empty air. Queer. And yet again . . . He stopped; listened.

Clop-p! clop-p!

Ah, he had mistaken his direction and crawled away from the wall. But where was the light—and Charleton? The niggers couldn't stop right in the entrance all the time. He strained to see. Blackness. He sat very still. Unconsciously he had visualized the cave as round; but these *kopjes* were honeycombed with caves.

"Charleton!" he whispered.

Clop-p! Clop-p!

Then in a very loud voice—

"Charleton!"

"—rleton!" came back to him.

"Oh, God!"

"—od!"

Spasmodically he pawed at his eyes. Utter darkness. Panic shook him. He controlled himself. All sense of direction was lost. The longer he tried to think the more confused he became. He clutched at his revolver—but there were no cartridges; and even his sense of touch appeared to have gone wrong, for his own body felt queer. And matches!

"Oh, God!"

"—od!" mocked him.

What had happened to Charleton? Where was he? Action clamored to stop imagination. He began to crawl—on and on—and on.

But perhaps he was crawling in a circle. He sat still. Fool! Why not walk? He stood up cautiously, queerly uncertain of his equilibrium. But he strode forward boldly, hands out fumbling; wincing at imagined obstructions. A blow on the head knocked him down.

He hit out wildly, thinking that he was attacked; then he sat still, scared, realizing that the roof was low. After ten seconds of pawing the air around him he began to crawl again. He was conscious of an unpleasant odor. At last his nail scratched rock. He stopped; listened; shouted strenuously.

"—rleton!"

The mocking echo drove him on in desperation—to the left, having no choice. He came upon a sharp corner. He wriggled 'round hopefully, staring for a glimpse of light. Odd things rattled beneath him with a musical twinkle. The wall curved 'round; made a sharp bend and came to another abrupt corner. Queer. He stretched out a hand—and touched the other side. Unconsciously he had crawled through an aperture not four feet wide.

Despair paralyzed him. The caves might be miles long like a bee's hive. He sat deadly still, listening to that infernal *clop, clop-p!* Was Charleton lost, too? Was he killed? What was this horrible stench? Thoughts tore through his mind—ever centering upon his own predicament—buried alive!

He started violently. Something was moving.

"Charleton!" he screamed.

"—rleton!"

He groaned; listened. Something was breathing. He stared. A dim spot of phosphorescent green kissed his aching eyes. The distant mouth of the cave! But there were two spots!

Charleton was . . . But human eyes do not shine. Blake remained rigid, staring. That stench! His fingers touched something smooth and light—and jagged. Bones.

He gripped the empty revolver. Frantically he fumbled in his mind. He clutched for his only weapon—a pocket hunting-knife; tore open the big blade and shrank against the wall of the lair.

What would the beast do? Would it spring? He desired to swear madly; desired to rush in and meet death half-way. The universe had dwindled to twin dim emeralds.

The breathing became quicker. A faint snarl quivered. He crouched as if imitating the brute. Suddenly the eyes grew bigger—and rose. At one green glow he stabbed with all his force.

A nightmare of writhing muscles and tearing claws; of stabbing desperately; of warm liquid—and of sinking through space.

A gale of innumerable suns—incredible murmur of voices. A spasmodic attempt to renew the fight brought excruciating pain. Distinctly a voice said—

"All right, old boy!"

He sank back, blinking. Slowly his eyes focused; he became conscious of the identity of a face bending over him against yellow sunlight on blue rock; Charleton's features with a bandage across the forehead. Another figure, familiar, loomed beside Charleton.

"Why, Doc—"

"That's all right. You must lie quiet, my boy."

But Charleton observed the bewildered demand in Blake's eyes.

"A splinter of rock or chopped wire, caught me on the head"—he touched his bandage—"and stunned me, old man. You must ha' got lost. When I came to I tried to find you, but matches gave out; so I cleared off and helio'd to Mrewa. We had a —— of a job to find you. You must have wandered half a mile."

Blake's eyes wandered as if in search of something.

"Yes," added Charleton, "you got badly mauled, old man; but you must ha' put up a —— of a scrap. He's a beauty, eh?"

He indicated a full-grown leopard strung by the feet to a pole.

"Now try to sleep. The ambulance will be here in about an hour."

Adventure, August 3, 1919

The Tree of Life

A VEIN OF PLATINUM on a jade ring was the river Mfunyaballa flowing through the forests of the French Congo. Above the place of a thousand islands is a slight rise of ground like a furry tongue protruding from the cavern of the forests, brown with the huts of the village of Basayaguru.

On a hot afternoon, when the only moving things were the scraggy goats, lazily scratching, open-beaked native chickens and chromatic lizards, a faint throb vibrated on the sulky air like the pulse of a distant drum. A yodeling cry from the steamy cavern of the forest caused the village to swarm with lithe ebon figures whose heads were decorated with frizzly hair, built a foot high above the forehead, streaming with long-bladed spears in their hands, like a flood of ants, to a point upon the riverside. Again came the cry from the forest from down the river. The distant throb grew into the "Eh! Ahh! Eh! Ahh! Eh! Ahh!" of the chant of paddlers. Presently around a bend appeared a canoe. As the host of natives squatted in silence, came stalking solemnly a tall figure with an ivory comb like a dagger stuck through the head-dress of hair and carrying an Express rifle. In the midst of his people he sank upon his haunches, gazing from a masklike face down the river with the eyes of a repressed child. The strange canoe hugged the far bank of the river, indicating by neglect of the rowers to avoid the sweep of the stream that they were uncertain of their reception.

Amidship of the leading canoe was a hood of woven grass from which protruded the helmet of a white man. When the canoe was immediately opposite the village, the paddlers backed water, and a tall man garbed in white calico with a green turban after the Arab manner stood up in the bow and chanted rapidly in a loud voice. The mob of natives watching gravely on the beach listened in silence. When the stranger had ceased, one cried back and was again answered by a chant and a signal made with the right hand raised.

Immediately the tall chief with the Express rifle rose to his feet, cried out imperiously and sat down. The canoe continued up-stream for fifty yards, swung round, came diagonally across the current and nosed its way through a flotilla of small and large canoes upon the village strand.

From the canoe sprang a short slender man clad in weather-worn khaki and wearing a small dark beard. The chief rose to his feet as the white approached and raised one hand, murmuring the Arabic word—

"*Salaama!*"

"*Salaama!*" responded the white.

As he raised his hand in the salute, his quick dark eyes were upon the Express rifle.

Solemnly the chief turned and led the way through the mob of his people up the hill to an open dusty space littered with goats, chickens and calabashes, where stood a thatched roof upon half a dozen poles, the palaver-house. Opposite to each other upon carved wooden stools, with the white man's interpreter in the green turban beside him, they began the formal palaver.

After more greetings and the solemn sniffing by the white man of the snuff proffered in a tiny gourd, the young chief indifferently accepted presents of several bales of cloth and a Snider rifle with cartridges. During the interview the white man's sharp eyes were unobtrusively noting details. The interpreter informed him that the chief had graciously permitted the strange white man to camp in the open space of the village.

The white recalled the topographical surroundings, and after swift reflection he consented, knowing that, except for field clearings in the dense forest, there probably was no other ground suitable for a camp. These matters having been arranged, the chief intimated that he would present the credentials to his august father, Basayaguru, which entailed the presentation of another Snider rifle. As the young chief rose to depart, the white man eyed the Express as the warrior handed it to his superior.

"Notice that .450, Ali?" he commented to the interpreter as they continued to sit in the shade while their equipment was brought from the canoes. "D'you think there are any white traders round here?"

"Allah is all-wise," responded Ali Mohammed. "Perhaps the person has traded it from the south, sir."

"South!" exclaimed the little doctor briskly. "These people are not nomadic, are they? I've understood from the agent at Kavaballa's that no whites have yet been here; district only touched by occasional countrymen of yours. Isn't that right?"

"Allah is all-wise," repeated Ali monotonously, blinking both eyelids. "But my countrymen are not disposed to carry weapons of that kind, Doctor."

"Um, um" muttered the little doctor. "*Hi!*" he shouted in broken Kiswahili, pointing his cane. "Make those men clear up this ground before you pitch the tent. *Fahamshi?* Tell 'em, Ali. This ground is nothing but a bug-preserve." He took out a cigar and lighted it. "What's the particular pet superstition here, Ali? Same as below or a new pope or something, eh?"

"Allah is—"

"I asked you what you think?" snapped the doctor.

"I do not think, sir," returned Ali imperturbably. "The savage think many things that they dream."

"Dream! Dream!" He glanced at Ali and grinned like a friendly terrier through his short beard. "Um. You're right. All this *ju-ju* business is merely the projection of a dream."

"In my country that is what our wise men say."

"Do they, begad? Then they're a —— sight wiser than ours! Um. Um. Ali, do you know what particular legend they have here?"

"No, Doctor," admitted Ali. "I do not. There are many strange and mystical things in Africa."

"Mystical tommyrot!" snorted Dr. Herdwether. "I don't believe you know much about it all."

"Only Allah knows the truth."

"I didn't bring you here to know Allah's opinion upon every —— thing from yams to folklore. As soon as you possibly can, get them to talk."

"They will not tell us," said Ali, "for these peoples always seek to hide their cult from the infidel eyes of strangers."

"Um. Um. Well, try, confound it, try!"

The energetic little man jumped to his feet, inspected the tent, sniffed disgustedly and walked with short nervous steps to the outskirts of the village with the object of seeking another site free from native garbage and the ubiquitous flea. But there seemed no hope, for the up-river side was as unpromising as he had observed the down side to be.

The river swirled around the small peninsula and away on its main course, leaving a series of flat swamps and tiny creeks, crocodile infested, worming into the dense forests in all directions; from the land side of the village was a vista of regiments of tree-stumps in native fields hewn out of the primeval forest, fields in which women—many with babies wrapped in skins upon their arched backs—worked diligently with the small native hoe preparing the ground for the annual sowing. Away high over the sullen edge of the forest soared lazily a pallid halfmoon.

Back through the village, noting the square hut of Arab influence surrounded by a small palisade with a large wild fig in the center, the little doctor tramped, batting at the myriad flies. As, perspiring and hot, he plunged into his green canvas chair, his personal boy emerged with whisky and a sparklet siphon. Each gesture of making, drinking, striking a match, lighting a cigar and the tones of the voice irritably demanding the preparation of his rubber-bath was observed solemnly by the circle of boys and warriors tickling their curiosity while their wives, mothers and sisters toiled in the blazing sun in the fields.

As the purple shadows elongated, came a procession from the hill, led by the tall chief, Basafingu. Advancing to within three feet of the white man, he squatted down. His followers placed before him two elephant tusks of great weight and good condition. According to the etiquette of a great chief the little doctor pretended not to notice their presence. For some minutes he continued to smoke his cigar, interested in the swelling of the sun as it sank within the humid atmosphere above the trees.

As silently and abstractedly sat Basafingu and his ebon retainers. From another green tent, the replica of the doctor's, emerged Ali in the green turban and a green gown and, stalking with much dignity, sank upon a stool beside the doctor without as much as a twitch of the eyelid to acknowledge the presence of the young chief. In impressed silence the audience of warriors and boys and children watched the statuesque poses of the actors. At last Ali gravely permitted his eyes to rest upon Basafingu and, turning very slowly, observed quietly:

"There appears to be some of the savages bearing presents for you, Doctor. Probably it would be as well to observe them now."

"Probably it would," assented the doctor. "This sort of thing gets on my nerves. You bargain and begin the debate, Ali."

"Permit your eyes to see them, and I will speak."

The doctor accordingly turned his head and regarded the gathering with a bored stare. After some five minutes of formal greetings Ali observed:

"The chief, Basayaguru, the father of this person, sends you these unworthy and trifling presents. Nod your head with the utmost carelessness, Doctor. Perfectly admirable, sir. He intimates that he will be pleased to receive you in audience upon the morrow before the sun is yet high. Nod again if you please, and I will dismiss these savages."

Ali made the set reply, whereupon the young chief, apparently impressed, responded and rose. But, when the bearers of the tusks had departed in his wake, there remained an old man whose head-dress was not so high as those of the young men and was like a bunch of greasy white wool. The face was wizened and as finely networked with lines as knitted black silk; on each side of the tufts of white wool which was his beard swung lumps of quartz as big as a walnut, suspended from the distended lobes; skeleton arms and limbs protruded from his robes of wildcat skins. He bent his head after the manner of an Arabic salaam until he revealed the scraggy wrinkles on the back of his neck; then he spoke, mumbling toothlessly—

"This exquisitely wrinkled person," observed Ali, "intimates that he is a doctor, sir."

"Not of divinity, I trust?" queried the little man with a twitching lip.

"It is injudicious to exhibit levity in the presence of the ignorant," admonished Ali gravely.

"Perfectly correct, Ali, perfectly correct. But what may the creature want?"

"He is, I deduce, the tribal medicine-man."

"Oh. A brother witch-doctor, begad! Um. Er—just the beggar we ought to make friends with, eh, Ali? What does he want?"

"As ever in this world among the infidel, he wishes undoubtedly a present of worldly goods of some denomination."

"Talk, man, for heaven's sake, talk," snapped the little doctor, "or I shall have to go into the tent to laugh. Ask him what the current *ju-ju* is."

"The moment is most inopportune," retorted Ali woodenly. "With your permission I will instruct Yamagulu to present him with two knives and a small bale of cloth and your most august respects."

"All right, but add a Snider to the respects. And find out how much we can buy him for?"

"The time is most injudic—"

"Never mind; try him."

"As you wish, Doctor."

After commanding the head man, Yamagulu, to bring the presents specified, Ali engaged the witch-doctor in polite conversation regarding the exalted status of the white chief, all that appertained to him and the imaginary objects of the expedition. The rifle and goods were brought and placed at the feet of the old man, who apparently remained unaware of them. At length Yamala, the witch-doctor, made his adieux and rose, leaving the presents upon the ground to be collected by his people.

"Well, what did he say?" demanded the doctor.

"In this case, Doctor, I have considered it inexpedient to obey you."

"—— you!"

"I wish to remind the doctor that I have lived and traded among such savages as these for a period of fifteen years; therefore it is to be presumed that I may possibly be permitted to be better acquainted with them and their minds than the doctor."

"Possibly, Ali, but—well, this confounded beating about the bush irritates me."

"The doctor will permit me to remark that, if he persists in applying the Occidental attitude to the Oriental mind, the chance of gaining the desired information, economical and social, will be considerably diminished thereby."

"You're a dear!" exclaimed the little doctor, showing his teeth in a grin. "But—all right, Ali, go your own way, but for heaven's sake don't mull it."

"As Allah wills!" observed Ali and turned his bronze Arab-Somali features toward the two tusks, appraising them with bright expert eyes. "Have you remarked, Doctor, the exceptional generosity of the chief? These tusks are considerably over one hundred pounds each and therefore, at the present market-price, of value considerably over one hundred guineas. Never have I known any of these savage chiefs to recompense a stranger so disproportionately to the value of the present bestowed. Never, Doctor."

"All right, Ali; so much the better for you. Keep 'em, my boy; only don't forget to pump my ancient medical colleague."

"A thousand thanks to you, Doctor," said Ali, salaaming. "I will assuredly endeavor to recompense you to the best ability."

"Oh, shut up, Ali. I like you, but you're a bore sometimes. Hi, Yamagulu, whisky soda. *Upesi!*"

II

VIOLET TWILIGHT stained with green died hurriedly, leaving the dented moon as if battered with the boredom of the chiliads to gaze incuriously upon microcosmical contortions. From the village of Basayaguru rose continuously, like puffs of invisible steam from an engine-exhaust, the rhythm of a drum above the murmur of the forest and the swirl of the river in the sulky air.

Like the red eye of a familiar, winking in masonic import to old Yamala, the witch-doctor, squatting like an idol carved in ebony, was the glow of the little doctor's cigar as he sat in the doorway of his tent in the lee of the greenwood fire. Half in shadow beside him was Ali, his robes a volume of carven turquoise supporting the dignity of his turbaned head, a cameo in lazulite.

"Now, Ali," said the doctor, "it's really about time you got to business. We've had a week of this fooling. We've got a general idea of the supply of ivory and that your confounded people ruined the vine rubber ages ago. But we could have got that almost anywhere. Now try to find out exactly what is the basis of their cult—whether it is the same in this part as down-country. Understand?"

"It most usually is so, Doctor," responded Ali.

"Well, but you don't know. I want facts, not suppositions."

"I still venture to doubt whether the moment be expedient yet," objected Ali tonelessly.

"Do as I tell you, confound you!"

"The Occidental and the Oriental—"

"Shut up!"

"Very good, Doctor. But you will please note that I do not take the responsibility. I obey."

As tonelessly as an oracle Ali spoke fluently to the old man Yamala, who at length replied as monotonously.

"The witch-doctor states that they have a goddess who dwells in the woods."

"Well?"

"Please to contain your most natural emotions," reproved Ali. "It is not the custom of the Orient—"

"Oh, —— the Orient!"

"Please to be patient," remonstrated Ali and began anew to talk with the witch-doctor.

The old man rumbled on in periods, punctuated by assenting grunts from Ali. The doctor finished his cigar and lighted another. Yet still the two voices blended as if in a liturgy to the rhythmic throb of the single drum and the faint anthem of the mosquitoes. The old man ceased and relapsed into immobility.

"Well, well? What is it?"

Ali was undoubtedly in a state of excitement indicated by a slight half-tone raise in the timbre of his voice.

"These peoples have, as you know, Doctor, been much influenced by the incursions of my own people. They were at one remote period the storehouse of our slaves, although in these days of your exquisite civilization one is compelled to take tribute in the form of merchandise only. I desire to point out that our ancient truths have influenced even these savages."

"You have," interrupted the doctor dryly. "Get on."

"The Occidental are not the ways of the Oriental—"

"Ali, shut up and get along with the yarn!"

"I hasten to obey, Doctor. I desire to state that these savages have confused an ancient philosophy with their own ignorant superstitions."

"Never mind that. What is the superstition?"

"As you will doubtless have read or learned, Doctor, each of these peoples have, with scarcely any exception, a belief in the spirits of the trees and the rivers. The correct word flees from me."

"Animism."

"Thank you, Doctor. Animism. But in this case they have confused—"

"Confound it," grumbled Herdwether, "never mind that!"

"They, as I wish to express, believe in the spirits of the wood and the plants. They have, the priest tells me, here a sacred and holy tree, which is the mother—I desire to express that it is the mother."

"Well, you have. What about it?"

"Because all other trees are male."

"The devil they are! Trees have sex as well as anybody else."

"Indeed true words as your exquisite education has taught me. But not with these peoples. It is that I wish to express that they have confused their superstition with the truths of my peoples, the Berbers. As may and yet may not be known to you, Doctor, the Berbers of the Atlas before the coming of the true believers—"

"Meaning your crowd, eh?"

"Indeed surely, Doctor. The Berbers, I may state, had faith in the mother of the universe, the sun, which is, they said with admirable logic, the source of heat and therefore of all things and therefore was fecund and therefore was a female, the mother of all."

"What the devil's that got to do with this *ju-ju* idol?"

"There is no idol, Doctor. It is a tree."

"What?"

"Truly indeed what, Doctor. The priest here informs that upon the mother tree depends quite, and undoubtedly logically from their point of view, the crops and all that is grown and therefore their alimentation."

"Yes, yes, the old idea from Jack in the Green to the Flamen Dialis. Well?"

"And therefore, with exquisite logic, that it is necessary for the tree to be fertilized and therefore to be married. At the first moon of the sowing, which is close unto us now, is the ceremony of the marriage of the magic tree."

"Married? To whom?"

"To whom the sacred tree is married I can not say. Such is without doubt as in all religions a matter forbidden to infidels and the ignorant."

"Well, buy the information then."

"It is not possible to buy faith. With one thousand pardons I will express myself for the reason of my excitement," replied Ali as coldly as the liturgy. "According to my way of thinking, the priest is most friendly disposed toward us. Indeed, he has invited—even more in the limits of his language—he has prayed that we stop to see the ceremony of the marriage of the sacred tree."

"Um. Um," mumbled the doctor, scratching a mosquito-bite on his left ear. "But do they usually invite strangers to witness these sacred rites?"

"Undoubtedly not. Undoubtedly not, Doctor. That is also one reason for the state of excitement in which you see me."

"Um. Um." The red eye of the doctor's familiar glared ferociously at the carven image in ebony by the dull embers. The throb of the drum pulsed steadily. "It appears to me that there must be a reason behind the invitation. What can it be? Is it money? I mean more presents? Yet they've been most unusually lavish already, haven't they?"

"More than exquisitely lavish," asserted Ali. "The reason is known to Allah."

"Confound Allah!"

"The doctor is unconsciously blasphemous," reproved Ali.

"No; it's a gift, I assure you," grinned the doctor. "Um. Um. Well, about the ceremony business. What else did he say?"

"Is it not sufficiently astonishing that he should tell us these things? The doctor does not perceive the exquisite abyss between the Occidental and the Oriental."

"Exquisite twaddle. Is there a sacrifice? These devils invariably want lakes of blood to bathe their gods in."

"That is unknown to me, Doctor."

"Well, ask him, confound it!"

"His lips will be tighter than the shell upon the ocean shore, but, if it amuses the doctor, I will hasten to obey."

Again there followed the solemn liturgical conversation. The doctor moved restlessly as if the continuous beat of the drum sought his pulse.

"The doctor will observe that my words are as true as the Koran. The tongue of the black priest is swollen, which is to say, as the doctor will perceive, that he refuses to speak concerning that which is to him sacred and forbidden."

"Tabu, eh? Um. Well, ask him directly why he wishes us to see the ceremony; whether all strangers are invited, or whether he has just taken a fancy to our pretty faces?"

"I hasten to obey, but the product thereof will be excessively more lies than the leaves on the sacred tree. His ears, as I have intimated, are made deaf by the clamor of our words," reported Ali. "He intimates exquisitely politely that he would retire with the offerings of the white chief, saying that the bird of happiness will bang her wings in his breast so excessively that he will not be able to sleep, because the white chief has willingly taken the acceptance to the marriage-feast."

"Um. Well, tell Yamagulu to give him whatever you think, Ali, and bundle him off to bed."

Ali's voice raised to summon Yamagulu, then appeared muffled as if deliberately hushed by clammy hands of the air on which rolled, with the rhythmic certainty of an Atlantic swell, the somber notes of the drum.

"What the devil's that drum for, Ali?" inquired the doctor irritably as he gazed at the fire, pondering.

"It is designed to prepare the mind and the body for the marriage-feast upon the full moon, Doctor."

"Why, that's about tomorrow or the next day, isn't it?" observed the doctor, glancing up at the battered moon.

"Two nights more yet."

III

IN THE STEAMY HEAT of the morning the first conscious impression of the doctor was that a pulse was beating in his brain. The mental effort of an automatic medical diagnosis awoke him to the reality of the merciless beat of the drum. He swore violently and shouted for coffee. Outside the net the flies had already taken over the duty of torment from the mosquitoes. The doctor breakfasted on river-fish in an exceedingly bad temper.

The inconvenience of the camp-site began to weaken his resolution to stay even the few days. In the jungle one had not to scratch all day as well as all night. He consulted Ali but as ever merely elicited the imperturbable, "Allah only knows." The doctor gulped the quinine he was in the act of swallowing. The brilliant black eyes of Ali in his bronze cameo features regarded him coldly.

"If the doctor would permit himself to meditate upon the Occidental and the Or—"

"Meditate!" spluttered the doctor, coveting the irrefragable composure of the Arab. "—— it, I believe I've a touch of malaria. Tell Yamagulu to get me the thermometer."

But his temperature was normal and his pulse as steady as the drum-throb. Later in the morning he persisted in visiting the old chief, Basayaguru, in spite of Ali's assurance that no more information would be forthcoming. But at any rate an audience would serve to fill up time. The old man, in token of his greatness and beauty, was so fat that he could scarcely walk. He lay like a baby hippopotamus upon his skins in the perpetual shadows of his square hut and appeared to do nothing save eat, drink, snuff and sleep, leaving affairs of war and peace to his son and politics perforce to Yamala, the witch-doctor.

To each of the questions put by Ali on the white man's behalf, he merely grunted non-committally, a process which led one to suppose that he was innocent of every crime as well as virtue that the black mind could conceive. The only articulate sentence elicited was an order to a slave to send the white chief another present of a large tusk of ivory. The doctor regarded the tusk in dismay.

"What's the meaning of this?" he demanded of Ali. "We can't possibly make return presents of anywhere near the value of these three tusks and the small ones. What do you think he's after? My Express? Because he won't get that, naturally."

"Allah only knows."

"Oh!" The doctor plucked savagely at his beard. "Ali, I ask what you think, not what Allah thinks."

"It is impossible to state, Doctor. Never have I witnessed such exquisite generosity from a native negro."

The little doctor returned to the camp, feeling, as he remarked to Ali, that there was something in this confounded country that would make a saint irritable. And, as he retired beneath the mosquito-net for a siesta, he grinned at the recollection of the sage advice based on theoretical knowledge he had given to clients about to leave for the tropics, to guard against irritation and liquor. During the hottest hours, when man and beast and bird, but not woman, made obeisance to the sun, the heart-throb of the drum continued mercilessly until the doctor in his sudorific bath struggled with an impulse to seize his Express and make an end of the tormentor.

At about four he suddenly grabbed the gun and, summoning Yamagulu, decided that he would seek something upon which he could wreak his exasperation. Yamagulu very naturally protested that neither bird nor beast would be stirring before the cool of the sinking sun, but the little doctor felt that in such a country to thrust forward reason was positively indecent and as incongruous as a Socratian debate in a lunatic asylum.

In the village not a body stirred. Unnoticed they selected the small canoe and embarked. The doctor directed the sullen Yamagulu to paddle down-stream along the bank until they should find fairly solid ground to land. About half a mile away, as they coasted just outside the guardian swamp, he perceived a narrow passage in the dense reed as if made by canoes. Up this turgid waterway the doctor insisted upon going. Fifty yards' paddling and reed hauling brought them within the line of the great trees and upon fairly solid earth beneath the dense jungle.

The doctor and the sullen Yamagulu landed and tore their way for some distance, earning a bath of sweat in the process. But this did not deter the doctor, who had obstinately made up his mind that he wanted distraction from the deadly ennui of the village. Farther on they struck higher ground and came upon a grove of considerable size.

Suddenly the sulky Yamagulu came to life and, touching the doctor's arm, pointed with his spear down the grove. The doctor failed to distinguish anything in the tangle of grass and bush. Then, just as he was about to whisper, he detected part of a bush that seemed to move. Slowly grew the form of some large animal. Calculating for the region of the heart, the doctor fired. A convulsive motion of the bush, and there leaped forth a big buck, high in the shoulders and dappled like forest light and shadow.

Again the doctor fired. The beast swerved to the right and disappeared. Yamagulu raced forward. The doctor followed and found him beside the buck. The first shot had been a fluke; striking the animal in the quarters as it had turned to flee, the bullet had lodged in the spine, killing it instantly.

"Okapi!" gasped the exultant doctor.

But, as he stooped, Yamagulu, grinning delightedly, drew his attention to a broad spoor through the dense grass which ten yards from the kill was streaked with blood, revealing that in all probability the mate was severely if not mortally wounded. Excitedly the doctor bade Yamagulu to stay and skin the slain animal and hurried off on the trail.

The beast was big and evidently bleeding heavily; so the spoor was easy to follow even for a white man. On panted the doctor, forgetful, as ever a hunter is, that time after all is an arbitrary affair. The ground rose steadily. The going became better at every yard. Where the trail led through thick bush, the beast had already forced a passage. As the ground sank into a slight valley, he caught a glimpse of the okapi as it dashed off from a shelter where it had apparently rested for a moment.

Wiping raining sweat from his eyes, the enthusiastic doctor plugged on down into a bog to his waist, dragged himself up the other side and on—and on—and on the little man struggled until quite suddenly the trail disappeared in a patch of jungle as thick as a grass mat. The doctor hunted furiously about—then with more care. No sign of blood; the blood-trail had disappeared entirely; not even a broken grass stem or twig could he find. Perhaps he had overrun the trail?

He cast about in circles. Fatigued and panting, he sat down to rest and wipe his streaming face. Just as he was about to make another effort, it suddenly occurred to him that the shadows seemed very dense. He glanced up through the leafy roof. The glittering ball of the sun was topping the trees. In a panic he snatched his watch. He stared incredulously at the hands pointing to a quarter past five. Only another three-quarters of an hour to sunset.

"——!" he muttered disappointedly. "I'll have to give him up now. I'll go back and help Yamagulu finish the skinning."

A rational and wise decision of the doctor's. He stepped forward briskly, hesitated, made a pace and stopped altogether. He glanced about in a bewildered childlike fashion at the wall of tree trunks festooned with creepers.

"When the devil—what the—oh."

Again he stared around more incredulously. Then very softly he said—

"Oh, God!"

He had no more idea of the direction from which he had come than of the secret of the cult. He was fatigued. So he sat down again, sagely concluding that he might as well rest while he thought the matter out systematically. Yes. Systematically; that was the thing to do. Now where was the sun when they had killed the buck? Um. Ah. At first he was sure that it had been over his right shoulder; then as equally positive that it had been behind him. Finally he concluded that there hadn't been any —— sun at all.

For a few moments the doctor was occupied in informing himself exactly how many different kinds of a fool he was; he bethought himself of Yamagulu and proceeded to inform the African continent what particular species of criminal idiots it produced. Then he plucked at his beard and glanced at his watch again. Remained about forty minutes of daylight—that is, forest semi-gloom. Tropical twilight was the only thing in Africa in a hurry, decided the doctor bitterly. Then he rose determinedly and, choosing a direction at random, made the amusing assertion that he would continue in a straight line.

Within twenty yards he was bogged; he tried another direction and found impenetrable thicket; a third attempt found another bog. A puzzled wonder as to how the deuce he had ever arrived where he was if the confounded jungle was nothing but swamp-holes was broken by a brilliant idea. Of course! He would just fire a few shots which would bring the fool Yamagulu to him. Accordingly at intervals of half a minute he proceeded to carry out the scheme, which, however, was arrested by the appalling discovery that he only had left another ten cartridges—with the probability of spending the night in the jungle.

For a while he stood still, trying to concentrate upon listening for the expected yell from the succoring Yamagulu. In a few moments he became aware of the voice of the forest: a continued twittering hum, murmurs like lachrymose sighs, tiny squeaks and whispers, mysterious rustles, a sudden chatter and a harsh squawk, then a faint hooting. He fired another two cartridges in rapid succession. The echoes appeared like derisive laughter. A sudden screech behind him made him start convulsively.

"——!" he muttered as if afraid to speak too loud lest some one hear. "I need a dose of bromide."

The gloom appeared to be deepening with a hissing noise as if it were slithering through the leaves. Erupted unbidden into his mind an exact knowledge of African carnivora. He glanced questioningly toward a tree. Images of gorillas and snakes shuttered his eyes swiftly. He grew violently angry with himself at the discovery that he was searching for things in the darkness. Suddenly he cursed aloud, as if challenging the whole menagerie of animals, and started off swiftly straight ahead of him.

Fighting with an impulse to run, struggling to suppress imagination, the doctor plowed on, tearing far more desperately than he realized, through thickets of creepers, tacking beside swamp-holes. Firmly he persisted in telling himself his exact medical condition. The forest appeared to overhear his thoughts and to laugh in rustling, weeping, insidious chuckles. Against his will he pulled out his watch repeatedly to peer at it in the gloom. Then he tore on to stop a moment to listen for Yamagulu's cry, only to hear the forest tuning up for the nocturnal anthem.

The gloom was so dense now that he could not see ahead of him. The canopied roof seemed writhing with innumerable arms, groping down—down. He crashed hastily through a tangle of creepers which seemed to be trying to strangle him, splashed in water and saw the gleam of moonlight on water. He stopped, drowning mosquitoes in his own sweat, wondered where he was, hoped that it was the creek and shouted—

"Yama-gu-o-o-o-o-o."

"Oo-oo-oo-o!" answered him.

A violent squawk brought him face about with his rifle to his shoulder. The forest murmured and sighed; mosquitoes buzzed in clouds.

Yie-e! squealed a bird at him.

Muttering something about a tree, he blundered on along the swamp edge, fell over something and grabbed. His hand clutched the edge of a small canoe drawn up on the swamp grass. At first hope made him think that it was his canoe and that Yamagulu was in the forest looking for him. He gave a mighty yell. That sobbing echo closed his mouth. A short investigation showed him that the canoe was smaller than his own. He glanced across the glimmer of water at the dense wall of the opposite jungle. Then suddenly like a caress he became aware of the regular pulse of a distant drum.

Desire carried the conviction that he had landed on the farther side of the creek from the village and that therefore by crossing he could make the camp by following the drum. He placed the rifle in, pushed the canoe hurriedly over the swamp up to his knees and clambered aboard. Pulling the canoe along the swamp-grass, he made deep water and began to paddle with his hands. A dark object near the other side, which he thought was a floating log, suddenly splashed and disappeared.

"Crocodiles!" he gasped and paddled furiously.

He landed without mishap, dragged the canoe up as far as possible and stopped to listen for the drum. He could hear nothing save the weep of the jungle. The curtain of the trees cut off the vibrations. He hesitated a moment before plunging into the dense shadows. The ground became firmer; it began to rise. On and on he struggled, scarcely conscious of the mosquitoes. Again he saw the moon and a few paces farther on stood on to the edge of a great glade. A glow caught his eager eyes. He hastened toward it. In the moonlight was the faint outline of a hut.

"Thank God!" he muttered. "The village!"

As he hurried on, he perceived a great fence around the hut in which was the glow of a fire at the base of an enormous tree. The doctor reached the fence and peered through. He put up his hand and wiped his eyes.

"My God!" he murmured. "Am I crazy?"

Seated beneath the great tree in a camp-chair in the moonlight was a bearded white man in full evening dress; an opera hat was tilted on his head; the firelight glowed upon the expanse of shirtfront.

IV

"HALLUCINATION!" muttered the doctor and pawed at his damp face again. But the image remained. The head was sunk forward slightly; the brown beard straggled over the shirtfront; one black-sleeved arm hung listlessly outside the chair, the other upon the right knee. In the moonlight the eyes glinted blue as the man stared at the fire.

"But a white man in evening kit!" whispered the doctor incredulously. "Here! Good God! No, no," he added after peering at the outline of a square hut built beneath the enormous boughs of the giant tree. "It is. I'm not crazy. The feller's crazy. Evening kit—good God! What the—he must be crazy, poor devil!"

The impulse to call out was inhibited. He began to form excuses to himself.

"I mustn't call out suddenly," he reflected, "or maybe I shall scare the life out of him. I must humor the poor devil. Yes, yes. Of course—unbalanced. They do go that way out here. Queer. Understand it, too, begad! Been in the forest all night perhaps, poor devil," he added, quite as unconscious of the ludicrous as of the fact that he was in reality talking about himself.

He opened his mouth and drew in his breath, yet he did not call out. He wriggled his shoulders as if trying to shake off an incubus. Then he realized that he was fearful that, if he shouted, the vision would disappear and he would know that he was crazy. He peered silently for a few moments, blinking his eyes.

"No," he decided. "It is real. —— queer. That bloody forest upset my nerves. Um, um. Better find the gate and let him see me when I shout. Mustn't scare the poor devil."

He began to move cautiously along the palisade, six feet high, made of stout saplings, swallowing and muttering excuses to account to himself for not shouting. Stopping occasionally to peep through the interstices, he followed the circle until he came to the great trunk of the tree, fully fifteen feet in diameter. He paused again for another look. That the vision was still there he noted with a feeling of reassurance. As he walked around the trunk, he was vaguely conscious that it faced an open expanse of the great grove, a cavern of basalt floored with jade and topped with fantastic pinnacles of chrysoprase.

On the other side he came upon the gate barred with great heavy balks of timber. The man sat exactly in the same position; had not moved a finger apparently. A wild thought that he was dead flitted across the doctor's mind. He began to draw breath to shout but stopped in indecision. What should he say? "Hi? Hullo?" Perhaps the man was not English. Probably not? What then? The question grew into absurd importance. Still the doctor stared through the balk gate. The rustle of something in the grass behind him evoked an uneasy movement and a clutching at the rifle, destroyed the fascination in the ludicrous argument as to exactly what he should say.

"I say, hullo!"

The man did not stir. Then the doctor was aware that he had whispered. He gripped his rifle tightly and with effort shouted—

"Hull-o!"

"O-o!" repeated the grove.

The doctor glared anxiously, dreading that the figure would disappear. But the head rose slowly; the eyes moved. Again the head sank despondently.

"Thank God, he is there," muttered the doctor, "but he thinks I'm an owl."

"I say—er—hullo!"

Once more the beard rose slowly.

"I say, I'm here!" continued the doctor fatuously. He could see the eyes staring as if mildly inquiring in the moonlight. "I say, old chap, are you English? It's all right! Er—would you mind letting me in?"

He perceived the beard to part suddenly, disclosing white teeth. The man was smiling.

"Good God," murmured the doctor. "He is crazy. Poor feller!

"I say," he began again, enunciating carefully, "I've lost—my—way, y'know. Would you mind—letting me in? I'm Herdwether—Borden Millar Herdwether. Oh ——! Hi! I'm an English doctor, Magdalen and London. I say, aren't you English? *Parlez-vous français?* Eh?"

Still smiling distinctly in the moonlight, the man raised a white hand and slowly waved it toward the doctor.

"My God!" ejaculated the doctor, shuddering involuntarily. "Am I crazy or are you?"

He stared. The eyes resumed the despondent contemplation of the fire.

"What on earth am I to do? He thinks I'm not here, and I thought he wasn't." He pawed at his damp hair. "If I throw anything to attract his attention, he'll think I'm a lion or some wild animal. And I'm not." The little doctor was unconscious of the whimper in his voice. "I can't stop out here all night, —— it, and who is he, anyway?

But what's he want to dress for?" he complained bitterly and glanced behind him at the cavern of the grove.

The doctor became aware of an illusion that he was within a barred cage like a captive monkey and that the man inside the fence was free. "There must be wild animals, or else he wouldn't have this confounded fence. Um."

The strange man rose to his feet, yawned and stretched his arms.

"O God, he's going to bed!" muttered the doctor resentfully. "It can't be more than nine o'clock." Then desperately, as the tall black back revealed the swallow tails, he shouted: "*Hii!* For God's sake, let me in!"

The tall figure turned sharply in his direction.

"Yes!" bawled the doctor. "It's all right! I'm here, I tell you! Herdwether!" The man was staring in his direction. "Yes, yes, come and let me in, and I'll explain!" The beard waggled slowly as if in regretful dissent. "I am here!" yelled the doctor frantically. "Englishman. Doctor. I'm lost. Help!"

The man took two paces, stopped, and spoke incomprehensible words.

"No! no!" screamed the doctor. "Speak English! *Parlez français!*"

He could see the beard move as if the man were talking to himself. Suddenly the fellow stooped, picked up a glowing firebrand and slowly walked toward the gate.

"God, he thinks I'm a gorilla," muttered the doctor and involuntarily brought up his rifle.

"For God's sake, speak, man!" he yelled. "I'm real, I tell you! I'm a white man!" The bearded man in full evening dress with a firebrand in his hand stopped abruptly and stared toward the fence.

"A white man!" he exclaimed. "Where? Oh, my God, where?"

"Here! Here! I'm lost! Let me in! I'm lost!"

The man hesitated, moved as if to throw away the brand, arrested his arm and stooped again to peer at the fence.

"Who and what are you?" he demanded. "Are you real—or am I crazy? Speak!"

"No. No. I'm real!" shouted the doctor. "I'm English, I tell you."

The man appeared satisfied, for he threw away the firebrand and advanced with long eager strides toward the gate, wrenched up the balks of timber and then, as if suddenly suspicious, leaped backward clear of the entrance. The doctor walked through, took off his helmet and held out his hand.

"How d'you do, sir! I'm Herdwether."

The big man gazed down at him and placed a hand to his forehead perplexedly.

"I suppose it's all right," he mumbled. "—— if I know. Er—how d'you do!" He touched the extended hand perfunctorily. "I—er—don't quite understand—yet. You said—are you a white man?"

"Yes, yes," said the doctor soothingly. "White, I assure you. English doctor, y'know. I—er—lost my way and—and saw your fire; so I just came along."

"Oh."

The eyes were still regarding him rather like a great child, uncertain as to whether the visitor was a tramp or an angel.

"My name's Herdwether—Borden Millar Herdwether. I'm here on a commission, y'know. Forgive me. I haven't the pleasure—"

"Eh? Oh."

Gazing incredulously, the man shook his beard as if trying to throw off an illusion. "Sorry. Er—I'm Dukely—Warren-Dukely, y'know."

"What! Warren-Dukely, the explorer?" exclaimed the doctor in astonishment.

The man giggled, throwing back his head.

"I beg your pardon!" he added more rationally.

"Not at all," said the doctor. "Not at all. Er—I wonder if you'd mind if we sit down? I—er—I'm rather fagged out."

"Fagged out, what?" The words appeared to act as a restorative. "I say, I'm awfully sorry. Of course! Come along." He started off toward the fire, stopped abruptly and, murmuring, "Forgotten the door, old boy!" hurried back and readjusted the balks.

The doctor waited for him, trying to catch a glimpse of the face. The man returned with great eager strides and to the doctor's amazement caught him by the shoulders and spun him around face to the moon.

"Good God Almighty!" he exclaimed. "That's good!" He dropped him as suddenly. "I say, I beg your pardon! You must forgive me, I—er—I'm a little off my chump, y'know. I—well, as a matter of fact, I haven't seen a white man for years. I don't know. I—but come and sit down." He strode forward to the hut, his swallow-tails flirting in the moonlight, and emerged, dragging another camp-chair. "Sit down, old man. By the way, I didn't quite catch? Herwether?"

"Herdwether," said the doctor, sitting, and he almost giggled as he saw the man pick up his tails as he sat as if he were in a club.

Dukely still stared a little incredulously. The doctor observed in the fire-glow the gauntness of the cheek-bones and the sunken eyes. Embarrassed, he looked at the fire, thinking—

"He can't be quite crazy if he knows it, but what on earth is he dressed for!"

Conscious of the eyes devouring him, he sat still, considerately waiting for his host to speak.

"My God, it's good to see you!" exclaimed Dukely at length. "I—d'you know I heard your voice calling, but—but, —— it, I thought I was dreaming."

"I understand," said the doctor quietly.

"One gets rather ratty after a while. Begin to see things if you're not careful. Er—'r' you camping near here?"

"Yes," assented the doctor. "Down at Basa-something's village, wherever that is. I was out shooting, y'know, and got lost."

"Oh yes."

As he stole a glance at the man, a black sleeve crept out, and a hand lightly touched his arm. Involuntarily the doctor started. Yet he had noticed that the hand was well kept, the nails polished.

There was silence for some minutes. The forest murmured and whispered and wept. Yet the sinister note was missing to the doctor's ears. Twice he glanced up at the bearded gaunt face. The man continued to stare almost like a yokel gawping at a circus fat lady. The doctor was embarrassed. A thousand questions leaped to his mind.

"Er," he broke out at length. "I wonder whether you have such a thing as a glass of water? I'm simply parched."

Dukely leaped from his chair as if galvanized.

"Certainly, certainly!" he muttered. "I'm an awful rotter!" and he disappeared into the hut to emerge with a calabash of water.

"Oh, thanks very much!" The doctor hesitated, glanced at the hut and up at the tall man in evening dress. He fumbled at his hip pocket. "Um. I—you don't mind if I—do you care for whisky?"

"Whisky!" echoed Dukely. The eyes brightened at the glint of a silver flask and were masked politely. "Good God, I haven't tasted whisky for—oh thanks!"

He almost grabbed, swallowed at a gulp, the tot of spirit which the doctor had proffered in the screw-cap; then he gasped, shaking his head at the calabash. The doctor took his share and a deep drink of water. As he placed the calabash on the ground beside him, the man sat down slowly and fell to gazing at his visitor again without speaking.

"Good God," thought the doctor, "is he going to stare at me all night?"

"Er—by the way," said he desperately, "have you—are you staying here long?"

The man started and seemed to shiver. He said slowly—

"Well, I'm going to be married in a day or so."

"Oh, yes, ah, of course," assented the doctor politely.

"I'm the King of the Wood, y'know."

"Oh, yes, yes," ejaculated the doctor as he thought, "My God, he's as mad as a hatter."

V

THE MAN WITH THE BEARD laughed, a rusty throaty sound, and stroked his nose delicately.

"I beg your pardon," said he. "I'm a little ratty. I mean I've been so long—er—here that—I forget that everybody doesn't know—well, who I am and that sort of thing."

"Quite so, quite so. Very usual phenomenon."

"Of course," continued the explorer, gaining more rationality in the tone of his speech and leaning forward in his chair; "you probably think I'm as mad as a hatter." The doctor looked away. "Not quite—yet." He stared at the fire meditatively. "By the way, what did you say you were here for, sir?"

"I'm on a commission; economic and social investigation, y'know."

"Social, eh? That's good!" Again he emitted a throaty chuckle. "We're frightfully keen on sociology here. Oh ——, yes! Er—but didn't you say you were a medical man?"

"Yes."

"H'm. Perhaps you'll understand a little better. Although I don't see why you should. I mean you won't be so inclined to think I'm quite insane."

"Not at all. Not at all."

"But you do! Oh yes. Quite natural. I should myself. By the way, you're not in a hurry, are you?"

"Oh no, not at all."

The teeth gleamed through the beard in a smile at the fire. Dukely shifted restlessly and looked up again.

"That whisky of yours, Doctor, has bucked me up a lot—pulled me together. I ran out six months ago. You know I'm not insane."

"No, no," assented the doctor, still wondering. "But have another."

"Thanks, old man!"

The skinny white hand again just refrained from grabbing the screw-cap.

"By the Lord, that's good!" he gasped as he handed back the flask. "Queer how the bally stuff stings after so long. Er. H'm."

"Have a cigar?" added the doctor.

"Good Lord!" Heartiness was creeping in to the voice. "That's awfully good of you! No, don't bother for a match."

He bent forward, picked a firebrand with delicate fingers and sighed at the first puff. He sat back seemingly absorbed in the joy of the inhalation. The doctor began to note details: that the shirt was soft and yellow, frayed; the parched skin drawn tightly over an aquiline nose, and the care bestowed on the hands; even the beard had been trimmed.

"Yes," began Warren-Dukely reflectively. "I'm the King of the Wood." Again the doctor was conscious of the thrill imparted by insanity. "No, I'm not insane, Doc. I—am exactly what I say. Let me see. Confound it, there is something the matter with my mind. Difficult of—er—grasping what I want to say. You ought to understand that, eh?"

"Perhaps you haven't spoken English for a long time. Do you think in English?"

"No, that's it, by God! Good Lord, I never realized it until now. Never realized that I was so far gone. H'm. Now I will get started! Are you listening, Doc?"

"Yes, yes, of course."

"Well, I was—or am, I suppose—am Warren-Dukely—I told you that, didn't I? Yes. All right. Now I'm the King of the Wood. —— it! Do you hear that drum?"

The doctor listened and was aware of the faintest possible vibration.

"Yes. It's the drum in the village, isn't it?"

"Oh yes, the drum all right. Only—" He sighed and suddenly placed one hand over his eyes as if shutting out a vision. "I beg your pardon, I'll try to get on—and tell you what a mess you're in."

"I am?"

"Oh, I'll tell you. Er—about three years ago—or was it four? What's the date, old man?"

"Date? Oh—er—about the fourteenth of February, I think."

"God, yes, my stick's right. That's the drum."

"What drum?"

"My drum. But never mind. Er—well—oh yes. —— it, I wish you'd give me something. But, of course, you can't—here. I mean I boggle so. Don't you notice it?"

"A little. Take your time, old man."

"Malaria, I suppose. And my quinine ran out some time ago."

"Oh, I shall be glad to let you have some."

"Let me have some?" The eyes stared at the little doctor. "That's good—all right. I'll go on. By the way, did you say you were Jesus?"

"No; Magdalen."

Warren-Dukely smiled at the fire and puffed at his cigar, seeming to have forgotten his guest. The pulse of the drum was so faint that it appeared like the strokes of an invisible baton conducting the nocturnal anthem. A cricket shrilled piercingly and ceased. A distant prolonged yowl was just audible. The doctor was watching Warren-Dukely with professionally keen eyes; he observed certain spasmodic twitches of the bare toes and a persistent scratching at the chair arm with one polished finger-nail.

"I guess I must have been before your time, anyway," he said conversationally.

"Eh?" The start was convulsive. He stared at the doctor; then the eyes smiled. "Oh, I beg your pardon. One gets to dreaming—more or less. Er—what the mischief was I gassing about?"

"You were going to tell me how you became King of the Wood."

"King of the Wood? Did I say that—really? This cigar seems awful strong, by the way. Still, years since I smoked one."

Suddenly he sprang to his feet and, bending over the doctor's chair, touched his bare hand as he picked up the calabash. He stood with the water in his hand and smiled down at the visitor in a relieved manner.

"I wonder whether you could spare?" he insinuated.

"I don't think you had better," observed the doctor quietly. "A little later perhaps. You're not accustomed to it, y'know."

"Quite right! Quite right! And you'll need it yourself. I'd forgotten that."

"I'll need it? Oh, you mean—it isn't that. I've a good supply with me."

"So had I, old boy; so had I," muttered Warren-Dukely as he turned away with the calabash of water in his hand. By the chair he stopped, glanced at it and threw it away irritably. "—— it, I continually do that. Carry things about. Still what does it matter?"

Sticking the cigar in his mouth, he began to pace up and down before the fire, staring at the ground. The doctor did not disturb him. Presently he began with a jerk:

"I've got it, by Jove. I know. I began yarning about that first expedition, didn't I? Well, after that Africa seemed to get in my blood. I broke off the engagement with Sybil. Had to, only decent thing to do. Can't expect a woman to wait—like a sergeant's wife? An' one can't drag her around here, eh? 'Sides, I'm not a marrying man. Never was. Poor old Sybby. I wonder whether she's still running the Cheshire?

"Oh well, on the second trip I had a mania to come through Tchad, pick up Boyd Alexander's trail—poor old boy—and zigzag down through the Albert Lakes and land eventually in Rhodesia. I circled Tchad and went off to the Dinka country. Told you all that though, didn't I? Well, never mind. I tacked back here an' barged into old Basayaguru as you did, eh? An' the —— old cutthroat made me King of the Wood!"

He stopped to raise his head and emit that throaty chuckle. The doctor, watching him keenly, began to revise his opinion of his sanity. He wheeled round, one hand stuck under the tails of his coat and the other holding the cigar.

"Bally idiot, ain't I?" he demanded. "You wait, ol' boy! Your inning's next for King of the Wood." He barked rather than laughed this time.

"Still, I've played the game, —— your eyes!" He appeared to be addressing somebody unseen, but he said, "No, I mean you, Doc." He began to pace again moodily. "Sorry, ol' chap," he said as abruptly. "You'll understand as soon as I can spit it out. I say, the old boy's very generous with his ivory an' stuff, isn't he?"

"Yes."

"H'm. Thought so. Invited you to witness the Marriage of the Sacred Tree, didn't he?"

"Y-yes," admitted the little doctor, wondering why he felt uneasy.

"Same hellish trick. Still, it would have been the same anyway. How many men have you, Doc?"

"Twenty-five. Three canoes."

"All armed?"

"Well—Sniders enough for all of 'em, but—"

"Oh pish!" he waved an impatient hand. "What bally rot I'm talking. Isn't a dog's chance. My dear old boy, I had fifty—all armed with Martinis."

"I'm afraid I don't understand."

"Good God, of course you don't! I say, know anything about folklore?"

"A little."

"Talked about the Sacred Tree, didn't they?"

"Yes."

"Well, that's the bloody thing there!" He raised a hand to the giant tree above him. "Mother of all an' has to have a husband every year."

"So I understand. My head man, Ali Mohammed, told me that they have muddled some ancient Arab philosophy with their own superstitions. Very interesting ceremony, I should imagine."

"Interestin' ceremony! ——!"

Agitatedly the tall man began to pace up and down before the fire again, sucking fiercely at the stump of the cigar.

"I'm to be the —— thing's husband," he jerked out.

"Indeed," said the doctor interestedly, for he knew of many ceremonies prevalent in Europe as elsewhere of the symbolical marriage of a girl to a tree. Then suddenly, "Oh, you mean that they've kept you here a prisoner for this ceremony of theirs? But that's nonsense. I mean of course I'll help you to—"

Warren-Dukely wheeled upon him swiftly and, pointing his cigar at him, cried:

"But you —— fool. I've told you you're trapped for the next husband."

"Husband!" repeated the little doctor bewilderedly.

"Yes, yes."

"But what—what happens to you?"

"Me? I'm sacrificed to this confounded *ju-ju*. Are you blind? The night of the marriage orgy they carve me up, wipe out your camp and stick you here to make magic for twelve moons."

"My God!" ejaculated the little doctor, half rising to his feet.

VI

WARREN-DUKELY hurled his cigar stump into the fire, turned on his heel and flung his body into his chair. The doctor remained for a moment, staring incredulously; then, as if he had grasped the import of the man's words and had decided that they were sane, he stood up abruptly and came over to Warren-Dukely.

"This—this seems incredible! In the twentieth century! I—"

The polished nails gleamed in the firelight as the delicate hand patted the doctor's arm half-caressingly, half-reassuringly.

"It isn't, my dear old boy; this isn't! It's before the flood. Sit down, Doc; I feel better now I've got that off my chest. For twelve moons I've been dying to tell a white man that! My God!"

"But—is it true?" demanded the doctor, conscious of the fingers spasmodically clutching his arm.

"It's true, all right; true as death!" The eyes gleamed as the beard emitted the throaty chuckle. "Sit down, old boy."

Doctor Herdwether returned to his chair confusedly, unable yet to decide whether or no the story was the result of a disordered brain. Warren-Dukely dragged over his chair close beside the doctor's and leaned forward.

"My brain's all right now, Doc. Er—forgive me, but I can't resist touching you—to see if you're there, y'know. By the way, that's why I dress sometimes. Just to try to keep myself sane. Helps. Can't fool around all day an' night doin' nothin'. I mean even cleanin' oneself an' pretendin' things keeps—oh, reminds one of what one was. Otherwise—well, it isn't done, is it? Not playing the game."

"But if—what you inferred—we might escape—ought not to lose any time."

"Time! You dear old thing! I've been sitting here for twelve moons wastin' time, ain't I? This is an island: crocs all round."

"But I've got a canoe!" exclaimed the doctor. "I came in it."

"Really? An' what the blazes 's the good of that? I tried, old boy. You bet your life I did. I hadn't got a canoe, but I got across on a log in spite of the bloody crocs. I wished I hadn't. They got me three days—or centuries—later. I dunno. Want to live in the jungle, eh?"

"God!" said the doctor and shuddered. "But we could make my camp an'—"

"Your camp! In the village, isn't it? 'Sides, did you blaze your trail here, eh? Which direction did you come from?" The little doctor made an inarticulate noise as he glanced over his shoulder. "No, it wasn't that way. That's where the village is. And, I say, for how long d'you think we two an' your twenty-five rats could put up a scrap against the mob? My dear old boy, we haven't got a dog's chance. I've known it for twelve moons. Come, buck up' an' we'll have a chat before we go—or rather I go! But I'm not goin' that way, by God! Playing the game or not!"

"What do you mean?"

One long arm shot up like a salute to the great bough above them.

"You'll see in daylight. Has a pod thing. Poison."

"But—but—" exclaimed the doctor, jumping to his feet.

"But! But!" mocked Warren-Dukely harshly. "What the devil's the use of butting? We're not goats. 'Sides, I've butted for twelve bloody moons. Come, old boy, let's have a drink, an'—an' we'll toddle along to Stone's an' finish up at the Empire! ——! Sit down, man!"

Suddenly he sprang to his height and slapped the doctor on the shoulder so that he sat down hurriedly. Then, tilting the opera hat upon the side of his head like a comedian, he lifted up his beard toward the moon and trolled in a husky tenor:

"Come, landlord, fill the flowing bowl until it doth run over—ove-er!
For tonight we'll merry, merry be!

For tonight we'll merry, merry be!
For tonight we'll merry, merr-y b-e-e-!
Tomorrow we'll be so-ber!"

At the last word he snatched off his hat and stood bareheaded in the moonlight as the forest answered coldly—

"O-be-r."

"Listen!" he cried, gesturing largely. "There's my faithful pal! Never goes back. Always agrees with me! The only English voice I've heard for fourteen moons! Come on, old boy! Let's have a drink. God knows I'm dry enough! ——!" he exclaimed, crushing the hat beneath his arm and bowing satirically to the doctor. "For God's sake, buck up! I'm neither drunk nor crazy! But, Lord, you're the first entertainment I've had for twelve moons! Fourteen moons! Moon! Moons! Moons! Nothing but moons! Wilde knew —— little about moons to what I know! I've watched; I've studied; I've wooed—every bloody one of the fourteen moons!"

"Sit down!" said the doctor sharply.

"Eh."

The tall figure wheeled toward him.

"Sit down, and we'll have a drink. But don't get excited."

"Excited! You dear old duck, I haven't had such a time since ma died!"

The hat went careering wildly through the moonlight, turned a somersault and settled drunkenly on one rim. Warren-Dukely dragged his chair a foot, lumped into it and caught his hand to his eyes.

"Sorry, old man; I'll be good. Fire ahead with that drink though." Then in a dreary voice as the doctor pulled out the flask, "You know you haven't an idea as to what this means to me. One gets used to anything in life. But—well, I did want to speak to a white man once more. Tribal, of course, but—" He dropped his hand to watch at the gurgle of liquid. "You know, Doc, old pal, I'm so —— glad to see you! I feel like a bally woman welcomin' her lover an' all that sort of thin'. I'm glad, but I guess you ain't."

"Here, drink this, and you'll feel better," said the doctor, proffering the screw-cap.

"Thanks!" Warren-Dukely gulped the liquor at a draft. "Lord, how it bites! Now you have a drink, an' I'll try to tell you what sort of a picnic you're in for. Oh, thanks a million times!"

He accepted the cigar, lighted it with a brand, leaned back and puffed reflectively. The distant anthem pulsed steadily. A night-bird squawked persistently. The faint vibration of the drum just reached them. After lighting his cigar, the doctor said quietly:

"You know, Dukely, I can't quite realize this. I—"

"Of course, you can't! It's taken me twelve moons to realize it. Oh, —— those moons."

"No; I mean there must be some way out of it. We can't be murdered by these savages."

"I object, I admit." The throaty chuckle was repeated. "Now let me tell you, an' then you'll understand, I'll guarantee. Er. H'm. My mind's foggin' again. Oh, yes, I know."

He stared up at the sinister boughs of the giant tree. The eyes hardened.

The nervous twitching of the fingers began again.

"Yes, I think I can do it. You need it, anyhow—to understand." He leaned forward, kicked the embers of the fire into a blaze and plunged abruptly:

"I told you how they caught me, eh? With the same trick of apparent friendliness. Invited me to the show, y'know. Very well. Two days before that drum there began. Sound physiological idea. Works 'em up. All right. On the openin' night I was led here an' given an orchestra stall while the orchestra was tunin' up. Same moon. Same tree. Whole crowd of 'em here. Mumblin' an' chantin' just beyond there in the open space. Old chief on his bally throne thing an' the young 'un. Master of ceremonies—your pal— Yes, I'll bet he's been your special friend, eh? With his head-dress—looked like a lord mayor's hat.

"Well, whole bunch of young girls an' my illustrious predecessor, the King of the Wood. He sat beneath the tree there just outside the gate. Of course, I didn't twig the game—then. D'you see 'em in the moonlight? Then that —— drumming—all the time—persistent—seemed to get in your bally head, y'know, or your veins—heart. I felt excited myself. Seen various sort of dances before an' all that. But—somehow this was different. Real thing, I suppose.

"Sort of thing they never do for white men except when they're—they're to be the *pièce de résistance*, y'know. But I didn't. They had told me somethin' about the principle of the thing: the marriage of the husband person—a great big devil by the way, more negro than these people. Came from the Kameroons, I believe; prisoner of war. They have an amusing idea that the bigger the man, the more the lady—I mean the tree—is pleased. More power, I suppose. Of course, white man an' white magic an' all that.

"Well, they kept up this —— drumming an' wrigglin' about—usual witch-doctor business—for the devil of a time. Drinkin' all the time native beer, y'know. Fermented corn. Then the girls' stomach-dances an' all that. Meanwhile the big feller sat up there in the shadow of the tree, sulky, silent. God knows whether he knew what was coming. I began to get bored." Again that throaty chuckle with a harsh rasp to it. "God—see the same old thing all over again. Then, just as the moon spilled over that big bough there and covered the big negro, there came a change. That must have been the mystic sign, I suppose.

"Well, your pal, Yamala, prancing about suddenly ceased his croonin' row and darted at the fellow, together with a crowd of other black devils. I heard the scream. I didn't realize what. They had him stripped over there in the moonlight—an' a knife— old Yamala." The beard jerked as if he were biting his lips.

"God—I've seen things. Of course, you're a doctor an' used to carvin'—but, God, it would have made you sick." Again he moved restlessly in his chair. "They cut him alive—screeches—poor devil—then they—they put it up there." He actually pointed to the exact spot. Up there in the fork of that bough. See? I vomited."

The hum of the insectile anthem continued remorselessly to the beat of the invisible baton. A cricket sang a shrill solo and ceased. Far away was the effect of sorrow in a hyena. Only one cigar glowed like the fierce eye of a dragon. From the doctor came an inarticulate noise.

VII

WARREN-DUKELY stooped for a brand to relight his cigar. He puffed thirstily.

"Twelve moons ago. The Cycle, eh? Still. Well, then I wanted to go. My head man was with me—poor devil! They were too busy to notice me. Then—I went off and down to the canoes. But there weren't any canoes—at least not where we had landed. They must have hidden them somewhere else on the island. Of course, I didn't know then that it was an island. Well, I was in a —— of a rage. I came blunderin' back here. Blood-drunk an' crazy. Orgy, of course.

"Just over there cookin' parts of the body on great fires. Blood an' hair and women all over the place. Saturnalia. I might as well have expected a rational answer from a lunatic asylum. My boy was gone. I wish to God I'd shot 'em. I couldn't have got 'em all, of course, but most of 'em before they had come to their senses. But I didn't know. I cleared off an' walked about all night. Then—of course, I had not a notion—what—what—well, you know now.

"I came back in the dawn. The drums were going. Some still dancin' like stuffed vultures. Others gorged, slept. They made me sick. I went off an' sat under a tree—that one over there. I decided to clear out next day, as I couldn't undertake to wipe out the tribe. Yet I recollect that I thought what a toppin' account it would make in a book. Queer ideas one gets—when Fate's playin' round. Oh God! Y'know, Doc, I've wondered sometimes—since—when I've been wooin' the moon there, whether we aren't all merely characters—an' —— rotten ones mostly, eh? In a book? What? But, Lord, I'd like to get my hands on my author who put me here—an' you. Sorry."

He ceased abruptly, puffed twice and shot out—

"Well, what are you goin' to do about it, Doc?"

"I really don't know." The little doctor's voice had lost the irritable note; he appeared to have regained his consulting-room tone—suave, impersonal. "But what did you do then—in the morning?"

"I do? —— an' Tommy, what d'you think I could do? They pinched my rifle while I slept. Then they trotted me up to this place. Oh yes, I objected. Still, they were an ugly crowd, an' lots of 'em. Of course, I didn't know what was up at the time. As a matter of fact they flung me in here and then skedaddled. I roamed around to find out that the darned place was an island. Among other things I found were about a couple of dozen heads of my men, on the trees down there, courteous reminder, y'know.

"They starved me for three days, an' then I began to find goats left in the stockade here while I was away huntin' round for some one to kill. After about ten days of that sort of thing, I dunno—they brought one of my men in a canoe an' made him interpret for me. Of course, I got as mad as —— when the feller told me about the husband business of the magic tree an' all that. He said they had all been wiped—except himself—and eaten.

"After that I tried to escape. I told you, eh? That cured me—or broke me. I dunno. I was delirious when they brought me back here. I pulled through an' found all my gear here—more or less—except guns. The other things they thought were magic an' were scared to interfere with 'em, even the whisky, thank Heaven."

"The whisky?" queried the doctor sharply. "Didn't they drink that?"

"No. Brought up all, nearly all, my gear except my rifles. Didn't know what whisky was probably—or thought it was magic stuff.”

“Oh,” commented the doctor. “Um. Um. I say, how about your medicine-chest? Have you got it still?”

“Oh yes; quinine all finished.”

“Um. How about opium?”

“Finished, too. You see, old boy, that was rather useful sometimes—when the whisky had run out. Gives you sleep at any rate.”

“Got any aconite?”

“No.”

“Laudanum?”

“Finished, too. Partly for same reason; also had dysentery, y’know. Why?”

“Why because I don’t intend to provide a post-mortem lecture for your witch-doctor friend.”

“Oh, well you’ll have twelve moons to think it over.”

“Nonsense.”

Warren-Dukely yawned lazily.

“You’ll find out, old boy, same as I did. A year of contemplation sobers you up a bit. What’s it matter after all? I don’t care what they do afterward.”

“Look here, Dukely; get that out of your mind.”

“That’s all right, Doc. You’re fresh an’ eager—same as I was then. I was mad to see a white once more. An’ you’ve given me that. Of course, I’m sorry that you’ll have to pay such a price for my amusement, but, —— it, old man, I didn’t lug you here, did I? I wish you better luck than I’ve had. By the way, you’ll find in my effects various letters an’ things for my people. An’, Doc, if God’s kinder to you than He is to me, I want you not to give away the cheap horrors to—to my own people and pals, an’ don’t let the papers get hold of the yarn.”

“I’m not dancin’ round in hell to make a journalists’ holiday. All details of my trip an’ notes on customs, particularly the legends an’ practises among our dear friends here, are together in the canvas-covered book addressed to the R.G.S.” He glanced at the doctor, who was leaning forward, elbows on knees, staring fixedly at embers. “Don’t seem interested, eh, Doc? You’re right. Talkin’ rot, ain’t I? I mean, how the blazes ’re you goin’ to get ’em out yourself? I tried—all sorts of crazy ideas.

“Put notes in bottles an’ chucked ’em in the swamp. Island don’t touch the main stream; of course they stopped there—unless old Surgeon Yamala has found ’em an’ turned ’em into *ju-ju* medicine or somethin’. Well, I’m goin’ to turn in. Get plenty of rest for the show tomorrow night—or is it today.” He glanced at the moon. “No; can’t be more than eleven. Ha! All the theaters comin’ out, eh? Poor old Piccadilly. Recollect that night I was chucked out of the Empire! Ah well—I can give you a dose on the floor, Doc, same as me.”

“Sit down,” snapped the doctor as he began to rise from his chair. “I’ve got an idea.”

“Sweet infant! So had I, by the dozen. Brilliant ideas every ten minutes. I know.”

“Shut up and sit down!”

“All right, old man. I’m not pressed for time. Fire ahead!”

“Look here; as far as I can make out from what you tell me and what I’ve seen, we may have a sportin’ chance.”

"—— sportin'!"

"Shut up, Dukely! You're fagged. With twelve months of this an' fever an' all that your nerves are in a rotten condition, naturally; your constitution's undermined, which affects your will. You see things—"

"See things! Oh my hat!"

"I said see things as they are not. Now try to pull yourself together an' answer my questions."

"Certainly, old boy. Fire ahead!"

"Sit up in your chair with your head forward and your back stiff, Dukely," commanded the doctor. "Get that spineless despair out of your mind—just for five minutes—and I'll give you a tonic that'll buck you up. That's it! Now! What time exactly do they begin the—the show?"

"Eight-thirty; early doors seven!"

"Don't be a —— fool, Dukely. I'm serious."

"Sorry, old boy; thought it was a joke!"

"Well, what time? Before sunset or after?"

"At the rising of the moon. But what that's got to—"

"Shut up and listen! Do they start drinking immediately?"

"You bet they do!"

"Good. What's the beer kept in? Large calabashes?"

"Yes."

"Where?"

"All over the place. Mostly near the tree."

"When do they bring the beer?"

"Bring the beer? Why several days beforehand. Has to settle, y'know."

"Is it here now, then?"

"Yes." Dukely gestured behind him. "At the back of my hut there. Gallons of the stuff."

"Um." The little doctor wriggled slightly. "Now about this tree. What is it?"

"The magic tree. Tree of Life they call it."

"You said it was poisonous?"

"Yes."

"Of what species is it?"

"I dunno. Seems to be of the same family as the baobab—Andansonia, y'know. But yet quite unlike the baobabs of the south. Never seen one like it before."

"Um. *Citric tribasic*," muttered the doctor. "No good." He stared up at the great boughs and, jumping to his feet in his nervous manner, went across and began to pick at the bark of the great bole. "That's not Andansonia!" he commented with a leap in his voice as he returned to his chair. "Don't know what it is. Unclassified, I should say."

"No, I don't think it's baobab. Wouldn't be poisonous if it were."

"Do they ever use it?"

"Yes. On the—husband. They say that it is the blood of the mother which he must eat before he is—married."

"Ah! What's the effect?"

"Oh God, Doc, that's what I want to know. They—they don't give the poor devil a chance to die. The stuff of the pod is thrust down his throat an' then—what I described.

But what's the scheme? Shove it in the beer an' poison the swine? My hairy aunt!" Dukely leaped to his feet with a yell. "You've got it, by God, old man!"

"Wait a minute," said the doctor quietly. "Not so fast."

"By God, I feel alive once more! We must do it, Doc. That'll fix them."

"That's the—sit down, Dukely. The point is: will it fix 'em? How do we know what poison it is? What quantity is required to produce the desired effect?"

"Oh the devil! Oh, it must."

"Desire has no effect on organic matter, my friend. Um. Um. Haven't got any animals around here to experiment on?"

"Not a thing. They bring me food every morning: fowls and sometimes goats but always ready killed."

"Um. Wish to heaven we knew what family it is." He stared at the great tree by which the moon in midarc was almost obscured. "Have you got anything to knock down one of these pods?"

"No, but I've some here," said Warren-Dukely, fumbling in his pocket. "I—I thought they might be useful in case anything happened before schedule, y'know."

The doctor took one, split it open and examined the contents: seeds embedded in a yellowish creamy matter.

"Um. Um," he muttered, sniffing it. "Wonder what the devil it can be. The odor seems familiar. Very. What the—— if I know. Tastes sweetish," he added putting a grain upon his tongue-tip.

"For God's sake be careful, old man!" cried Warren-Dukely.

The doctor held the pod in one hand and stared at the moonlit glade.

"If only I could think what that reminds me of. I might get a clue. I've half a mind to try. Have you any mustard for an emetic?"

"Don't be crazy, Doc! And I haven't any, anyway. It may be anything; maybe the stuff some of these devils poison their arrows with. I know that's a vegetable poison of some sort and absolutely deadly."

"True!"

"Besides, if it takes a long time, the actual knowledge won't do us any good. I mean that's our only chance either way."

"True again. What time do they come in with food?"

"Sunrise or before."

"Well, we'll have to take the chance, that's all. Come, we must fix up the stuff now. Grind it up, I suppose, as much as possible, and stick it in their beer. Thank heaven it's sweetish. They probably won't notice it or rather like the sweet effect. How much have you got there of the stuff?"

"Oh, only about a handful. I thought that would be enough for me."

"Put that idea out of your head," said the doctor sharply. "Now come along. I'll bunk you up on that bough and you grab the pods. About a quarter of a pound per gallon ought to be enough. If it were aconite, it would knock 'em stiff at the first gulp."

Into the gloom of the great tree's interior disappeared the coat-tails of Warren-Dukely, looking like some monstrous white-breasted bird clumsily seeking to roost.

VIII

As a lover hastens to a tryst, so rose the sun and rising seemed to dally in the pleasance of his love. With the hot kiss upon the dew-tipped crest of the giant tree the two white men hustled the last of the empty pods into the latrine behind the hut. Just as a bird raucously announced the capture of his prey to his nearby mate, Warren-Dukely, peering through the fence, saw the first of the six young girls who daily brought his food, for to a layman or woman of the age of puberty was it worse than death to come within the orbit of the sacred magician's sight, the husband of the Tree of Life, arbiter of fecundity in crops and women, mother of all, potent and terrible.

Across the glade they came: lithe young forms of ebony moving lissomely from their slender waists, bearing upon their immobile heads a slain goat, chickens and calabashes of sweet water, milk and eggs—for must the holy mate of the goddess be propitiated and fed sumptuously to avoid his great displeasure.

"Better lie perdue, Doc," warned Warren-Dukely, "while I find out whether they know where you are or not—that's if these children know."

At the entrance to the palisade the six stooped and, having placed the loads upon the ground, called shrilly the prescribed greeting. Dukely replied. One responded in the chanting speech which was obligatory in addressing a sacred person. Then in single file they turned and glided down the glade as if well content to have completed their dangerous duties.

"As I thought, old man," reported Dukely, returning into the hut with the groceries. "They know that you're here. And, by way of precaution, I instructed 'em to tell our invaluable friend, Yamala, that I had summoned you, my brother, to take my place after I had—entered into connubial felicity."

"D'you think they'll swallow that?" inquired the little doctor, squatted upon an overturned calabash, stroking his beard.

"Oh Lord, yes! You haven't learned as I have the great prestige of a medicine-man. They will expect crops an' what not as never before by the union of such a great white magician as I. God, so thoughtful, too! I even provide a successor as mighty!"

"Why," demanded the doctor with a calabash of milk in his hands, "don't they cultivate the glade here near to the source of magic power? Seems queer."

"Oh no. They dare not do that. The island is sacred, as I've told you. They seem to look upon the ground here as a part of the body of the great mother and 're scared to hurt her feelings by scratchin' her skin. That's the idea as I've understood."

"H'm, homeopathic magic as usual."

Dukely sank down upon the camp-bed.

"Phew! I'm fagged out. Sorry, old man," he added swiftly, "I'm forgettin' my duties. You must be starving. There's some cold goat in that calabash beside you an' some cornbread of a sort—sourdough, y'know. When you've eaten, we'd better have a sleep. You must need it, by Jove—so's we'll be fit for the—Diamond Sculls tonight," he added with a chuckle that was less harsh. "Oh, by the way, we'll need your gun, Doc; so let me have it, and I'll toddle along an' hide it in a bough near where I know now the canoes will be. We can pick it up as we go."

"Good. And you may as well take these few cartridges in case they should take a fancy to them, eh?"

As soon as he had gone with the rifle and the belt, the little doctor, whose curiosity had been excited by the first glimpse of the interior of the hut by daylight, rose to note the contents. At one end was the camp-bed with a bepatched mosquito-net; in the middle, facing the door, was a chair beside a crude bookcase of shelves formed of sapling logs burned off and strung together with bark fiber, containing about a dozen volumes, of which the most conspicuous were a volume of the Royal Geographical Society's journals, a Swinburne and a Rabelais and some chunky volumes bound in canvas; at the far end was a green canvas table on which, set in orderly array before a shaving-mirror, were a number of small objects which gleamed in the half-light.

Chewing a rib of goat, the doctor rose stealthily for a surreptitious peep at a complete manicure-set and hair-brushes in ivory, gold inlaid. As he handled them curiously, he observed on each one a crest of what appeared to be a naked scimitar blade clasped by a mailed hand. The little man took the bone from the nest of his beard to grin as he remarked:

"Totemism! Complete case. Most interesting, bless the dear! No wonder they wanted him for a medicine-man!"

The sound of the balks of the gate being dropped into place sent him scuttling back guiltily to his seat on the calabash.

"Do yourself well!" he observed as Dukely entered.

"Oh yes. But, by the Lord, Doc, old man, if it hadn't been for my pals there, I couldn't have stood it. My God, no!" The expression in his eyes as they glanced at the primitive library was almost like a dog who knew he is about to be parted from his master. He swore quietly and remarked, "D'you know, Doc, the hardest thing's goin' to be to leave my pals there tonight."

"Rot," said the doctor with the rib of goat in his beard. "You can get other editions." But with a glance at the bulky canvas books, "It does seem a pity to leave these note-books. They are, aren't they? Um."

Warren-Dukely sighed as he stretched himself on the bed.

"Queer," he observed, staring at the grass roof, "a while ago I was willing to—oh, cut a dean's throat to get out of this hell, an' now, when I think I'm good as free, I'm wanting to raise Cain 'cause I can't take my worldly goods an' chattels with me."

"Human nature, ol' boy," commented the doctor, chewing away as contentedly as a terrier at the bone.

"Oh, I beg your pardon, ol' man!" suddenly cried Dukely, springing from his bed. "Look here, you make yourself comfortable here! Yes, yes. Courtesy goes to the devil an' all here!"

"Umgh, umgh," grunted the doctor through his bone. "Sit down an' don't be a fool. I'm all right."

"No, no." Dukely dragged one yellow pillow from the bed and sprawled on the floor. "Turn in when you feel like it. Anyway, as soon as you've finished sitting on my wardrobe, I'll change. They'd probably put me in gaol at Kavaballa's if I arrived in this kit!" he added with a slight return of the hysterical note in his voice.

The doctor, who appeared to have lost every trace of his normal irritability, did not dispute the point but, having finished another bone and drunk some more milk, rolled on to the bed and was asleep in five minutes. Flies buzzed in freedom, walked upon the doctor's nose and danced upon his eyelids with impunity; they essayed to hold a carnival upon the long figure in khaki crouched upon the floor but were repulsed by the bony hand of perfect nails. Shadows dwindled toward the west. Parrots began to squawk; a wart-hog and his family nosed inquisitively around the palisade and went a-truffling farther up the glade.

Hornets played busily between the forest and a nest of clay beneath the eaves. A lizard progressed in suspicious darts across the earthen floor, reached the calabash of goat abandoned by the doctor and feasted most lizardly upon the swarming flies. Suddenly a streak of cobalt blue struck the empurpled lizard like dulled lightning, and a small snake, startled by a throttled gurgle, slithered into a hollow in the wattle and daub wall. From the southern end of the glade parrots streamed, screeching a pessimistic warning.

Warren-Dukely stirred and arose as his keen ears caught a distant chanting. He awoke the slumbering doctor.

"What the—" mumbled the doctor resentfully. "Oh." He sat up abruptly. "Oh Lord, yes, I'd forgotten. What's the matter?"

"Curtain's going up, old man. Pull yourself together. You stop here an' don't come out unless I call. I've got to go an' parley with our pal, Yamala. He's chanting Gilbert an' Sullivan stuff down there at the end of the grove."

"What! Are they beginning already?"

"Not until sunset. My magic is too powerful for any except the anointed sorcerers or whatever you like to call 'em while the sun is up. Then the crowd comes with a rush, an' they start with a song an' dance act."

"But—Dukely, d'you think that they've already wiped out my camp? That Arab of mine, Ali, will put up a fight if he gets any warning, an' he's no slouch."

"God knows! Perhaps they'll bring him up to see the show an'—or—else they may take it into their heads to keep him for the next year's magician—particularly if he's a pure-blooded Arab; that is, looks it."

"Um. If he knows, he'll fight like a wildcat. Fine chap, Ali, even if he is tiresome sometimes." A smile twitched the doctor's shaggy eyebrows. "I hope they do bring him along if only to see a carven image get excited for once. Dear me, how sentimental one becomes in post-mortem contemplation."

"Oh, shut up!" exclaimed Dukely sharply. Then, turning away abruptly, "Look here, I'll toddle along!"

As he strode from the hut, the little doctor watched him keenly.

"Um," he remarked *sotto voce*, "careless of me—very. Nerves in rags. Still, rather natural. Um. That food and sleep did me good though." His eyes wandered over the ground and alighted on an empty pod of the Tree of Life. He picked it up and sniffed at it again. "Queer, familiar odor." He stared reflectively at the glare of sunshine without. "—— if I can recall what it reminds me of. Um."

From without came Warren-Dukely's voice pitched in the high native chant. As it ceased, above the recurring buzz of flies came the response like a thin streak of troubled sound from a distance. The doctor moved toward the door and saw the bearded white man turn away from the fence to regard the giant tree; he noted a certain rigidity in the body and the clenching of the fists. The doctor dodged back swiftly as Warren-Dukely came to the hut.

"Come on, old man!" he shouted a trifle boisterously. "It's about an hour to sunset. Let's feed, an' I'll fry some eggs an' goat. We can stuff 'em in our pockets for the trip tonight." Averting his eyes, he plumped down into the chair by the library. "An', by God, we mustn't forget to stir up the beer before—before the bar opens!"

"Certainly," assented the doctor, "an', talkin' about bars, there's another wee droppie left, laddie!"

"Thank Heaven!" exclaimed Dukely. "Let's drink to—to the holy estate of matrimony, by the Lord!"

"Um," reflected the little doctor as he unscrewed the flask, "he's fightin' it through, but he may collapse on my hands at any moment. Confound it, what does that stuff remind me of?"

IX

IN A FIELD OF MALACHITE within a cañon of the basalt forest before the domed majesty of the Tree of Life was spread a quivering fan of ebony, whose writhing squirming figures were sheened in the blue flood of the moon. In the center upon a carven stool was draped the girth of the chief, Basayaguru; upon his left squatted his son, Basafingu, and upon his right, a bearded face of ivory and jet, squatted the little doctor beside the immobile carving in turquoise of Ali Mohammed.

Before them pranced Yamala, smeared in clay, a frenzied skeleton of chalcedony from whose high-crested head streamed a pennant of red parrot feathers, dancing in the humid air as if in wild pursuit of the glittering snake which was the sacred spear, to the screeching chant and the throb of the drums. Beyond him, beneath the great bough in the blue womb of the tree, was the glimmer of a white body crouching.

Around a wriggling group of the six doomed and holy maidens leaped the men and shuffled the women, grunting and squealing to the impulse of the drums. On every side like giant mushrooms stood the great calabashes of the beer from which he who willed could drink his fill.

"God," muttered the doctor, nervously plucking at his beard, "when is this confounded stuff going to work? I don't even know what reactions to look for! Ali! How far do you reckon that moonlight is from Mr. Dukely now?"

"Undoubtedly within one foot, Doctor."

The doctor glanced at the clear-cut features which were as cold as rock, and he swore resentfully.

"Dukely," shouted the doctor above the racket, "are you all right?"

"Yes," came the reply in a steady voice. "They'll get me in a minute or two."

Continuously the blue-sheened limbs pranced on; untiringly yelled hysteric voices; remorselessly the blue tide of the moon rose nearer the bole of the Tree of Life, the Mother of All, where crouched the unwilling bridegroom.

After an anxious stare about him the doctor fidgeted restlessly and gazed fascinatedly at the line of creeping moonlight.

"Is that stuff ever going to work? Ali," sharply, "d'you think we've made a mistake? Perhaps it's merely harmless—just citric acid of the baobab? Ali!"

"Allah only knows," responded Ali tonelessly.

The doctor swore and began again to pluck at his beard.

"God, this tension's—look!" he whispered and clutched at Ali's robe.

The enormous bulk of the chief, Basayaguru, beside him was heaving convulsively; the head was thrown back until the head-dress was almost perpendicular, and the mouth was wide open, the jelly face creased in a thousand wrinkles; the eyes were dilated, flashing the blue whites; the blobby hands clutched at the flabby mass of the strained throat.

"He is drunk, Doctor," said Ali gravely. "He wishes to laugh—exquisitely."

"Laugh! Good God, what at?" exclaimed the doctor.

As he spoke, the ghostly figure of Yamala, the witch-doctor, doubled up in front of him, holding his sides as his open mouth gasped in a paroxysm of laughter. As suddenly as if indeed a magic wand had been waved above them, the drums ceased— the screeches died away. Five leaping warriors turned in amazement and stared. A yell was turned into a gasping sob.

Astonished the doctor stood up. Every savage except the six holy maidens was rolling about in the grass, holding his sides and gasping with laughter. The chief beside his son was kicking his fat legs like a baby hippopotamus. Into the moonlight stepped the ivory figure of the bridegroom. Several figures ceased to struggle. They lay quietly in the grass.

"For God's sake!" began Dukely. "What on earth—"

"Come!" yelled the doctor. "Run for it, Dukely, for your life! Ali!" And without explanation the doctor sprang over the squirming figure of the chief, followed by Dukely and the sedate Ali. Not until they had reached the tree where the doctor's gun was hidden did he have breath to explain.

"That smell! 'Course I knew it!" he gasped as they trotted through the forest to the canoes. "Dentist!"

"Dentist! What on earth—" panted the ghostly form of Warren-Dukely.

"Yes, yes, nitrogen monoxid—probably form—pentoxid—Laughing Gas, y'know! Asphyxiate 'em for hours—if doesn't—kill 'em! There's the canoes!"

Adventure, August 18, 1919

The White Frog

"WISH I HAD LIVED in those days!" exclaimed young Charters, closing a magazine he had been reading by firelight.

"What days?" I demanded, sprawling on my blankets, staring at the stars through the canopy of leaves.

"Oh, these Indian days your tribe is so fond of scribbling about."

"I'm mighty glad I didn't!" remarked Mandeville from the other side of the fire. "They were no more romantic than these days. Only the smoke of time."

"Out of the mouth of babes!" I quoted laughing.

"Oh, rot!" persisted Charters. "Half of the things never happened, except in imagination. What I'd like to know is just what percentage of mendacity is added to the real thing to make it palatable to—

"Unsophisticated youths, huh?" I inquired. "You talk like an immoral milkman studying the pure food regulations! Just what's the matter now? Rotten yarn?"

"No; quite a good yarn. But it is obviously a yarn. That's the trouble. You know you fellows can't get away with the 'queer,' unusual happenings. They just don't happen in these prosaic days of flivvers—if ever they did."

"They do, young Solomon!"

"Yes; on the order of I know a man who had a cousin whose maternal aunt—"

"Sometimes yes, sometimes no, Mr. Socrates! Of course, if in your extensive travels in a Pullman between New York City and Syracuse—"

"Oh, cut it out!" butted in Mandeville. "Have you got a personal yarn of the marvelous?"

"Marvelous? Well, uncanny rather. But—"

"Oh, you're a professional liar," observed Charters somewhat crudely. "If it's a good yarn, why haven't you written it?"

"Because I have respect for my clients," I retorted sharply. "I always try it on the dog first!"

"All right!" laughed Mandeville. "I'll be dog!"

"Me, too," agreed Charters.

"Well, this yarn's about a frog," I began, after stoking my pipe. "Kick that log on to the fire. It's chilly."

"One moment. Is this yarn of the 'aunt-cousin' order, or did it happen to you?"

"The fact that I am about to attempt to tell the story precludes the possibility of my having filled the principal role," I said severely. "But I had an orchestra stall for the show. Now will you be good?

"The stage is set in Central Rhodesia and at a fort of the British South African Mounted Police, a small granite hill like a hog's back sticking out of a swamp surrounded by *kopjes*, as they call 'em there; hills running from about five hundred to a thousand feet high, mostly timbered, with huge boulders and stones showing through like the skin on a mangy dog's back. The hill nearest the fort was rather like the back of a bald giant's head rising sheer out of the swamp with a fringe of hair just above his collar, where hundreds of baboons lived.

"Well, on one end of the hog's back, perched on the rump as if it were slipping off, was the white man's camp: six *kiers*—huts, you know—made of *darga*—mud, I mean—and sticks, and with thatched roofs, forming a tiny square with lumps of granite sticking through. Sergeant Trotter's was at one end and the mess-hut at the other, and we four troopers, Hugill, Barnet, Lemare and myself, on the flanks. A little farther along, over the loins as it were, was the Black Watch, the native police, about a hundred of 'em and their wives. After that the rest of the hill was covered with a short scrub and thorn-trees which always suggested the hair on Baboon Hill.

"Oh, that Baboon Hill! I can see it now. I could draw every blessed crack and water fissure, every odd whisker on that —— cranium today! Right on the southern edge against the sky was a dwarf tree which looked like the single hair of the comic supplement sketches. I used to stare and stare at it until I began to giggle!

"Well, this was Fort Mutoko's, an out-station of D Troop. Our headquarters was at Inyanga, about a hundred and fifty miles to the east on the Portuguese border. Our nearest station was Mrewa, about eighty to the southwest, but with the usual brilliant reasoning of administrations D Troop had to furnish the detail for this station. The trail crossed four rivers which were impassable in the rainy season, whereas to Mrewa there were only two rivers and almost a real trail. The point of this is that for two or three months we were completely isolated; even the mail only turned up about once in three weeks.

"We were supposed to patrol the district once a month with a platoon of the Black Watch. But half the time we hadn't any horses available. Originally we had two; one great gaunt beast who had been a water-cart horse in the Tenth Hussars during the Mashona Rebellion, the Camel—and, my God, to ride he was like a camel or at a gallop more like an earthquake—and the other was a little polo-pony. But usually they were sick so that whoever did the patrol had to go foot clogging.

"Johnny Lemare and I did most of the patrolling; used to beg of Trotter, lethargic and *dop*-soaked, like a dog for a piece of sugar just to get away from that infernal camp. The patrol merely consisted of ambling along from village to village around a great circle and back. Nothing ever happened except shooting along the Ruenya, for the Mashonas are a poor race without the guts of the Matabele—skinny little devils.

"Well, Lemare had been on that station nearly two years and I only eight months. So I had some life left, and he, like Trotter, had been inoculated by the country, I suppose. Anyway, he was mighty dull, sulky and taciturn. Taciturn! Why, for a week you'd get nothing out of him but 'yes' or 'no.' After that I gave up and tried 'Nosey' Hugill, a cheerful sort of chap, but he spoke the local lingo rather well and preferred to sit and talk, when he did talk, to the natives.

"That riled me, because I knew very little at all—merely enough to ask for things and make official inquiries. As for Barnet—'Pasty,' we called him—he never wished to go on patrol or do anything; his forte was eating and sleeping. He was too lazy to ride the Camel even when the beast was fit.

"Trotter was nearly always half-drunk. He'd sit—Lord, how often I've watched him—like a squat Buddha in his pants and half-dirty shirt on a bit of rock, which I could see from my *kier*, outlined against the bald *kopje*, never moving except to shove a pinch of Boer tobacco from the little bag tucked under his belt into his mouth and then take a swig of *dop*—Cape brandy—and chew the mixture.

"Trotter was rather amusing when he felt good. He'd chew and drink for hours, yarning about the customs and ways of various tribes. He was a Colonial and he certainly knew the natives from A to Z. Lemare and Hugill would sit in the mess-hut, Hugill with that long melancholy nose of his, and drink it all in.

"When I had arrived, Trotter, Hugill and I messed together. Trotter said Barnet's table manners made him ill. But three months afterward our mess broke up. Trotter said he couldn't stand our faces at every meal; it was like being married, he explained, and he hated that. So we fed in our respective huts and had meals cooked by each one's private boy, except Barnet and Lemare. Sometimes we asked each other to dinner. It made a change.

"There was absolutely nothing to do. Of course, we were supposed to do many things. Even the Black Watch only drilled when their sergeant felt inclined. Looking back, I scarcely know what on earth I did with myself all day. The chief amusement seemed to be sitting on a rock—each one had his own rock and bitterly resented any of his mates daring to use it—and staring at that bald *kopje*; that and potting at the baboons in the whiskers of the bald head.

"Sometimes Lemare and I used to wander out with a gun. We could invariably get a buck and any amount of birds down in the swamps. But gradually even that sport began to pall. Barnet confined his sportsmanship to eating. Only once do I remember Trotter ever going out with a gun. Then he got nothing—which was enough to discourage him for life apparently.

"We'd get up at what time we liked. Dressing consisted of climbing into a pair of pants and a shirt. One's boy kept rifle and gear clean. That sitting on a rock business developed into an unconscious ritual. Nearly every sunset would find us white men squatting on our respective rocks, each taking no notice of the others and each staring at that Baboon Hill. Oh, except when a mail might be due, and then we sat on the opposite side of the rump like five dirty crows, staring out across the swamps trying to catch the glimpse of the mail-runner crossing a bare patch in the scrub about a mile away.

"Most of the day I'd lie around in my *kier* and read papers months old, a few books and magazines; read and read 'em over and over again. Always at my solitary meal I'd stick up a tattered magazine and read the ads. Queer! You get a perfect mania for ads; I mean, you find yourself having favorite ads which appear to afford you infinite satisfaction to read over and over again. I recollect that one was of some smoked ham. I think I read that —— thing until bully beef or venison tasted of ham.

"At night I'd hear Trotter in the *kier* across the tiny square, jabbering away in Mashona or Sindebele to some native, and Hugill's cracked baritone singing ditties to himself or mostly talking. He had the walls of his hut plastered with cuttings from Sunday supplements and would sit and literally chatter away to one or a group of 'em for hours. It seemed uncanny at first. But then I began to do the same thing. Every one living alone does, more or less.

"Of course there was the local amusement to entertain us frequently. Malaria, I mean. One or two of us would often be down with a go for a week or ten days. It became quite ordinary. So much so that one would hardly take any notice of the other who was sick. I recollect my first 'go.' I was delirious for ten days. Trotter, I think, gave me quinine and phenacetin, but otherwise my boy looked after me. Once I 'came to' under my bunk, hugging a seven-pound can of beef. Another time Hugill in delirium ran off the *kopje* and nearly drowned himself in a swamp hole. Such a life would kill most. But yet it didn't seem to kill us—then.

"One day Trotter was yarning to Hugill and me about a native legend that the top of Baboon Hill was haunted by a particularly malignant spirit. I suggested to Hugill that we go and explore, and to my amazement he was keen. We set out with our boys and a couple of the Black Watch. From the north the hill was shaped rather like some enormous animal lying down with his head erect. We made our way around to the tail, where, climbing through boulder-strewn undergrowth, we got on to the rump. But the devil himself couldn't persuade any native to follow us farther.

"We went on walking over a saddle of boulders, but at the base of the neck, as it were, we had some fairly tough climbing to do over bare slippery granite. Finally, by taking off our boots, we gained the summit to find to my surprize that it was a hollow basin which at that time, just before the rainy season, had small pools of stagnant water. Around the edges was a good deal of vegetation and quite a bunch of trees unseen from the swamps below. There was no sign of baboons, as I had half-expected, to explain the legend of the malignant spirit. Either it was too far from food supplies, or they didn't care for the climb over the bare granite slopes. There were a few birds and any amount of bright-hued lizards.

"When I was poking about in a crevasse looking for fossil shells, which I knew might be found there, I came across a tiny white frog. Funny little chap, he was, about an inch long with pink eyes and pink feet. Hugill decided that he must be the evil spirit of the mountain and that he was going to take him down with us for luck. He put the frog in a match-box. We hunted about for a long time, but we couldn't find any more of 'em.

"When we got down, our boys and the two policemen were astounded to see us alive. Now, although this was a local legend, they appeared to be convinced as much as the Mashonas. While we were having some grub, Hugill showed them the white frog. Lordy! It was all we could do to stop a stampede—and by the row they kicked up the frog might have been the devil in person. Hugill was all cock-a-whoop saying that he was right; that they said that the white frog was the real devil of the mountain. He laughed at their superstition. After a while they got sulky and wouldn't talk about it any more.

"Of course, Hugill showed his prize to the other fellows, who weren't a bit interested—except Barnet, who wanted to know whether it was good to eat, and Trotter, who told Hugill to get rid of it else we'd have bad luck as the natives believed. Hugill said he would, mumbling to himself that Trotter was half a native anyway. But, of course, he didn't.

"The first thing that happened was that Hugill's boy refused to go into his *kier* to clean up because the devil was there. Hugill beat him. But he would not enter at any price. Hugill fired him, but he couldn't get another boy and so had to do the work himself—and that wasn't much. My boy began to act queerly, too, always glimmering his eyes at Hugill's *kier* across the square, as if expecting to see something. I told him not to be a *mompara*—idiot—but he mumbled that things were going to happen.

"Next morning, as a matter of fact, the pony slipped going down the *kopje* to the grazing-ground and broke his foreleg. Of course, we had to shoot him. That night the black sergeant, Munyangombo, came to me as the senior trooper—Trotter was ill or drunk—and complained that 'Ugilli' was cursing the camp by having the devil frog and that the accident to the pony proved it! Naturally I told him that he was idiotic; just as if a pony couldn't fall down a slippery *kopje* without being pushed by a devil god, and the beast had always been as clumsy as a clothes-horse, anyway.

"But the sergeant complained to Trotter next day, and Trotter ordered Hugill to get rid of the thing as being calculated to demoralize native discipline. Hugill said that he had, but I knew, as every native did, that he was lying.

"Life ran as monotonously as ever for a week. I had just told the Black Watch sergeant that he was a Mashona fool when I went down with malaria. Well, that was nothing unusual, and it was a very mild dose anyway, but one night I was a bit light-headed, and I awoke with a crazy idea in my head that two lions—oh, there were lions around—were trying to get through my roof! I had a night-lantern going and I could have sworn that I saw one paw, claws as well, sticking through the thatch. I lost my head and, sitting on my bed, began blazing away through the roof and yelling blue murder. The next thing was that, seeing the reed door opening, I mistook Trotter for another lion. I didn't bag him, fortunately.

"This was, Sergeant Munyangombo persisted, another proof of the working of the frog. Trotter said that he was going to search Hugill's *kier*. He did, but he found nothing, as the obstinate idiot had hidden it. Then the devil thing began to get real mad, or it seemed like that, for of course it couldn't have been really; still— You fellows needn't laugh! But within four hours Trotter went down with black-water.

"Now the main treatment for black-water is to keep the heart going as well as to clear the kidneys, but poor old Trotter might as well have drunk milk and water for all the stimulation that brandy and champagne from the medical comforts could afford him. I got badly scared for Trotter. The only chance to get a doctor was at the Kaiser Wilhelm Mine, sixty miles to the north and with fortunately no big rivers to cross. But that was only a chance, as there was no resident medico there. However, I decided to take it.

"So I saddled up the Camel, who happened to be fairly fit, and rode off. Poor old Camel; he had never been driven as he was then in all his hoary life! As usual, about four o'clock the rain came up. There was no trail except the Kaffir paths from one village to another. But, as the luck had it, the weather did not clear up at sundown, as was usually the case, but poured harder than ever. We pushed on at a walk in the inky blackness. Fortunately I knew that road well. But it took me all my time, steering by the contour of the hills in the flashes of lightning, to keep anything like the right direction. The Camel didn't like it; neither did I.

"A dozen times we lost all track of a path. Sometimes feeling with my hands in the dark, sometimes with the aid of a match, I found some path that seemed to lead in the right direction. Once, crossing a swamp, we got badly bogged, and the Camel was a heavy beast. But we got through somehow, and, when daylight broke, I found myself a little on the wrong side of a line of *kopjes*. The poor old Camel must have imagined that I thought he was a baboon by the way I chased and led him, persuaded and cursed him over dongas and rocks through a slight gap in these hills. Indeed his poor old creased body and limbs looked more like a prehistoric leviathan recently dug up than a horse who did amazing stunts.

"But we did it and arrived in time for breakfast to discover that, of course, the doc had left for Salisbury the week before. However, Goddard, the mine secretary, who said he had been a medico at some remote period, offered to come along, and I accepted. We started right back. Goddard rode in a *machilla*—a hammock carried by natives, you know—and I hardened my heart and drove the old Camel at it again.

"We got in late that evening. The Camel couldn't walk for two months after that, but Trotter was still alive. The whole trip was really wasted, for the only medical lore that Goddard had was his kind heart—and that wasn't much of a stimulant for poor Trotter.

"He was very weak. Goddard was sure that he couldn't last long. We stayed with him in that little mud hut. He was conscious most of the time and mighty cheerful, although toward morning he smiled feebly, said that he was going out this trip and asked for one last chew. Goddard gave it to him. What did it matter? And also another 'go' of *dop*. The favorite combination cheered him up. He grinned. Just as dawn was filtering through, he looked at us, tried to turn over, said, 'Hell!'—and then he had gone.

"I suppose I was young, and you fellows will think superstitious, but the black sergeant's words and that —— frog began to get on my nerves. I knew that Hugill still had him, for I saw him catching small flies to feed the beast. I mentioned the matter to Goddard, but he—well perhaps he thought he had his alleged medical reputation to keep up, for he merely laughed at me and maintained that Trotter had gone under from too much booze, which had induced black-water. As a matter of fact, thinking things over calmly, that diagnosis sounded mighty convincing, for booze kills more fellows out there than ever malaria did.

"Well, we buried poor old Trotter down below in the swamp; a horrid job, and he was awful heavy. After that Goddard went back to Kaiser Wilhelm Mine, and we settled down once more. As it was the beginning of the long rainy season, I could not expect another non-com to come out to take over for two or three months, and somehow, even then, I didn't relish my job. That evening Sergeant Munyangombo stalked up and solemnly denounced the white frog once more for the death of the *umlungu*, but I was reassured by Goddard's opinion and dismissed the silly fellow.

"Well, things ran on quite smoothly for ten days or more. We began a general mess again, too. I don't quite know why. Sort of more companionable in a way, and Trotter had been a little domineering and cantankerous at times, although even I had to admit that Pasty Barnet was enough to make a man sick to see the amount of grub he shoveled into that pallid fat face of his. A week later a call came from a native commissioner about half-way to Mrewa for an escort to arrest a Jew trader who had slipped across the Portuguese border.

"Usually the N.C. called on Mrewa, but the Inyadiri River was in full flood. I wanted to go myself for the change but could not, as I was senior trooper in charge. It was Lemare's turn for duty, but he happened to be convalescent after a go of fever; so I detailed Hugill. Hugill scowled and complained that he hadn't got a boy. I offered to lend him mine, but my boy refused point-blank. I couldn't make him, as, of course, he was not in the service; so I told Hugill that, if he would keep that fool frog, he would have to put up with the consequences.

"He grumbled and began to prepare his kit. Then he came over to my *kier* with Pasty Barnet; said that he was sick; that it wasn't his turn, anyway, and that Barnet wanted to go. That Pasty wanted to do anything except eat or sleep was almost incredible, but he corroborated the amazing statement. I supposed that Hugill had squared it with him; anyway, it didn't matter which one went, and I was feeling a bit rotten, too.

"So Pasty trudged off next morning with a platoon of the Black Watch, for the Camel was still on the sick-list after his trip to the Kaiser Wilhelm Mine. I was lying in my bunk smoking and reading some station papers I had had to take over from Trotter when about noon a perspiring Black Watch suddenly stood in my hut door, saluted and stuttered out that the *umlungu* was *kufa*—dead.

"At first I couldn't comprehend what could have happened. A rising of natives occurred to me; the Black Watch had killed him. But no; as far as I could make out Pasty had insisted upon taking a short-cut across the swamp through a part where all of us who went shooting knew it was dangerous. They came to the dangerous part, an open *vlei* of sweet and short green grass, which any born fool knows is suspicious; for that usually signifies bog formed by a basin of granite beneath the alluvial which holds the water there.

"The Black Watch apparently mutinied outright. He called them cowards and *momparas* and laughed at them and began to run across! The Black Watch shouted, '*Ikona mushla!*'—no good—but he ran on; Pasty weighing a good two hundred and twenty pounds! Of course, within thirty yards he was up to his knees. But he struggled on, and, as far as I could gather, he must have struck an outcrop of rock, which often occurs in the middle of the basin, for suddenly he was capering about—dancing, they said—on dry land, shouting and waving to them to follow him. But they wouldn't. They yelled '*Ikona mushla*' again and again.

"Then Pasty got mad, apparently, for suddenly, after calling them more names, he shouted to them to go around, as they were Mashona curs, and tried again to rush across. The man said a devil got him by the feet, which probably meant that he slipped; anyway Pasty plunged headforemost into the swamp! They saw his feet kicking for some time and the rifle sticking up. Then everything disappeared.

"Got a cigaret, Charters? Thanks.

"Well, that made me feel rather queer. I walked across to the mess-hut, where I found Lemare and Hugill having lunch. When I told them, Hugill stroked his big nose and said, 'Bloody glad I didn't go!' But Lemare sat silent for several minutes, sighed and rose, remarking, 'Lucky swine!'

" 'What the devil's the matter with you?' I demanded testily.

"He turned in the door and stared at me with that melancholy bilious look usual to him.

" 'Bloody sight better to be buried in a swamp than be buried alive, ain't it?' he drawled and mouched away, chewing a biscuit.

"Hugill began to snicker.

" 'What the ——'s the matter with you all?' I shouted, exasperated at I did not know what.

" 'Can't I laugh if I'm having a good time?'

" 'If you don't like it, why the devil don't you get a transfer then?'

" 'Mebbe I will,' he retorted, 'but not the way Pasty went!'

" 'Don't know so much about that!' I snapped, conscious that I was so irritated that I expected another dose of fever. 'Anyway you're detailed for duty tomorrow. Johnny's sick—and, for God's sake, take that —— frog with you and see if you can't follow Pasty's road.'

" 'Superstitious old woman!' he sneered. 'You're as bad as the blacks. More likely Johnny'll sign on in the winged police than me. I've had enough 'f a cop's job.'

" 'Oh, shut up!'

"I bolted my piece of everlasting bacon and chicken and went back to my *kier*, wishing that the gathering afternoon storm would break and cool off the air.

"About six o'clock I heard the drums in the native quarters begin to beat. I got up, intending to stop them, but then I recollected that it would be the night of the full moon and that the Black Watch was allowed, according to native custom, to hold a dance. I went across to the mess-hut, intending that after the morrow I would revert to my old custom of feeding alone. Lemare wandered in a few minutes after, but Hugill did not turn up.

"Lemare was more taciturn and melancholy than usual, although I did not notice it particularly, for frequently we would feed all together without exchanging a word. We all knew each other's jokes, life histories and disappointments to boredom. Hugill, I imagined, if I thought of his absence at all, was ill or playing up to being ill to avoid the morning duty. When the mess-boy brought in the coffee, Lemare looked up from contemplating the door through his hands and said quietly:

" 'I feel rather rotten. D'you mind if I have a small bottle from the comforts?'

" 'All right,' I said shortly, giving him the key; 'only go easy, for there isn't much left—after old Trotter.'

"Lemare grunted, went off to the storehouse and came back with a small bottle. I was drinking the usual *dop*. But, when I heard the pop and the fizz, I sort of got thirsty, too, and anyway I was really only convalescent, which accounted for my unusual irritability. I don't mean that I'm a saint at any time, but malaria does wear your nerves. I sent the boy for another bottle of *manzi muti*—medicine water—and threw away the *dop*. When Lemare heard the message, he filled my empty glass and stood, with as near a smile as I'd ever seen on his face, holding up his glass.

" 'Here's to the next transfer!' said he. 'And I hope to —— it isn't as rotten as this hole!'

" 'Here's to!' said I.

"We finished my bottle in silence, staring out at the bald skull of Baboon Hill with a halo of gold around it and listening to the throb of the drums. That champagne appeared to run through my veins. I began to feel good once more. I called the boy and threw the key at him, telling him to bring a big bottle. That pop seemed better than the last. Lemare drank a glass and then suddenly began to talk in a quiet rambling sort of tone. He talked about himself, of course; although, by the way, he was the only one in the station who hadn't bored every one else with family stories and personal troubles. I sat on, sipping, smoking and listening.

"He was really an Austrian, had been in the army and had married a wonderfully beautiful woman. He rambled on describing exactly how beautiful she was and all the rest of it. Sentimental, of course, but I didn't see that then. And—and—well, we did have another bottle. I felt so much better, and I had felt so rotten. You know. Well, with the second bottle he came out with the fact that he had had to leave the army because he had married a woman with no money—not of the caste and all that, and then, so he said, to save her he had embezzled some money and had had to clear out.

"She had married or gone off with some one else. That was why he was in the police—and he couldn't forget it—and all that. Well there was nothing extraordinary in the yarn, for men of all sorts were in the B.S.A.P. 'Duke's sons, cook's sons (Pasty, by the way, was the son of a cook and a confectioner by trade—that's why he loved eating, I suppose—still he could make splendid tarts!), sons of a belted earl!' as Kipling has it. Well, he wandered on, talking away, and then became horribly sentimental. Said life wasn't worth living.

"You know how emotional some of these foreigners are. As a matter of fact, he began to weep. I felt uncomfortable—and, well, alcohol has the devil of an effect on fever-weakened people. However, he suddenly streaked out a string of oaths in Austrian or something, threw a bottle on the floor, tragically announced that his wife had used to bathe in the —— stuff and stumbled out of the hut.

"As I walked across to my hut the great moon was rising above the swamp, tinting the bald head of Baboon Hill with blue, so bright that you could see each leaf on a tree. I had a chair just under the eave of my hut, which I had made out of elephant grass and branches. I sat down, sort of fascinated by the moon. No; I wasn't drunk by any means, but I had needed that champagne, and it had put some life into me. To the right was Trotter's old hut, and to the left Pasty Barnet's. The suggestion made me—well, queer. Forty per cent death-rate in a few hours was fairly high even for Mutoko's.

"I had just remarked how yellow was the glow of Lemare's candle against the green sky when I noticed that Hugill's hut was in darkness. Perhaps he was not malingering after all. I went out and sat upon my own rock, staring at the *kopje*. The rhythm of the drums began to affect my mind. I found myself humming some idiotic ditty to the beat.

"A shot which sounded like a big gun crashed out behind me and was caught up and echoed time and again by Baboon Hill. I leaped to my feet, nearly scared out of my wits. I stood for a moment wondering what on earth could have happened. The rhythm of the drums continued. Nobody seemed to have noticed. After all it was not extraordinary for some one to take a pot at a baboon or a hyena. Still, why didn't Lemare come out to see what it was about? I walked across toward his hut, crying:

" 'Johnny! Johnny! Who the devil's—'

"Then I saw through the door a figure lying in a crumpled heap. Ouf! A bullet through the mouth makes an ugly mess. He had pinned a piece of paper on to his table which read—'Here's to the next transfer.'

"The spirit of the champagne left me. I felt weak and sick. I came out, mumbling: 'Good God! Good God!' Then I went across to wake up Hugill. I shouted at him but got no answer. I struck a match. No one was there. In a sudden panic I rushed back to my own hut. I felt uncanny. Scared at the shadows of the moon. I shouted for Sergeant Munyangombo. No answer. Angrily I hastened toward the native camp.

"The quarters of the Black Watch were formed on two sides of a square, and in the middle they had lighted fires around which they were shuffling, the women one way, the men the other, crooning some everlasting chant. I felt eery and unnerved. These figures, with blue and red lights of moon and fire sheening them through the wisps of smoke, seemed sinister: some devil's dance. The moon was so bright that I could distinguish the different men.

"Just as I reached the sergeant's hut, the first, I noticed a stranger seated by the fire, a wizened old man, who was chanting away like a gramophone. That he was a Mashona I could see by certain bracelets of copper wire. His hands were waving to and fro. Just as I was wondering what on earth he thought he was doing, I saw another figure squatted in front of him within the circling group of men. He was white and clad in only a shirt. I recognized Hugill! I stopped, more scared than ever. As I looked, the old man daubed Hugill's neck with some stuff from a calabash.

"For the moment I was so amazed that I merely gasped. No white man does that sort of thing—unless he goes 'fantee'—native, you know. I concluded that he must be drunk or delirious with fever, but, just as I made toward him, a voice murmured—

" '*Inkoos!*'

"The figure of Sergeant Munyangombo in his loin-cloth and bangles loomed so big and savage in the moonlight that for a moment I didn't recognize him.

" 'What do you mean,' I began, pointing at Hugill, 'by letting the *umlungu* come—'

"But Sergeant Munyangombo had begun to talk in a low serious voice which made me listen. The *Inkosi*—that's me—knew that, as he had told me, the white frog was the devil of the mountain, who was very angry at being taken away by a stranger and that therefore he was very dangerous, as everybody knew; again that, as he had told me, the devil spirit had killed the pony and then the big sergeant *Inkoos*. And after that had he not made the fat *umlungu* to run into the swamp so that he could catch him by the leg and drown him in the bog?

"I exclaimed at this statement, but somehow I could not help listening.

"Now the devil spirit was very angry indeed and would kill me and everybody in the station and after that all the people in the villages about. So in their fear they had consulted the great witch-doctor, who everybody knew was the greatest wise man in all Mashonaland, and he had said that the only way to prevent the evil spirit from making all this trouble was to make such magic that he would enter the soul of the *umlungu* Ugilli, for after that he would be unable to make black magic against anybody else. This good magic the celebrated witch-doctor had just made so that now the devil spirit was in Hugill and Hugill's soul was in the white frog.

"For a moment I was both angry at this absurd statement and terribly scared. I was about to tell him that he was under arrest and that I would send them and the witch-doctor, too, to the native commissioner for punishment for having broken the law which forbids the practise of witchcraft. But I saw the image of the crumpled bloody heap in the hut. I didn't believe the silly superstition, of course, but yet—well, I tried to tell myself that this idiotic ceremony, whatever they had been doing, didn't amount to much, anyway.

"I must get Hugill back to his hut and see to the other business. Also it occurred to me that probably Munyangombo had gotten some native beer, which was supposed to be forbidden in camp. So I said it was '*Mushla*'—all right—and told him to tell the *umlungu* that I wanted him.

"Munyangombo seemed very pleased with this and went straight up to Hugill and quite familiarly pulled him out of the circle of the dance and said something to him. Hugill replied. I couldn't catch what he said, but Munyangombo refused energetically. Then Hugill dived forward through the crowd, which parted right and left, and stooped over something before the fire.

"As he picked it up, I caught the gleam of the match-box. He had undoubtedly had the white frog there for the witch-doctor to mumble incantations over. He came toward me, looking in his shirt in the moonlight like a walking corpse. His eyes were shining, too, as with fever, and he reeled slightly. I said as cheerfully as I could, wishing to pacify him—

" 'Come on, old boy, lights out!'

"He stared at me queerly and followed without a word, but, when we had reached our own quarters, he stopped and began to laugh.

" 'I've been having a devil of a time!' he informed me, holding up the match-box in the moonlight. 'Rummy—they've been making me chief; —— of a chief! Me and the —— frog! No more —— cops! I'm going to live on the —— mountain! Hooray!'

"I glanced at him sharply, caught the glint of his eye and decided he hadn't been malingering but really had a bad go of fever on.

" 'Come on, Nosey,' I said soothingly. 'Time—'

"But the absent-minded use of his nickname infuriated him. He ripped out a string of oaths and flung himself upon me.

"We grappled. But I wasn't as strong as I had thought I was. Neither was he. We fought weakly to and fro. My knees collapsed. He fell on top of me and hit me in the face. We rolled over, and I punched him. We struggled on until we were both so exhausted that we couldn't scrap any longer. While we lay opposite to each other on the sandy square in the moonlight, panting and glaring at each other, a silly idea came into my head that the witch-doctor had done something; that perhaps the devil spirit was in Hugill, which had made him crazy.

"He spat some incoherent names at me and laboriously began to crawl toward his hut. Shambling on his hands and knees, he looked like a white bear in the moonlight. I laughed or giggled. He stopped, turned his head and called out a name. I rose to my knees in anger. Then I saw something move. Beside me was the match-box half-open and partly broken in the fight, and distinct in the moonlight was the white frog, which jumped again as I looked.

"In sudden futile anger I raised my boot and brought it down on the frog, squashing it flat. I heard a groan and, looking, saw Hugill lying flat upon his face.

"I got up and went across, cursing the frog. I thought Hugill had fainted. Then I got scared and called Sergeant Munyangombo. Hugill was dead."

Adventure, January 18, 1921

The City of Baal

WILL LANGSTER always somehow reminded me of a thimblerigger's pea; not that he was very small, but that he was never where you thought he was. One moment when you were sure that he was in Timbuktu you would meet him as you strolled into Sherry's; if you were certain you would be able to find him there, you would see him coming out of a Busy Bee in the Bowery; when you were ready to bet that he was dead, a concussion on your shoulder-blades disillusioned you; and when you were convinced . . .

I was a trooper in the British South African Police and was encamped in the middle of the ruins of what had once been, so they said, a Phœnician town. Anyway there are ruins all over the place around there; walls about two to three feet high marking out circles, squares, quadrangles, triangles and what not, as if a god had been teaching geometry to a school of giants. The *kopjes*, too, around this district, as at the great ruins at Zimbawbwe in the south, are full of old fortifications, and the steep hillsides are terraced, undoubtedly for cultivation, as in Syria and Greece.

I was stationed at Mutoko's, some ninety miles from Inyanga D Troop depot. According to instructions, some one had to go out to arrest an alleged murderer. There were three troopers and a sergeant at this out-station; one was sick, another was tired, so the youngest had to go. It was my turn anyway.

That the Mounted Police should be expected to arrest anybody save one another was considered a vast joke; we had always imagined that we were the goat.

However, this fellow, one Matakini—which being interpreted means the chigger flea who burrows in your toe-nails and there lays his eggs which your boy digs out with a needle—had come across the Portuguese border and was suspected of having killed a prospector who had disappeared about a few months before.

Another man, a stranger, was to meet me about half-way. I had information that the wanted man was somewhere hidden in the *kopjes* around and, being young, I was much excited, hoping to get him alone before the Inyanga man and my senior joined me.

Matakini had, according to report, some dozen of his own natives with him, well-armed, and was marching swiftly, avoiding *kraals*—though in this region there were very few villages—to get over the border again where we could not follow him. Next morning I intended to mount the best *kopje*, taking a signaler and leaving the other Black Watch hidden below, to watch a gap which I reckoned he was bound to pass through, and then ride to head him off, for he had no horse, of course.

But as I was cooking some *kabobs* in front of my patrol tent one of my men reported a mounted white man approaching. I cursed because I was conceited enough to think that I didn't need help. He proved a little chap whom I had never seen before; but then I knew that there were a lot of new fellows at the depot at Inyanga. He was very swarthy and looked rather Jewish; some sort of colonial I thought him, or possibly Italian with an accent rather like Corporal Manzini's at Inyanga. I didn't take to him much. For one thing he was sloppy and yet flashy in a way, sporting a chased gold bangle on his hairy, skinny arm like a woman. He was in shirt sleeves, carrying his tunic strapped across his saddle-bow as we usually did; but his riding-pants looked as if they were as the quartermaster had given them out—about three sizes too big.

Most of us liked to dress smartly, having our regimentals altered at our own expense to fit everywhere instead of only in the places where they touched.

Ford had, he told me, sent his detachment of Black Watch to a certain point on the border where he had sure information that the Matakini was to ford the Ruenya River. I was rather angry because I was certain that the fellow was in the vicinity, but as he was senior trooper I had no option.

We had supper and a drink of whisky which he had with him, and turned in; he was dead tired, he pleaded. He talked little; of Inyanga he said he knew nothing as he had only just been transferred from headquarters in Salisbury.

Next morning we made, as he insisted, for a point on the river where to my surprize was a large village. The chief, as usual, came out to greet us, as he was supposed to do, and sent us the usual food and moreover plenty of fish and wild honey. Ford seemed a sulky sort of creature and most of the time we had ridden in silence. The morning after that, according to his instructions, I dispatched my men to a point five miles down the river and I crossed with him.

Then no sooner had we landed on Portuguese territory, which we police were not supposed to do, than he turned suddenly and stuck a revolver under my nose. I was so startled at a man whom I had considered my fellow trooper turning upon me that for a few moments his words appeared utterly incomprehensible. Then slowly it dawned upon me that he was the murderer I was looking for—the Matakini!

He was. And he told me so with a grin and suddenly became very talkative. He thanked me sarcastically for having escorted him into safety, was very rude about my youth, wished to know whether the police ran baby-farms, ordered me off my horse and then commanded me to march in front of him.

I had to obey. To my demand to know where I was to go he laughed and refused to answer. I was young in those days. I cursed and wept with angry humiliation as I trudged along wondering desperately how he had obtained the uniform and what he could possibly want to do with me now that he was safe in Portuguese territory.

I was uncomfortably aware that he was a suspected murderer; and he looked it. The snarl of his mouth as he had jeered at me and the glitter of his black eyes were like a cat playing with a mouse. But what on earth could he wish to kill me for?

Ten miles farther on we came to a village, the chief of which was evidently in the pay of the Matakini. There I was ordered into a hut. As I entered a voice cried out—

"Thank God, you boys have come!"

In front of me was a fairish man standing in his shirt and underpants.

"Lord, but I'm mighty glad—" he went on, and then stopped as the Matakini's face appeared behind me.

"I breeng you another leetle infant for you to play!" he gibed and shut the door.

"Who on earth are you?" I asked bewilderedly.

The blue eyes glared at me angrily as if it were all my fault.

"D'you mean to tell me that that"—his words were regrettable if excusable—"—— put it over on you, too?"

"If you mean," said I, "that he captured me, I'm afraid he did. But who are you?"

"Me?" The blue eyes changed to a laugh. "Same sort of a darn tenderfoot as you! I'm D troop from Inyanga."

"Oh, my lord!" I exclaimed. "The chap who was to meet me?"

"Sure."

We sat down and looked at each other ruefully. He proved to be one Billy Langster, an American—we had divers nationalities in the B.S.A.P.—whom I had not met before and as young as, and possibly a little bit angrier than I. The Matakini had somehow—watched from a *kopje* no doubt—seen that Langster had divided his force, sending a squad right and left to search the hills whilst he and five men had continued up the valley and walked right into an ambush in which the Matakini had shot outright the five Black Watch.

"But for what," I demanded, "has he taken us both? He could have shot either one had he wanted to, —— him."

"Search me," responded Billy. "The point is we've got to get out, and mighty quick. Whether he murdered that prospector fellow or not I dunno, but I'm not asking for an early grave."

"Nor me!"

Late in the afternoon the Matakini sent us some food, of which we were rather scary at first. However, there seemed no reason to poison us if he hadn't shot us. In the evening we noticed that the Matakini was evidently giving a dance to the *kraal* and our hopes rose.

As soon as they had apparently left us for the night we broke a gourd they had left with food and began scraping a tunnel underneath the mud-and-wattle wall at the back of the hut. Luckily the row of the tom-toms and chanting of the natives drowned the scuffling noise we had to make. It was devilish hard work in the sticky heat, but we rested scarcely a minute.

About two in the morning when the dance was going strong we had broken through. Our guard had stuck to his post all right, but was squatting by the door with both his ears stretched toward his luckier brothers. Fortunately the moon came up a little after we were clear of the village.

We ran the major portion of that ten miles to the Ruenya, caring little for the lions that infest this district, and swam the river at the village with never a thought for a croc. We made the chief send runners to Mutoko's, for Billy couldn't walk, as his bare feet had been cut to pieces.

There was an awful shindy about the affair and we were court-martialed, but the case was squashed by "Lyddite," as our C. in C. was known. He ruled that our C.O. was at fault for having sent the most inexperienced youngsters apparently he could find. However, Billy and I became great pals and whenever we were together we spent our time plotting how we would yet get Mr. cube-root adjective Matakini; but we never found out what the Matakini intended to do with us then.

About eighteen months later the Boer War broke out; and while most of our troop was cursing because we couldn't join in the row we heard that poor Billy, who had been down at Umtali, had been chewed up by a lion. I was more than sorry, for I had liked him a lot and we had had a general agreement that when our time was in we would either go in trading together or set out to get the Matakini—whichever had depended upon the amount of exhilaration at the moment.

When I got my ticket I, with a bunch of bloodthirsty souls, went down south. At Durban we heard that Kitchener had started a nice little corps of irregulars which seemed very inviting, a lovely little outfit from an adventurer's point of view; no pay, own horses and seventy-five per cent of all confiscations, divided among the members of the corps, fifty-odd strong and all expert scouts.

The only trouble was that recruiting for this select party was in Pretoria only. I chanced my arm, as they say in the army, and putting up officer's tabs, bluffed my way up the line. I went all right as far as Elandsfontein Junction, where I was compelled to get a fresh pass for Pretoria, for the one which I had bought was for Johannesburg. Feeling pretty scared, for it meant three years at least if I were caught, I boldly walked into the office of the R.S.O. (Railway Staff Officer) and stared at a full-blown captain who was saying coolly:

"Hullo, Faxy, old boy! Where did you spring from?"

"For ——'s sake, Billy!" I gasped. "I thought you were inside a lion."

"I was, ole buck," he grinned back; "inside a steam lion that bolted all the way to Beira. I found a steam whale there that spewed me upon the beach at Durban like Jonah. They winged me at Kameel *spruit* and I got dysentery and things, so I'm here for a soft job for a month or so. How's the Matakini?"

"Dunno," said I, "and don't care for the moment; but we must get the blighter yet when this show's over."

Of course I told him what I was after and he threatened to desert by way of another lion in order to join the Scouts with me. Well, the war petered out eventually, but I didn't see Billy until several years later. It was in New York; I found him with many females in Sherry's, doing in, as he told me, the result of a trip to the Russo-Jap War.

We revived old times, of course, over a matter of several weeks, drinking the Matakini's health most gorgeously; and then he went south to see his people.

Again time ran on. When I was in Borneo I heard a lot of talk among the Dutch officials of some man who had been playing old Harry on their pearl-fishing grounds. It seemed that this fellow and a Chinaman under the pretense of trade had been swiping fabulous sums of pearls—so they said—without the formality of paying license and taxes, and when they had sought to remonstrate by means of a warship he had headed a party of natives and bagged the cutter too.

I didn't guess who this enterprising chap could be until I got to Singapore. There every one was talking about a crazy American who had thrown money about like cigaret-ends and had left by the Messageries for Marseilles. Well, while I was signing the register at Raffles I saw in bold, scrawling characters, "Billy Langster."

I wandered on my erratic path, and after trying in my turn to pinch an empire, found myself with six pennies in a London doss-house. As I came into the common room, where you have the privilege of cooking your penny bloater, a dirty-looking object crouching in a corner let out a yell and sprang at me.

"Matakini! You old son of a gun!"

Billy once more, of course—at the end of a dreadful bust. We left London and went on the road, where we saw something of English haystacks and damp weather and spent many pleasant hours telling yarns of our various adventures. At Liverpool,

Billy shipped for the States and I looked up a millionaire who had African interests and tried to be good in a job.

Old Dame Fortune gave the wheel another twiddle. Some three years later I found myself so short of ready cash in Port Said—I had taken the foresight to get a draft on Durban and had had the short sight to spend nearly all I had in Cairo—that I was compelled to take steerage to Mombasa on a German boat.

At Djibouti I met a mad Scot who had been up in the interior and would have joined in with him; but on our arrival at Beira, where we both went ashore to smell around for possibilities, whom should I see garbed in immaculate whites but dear old Billy. He was changed somewhat; fatter than usual and wearing a beard but not so boisterous as he had been, and at first more reticent. One thing I did notice was that he appeared to have forgotten the old war-cry of "the Matakini!" for all he said was—and that quietly—

"Faxy, by ——; the very man I'm praying for!"

He insisted upon dining us, of course, but purposely avoided any reference as to what he was doing. When he knew that I was at a loose end he urged me to stay over a few days at least. The crazy Scot, who had money, went on back to the boat bound for Heaven-knows-where to carve a fortune with a ridiculous sword he carried, which he said had belonged to King Robert Bruce of Scotland. When he had gone Billy turned to me as we were sitting on the veranda and said quietly—

"I'm getting even with the Matakini."

"What!"

"*Sssh!* Come up to my room and I'll tell you the yarn."

II

We had been sitting after dinner on the patio or veranda of the hotel on the street. From somewhere close came the tinkle of a mandolin and a throaty tenor wailing on the sticky night air. Billy's room was at the side with two fairly wide-open windows on to two streets, one very narrow with single-storied houses. Billy switched on the light—oh yes, they had electricity even in those days in Beira—and made me comfy in a wicker chair by the wash-basin; and when we had our cheroots going he sprawled on the bed, which occupied the center of the room. He grinned at me and began—

"Faxy, d'you remember that yarn you told me camping under a —— damp tree in the Springtime in England—about an empire you tried to pinch?"

"Of course," said I; "but—"

"Well, old son of a gun, I've got one! A sure bet because I haven't got to bump up against a regular he-man power as you had."

"An empire! Where? Here?"

"Not in Beira, old sport, but not a five hundred miles away all the same. Sure thing, I'm telling you," he added in response to my incredulous stare. "No, it's not a hop-dream either. And you're going to come in."

"You bet," said I; "but—"

"But me no buts, you dismal *Hamlet!* Look here!"

He drew back his white sleeve, revealing a gold bracelet upon his forearm.

"Did you ever see one like that before?"

I stared; and association brought to me a swarthy, hairy arm, nearly black, which had worn a bracelet also.

"By —— yes; the Matakini!"

"That's right. Did you ever examine it? No? Well, dekko now."

On examination I saw that it was heavily chased in simple design which vaguely reminded me of something.

"Greek, isn't it—or Etruscan?"

"No; Phœnician or whoever those guys were who made those ruins at Zimbawbwe and around Mutoko's. Remember them?"

"Certainly I do. That's where I met the Matakini."

"Sure you did! So did I!" He laughed. "That's mighty queer. Never noticed that before. That's where I met him again; I mean in the same surroundings. You recollect we could never make out why he took us prisoners? Well, I've got an idea. All right; don't get mad at me," he added as I exhibited impatience.

He slid off his bed to get some more cheroots, fixed another seltzer and whisky and settled on the bed again.

"Look here; so's you'll get the hang of the whole thing I'd better go way back."

"You recollect when I shipped away for the States at Liverpool? When I got over the other side I went as usual down to see the folks. Of course they wanted me to be good and all that. Man, to please 'em I tried as we all do. But you might as well expect a leopard to sit and lick himself in the middle of a hen-farm. Even went as far as taking a job in my uncle's office—the old man's dead, you know.

"I had never known what hell was before. For those three months—yes, I stuck it out for three months—coming home o' nights like a hen-pecked husband, listening to the whole bunch lecturing me and telling me that I ought to get married and all that! Me!

"Well, then I took a flying jaunt up to li'l ole New York; just thought if I could get away from the home-town I'd feel better for a bit. You know. Then in a hop-joint down the Bowery I fell across a guy who had been in our bunch—oh, away after our time.

"Of course, we got to yarning, and he came out with a yarn that set me by the ears. You remember the lie of the mountains at the back of Inyanga—the Mountains of the Mist, as Rider Haggard called 'em; the watershed of the Pungwe and the border? Well, according to him he deserted with a bunch of others from D Troop from Inyanga and bolted over the range into Portuguese country with the idea of cutting the rail the other side of Umtali and getting to Beira and a boat.

"But it appears that they were a pretty tenderfoot bunch and got lost in the dense forest. Their horses sickened as they would with tsetse fly, and they bumped up against a crowd of natives who nearly wiped 'em out.

"After wandering in the jungle for several days they climbed a bit of a hill, determined to seek shelter at the nearest *kraal* for the sake of food. Then, this fellow told me, he saw or thought he saw sticking out of the forest at what seemed about five miles away, a city of houses white in the sun. He says he began to cry, thinking he'd gone loony. Anyway the other fellows had got 'em too, for they saw the same thing."

"What!" I interrupted. "A city of houses near the source of the Pungwe! For Heaven's sake, you haven't come all this way to follow a pipe-dream like that, Billy! You said you met the man in a hop-joint. Why, Umtali's the nearest; and that must be several hundred."

"Shut your head, old buck," retorted Billy. "Anyway these fellows just naturally made a straight line as far as possible for this extraordinary city. They plunged on, weak as they were, all day; but down in the forest of course they couldn't see anything except trees.

"Just as they were beginning to doubt each other and think that the whole thing was some form of mirage they were surrounded by some fifty natives—big fellows, the man said—armed with spears and blunderbuses and Belgian Sniders, although some of them had modern rifles—Mannlichers.

"They were too done to think of putting up a fight and were too glad to have a chance for some food. What dialect the natives spoke he didn't know, for not one of the bunch knew more than a few words of kitchen-Kaffir. Anyway they were marched off to a *kraal* near by, a well-kept and heavily barricaded village, according to what he said, put in a well-built hut and given food. Of course there was a lot of *indaba* which none of the fellows could understand. Anyway after being bucked up by food they began to sit up and take more notice.

"First of all they decided that the city they had seen was undoubtedly a mirage, or rocks shining in the sun; secondly they noticed that some chiefs, who came as if to view them, wore gold bangles—no, not like this one," interposed Billy, touching the one on his arm.

"That just got most of them going, as it were. Gold must be there. But they were prisoners and disarmed, and anyway as they had seen they would never be able to put up anything of a scrap, much less raid anybody. So they began to figure out how they could make a getaway and get up a real expedition.

"But that little plan was mighty soon hit on the head. There seemed to be a lot of excitement in the village that day, and the next morning at daybreak they were taken out and led off down a Kaffir path through the forest. Of course where they were going they hadn't the faintest idea, but go they had to.

"About eleven, according to this chap, he was plowing along, feeling sick and suffering from sore feet, when the man in front of him literally yelped. He looked up; and there, sparkling in the sun, through a break in the forest high on a *kopje* was the walled city of houses they had seen before, and all about it was terrace upon terrace of—gardens, he called 'em."

"What!" I expostulated. "D'you mean to say one of the old Phœnician cities?"

"Yessir!" asserted Billy. "Of course when this fellow let this out down in that Bowery joint I thought, too, it was a hop-dream, but what shook me up was this fact: How the —— could he have imagined a Phœnician city or ruins so near the Inyanga district where I knew such ruins are, if he hadn't been there?"

"That's true, but—well, where's this fellow now?"

"In New York for all I know or care. He was a flabby-kneed creature anyway, and the hop had got him; but all the same a million dollars wouldn't bring him back here."

"But why—"

"I'm telling you. They brought the bunch of them into the town; and a town it was with regular streets and real houses full of blacks—of course—holding markets and the Lord knows what. There they were put into another prison built of stones fashioned like bricks—remember those ruins around Mutoko's? They were given more food and left alone. Of course they were in a worse pickle than ever; not only that, but they were sort of fuddled with the whole thing. He told me that he had a queer sensation as if he weren't alive or was somehow living several centuries ago. All they could do naturally was to talk and wait.

"For three days, bar the blacks who brought them food, they saw no one. Then on the fourth they were taken out and led up the hill—I told you it was like a medieval castle on a *kopje*, didn't I?—up the hill to a kind of fortress as he described it.

"The six of 'em were placed in a row with a guard of blacks who carried enormous spears like halberds and dressed in leopard-skins. They reckoned that they must be the king's guard.

"While they were kept like that a gang came out from a high door to inspect them, and what surprized 'em was that these fellows, evidently chiefs or something like that, were not black but an olive-bronze color with hawk noses and thin lips more like Arabs; and they were dressed in white robes not quite in the Arabian fashion, because each wore a kind of tunic or toga and on their wrists were gold bangles chased; yes, like mine.

"They came over, sat in front of the prisoners on stools carved with a similar design to the one I showed you a while ago and inlaid with gold, and began to discuss something among themselves in a language which my man says he suspected from the first was not a native lingo. Then an elderly fellow with a white beard and melancholy eyes leaned forward a little and shook 'em up by demanding in English but with a strong accent—

" 'What do you seek in this country?'

"Apparently they all answered at once. The old man held up his hand.

" 'Your chief, if you please?'

"One of the bunch who had been a sergeant, a cockney, said—

" 'We lorst ourselves.'

" 'But what were you seeking when you lost yourselves?' the elder asked.

" 'We was trying to get out to Beira, mister. We was in the police over there,' said the sergeant, and jerked a thumb vaguely, 'and we were fed up and wanted to go 'ome.'

"The chiefs listened to a translation of this and seemed mighty puzzled. Then while they were still chewing the fat a small procession came out of the big door. A man was sitting on a kind of wooden *machilla*. He was dressed up, so my man described him, like a Roman general with a gold helmet on his head. But it wasn't Roman"—Billy interrupted himself—"because I made him make a rough sketch of it. More like an Etruscan form or Phœnician, if you know the difference."

"I don't," said I impatiently. "But go on."

"Well, this fellow they reckoned was the king. He sat down in the middle of the elders. Then a little fellow—his features were slightly different to the others; more Jewish, he said—asked them in English—again with an accent—what they wanted. They tried to explain; but apparently he didn't want to listen to anything they had to say, for he began talking rapidly to the others. Several seemed as if they didn't agree, but finally the Jewish guy turned to them and said quickly:

" 'We're not going to keel you now but you can nevaire get out. You un'erstan'?'

" 'Good ——, what d'you mean?' broke in one of the party. 'You mean we're prisoners? What for?'

" 'You can't do it! Daren't do it!' the others hollered. 'The British government—'

" 'The Breteesh government will not do anyzing because God do not weesh,' the man announced. 'That ees all.'

"He sent 'em back with a wave of the hand, and they were herded back into their jail, kicking, but in a —— of a scare. They decided that the man was plumb crazy and talked all night wondering what was meant. In the morning they were surprized to be taken to a larger house with lots of gardens formed of the terraces—recollect the Inyanga ones?—and given more food and wine than they could eat or drink; even whisky, cigarets and cigars. They had nothing to do. The only thing was that they couldn't get out; were closely guarded by these big blacks with halberd spears day and night. They had nothing to do but eat and drink and smoke their heads off; but of information as to what was intended they couldn't get a word.

"They were forever making plans to escape even though the life seemed soft enough.

"For some months nothing happened. With no exercise—just lounging about and well fed—they began to get fat and lazy; that and the climate. Then one day the cockney sergeant disappeared. The last they had seen of him he had been in the garden smoking. They never saw or heard of him again. As a matter of fact they scarcely saw anybody save the black guards. Well, that happenstance scared 'em some.

"My man says he was there for about two years—and during that time two others disappeared. Then they became desperate and made a frantic stab at getting away. They got caught. But instead of being punished they were isolated in different houses. He says he began to think that he was going crazy, but within a few months he succeeded in beating it."

"But how?"

"A woman helped him. He must have been good-looking before the hop got him."

"But what did it all mean? Who are the priests and king people if they're not native negroes?"

"He never knew. Couldn't speak the lingo, remember; or even if he did learn it he never saw anybody but the guards and negro folk. That's just what I was determined to find out. I wanted him to come back; but as I said, he wouldn't for a million.

"Of course that yarn got me. Talked my head off to my uncle. Didn't dare tell him such a hop-dream, you bet! Said I was no good anyway, and if he'd advance me some few bucks on what would come to me on my mother's death I'd promise to disappear for keeps. For once he agreed with me.

"I'm supposed to be rubber-planting. Of course I made straight for here. I managed to dig out various rumors of strange things up-country and found a partner—Harvey, an Englishman; an awful son of a gun, but of course I didn't know that until after we had left Umtali. Then he developed an idea that he was running the outfit—you know the type, Faxy."

"I do," said I feelingly. Well I knew how different a man may be in town from what the wilds bring out.

Billy laughed and slid off the bed.

"Just to whet your appetite, old buck," he remarked, dragging out a steel uniform-case beneath the bed.

He opened it and held up what appeared to be an ampulla or flask, made of gold. As I exclaimed in astonished admiration the electric light failed. I heard an exclamation from Billy; and as I rose, thinking something about a short circuit, I saw dark forms in the window. Then a blow put me out.

When I came to I was blinking at the stars being washed out by the dawn, and a million mosquitoes were chewing my face. As recollection came back I sat up, wondering how on earth I had got there and where I was, and conscious of a sore head.

And Billy? Vague recollections of the strange story he had been telling me returned. Good Lord, I thought, what could have happened? Robbery? I felt my pockets. No.

I got up and looked around. Evidently I was somewhere on the outskirts of the town, for a stretch of swamp and sand was in front of me and low adobe sort of houses at the back. I hastened along and after some trouble in locating it found the hotel.

As I paused to be certain which was Billy's room the proprietor came out. I inquired for Senhor Langster's room. The man appeared puzzled. He did not know the gentleman, he explained.

"But yes," said I, "a *senhor Americão*," and described Billy as well as I could, adding that I had dined with him on the previous night.

Very unctuously the *patron* informed me that there were two German *senhors*, one French *senhor* and three Portuguese *senhores*, but most certainly no English or American. Irritated, I pointed out the room, judging by the recollection of the windows from the street.

"The room is empty," he explained; "but if the *senhor* insists—"

He led me up and opened the door. It *was* Billy's room; but the bed was uncreased and there was no sign of our drinks and cheroots; spotlessly clean—that is, for a Portuguese room. I was flabbergasted. I followed him mutely.

"The *senhor* is satisfied?"

Staring at him, I was taken by another idea.

"But where's *my* room? I took a room here last night."

The *patron* regretted exceedingly that he had never had the honor of seeing the *senhor* before.

"Oh my ——!" said I, holding my throbbing head. "I don't exist either!"

"But if the *senhor* requires a room—?"

"No; a cognac. That is," I added dismally, sinking into a chair on the patio, "if I don't melt into thin air before you come back."

III

WHEN MY PHYSICAL HEAD as well as my mental felt a little clearer I gave up wondering and began to try to piece matters together. I had difficulty at first when recalling Billy's yarn to realize whether he really had told that queer story or not. It was only by going back and linking up incidents from the time when I had stepped ashore with the mad Scot to my meeting Billy, dining and listening to the yarn up to the point when Billy had held up the golden ampulla that I convinced myself that it was really true.

First of all, I asked myself, what had become of him and why? Had he been killed or kidnaped? How had he been able to live in this mysterious city and come out alive?

Whatever had happened I saw that the greasy proprietor of the hotel was in league with the assaulters. From him alone could I possibly get any information. I decided that I would interview the gentleman, and at the end of a gun. But obviously I couldn't do that in the open.

I called him up and informed him that I had changed my mind and would take a room. He spread out his fat hands and professed to be delighted to honor the *senhor*. I rose, bidding him to show me to the room. He led me as far as the door and then called a servant. The cunning little man had evidently foreseen my move. I couldn't object, but decided to wait my chance.

I sat on the very bed Billy had sat upon and tried anew to solve the problem. It would be utterly useless, I knew, to go to either the British consul or even the American had there been one. I had not a shred of evidence in view of the fact that the proprietor and evidently his staff would deny all knowledge of Billy.

After I had bathed my head, which was not badly cut, I went down for breakfast. Diaz, as I learned his name was, was still mouching about the dining-room. As I drank my coffee I watched him. He appeared perfectly unconcerned, exhibiting none of the furtive looks and grimaces such as villains are usually supposed to make.

I got into conversation with him. Obviously from what I had heard of Billy's story the Matakini had something to do with it, although Billy had not mentioned him as far as he had gone except in opening the subject when he had remarked that he had "got even" with the Matakini.

I chattered about Beira and asked questions that a traveler would ask, and then suddenly inquired whether he knew the Matakini. Not a flicker of an eyelid was there as he affected astonishment, inquiring whether the *senhor* was pleased to joke about chigger fleas. I explained that I meant a man, but the test had failed. Quite possibly, I reflected, the Matakini was known in these parts, if known at all, under some other name.

I decided to wander around the town and tried to pick up a clue. After rescuing my bag from the customs I hired a trolley such as they push on rails in Beira about the sandy streets and set out on a tour.

I spent most of the morning sampling various bars before I found anybody who seemed likely, and that was a bullet-headed Irishman who ran a liquor-dive. He seemed as friendly as an Irish terrier and rather glad to chat with me.

Once he got going, he became fairly voluble, and from him I began to learn something about the manners and customs of Beira. Only six or seven weeks ago, according to his loquacious account, the governor of the province, his Excellency O Capitão-Gerale Dom Porfirio Fernandez Diaz—who was not related, I learned, to my innkeeper—had been held up by three Englishmen in his private train as he was returning from up-country with native taxes in gold. He was compelled at the point of the revolvers actually to escort the desperadoes on board a private yacht in which two of them had come. Since then foreigners had not been popular with the said Excellency.

I rather suspected that my host's Celtic imagination ran away a bit; nevertheless I guessed that there must be some truth in the yarn, which seemed to amuse him vastly. Finally I decided to confide in him, not giving away poor Billy's strange story, of course. I merely explained that whilst talking to this friend we had been attacked and described what had happened since that point.

O'Grath, as he had introduced himself, seemed to imagine that this was another joke, but he could give me little information or encouragement. Such things in Beira were not judged to be of a hair-raising vintage. As I had supposed, he said that if I went to the governor I would get little attention or none at all, particularly as I was of the same nationality as the gentlemen of the yacht who had so wounded the Capitão-Gerale's good temper, dignity and private purse.

However, I did strike something when I inquired whether he knew or had ever heard of the Matakini. At first he could not recollect the sobriquet, but after I had described him he did. A trader he was supposed to be who came from up-country somewhere. Little was known about him except that he was considered dangerous to monkey with. He was reported to have made a pile in ivory, and consequently had the means to gain the good-will with the governor and officials.

I asked O'Grath where this individual came from, but that he did not know except that he got off the line from Beira to Umtali in Rhodesia near the border at a station called Manzini. I made a note of the name and strolled back to my hotel with the object of interviewing friend Diaz the lesser, but he was not to be seen; and when I inquired for him I was informed that the *patron* had been called away on urgent business; up the line, they said, but I had good reason not to believe them.

I sat down and got my brainbox going again. That Billy had been murdered I did not think—in spite of the presence of the golden ampulla. The murderers might have been assistants of the greasy innkeeper. Such things have often occurred before. But then why hadn't they murdered me?

There seemed far more at the back of the whole situation than I considered, probably influenced by Billy's extraordinary yarn. Who and what were this mysterious city and the non-negroid priests or rulers, from whom evidently the ampulla had come as well as the bracelets?

I calculated the financial side. On me I had scarcely five pounds; but I had the draft on Durban for a few hundred with which I had originally intended to hunt for possibilities in Rhodesia. Now I could have the draft transferred from Durban, of course; but if I bought equipment and started up the line from Beira in search of the mysterious city and Billy something would be likely to happen swiftly and violently, as undoubtedly I would be watched by those who had been responsible for Billy's disappearance.

I decided to transfer the money to Delagoa Bay, go there and thence up the line through Rhodesia to Umtali, the place which I recollected Billy had said he had started from. But neither a mail-boat nor any other form of locomotion runs from Beira every day. I had to hang around three days before a tramp bound for Delagoa turned up.

However, during that time my precious greasy host of the inn did not show up; and I spent most of my time with the Irishman O'Grath. From him I got a bit of information which taught me that I wouldn't make a good Sherlock Holmes. A point which I had utterly forgotten to inquire about, and which he revealed in a casual remark while talking about the Matakini, was to the effect that he had heard that the Matakini had been in Beira about four days ago, down from up-country for provisions. That, thought I, settles the fact that the Matakini is at the bottom of the mystery; therefore to find Billy I must hunt the Chigger.

I could not find any likely partner whom I knew in view of general experience and Billy's hinted troubles with the man Harvey, so I decided to play a lone hand. A month later I set out from Umtali, intending to follow Billy as far as I could, heading for the head-waters of the Pungwe. As far as the Rhodesian border the trail was fairly easy; but fifteen miles within what was nominally Portuguese territory I lost trace of his passage and began to get in touch with tribes who were little acquainted with the white man and his ways, although they were friendly enough and eager to trade.

I had—wisely, I thought—not made any definite plan, deciding to wait until I got to the river, as the old adage says, before trying to cross it. My equipment was small—necessarily; and anyway as I knew from experience the bigger the caravan, unless heavily armed, the more the temptation to attack and loot it; also the more difficulty in traversing strange country to obtain porters either to go or fresh men there. I had only ten *pagazi* and two servants, one officially a gun-bearer—a retinue not large enough to attract undue attention.

Of Portuguese interference twenty miles from the rail I had no fear whatever. Occasionally the Portuguese made futile attempts to collect hut tax, but in the interior on the few occasions when they had sent a punitive expedition they had suffered repulses, in one case having practically the whole force annihilated. The whole of the upper regions of Portuguese East Africa north of the rail to the one-time German border was to all intents and purposes unknown territory; hence the Billy story, or rather the suggestion of Billy's unfinished story, was feasible—at least insofar as some unknown tribe's actually being there.

Ten days out I came to the village of a chief who was of sufficient importance and power to make it necessary to have his permission to enter his country. Fortunately I am fair, a trait which has helped me quite a lot with the natives in this region, to whom a Portuguese for very sound reasons is anathema. Since leaving Umtali this village was the first one I remarked as being really fortified; that is, it had a well-constructed stockade around it, indicating not a people who were timorous but a warlike tribe surrounded by other warlike tribes among whom there were, as is frequently the case, continual forays and raids.

The chief was a middle-aged man who seemed inclined to be suspicious as well as greedy. The *indaba* lasted several days, he continually making excuses to prolong my stay.

Although I made discreet inquiries as to whether Billy had passed through I could not gain any hint that pointed to him in particular until I saw by accident one of the chief's brothers sporting a Martini rifle. Now the Portuguese and most traders in their territory use either the Snider or some other make of gun. Such trade goods too as they had were, I knew, of Portuguese origin. As I knew that Billy had started from Umtali I took it as fairly certain that the gun had come from him, so that I became more anxious than ever to continue on.

On the morning of the fifth day I was summoned by a young warrior for an audience with the chief, whom I found in the usual clubhouse in the center of the village squatting with his elders and witch-doctors. As soon as I was seated on the campstool carried for me by my bearer I noticed—for you have to make it your business to remark such things apparently trivial, on which nevertheless your life may depend—that among them was a stranger, a youngish man to whom was paid in the native manner much deference. Upon his forearm was a gold bangle, the sight of which quickened my hopes considerably.

The *indaba* had been delayed, I thought, in order to summon him. From the fact that he was not of the same tribe, as was revealed by the difference in the form of hair-dressing and the tribal cicatrices, I gathered that these people must be subject to another tribe. This man carried too, I noticed, a Service rifle of the pattern with which the Rhodesian Mounted Police are armed, another point which made me sure that I was on the right track; for I figured that more than probably he must have been one of the chiefs who had captured and disarmed the party of six deserters from Inyanga.

After the customary beating about the bush, a prohibitive price for powerful magic was demanded on the ground that the evil spirits which were with me would be difficult to exorcise. I made the correct answer, and, smiling as if I were tickled to death, retired to consider what I should do. The amount—in goods, of course—was ridiculous; and moreover I saw that should I give way on that point others would immediately arise.

When I reached my camp I found unmistakable symptoms of real trouble brewing. There were no women and children squatting around for what they could pick up in the way of valuable old sardine-tins or legitimate trade.

I had lunch in the open before my tent and tried to find a way out of the tangle. Perhaps, influenced or ordered by the strange chief, they were about to attempt to disarm me or possibly murder me out of hand. But the latter I did not think was likely; rather it seemed to me that the former was the more probable course, as it was what the other natives had done with the police-party. But I certainly had no desire to enter the secret city as a prisoner to be tortured or massacred.

Throughout the day nobody from the village came near us. My twelve men were squatting around their temporary grass shelters, evidently discussing important news. From the look of them I began to think that they had got wind of something and might desert me at any moment—at any rate the ten porters.

I called up Magunga, my head boy and servant, and asked him what the porters were talking about. He said they were commenting on the absence of women and children and added that the chief was angry with their white men who, from remarks overheard of the villagers, had offended against some tabu. I knew what that meant— the usual excuse to justify themselves, sought by whites as well as blacks when about to do something particularly evil.

I realized that I had to act, and that quickly. If I made the slightest sign of striking camp I was pretty sure that they'd hurry matters—probably rush me. On the morrow they certainly would. "When you are menaced by an enemy, strike first," is a good motto; and I adopted it. I knew that I couldn't get far with my scheme; but at all events I might work out of this fix.

The sun was about an hour above the treetops when I went with Magunga, whom I did not tell of my plan, preceding me with a campstool, up to the entrance of the stockade and called out that I had come to give the chief my words in reply. I was apparently unarmed, though in reality I had two revolvers hidden beneath my coat. Several men came out of their huts fully armed, and grouped about me, watching curiously and chatting, but I couldn't follow what they said as I did not know their local dialect well enough.

I appeared as unconcerned as possible as I awaited the messenger, who presently returned and bade me to follow him. To my delight this time I found the chief squatting beneath a tree in front of his house with the stranger alone with him.

After the usual preliminaries I told them that I was a top-side number-one white man who was both a hunter and a magician; that I had just consulted my private oracle, who had informed me just what sort of blackguard he was; that because of that I wouldn't stay in his beastly country if he paid me—or words to that effect; that I intended to leave his village on the morrow at the hour of the monkey, or cock-crow; and added that he would give himself the pleasure to pass the night with me and escort me personally and alone toward the border for one day's long march. This—to him—extraordinary statement finally penetrated into his head and raised a guttural cluck of astonishment. While I was warning him that any resistance would mean certain death, I shifted suddenly to get my back to the hut wall in case any of his people were peeping through the reed fence, and whipped out both revolvers.

Instantly the young stranger grabbed for his spear. I fired, deliberately breaking the haft above the spot where he had clutched it. He grunted and remained still.

I heard cries and yells coming from the village. I told the chief to shout instructions to keep away or I would blow his head off. He did it somewhat hurriedly. Further I instructed him to inform his people that he would walk in front of me through the village to my camp and that if any one attempted to attack, both chiefs would drop dead.

Through the crowd of excited warriors brandishing spears and guns my two prisoners marched ahead with Magunga immediately behind me. At the gate I made my man warn them that they must not come within one hundred paces of my camp. He did so.

In the tent I tied the pair to the tent-pole with straps, sat on the bed with the revolvers on the little camp table facing them, told Magunga to do continuous sentry-go around the camp and to warn me if anybody approached, ordered the other boy to make much tea and light the lantern, and with cigarets prepared to pass the night.

To while away the time I attempted to get my prisoners to talk. The local chief, who was in an obvious funk, immediately began to lay the blame upon the other fellow, whom, he pleaded, he was bound to obey; but the stranger, even when menaced with the revolver within a few inches of his head, would not open his mouth, exhibiting not the slightest sign of cowardice.

From the village I could hear the hubbub going on all night. Some of them came close to my camp in the darkness in spite of their fear of evil spirits; mostly, I think, expecting to see some terrible demons prancing about the white magician's camp; but no one attempted to attack. At dawn I prepared to march.

As my men were striking camp I noticed that the hubbub among the villagers, which had increased at the signs of moving, had died down. With my two chiefs walking in front as security I started off.

About a couple of hundred yards from the village the back trail led through a narrow belt of swamp and forest. In the early light it was faint twilight at most in the shadow of the great trees heavily festooned with creepers, and the going was difficult, particularly for a white with boots on. The porters waded to their knees and sometimes to their waists in stinking black mud.

Scrambling with difficulty from fungoid root to root, I was compelled to stick my guns in my belt; but still there was no chance of either captive bolting, for before he could leap and scramble out of sight in the undergrowth I could easily have brought him down. In the very gloomiest portion just as I was balancing for a spring on to another root a voice shouted—

"Put your hands up or I weel shoot!"

I was so startled that I slipped and slid up to my waist in the ooze. Then I saw within five feet the muzzle of a rifle covering me and behind it a black-bearded, swarthy face beneath a ragged felt hat.

As I obeyed, the figure advanced from where he had been in hiding in the thicket, revealing a small man dressed like a native in loin-cloth and boots, a white man whose shoulders were burned almost black with the sun and upon whose hairy arm gleamed dully a gold bracelet.

IV

As, HOLDING THE RIFLE at the hip with his finger on the trigger, the Matakini disarmed me for the second time I squirmed with rage. But nevertheless I thought swiftly. The first thing to know or guess was, did the man know me? I didn't flatter myself that he would recollect the young trooper on the Ruenya; and anyway I had altered as he had. The question was rather, had he been present when Billy was kidnaped or murdered? And had he seen me in Billy's company? If he had then surely he would know instantly what I was after. I decided to pretend that I did not know him from Cain.

I noticed as my late captives came up that they did not seem at all surprised; and, recollecting that the hubbub had ceased that morning as I was striking camp, I guessed that the Matakini must have arrived, quieted them and lain in ambush for me.

Perhaps after all the delay had been purposely made to give them time to send for the Matakini; at any rate he seemed to have, as had the strange chief, control over the others; for as the warriors came yelling triumphantly from all sides about us he shouted at them in the dialect that they were not to injure me.

"What d'you mean," said I as he turned to me; "you, a white man, taking sides with natives?"

"Go back to villeege. I talk with you zere. Go!"

He motioned with my own revolver, and I was compelled to obey.

On that short walk to the village I did some more industrious thinking. I began to be certain that the Matakini did not recollect ever having seen me before either in Rhodesia or Beira; therefore apparently he had not conducted Billy's disappearance in person. The point was, what did he intend to do with me now? Why really had he interfered?

There seemed to be, as the story of the police deserters intimated, a regularly organized system among the natives to keep all whites or strangers away. Why? Billy's uncompleted story of the mysterious city might be a feasible solution. I remembered too that those six deserters had been taken straight to the city and condemned to some mysterious fate from which only one escaped. I seemed likely to follow their example.

Surrounded by the warriors, who already were driving my unhappy *pagazi* and two headmen with my goods at the point of their spears, we arrived at the village amid much hubbub and noise. The Matakini, who had not spoken on the road, ordered me into a hut just within the stockade, and, squatting upon a chief's stool a native brought, he announced:

"Now I talk wit' you. What you want come here for? What you want shoot my frien' for? You tell me or I shoot you; you see?"

"In the first place," said I, sitting down with my back against the wall, "who the —— are you? And secondly, what d'you mean by holding me up? You're white, aren't you?"

He tapped the revolver-barrel with a finger.

"You no talk what I tell you, he talk; you see?"

"Yes, I see; but any fool can murder a defenseless man. You as a white owe me an explanation for taking the side of a native."

"You say what for you want shoot my frien'?"

"I had no intention of murdering your 'friend,' as you're pleased to call him. I was merely taking precautions to prevent his murdering me."

"He no want keel you. He want keep you till I come, you see."

"I see. But who the —— may you be?"

"That not your beesiness. You say what you come here for."

"Well, if you must know, I should say it's pretty obvious, isn't it? What else would a man come here for but to trade?"

The sharp black eyes watched me keenly. That he had not seen me in Beira was evident.

"You have been in this country before?"

"Never. Rhodesia's my country."

"What you do in Rhodesia?"

"That's my beesiness," I retorted, mocking him.

"Ah! I know. You prospector. You want come here look for gold. You Breteesh. Then you send soldier here. But there ees no gold here, you see."

"You mean," said I unwisely, "that what there is you want to keep yourself, eh?"

"Who told you gold here?"

"The fact of your presence is sufficient guarantee."

"That no come from here," he said, noticing my involuntary glance at his bangle. "That come from Cypre. I Cypre man. I leef here twenty year. This my country. I no want other people come my country; you see?"

"You mean you're chief of these tribes; is that it?"

"I no chief. I *padrio*."

"*Padrio*? What d'you mean? That there's a monastery here?"

"Monastery, yes. Big monastery, but not what you b'lieve."

"What? Do you mean some form of the Ethiopian Church?"

"Much more old than Ethiopian Church."

"What? Some ancient Phœnician religion? Is there a Phœnician city there?" I exclaimed, forgetting my situation in my interest.

"Who tell you city there?" he demanded instantly.

"No one told me," I lied. "Aren't there tons of old Phœnician ruins over the other side of Inyanga there?"

"Inyanga! You been Inyanga?"

He peered at me intently and then laughed.

"Ah, it ees my leetle frien' who want take me for police at Mutoko's; *hein*? Ha-ha-ha! How you do again? What you do all time? You catch bad mans, yes? When I see you I t'ink all time where I seen that funnee face."

"That'll do," said I wrathfully. "I'll get even—"

"You forget my leetle frien'; you see?" he reminded me, tapping the revolver-barrel. "You want talk wi' him, yes?"

"Well, what d'you intend to do with me?" I demanded.

"What I do wit' ev'rybody come my country."

"You didn't with one anyway," said I angrily.

"Ah, you mean the other leetle infant whose boots I take, yes? You seen him then at Beira? They tell me he talk too much—you frien', yes. I know ev'ryt'ing, you see."

"I know a good deal too, Matakini."

"No matter eef you know somet'ing or you know not'ing. You come 'long me jus' same. I jus' keel you how I want, you see."

"That's awfully nice of you."

"Yes. One man of you frien's from Inyanga he get away; he tell your leetle frien's wit'out boots. No man leave who come here."

"But he did. Is he still alive?"

"Yes, he leeve all right; but he sure want to be dead; you see."

"You swine!" I exclaimed, half-rising. "You're torturing—"

"Seet down!" snapped the Matakini, pointing the revolver.

I paused half-way. If the maniac really intended to torture me to death as he implied I might as well force the issue now by rushing him. If he didn't "out" me right away I thought I could get my hands upon the little brute and then I would be confident of the result even before his people could rescue him; if not, then a quick death.

But then the thought of Billy being alive and being tortured intervened. I had to make an effort. God knew what might happen. I couldn't foresee any way out then. I sat back slowly.

"You may go to hell-hull-an'-halifax," said I slowly, "and do your darnedest. You've got the drop on me for the second time; but for the third look out the cards don't fall my way a bit."

"No fall your way," said the Matakini. "I make leetle meestake sometime when I 'low you 'scape on Ruenya and your frien'. All right, I pay. But I no make meestake 'nother time; you see. Now you stop t'ink what I tell you so you find me funnee mad, yes? I send you food, yes; plenty food make you nice and fat; you see. Ha-ha!"

After handing me over to the care of two buck natives—big fellows of the stranger tribe, both armed with modern rifles—the Matakini bowed ironically and left me to my own reflections.

• • •

Once more I tried to piece together the various points I had learned from Billy's decapitated story and the remarks of the Matakini. As far as I could make out now the city of Phœnician or other origin must really be existent; and apparently it harbored an organization that might be an African secret society based on superstition, like the Human Leopard Society of the West Coast, or, as the Matakini seemed to imply, some other religious system with an order of priests of which he said he was one. Also for some reason they—probably through this superstitious religious order—had complete control over the surrounding tribes and were determined to keep out the white world at any cost. I guessed from the Matakini's remark that Billy, who had apparently somehow won immunity from the usual penalty of death or slavery, had offended against the sacred tabu and had been kidnaped and brought back to be tortured. Beyond that of course I couldn't make head or tail of the affair.

Some young girls brought me, as the Matakini had promised, an ample supply of chicken and goat and milk, to which was generously added some of my own canned food. During the afternoon I could hear the hum of a big *indaba* going on in the clubhouse; but nobody came near me until about four, when a messenger brought orders to my guard, who told me to follow them. They led me through the stockade, where to my amazement I found a *machilla*, into which I was bidden to mount.

The Matakini must be insane, I began to think, thus to treat one who to him was obviously a dangerous prisoner. It did occur to me that possibly he was doing so in order to keep up the prestige of a white in the eyes of the natives; yet it could scarcely be that, judging by his own ways and his native manner of dressing. My bearers went off at the usual fast lope of a well-trained *machilla* team, and my two guards ambled on either side of me. Of the Matakini I saw no sign, nor did I on the whole trip.

That night I was placed in a better built hut in a larger village, which I thought belonged to the younger of the two chiefs whom I had taken captive—the one with the gold bangle. At any rate he was there, and even looked into my hut to greet me most politely. The local people showed no signs at all of hostility; merely the usual mild curiosity.

I don't think that I even planned to attempt to escape. They certainly did not give me a shadow of a chance. Their system among the tribes of barring out any stranger seemed pretty well organized; and anyway I might as well travel in luxury at the Matakini's expense. Perhaps after all he had some idea of a grim joke. Time enough when I got to the city and in communication with Billy.

We traveled fairly fast and long for two days, passing through a thickly populated district of a tribe which was obviously strong and warlike. Then on the morning of the third as I swung out of a fairly thick forest I, in spite of the fact that I had been forewarned, almost thought that I had gone loony as Billy's man in the opium-den in New York had done.

There at the head of a broad and fertile valley through which meandered a river, upon a *kopje*, surrounded by others wooded and boulder-strewn just as they are in Mashonaland, was undoubtedly a walled town whose flat-topped houses, dominated by a great square building evidently in the center, rose in tiers above crenelated walls, the whole white in the fierce sun against the mass of foot-hills of the Inyanga range of mountains.

As we swung down a well-beaten trail I noticed that the land was well cultivated down the valley; and in the open marshes large herds of cattle of the Madagascar kind with the hump were grazing. I forgot that I was under sentence of death—and a sticky one too if the Matakini was not jesting—in the excitement at having reached this mysterious city.

Between the silt of the valley and the walls was terrace upon terrace filled with plants and what appeared to be orange and olive trees. Figures were moving about the large arch of the principal gate, reached by a broad stair carved out of the granite hillside. As my bearers walked up these steps I saw that on each side of the gate, built of blocks of granite, were figures, carven with considerable skill, which appeared to be winged bulls.

The gates were enormous. They appeared to be made of planks of ivory yellow with age which were covered entirely with hieroglyphics and weird animals and cones. Immediately within was what I took to be the market-place such as they have in Oriental cities, the floor of which was of solid rock. There were no horses or vehicles of any kind. As I was staring round I noticed the sound of the trickle of running water and wondered where it came from.

Not many natives were about. The women and men seemed to be of the same tribe as that through which we had traveled the last two days.

At the end of this square between the walls of flat-topped houses a wide street ran straight up the rocky hill, with flights of steps wherever the path became very steep, to the great square building which I had seen without dominating the whole town, decorated with more winged animals like gigantic gargoyles.

Half-way up my escort turned into a side street flanked by high walls broken at wide distances by the blank backs of houses. Coming toward us was a procession containing what turned out to be a kind of cross between a sedan chair and a hammock. In this conveyance lounged or were seated a man and a woman. They looked for all the world like a scene in a movie; for the man had a kind of Roman toga on and was certainly a white man—fair, too.

Next to him was a woman in a kind of blanket wrapped about her obviously in the Greek manner. Her hair was black and long, and she was swarthy; but not more so than many Italian girls I've seen in Bleecker Street, New York, or Soho, London. As a matter of fact I was so engrossed in looking at her that not until we were almost abreast did I see the man's face.

"Billy!" I yelled and tried to leap out of my hammock.

One of my guards roughly hurled me back, but I shouted again. The woman was staring at me, and Billy turned too and deliberately looked me straight in the face without a glimmer of recognition.

At some order from my guard the bearers broke into a run and I was carried past them. I was so flabbergasted that I couldn't think. I sat peering out of the *machilla* at the back of Billy's fair head.

A bit farther along they took me into a house. Inside was a kind of bare hall. I was told to get out of the hammock and then, still in a maze, was led into a room on the right and a heavy wooden door was slammed and bolted upon me. Vaguely aware that there was a pallet in a corner on the floor, I sat on it, staring stupidly at a barred window high up near the roof.

Was he Billy? I was dead certain he was. But the Matakini had given me to understand that he was being tortured. Tortured! With a pretty girl doing a kind of movie Roman-emperor stunt and didn't know me? He *must* have known me. Of course he must! Why? What did it mean?

V

I FELT AS BEWILDERED and unreal as I did after the crack on the head in Beira and the denial of Billy's existence. Half a dozen wild surmises came up, but none that was tenable. Billy had been hypnotized; he had been tortured until he had gone mad; he had submitted to whatever demands the Matakini had made regarding my sticky end; or he had totally forgotten me.

That Billy should willingly desert me in any rational state of mind was incredible. Yet I felt myself grabbing as it were at reality with an uneasy sense that anything might be possible, granting that such a phenomenon as this extraordinary city did exist.

I gave up trying to solve the problem and made an examination of my prison. The walls were bare and made of stone dressed in brick-shape. The window was high up and heavily barred. The door was solidly made of some very hard African wood. The lock I could not make out from the inside.

The pallet or divan in the corner was made of some kind of woven material of a pattern I had never seen before and was well stuffed—I opened it to see—with dried moss of some kind. The walls, which were apparently extremely thick, and the gloom made the place quite comfortably cool even in the early afternoon. All was quiet save for the sound of trickling water such as I had heard on entering the city. What it was I could not imagine.

Like a caged beast I began to pace up and down the room, which was fairly large, vague ideas and plans fomenting me into a state of excitement. Presently the door creaked and opened, and the stranger chief with the flat gold bangle who had been once my captive came in unattended, greeted me and squatted down as if for an *indaba*.

After the usual form of polite inquiries, more after the Arabic manner with this man than in the ordinary native way, he informed me that he was deputed to be my guardian and to see to my needs. This statement didn't seem at all interesting to me.

However, I recollected that when we had entered the gate my servants and porters with my goods had disappeared. I asked where they were. He told me that they were all dead, having been slaughtered immediately we had arrived. When I angrily wished to know why, he said that that was the law according to the chiefs.

"What chiefs?" I demanded. "The Matakini? The man who rescued thee?"

"Nay, he is the first doctor" (using the word indicating magician).

"Who is the chief then?"

"That is but known to the Great Ones."

"Who art thou?"

"I am the son of Banfangala, chief of the children of Banfangala."

"Who are the Great Ones of whom thou dost speak?"

"That is known only by Those Who Have Eaten of the Fruit" (of initiation).

As I knew a little of the cults within cults among all secret societies, mystic or religious, I tried another tack.

"O son of Banfangala, who is the white man whom we met before we entered this house?"

"I saw no white man, for I was not with thee."

"He was a man fairer than I," I explained, recollecting that the man had disappeared somewhere between sighting the city and the house; exactly where or how I had been too interested to notice, "and wears upon his left arm a bracelet like unto thine, yet having certain marks upon it."

"He was of Those."

I controlled my irritation and said—

"I wish to see him."

"Thou wilt see him when the time is ripe."

After that I gave up, knowing I would not get any information even of the little, as I suspected, that he knew.

"What callest thou the man who rescued thee?"

"The Lord of the Temple Altar."

I could hardly repress a smile, thinking of the difference in this pompous title and that bestowed upon him by whites in Rhodesia—the chigger flea!

"And how is named the fair man of whom I spake?"

"The Seeker of Secrets."

Billy, the seeker of secrets! It seemed more confusing than ever.

"What would the One Bidden to the Feast require?" demanded the son of Banfangala, for native-like he would never mention his own name.

"The One Bidden to the Feast?" I repeated, bewildered; and then, realizing, as there was obviously no one else present, that this must be the name they had given me, I replied, "My private things (goods belonging to the body) that I may wash in the manner of my kind; water and food."

"These things shalt thou have," he answered and, rising, left me.

The acceptance of my wish gave me a ray of hope. For the *veld* I prefer a Colt or Webley, as they are not so likely to get clogged with dust and damp as the more intricate mechanism of an automatic; and in my steel suit-case I had placed an automatic with cartridges which I had quite forgotten until that moment. Would they break open the case and search?

I soon had my answer. The gods were good for once or my luck seemed changing, for the suit-case was unopened and my automatic quite safe; also I found a couple of sticks of dynamite with fuse and detonators, which like most prospectors I had always with me. I told the man who appeared with it that I wanted water. He bade me to follow him. Under pretext of taking out clean underwear, razors, etc., and hidden by the box-lid, I slipped the automatic and the dynamite into my pockets. He led me through the hall-like place and into an open courtyard with a square pool of water in the center and flanked by closed doors after the style of the Roman atria.

I stripped and began a badly needed wash. As I was wondering why the water was so cool and fresh I noticed that at the bottom was an inlet and outlet. Probably, thought I, the pool was kept replenished from some reservoir. After a shave in my cell and a smoke—another prize from my suit-case—I became much more optimistic, particularly with the reassuring feel of the bulge in my pocket.

I carefully went over everything I had been told by Billy, the Matakini, and the son of Banfangala to compare notes and try to arrive at some feasible solution. But, twist the evidence about as I would, nothing satisfactory in the shape of even a theory could I evolve.

I prowled around the room, but failed to discover any hope of getting out unaided. There was only one alternative—to hold up my jailer when he came in and chance whether he had companions outside. Of course the street door might be closed also. Anyway I decided to take the risk, and at night.

The latter idea was suggested by my pocket torch, which fortunately was still in my pocket. I had vague hopes that the torch might serve to scare any possible pursuers at night, when their superstitious minds would probably take it for the eye of a demon.

What I was going to do and where I was to go I hadn't the faintest idea, except to find some place to hide and eventually find Billy unless the old boy really had gone off his nut. Anyway the plan soothed me.

About sunset my jailer came with food. It was too light to make the attempt to escape, and the food looked good—roasted kid, bananas, fish, olives and wine in an ampulla, the replica in clay of the one Billy had shown me. Also the man brought in two lamps, shaped something like the Roman, with oil and a wick in the lip, and with tinder and steel lighted them. Again I wondered at the solicitude of the Matakini. After this splendid meal—for central Africa!—I smoked and matured my plans. Finally I decided to make the attempt after midnight well before I calculated the moon was due to rise.

When that hour had come I took my spare suit of breeches and coat and, cutting open the pallet, stuffed them with the dry moss so that in the dim light it would represent me to a casual glance as asleep on the divan. Then, standing behind the door, I began to moan and beat on the wood. I didn't want to yell loudly for fear of waking any possible sleepers, but as nothing happened I did so.

At last in between the yells I heard the faint patter of naked feet. The door opened. I did my best to do a ventriloquial act, saying that I was ill. The man, looking at the bed, advanced two steps, dragging his rifle-butt on the floor.

The opportunity was so good that I had no need to hold him up. With a spring I landed a full right just behind his left ear. I hurt my fist considerably, for no one's skull is so hard as a negro's; but he cushioned off the wall, which helped me; and before he could yell I got in another, which put him to sleep.

There were some braces in my suit-case; and with those I bound him, then gagged him with a shirt and dumped him on the divan. Naturally I didn't neglect to take along his rifle and ammunition.

I peeped into the hall, where one oil lamp was burning. The room was empty. In the atrium I could see the glimmer of the pool in the starlight.

I tried the street door and flashed my torch on the lock. There was an enormous key in it about the size of a large corkscrew. I tried various ways of working it, but the door would not open. I wasted some time in finding out that the lock was on the ratchet-bolt system and that you had to unwind by turning the key a number of times.

At last I got the door open and was in the street. I stole down toward the main-road with the flights of steps. Peering round the corner, I saw the yellow of dim light. At first I couldn't imagine what it could be until at length I made out that all the figures I had noticed decorating the temple or whatever the great building was, were illuminated—with the little oil lamps, I supposed—and I just could hear a distant sound as of chanting.

I paused to ponder which way I had better go. I could not see a soul about. Curiosity urged me to go up and investigate the temple and see what the singing was about, but prudence suggested otherwise. However, in the darkest side of the wall I began to venture up.

Half-way, just at the foot of a longer flight of steps than usual, I came across a door ajar. Peeping within, I could vaguely make out in the darkness a curious garden formed of terraces evidently cut in the granite and filled with soil.

I paused to listen. Only the distant chanting and the trickling of water could I hear.

I stepped inside a few paces. Behind a clump of trees I saw a faint light. I crept cautiously forward with the rifle under my arm, the automatic in one hand and the torch in the other. Hearing no other sounds, I advanced farther and peered through the branches.

In the dim light of oil lamps I saw five women, nude and apparently oiled, kneeling in a posture of prayer before a wall of granite upon which was carved a figure of a winged bull such as I had remarked on the town gates. Then as I stared I made out a pile of some white objects upon a slab at the feet of the bas-relief. What they could be I couldn't guess, except that they were evidently offerings of some sort. As for the image, it was obviously the tribal god.

Then a twig on a branch which I had parted snapped under my hand. Instantly the five leaped to their feet like startled antelope. I remained motionless. Whether or no the starlight was reflected on the barrel of the gun or automatic I don't know, but one began to walk toward me.

Poking the torch through the screen of branches, I switched it full into her face. She stopped. For an instant there was the hiss of inhaling breath. Then the five turned and fled, uttering appalling screams.

I heard answering shouts from below. I looked around hastily. Each terrace was about five or six feet wide and three to four feet high. Instinctively I made upward, where the bushes and trees seemed thickest at the back of the image. I scrambled over some boulders which seemed to have been left as they were naturally. In the midst I crouched and listened.

I heard some men calling and women replying agitatedly. Gradually the voices died away and there were no sounds save the trickling of water and the distant continuous chanting.

I thought about regaining the road and continuing my explorations, but a green pallor in the east warned me that the moon was coming. So I hunted about for a hiding-place. For some reason or other quite a large patch of land had been left in the natural state behind the bas-relief, due, I supposed, to some tabu.

The suggestion gave me an idea. If I were now standing on tabu ground it was very unlikely that anybody would ever come there; searchers might not dare to walk over the ground in search of me even should they arrive at the conclusion that I was the one-eyed demon who had scared the women. For that reason it would be a good place to hide.

I began to hunt about but in the darkness I could find no better spot than a crevice between two enormous boulders. There I lay down, wishing that I dared to smoke.

I must have dropped off to sleep—thank Heaven there were no mosquitoes up on the hillside! A slight noise awoke me to find the moon well up. I had just noticed that the chanting had ceased when I heard again the noise.

I listened. The sound resembled a faint tap as of a blind man's stick on a pavement and moreover appeared to come from underneath me. I stood up, peered over round the boulder—an enormous one which leaned lopsidedly against its brother; such are on nearly all Rhodesian *kopjes*, forced by pressure into fantastic positions in the ice age.

I could not see anything moving, and the tapping had stopped. Farther up the crevice which formed my hiding-place was a gnarled tree growing between the great rocks barring my passage.

Now, nearly every Mashona village is built on a *kopje*, which is frequently full of caves used variously for grain-bins, witch-doctor practise and bolt-holes when attacked. This was probably the case here. I squirmed my way round the tree. There, sure enough, under one of the tilted boulders was the dark of a cave-mouth.

However, before investigating I reckoned I had better have a look around. Along the crevice I discovered quite a well-beaten track. The entrance to the cave was well screened by a clump of trees. Beyond them I could see the customary terraces, and not far off one for pedestrians, probably the continuation of the same which I had followed from the door to the shrine.

Being satisfied that no one was around, I laid my rifle on the ground and flashed my torch beneath the boulder. The ordinary cave-mouth had been enlarged artificially, for it was square like a door. Within were steps leading into a corridor in the rock.

Just as I stepped forward, into the white glare of my torch walked a small figure clad in a white robe. Startled, or rather amazed, black eyes stared at the light. I caught a glimpse of a swarthy face with a gray beard and hawk-like nose. Upon his arm the figure bore something like a shield which gleamed yellow.

I fired straight at the high light of his forehead. The crash of the automatic reverberating in the confined space and the corridor seemed enough to awaken the whole town. He crumpled upon his face and never knew, I think, what or who had slain him.

Lord, I thought, as I looked at him, one of the Phœnician elders that Billy's hop friend spoke about; and I regretted that I had had to kill, for the face seemed so venerable and wide and the eyes still retained that mild look of amazement.

The shield proved to be a mask reaching from the forehead almost to the navel, beautifully made of beaten gold. As I hastily took his robe I noticed that he too wore a golden bracelet like the Matakini's, but it seemed a more intricate design with more hieroglyphics. It was too small for me, so I threw it away. The body I took out and thrust beneath one of the great boulders; and, wrapped in the robe with my rifle strapped underneath it, I hastened into the cave, carrying the mask.

VI

AT THE BOTTOM OF THE STEPS I found a narrow corridor running at a fairly steep angle downward. Scared lest the report of the automatic had aroused some one who might come seeking the cause, I hurried along pretty fast without stopping to examine the drawings with which the walls were covered. Now that I was in the city I had no doubt that in all truth it really was built by the Phœnicians or whoever were responsible for the Zimbawbwe and other ruins in Rhodesia.

Presently, flashing my torch in front of me, the beam was lost in darkness. I was standing within a large cavern. I shut off the torch and listened. The sound of trickling water puzzled me; how could it possibly be within these caves?

I chose the left wall and began to follow along that to find out how big the cavern was. After I had gone perhaps fifty yards the flash of the torch glinted on water and I found a subterranean conduit about two feet wide which was obviously of artificial construction, but for what purpose it had been made I could not imagine.

A glance at my watch told me it was half-past four. In these latitudes the sun rises all the year round within a few minutes of six o'clock. I could not see any likely place where I could possibly hide. If the dead elder had passed through these caves, evidently others might come. I decided to go back to my crevice between the great boulders. I arrived there without mishap and slept on the other side of the gnarled tree until the brazen sun nearly overhead awoke me.

I was very thirsty and dying for a smoke. The latter I enjoyed very cautiously beneath the boulder. Then I peered out and around. I expected to find men or some slaves working on the gardens, but I could neither hear nor see any signs of them. Then I recollected that it was just afternoon, the hottest part of the day.

Wrapping myself well in my robe, leaving my rifle and mask by the rock, I stalked boldly out in search of water and food. I made for the pool near the bas-relief. After I had drunk my fill I looked curiously for the white objects upon the slab of the altar that I had seen the night before. They were the bones of a small child. What their presence meant I could not guess.

As there was still nobody in sight I strolled along the terrace path, looking about. I had hoped to see something of the lie of the houses; but the olive-trees, which were thickly planted hereabout, prevented any more than an occasional glimpse of flat roofs below me. Once looking upward I caught a vista of the great building on the top of the *kopje*.

I did not feel very hungry in the heat, but cast about for a way of getting food. Farther along I spotted the fronds of bananas and walked toward them, hoping that they were in fruit.

The next moment I saw a big native in dirty robe coming straight toward me. I had no opportunity to run for cover. With my automatic ready beneath the robe I strolled on steadily, holding my head down as if in meditation or prayer, a posture suggested, I suppose, by the association of the place and the monk-like dress. I did not dare look directly at him, but I saw from the edge of my vision that as I passed he dropped upon his knees by the side of the path and softly called some greeting.

I refrained from looking back for some fifty yards, and then he was out of sight. I was rather bucked up by the success of the stratagem and determined to try it again. Evidently my costume was that of a very high official or priest, to whom the natives were taught to do homage.

The bananas were not in fruit. But near them was a small house or rather stone hut which I judged to be the home of the man who had passed me, a gardener or something of that sort.

I walked up boldly and looked within. A native woman in a filthy robe was stretched out asleep on a mat with a child beside her. In one corner I saw some ordinary native cooking-gourds and clay jars. I tip-toed over with an eye on the sleeping woman and found some milk, of which I drank as much as I could.

There was a bunch of green bananas and some dried olives and cobs of corn. I loaded up all I could carry and got away without shaking the native lady's slumbers. Then I made straight back to my hiding-place and had a good feed. I now had a store enough to last me several days at least.

Lying in the shade well under the same rock which sheltered my poor victim I smoked and planned. If I attempted to go through the streets I would be sure to encounter many people and probably have my disguise penetrated sooner or later. I might be fairly free to wander about at night; but I was sure, since the elder had come from the caves carved and so decorated, that I would be more likely to discover something of value there than in the streets.

This argument was supported by the theory that the ground behind the image at the pool hiding the cave-mouth was tabu, which meant of course that therein was hidden the secrets of the cult from the vulgar eyes. I decided to continue my subterranean exploring that night and early. Then I went peacefully to sleep.

I awoke about an hour before sunset and was immediately aware of the sound of drums and of some wailing instrument as well as of the chanting from the building up on the hill. An hour after sunset I set out, clad in the captured white robe and with the golden mask upon my arm. Under the robe I carried in my pockets the flash-light, the automatic, and the dynamite, together with the rifle in an improvised holster. As soon as I entered the cave-mouth I found the corridor illuminated by the Roman-like oil lamps set at intervals of about fifty feet apart. This confirmed my suspicion that the early hours of the night must be the time of principal activity.

Very cautiously I crept on in my sandals until I was in the shadow at the corner. The cavern was not so large as I had imagined nor so high. Glimmering in the light of the lamps set at each entrance were some dozen or more doors which presumably were like that to my corridor, and in those that were nearly opposite to mine I could see that similar lamps were posted at intervals, evidently to light the way of some one's progress. The conduit of water passed through about the center of the cavern and ran into an unlighted tunnel.

I tried to work out the situation. Evidently, I thought, each priest or whatever he was had a private tunnel leading apparently to his own residence through which he passed to the secret ritual. As all the tunnels converged on the cavern I thought at first that this must be the meeting-hall, and decided, as the man whose robes I wore was dead, that unless they had discovered the body no one would be likely to interfere with me if I stopped where I was. Yet there might well be servants or colleagues.

The only other place to hide was the conduit passage, which was in darkness. I took the chance and ran for it. Fortunately on one side of the water there ran a narrow path, possibly for workmen.

Scarcely had I taken up a crouching position in the shadow when from one of the corridors a hooded figure emerged, garbed exactly as I was, or as the elder whom I had slain had been. The figure walked slowly in a direct line for the door of another corridor, up which it went.

Five minutes later another figure emerged from another door and passed up the same passage. From this I gathered that this cavern was not the meeting-hall, but was merely the hub of the radii formed by the corridors.

I decided to wait until each corridor had given its man, except of course the one I had used. It suddenly occurred to me that Billy, whom the son of Banfangala had said was One of Those, might pass, and I determined that if he did I would follow or call to him. At intervals of minutes and seconds they came along, and I began to get mixed in keeping check. But none had the remotest resemblance to Billy's walk.

At last according to my tally there remained but one door except my own that had not given a man, and that was within some fifteen feet from me. Five minutes passed; then there emerged a slight figure whom I knew instantly—the Matakini!

I felt so angry at the sight of him that I very nearly let drive. I hesitated whether to run after him and hold him up or not.

Ideas of taking him as a hostage flitted through my mind. Yet I couldn't trust his word; and where on earth was I to keep him prisoner?

According to my calculation he was the last man due. As soon as he had turned the corner of the passage I followed swiftly.

That this corridor led to some particular cave or temple or whatever it could be, was indicated, I noticed, by the guardian bull's heads carved on what would have been the door-post; and as soon as I was inside I heard again the wail of instruments and the drums.

None of these corridors was entirely artificial for they wound most erratically; probably they were small natural caves enlarged and tunneled when necessary. But how at that period without drills and dynamite they had done the blasting I could not imagine. I recollected that none of the gold-workings in Rhodesia showed any sign of rock-mining as we moderns know it.

By reason of the tortuous passage and my sandals I had little difficulty in stalking Master Matakini. Quite abruptly the corridor began to mount steeply, and finally it came to a flight of steps, at the top of which I saw brighter light and simultaneously caught the smell of sweet incense.

I hung back a little until the figure of the Matakini had disappeared. Then, crouching, I ran swiftly up the steps and, lying flat, peered over the top, and gasped in amazement.

I had been astonished at the realization that the story of the mysterious city had come true, but the complicated sight—for I couldn't take it all in at once—produced an even more profound emotion—awe.

The first impression registered was of enormous flambeaux burning steadily beneath the bright stars away overhead, grouped in threes about an enormous square of rock, the sides of which were carved in mighty columns like an Egyptian temple, and covered with intricate hieroglyphics; and between these columns were enormous bas-reliefs of fantastic figures, suggesting Assyrian origin, of winged beasts of all sorts, although at that moment I had no time to notice that.

Priests in the shield-like golden masks were emerging every moment from doorways around the sides of evidently similar corridors to that by which I had come, making toward the chancel, which was guarded by a low palisade of ivory and gold. Where, grouping upon their knees, were the other arrivals flanked by statues of more winged animals. Each of these statues seemed to be half-turned as if praying or doing homage to a figure of a bull with the body of a man having the hands held out in front as if bearing a burden—a colossal image whose mass gleamed dull gold in the light of the restless torches.

VII

THIS COLOSSAL GOD upon a pedestal or altar or rock with his arms outstretched over the chancel and illuminated with a profusion of trident flambeaux sat within an enormous alcove or chapel decorated with figures and columns. Away at the back of the temple, which was quite five hundred feet long by about two hundred broad, I could see dimly a body of natives who were evidently chiefs by the occasional glint of a gold bangle on their black arms.

Where the rhythmic throb of drums and the wailing of some reed instruments came from I couldn't determine, but although to my ears they were chaotic the wild strains were somehow not unpleasing. Several times I was compelled to slink a little down my corridor to avoid blacks nude and oiled—eunuchs, I learned later—who patrolled around, some swinging golden censers and others bearing small ampullæ of gold filled with olive-oil for the lamps and torches.

Gazing upward as my eyes got used to the light, I remarked that the site seemed originally to have been several natural caverns which had been knocked into one and the roof broken in forming this vast sunken temple. On the top of the rock walls I could make out the continuous square roofs of buildings with gargoyle decorations against the stars.

All the time I was observing these things, robed and masked figures were appearing from the gloom of the blackness between the carven columns of the temple and joining their brethren just within the gold and ivory barricade guarding the sanctity of the chancel, which was raised some two feet above the level of the transept. I hesitated whether to risk going among them. If Billy were there I might be able to recognize him at close quarters in spite of the mask. Yet, I reflected, probably each priest would have his appointed place, and if I could not strike by some lucky chance that of the man I was supposed to be, I would instantly be discovered.

I waited, hoping to see a vacant place, but at that distance I could not find one. Then when all the priests were apparently assembled—some three or four hundred of them—the wailing ceased although the drums continued, and a procession emerged from somewhere.

A figure in a wooden *machilla*, such as I had seen on the street but heavily decorated with gold, was borne by black guards carrying the halberd-like spears that Billy had described. They advanced slowly to the entrance to the chancel, where a man in a toga kind of garment without a mask and wearing a golden helmet after the Etruscan pattern got out, bearing some article of gold which glittered in his hands. As he went upon his knees there arose from the congregation of blacks in the body of the temple a long wailing moan like the wind through trees.

Then one of the masked priests took up the golden vase, which seemed to be a kind of pyx, and, walking slowly to the feet of the god, cried out in a loud voice. From the nostrils of the bull issued smoke and fire and a voice roared deeply seemingly within him. From the pyx the priest poured upon the base of the pedestal a libation which left a red stain. Immediately the smoke and flame stopped, and from the negroes in the back came another howl, wilder and fiercer than before.

As, retiring backward, the priest resumed his place the hidden orchestra burst into skirling music like mad bagpipes; and from the gloom behind the flambeaux in the back of the god's chapel there darted one after the other nude girls—evidently, I guessed, the sacred women of the temple—who began wild gyrations before the image, reminding me of the Indian nautch dances.

I had not forgotten Billy nor the Matakini, and while this dance, which suggested a crazy Russian ballet without the color, was in progress I cast about for a way either to mingle with the throng when the priests dispersed or somehow get on to the other side, as I was fairly certain that Billy did not belong as it were to the group on my side, if indeed he were there at all. I had decided that it was more important to get into touch with Billy than to kill or capture the Matakini.

Between the walls covered in bas-relief and the Egyptian-like columns carved out of the rock was an aisle about ten feet wide. I began to wonder whether I dared risk run from pillar to pillar and thus make my way around the temple while the people were engrossed in the dance.

I realized that should any of the blacks see what was apparently a priest out of his proper place within the chancel he might be suspicious. Yet, as the son of Banfangala had implied, they were allowed to know little and taught to have much respect for priest-craft. Waiting until a gang of four eunuchs with golden censers had passed down toward the back, I followed, flitting at intervals of a minute or more, from column to column until I had reached level with the black worshipers, when, remarking that I had been seen, I marched boldly along, trusting solely to the mask.

The ruse succeeded well; for beyond some of the eyes, which looked like white butterflies in the gloom of the body of the temple, fluttering curiously in my direction, nobody took the slightest notice. In this manner I passed four large corridors with tall carven doors, which, I saw in the light of the lamps, ascended—evidently public entrances to the pit as it were—and arrived at the center of the temple on the opposite side, where I hid in the nearest corridor.

In my anxiety to find Billy I had omitted to think out where I was to go when the priests returned to their respective tunnels. I felt extremely uncomfortable at the realization of my hasty action. However, there was nothing to do now but wait and see what was about to happen.

The dance was still going on, and the action and the music were becoming more hectic. I began to wonder whether the congregation was to be worked up to some form of religious mania, but they remained the whole time perfectly motionless save for a low grunting in rhythm to the drums.

Just as I was trying to imagine what the meaning of the performance could be and how long it was to last, one of a passing band of eunuchs came directly toward the steps upon which I was lying. To shoot would advertise my presence and probably bring the whole mob of blacks and priests upon me. I scuttled down the steps, intending to run around a bend of the corridor. Whether he had spotted something foreign in my walk or not—and as a temple eunuch he would probably know every one of the legitimate priests—I never knew; but at any rate he started to run after me.

I took to my heels and sprinted along the corridor down flights of steps and around corners. Suddenly I came out into a similar cavern to that on the other side, a hub of radiating corridors.

I dodged behind the carved door-post. As he dashed out I leaped and swung my rifle-butt. But I missed his head and the blow glanced off his shoulder.

He stumbled to his knees, came round as swiftly as a leopard and sprang upon me before I could recover to strike. He was fairly fat, but agile; and his oiled, nude body felt like the coils of a serpent. I was hampered by the folds of my robes; but the mask aided me, for he couldn't get his fingers on my windpipe.

He began to yell for help. I slipped backward, dragging him on top of me. As we fell the mask came off and I squirmed so that he came sidewise across me. Then with a desperate effort, grabbing a mass of woolly hair, I managed to get his shoulders across my knee in the neck hold; and, cupping his chin with my right hand, I thrust with all my strength and broke his neck.

Scared lest some of his fellows had heard his cries and would arrive, I glanced around anxiously for a hiding-place. In the center was a similar conduit to that in the other cavern, running into its own tunnel. Seizing my rifle and mask, I pulled him by the shoulders into the darkness, and, panting, sat watching while I recovered. I was relieved that I had settled him; for I had reckoned that the last place which they would search for me would be underground, and had he escaped or had they found his body my whereabouts would be known or guessed.

After some reflection I decided I had better stop where I was. Perhaps if Billy were among the crowd in the temple he would pass through this cavern and I could spot his corridor and follow; or if not I could wait until the eunuchs had put out the lamps, which evidently they did every night or morning, and explore on my own. My fears that some of the eunuchs' comrades would arrive in search of him were somewhat soothed by the reflection that the sound of drums and reed instruments which penetrated down the corridor to this cavern had probably drowned his cries.

I must have been squatting there some two hours before the first robed figure of the returning priests entered the cavern. Eagerly I watched each take off his golden mask, and, mumbling words of salutation, separate for his respective corridor. I had almost given up hope of locating Billy when in the last group his fair beard stood out against the swarthy Phœnicians'. To my dismay, instead of walking alone to a doorway as the others did he was accompanied by an elderly priest. I had intended to follow as soon as the cavern was free, but this unexpected incident upset my plan.

While I hesitated there came a mob of eunuchs who hastened in the wake of their masters. At first I thought that they had come to extinguish the lamps. But a moment's consideration showed me that perhaps these people were dedicated to the temple and had to live always underground; or perhaps they had another exit, in which case they would obviously begin at the open-air entrance and work back. Very carefully I noted Billy's corridor, which was the fifth on the right from the bull-guarded doorway. Within a few minutes the first eunuch returned.

Squatting there beside the corpse, I began to feel most uncanny as light after light went out and the dense blackness of the cavern seemed to be descending upon me like some vast octopus intending to devour me and the corpse by the gurgling stream. So intense was this feeling of being abandoned in the bowels of the earth that I had to restrain myself from crying out when the last attendant disappeared up the main temple corridor, dousing the wick with his fingers as he went.

I have never been particularly imaginative, so I suppose the echo of the light from the lamps still remained in my eyes; perhaps the weird spectacle I had witnessed had overstrung my nerves; but I could have sworn that ghostly figures, sometimes human and sometimes animal, were prancing about in the utter darkness of the cavern.

At last I was certain that I could hear the *pad-pad* of paws. I could endure it no longer. I switched on the torch. Within fifteen paces of me was the figure of a woman with a wild maze of gray hair to her waist prancing across the cavern. Bony hands with inch-long nails were making passes in the air. As she came to the conduit she leaped over, making a horrible gesture like that one would imagine a hag to make on a witches' sabbath. Her body was wrinkled like the neck of a tortoise and was of a corpse-like wax color in the glare of the torch. I could not see her eyes for the tangled hair, but the jaw was sunken gum to gum.

Instead of turning toward the beam of light as I expected she continued straight on in her ghastly dance and disappeared up a corridor. Who or what this horrible hag might be I could not imagine, but the sight had effectually shaken my nerves. I felt that I must get out of this sticky and horrific mystery instantly. As I ran across that cavern I switched the torch around on all sides, expecting some new atrocity to rush upon me.

To my further confusion, at some fifty paces or more I found myself instead of in the open air in another small but lofty cave out of which ran three corridors. Down which one had Billy gone? I was annoyed and angry and jumpy.

Hastily I chose the left-hand one, which, I found, bore round to the left as if it were going back in the direction of the temple. I hesitated, turned back and took the middle, which sloped downward and then to my dismay ended in a steep flight of stairs. I was certain that to reach the open it should trend upward as the first had done. What to do, I didn't know.

I might discover something if I went on. On the other hand I might well lose myself, or come across some of the temple slaves or that awful hag. I went back. As I approached the first cave I thought I heard the *pad* of sandals again. I listened.

Very cautiously I felt my way to the edge of the door. I saw a light glimmering in the corridor on the right and crouched low with the automatic ready. Again I hesitated whether to run back or not.

A masked figure carrying one of the usual lamps of the corridor emerged and walked quickly down the opposite corridor. The quickness and energy of the walk aroused my suspicions that he might be Billy. I dared not call out, but I followed.

In the big distributing-cavern instead of taking the temple corridor he went up to a portion of the decorated wall. I stood in the shadow and watched, wondering what on earth he was going to do. He began to paw about the figure of a bull in bas-relief. Then, evidently having trouble to see, an irritable exclamation came from him and he unbuckled the mask, revealing a fair head. Recollecting at that moment that the last time I had seen him he had ignored me and what the Matakini had said, I had a sudden panic.

"Billy, old man!" I called softly.

He stared, turned his head and looked around incredulously.

"It's all right; it's me," I continued, stepping out of the corridor.

"Faxy!" he exclaimed; and I knew that he was sane.

VIII

"MY ——, BUT IT'S MIGHTY GOOD to see you!" ejaculated Billy. "But how on earth did you get here?"

"Oh, that's a long story," said I, conscious of a haggardness in his features. "But why on earth didn't you recognize me the other day? I—"

"I daren't, man. I daren't," he began eagerly. "I knew you were here, or I guessed that it was you, and— But say, we can't stop here. Let's get up top."

He glanced around hurriedly, almost fearfully.

"This is a —— of a place," he added vaguely. "Fell for that —— Matakini again. But come on."

He led the way to the right-hand corridor, the one from which he had come; but in the entrance he stopped to look at me again incredulously.

"My —— man, I can't understand how you've got here—alive, I mean; and— Oh, come on!"

He started up the corridor hurriedly; every action was so unlike the cool, self-possessed Billy I had known. Recollecting the grinning Matakini's words, I began to wonder whether they had been torturing him. Farther on, the ground sloped up and ended in a flight of stairs, at the top of which I could see the silhouette of trees against the pallor of moonlight.

"They're devils," he muttered as he doused the wick and replaced the lamp at the bottom of the steps. "Didn't they find you?"

"Who?"

"Those black fiends?"

"Eunuch attendants? Yes. I—er—had to kill one."

"You did! You did! But, man, they're sacred!"

"Never mind," said I, beginning to doubt his sanity again. "Go along up and let me have some fresh air."

He stretched out his hand and touched my shoulder.

"——, but it's good to see you, Faxy, old boy! I can't believe— But how did you get the robes?"

"I took them from a priest or whatever he was," I replied. "But go on, for Heaven's sake. We can't stop here all night."

"No, no. That's right; that's right. They may come at any moment."

He scampered up the steps and I followed, glad to escape from the thick subterranean atmosphere to the comparatively fresh air in the open. I found myself in a small copse, through which I could see below in the faint light a long valley and immediately to my right the gleam of a flat roof.

"That's my house," whispered Billy. "I'll take you there; but you won't be able to get out till tonight. Put on your mask if anybody shows up. This is tabu here, and—"

"Yes, I know. Go on."

We descended from the copse and boulder and came upon a terraced path which led to the house. As we walked I gazed about. We were, I had thought, directly on the other side of the *kopje*, but to the left I saw what appeared to be in the moonlight a huge wall completely blocking the natural valley, built apparently from summit to summit of two *kopjes*. I asked Billy what it was.

"An aqueduct," he replied. "The ancient guys built it to bring water from the plateau yonder. Runs through the whole city inside and out."

"What! A water-sewerage and that sort of thing?"

"Yes; flushes the town and comes out below into the river. Sssh!"

At a little distance from the larger house was another, the quarters of the servants or slaves, so that each owner and his family lived entirely alone. In front was a small artificial plateau planted with oleander and other flowering shrubs.

Billy pushed open the gate which he had left ajar. Within was the hall; and beyond, the atrium in which lamps were burning, an exact replica of my prison house. Into a spacious room on the right he led me to a spot where were a solid stone table like an altar profusely decorated with figures and cones and a divan built upon a slab of rock against the wall.

"Wait a moment," said Billy as I put my rifle in a corner. "Before we begin I want a drink."

He drew from a corner somewhere a golden ampulla and some golden goblets. He set them on the rock table and poured out some yellow fluid which he diluted with water from a stone vessel.

"Good Lord!" said I as I brought the goblet to my lips, supposing it to be wine. "Whisky! Here!"

"Sure. I told you so, didn't I?" said Billy, and gulped; and then to my further astonishment he proffered a box of Turkish cigarets.

In this cool, quiet room I began to lose my sense of horrific mystery, and the little touches of civilization were soothing. Billy seemed to experience the same effect.

"Phew!" said he with a sigh of relief. "I feel better! I was badly rattled tonight to tell the truth; and then you scared the life out of me. I thought you were your own ghost, old boy, for I was sure you had either gotten away or were dead.

"Yes, I knew you were a prisoner, and I made plans to get you out; but before I could do anything I heard you had escaped. You see that's why I daren't recognize you, for if the Matakini knew that I knew you—"

"He must have," I interrupted, "for he remembers me from Inyanga days."

"The —— he does! Man, but this is some complicated outfit. Faxy, old boy, I've fallen down badly and I'm mighty sorry that I've brought you into it."

"But you haven't. I came poking along on my own."

"Yes; but you wouldn't have if I hadn't tried to tell you that yarn about—about this place. What time is it?"

"Quarter to three."

"Quarter to three? Oh, well; it doesn't matter. We're safe here to talk all day unless the Matakini comes butting in. But that won't be until after the siesta unless he knows you're here. I'm never sure what that brute does know.

"Now get busy and tell me how you've gotten here anyway. Then we'll try to clear up things a bit. I hate admitting it, but the Matakini has had me badly and now I'm —— if I know where I'm due to get off. But fire ahead."

I related all that I've written from the time Billy showed me the golden ampulla in the hotel room at Beira.

"That old hag is Mannagi-Arbela," Billy explained when I had finished and the dawn had come. "She's sacred. She's called the mother of the tribe and is blind, deaf, dumb and mad and supposed to be a hundred and forty years old and immortal. And you were right about the system of defense; they have rings of tribes outside this one who are absolutely faithful under the tabu and the degrees of masonry. That's why the Portuguese have had every expedition they've sent anywhere in this neighborhood wiped out, for the natives were organized and equipped by these—these people."

"Are they really Phœnicians?"

"Sure they are— What's left of 'em. That fellow you shot was Ishtar Iddina, one of the inner cult. Probably they haven't missed him until last night or this morning. ——, man, what a pity you didn't take his bracelet!"

"Why?"

"Why? It's the mark of the inner cult, the thirty-third degree."

He thrust out his bracelet.

"Mine," he continued, "is only the thirtieth. I was planning to get you in here with me with one of these bangles; but look here, the thing's so darned complicated I'd better tell you the yarn straight so's you can thread things together. Where had I got to when they shanghaied me in Beira?"

"You hadn't said a word about yourself. You had merely told me the story that the hop fiend told you."

"That's right. Well, here; have another drink. We need it, I reckon."

"But wait a moment," I said as he was lighting a cigaret. "Clear up my trip first. What was this hokum-pokum in the temple last night?"

"Sunday evening service," said he with a sudden harsh laugh.

"What the —— d'you mean?"

"Exactly what I said. I've told you these people, the priests you saw, are really the last of the Phœnicians and their religion is older than the Passover; dates, as you ought to know, to pre-Old Testament days. 'And the Lord God rested on the seventh day.' Yesterday was their seventh day."

"Good Lord!" said I, feeling, I don't know why, rather shocked.

"Semitic, of course, like the Moabites; but founded on the same idea, I think."

"But the idol—the bull; what does that represent?"

"Why Baal, Moloch, the Golden Calf! The same thing that the what-do-you-call-'ems were worshiping when Moses came down from the mountain with the tablets of the law."

"Good ——!"

"Man, you're 'way back here about twenty centuries or more before Christ. It's the original masonry from whom Solomon must have pinched the idea, or they say he did. These people are the children of Abraham. Don't you remember that passage—in Exodus, isn't it—where God calls on Abraham to sacrifice his eldest born, Isaac, and the old man is just about to do it when the angel speaks to him and he finds a ram stuck in a thicket near by which he substitutes? Well, these people are *before* that! They haven't arrived at the substitute!"

"What!"

Then I recalled the baby's bones upon the altar which the women were worshiping in the garden before the bull-headed god.

"D'you actually mean," I gasped, "that they still sacrifice their eldest born?"

"Their people, the blacks, do. But whether the Phœnicians do or not I don't yet know. *That's* the point."

He leaped up in his excitement.

"I was just about to be raised to the thirty-first degree," he went on, "when that cursed Beira trip spoiled me. It was a trap, a test. Man, you don't know. It's the twenty-first of September—the vernal equinox on this side of the equator—and the great sacrificial feast of the year commences tonight and I'm not raised. They have the show in the grand temple. I wasn't even allowed to see it last year. The populace go crazy. But beneath that temple is another temple only open to the inner cult, the thirty-first, thirty-second and thirty-third degrees."

"Do those only wear the mask?"

"No; only the priests; but they're all that now except Tchelkonos, the king—the fellow in the golden helmet—and he can't be. The laymen—natives—think that the masked priests are the demons of Baal and that to see their faces would be death. That's why each priest enters the temple secretly by the tunnels. By day they're just ordinary elders of the tribe."

"Like the West African bull-roaring masked priests," said I, "who are supposed to turn themselves into leopards or something."

"Sure, that's the idea."

"But how many of them are there?"

"Several hundred."

"But they were all old men."

"That's it! That's it! They're the last of 'em. They came here over two thousand years ago. All over Inyanga way, Zimbawbwe, are ruins of their old cities. This is the last. They've nearly died out and they can't get any children. They have a few young girls, but no young men.

"Don't you see? *No young men.* Always they've sacrificed the eldest sons, which naturally hastened the race-suicide. The only male children are a few of the Matakini's. Man, they wanted me to marry a dozen or more of their wives. Nothing doing, of course."

"But you're not a Phœnician."

"They pretend I am because of the sacred bangle. That's why I'm not dead or— That's it; that's it!"

He leaped up excitedly again.

"You remember those fellows the hop fiend spoke about who disappeared? Don't you see? Harvey—you know, the English partner I told you about whom I thought was dead. But he *isn't!* I only found it out today from that girl you saw me riding with. *Whom* do they sacrifice?"

"You mean that they are going to sacrifice that chap Harvey?"

"I don't know. But if they accept me as a genuine Phœnician they may wink by necessity at other things. They may have found a substitute for the sacrificial firstborn. They can't pass off a black for the body of a Phœnician."

He stopped short and sat down quietly.

"Say, I'd better tell the story so that you'll know where you're at, as they say."

IX

"WELL," BEGAN BILLY, "I stopped off at Beira and pottered around but couldn't get a line on anything. The Portuguese had just had another expedition wiped out and weren't keen on giving any information about their alleged territory anyway.

"I went on through Umtali up to Inyanga. Just the same, except that they've got a stone-built store across the *spruit* and the camp's much bigger. Scarcely any of the old crowd left. Daycomb got a commission and is down at Bulawayo. Pete's dead and Mac's gone.

"By chance I found old Wilkie there. He's got half a dozen stores all over the country now. I merely hinted at the yarn and he turned it down flat. He always was a skeptical old cuss anyway.

"But a point on which I did get information of my man's yarn in the hop-joint was that a party of six men actually had deserted from Inyanga troop and were supposed to have reached Beira and made their way to England. Any rate they had never been heard of again.

"Another point was that since then two of our fellows had disappeared somewhere around the Ruenya—supposed to have been killed by lions—and also two prospectors and a missionary. But then as you know fellows are always disappearing somewhere or other.

"Two of the prospectors were reported to have been seen up in Nyassa way so the supposition was that they had merely taken it into their heads to go to Uganda or somewhere north. Taking into consideration the normal conditions of frontier life, there was nothing remarkable about it all.

"I went on across to Mutoko's. Don't quite know why. Just to see that bald-faced *kopje* again, I think. But passing through the country of the ruins I just naturally had to fossick around, not expecting really to find anything worth while. D'you recollect the country between the Musisi and the Inyadiri where the ruins are pretty thick?"

"Lord, yes," said I. "That was where I met the Matakini dressed up in your pants."

"That's right. Sure. Well, there's a very fine specimen of the fortifications and terraces up on a *kopje*—that is, fine for that portion of Rhodesia. Most of the terraces have, as you know, been nearly obliterated by the action of rain and what not.

"I got kind of interested in one of the better preserved and while examining it noticed a queer kind of hump or mound. I set my boys digging around it and found that it had been what I now know as one of the tabu places. The mound had been caused by the earth piling up over a local shrine of the Baal. Of course that excited me some, and I fossicked more with the result that I came on this bangle here.

"I hunted about like mad but didn't discover another darn thing except some broken shards and clay ampullæ. I guess the other stuff must have been looted centuries ago.

"Well, I was all up in the air, you bet. But I went on to Mutoko's and saw Peacock and Win Head, hoping that I could work one or both of 'em up to come with me. But Peacock was down with black-water. I stayed with him long enough to pull him through and then went on to see Win. Nothing doing. He always was a cantankerous old cuss and he was frankly skeptical.

"However, in talking he mentioned that he had known the Matakini for about fifteen years. Said as far as he knew that he was one of the first whites in that country to the north of the Ruenya and back of the Inyanga; also said—which was more interesting—that many years ago the Matakini had wanted him to go in with him on a prospecting expedition over the Pungwe, and by way of heating him up had shown him some splendid samples of nuggets and talked a lot about a rich alluvial field he'd located.

"But Win said he didn't like him, and anyway he was just getting over a bad spell of malaria and dysentery and wasn't fit to take the field. Later he had heard vaguely that the Matakini had found a partner in Salisbury, but who he was and what happened to him he didn't know. Beyond reminding me that I owed one to the Matakini the name didn't interest me, for of course I didn't connect him with this yarn at all at that time.

"I had half a mind to start on my own from Inyanga and try to follow the trail of the deserters; but anyway I had to return to Umtali to outfit, and from there I could more easily, I reckoned, work along the eastern slopes of the Inyanga. And another thing: I thought a partner or two would be more likely to succeed than playing a lone hand.

"Well, there I met Harvey. Big fellow about forty—regular roughneck. Don't know whether you'll remember him or not, but he used to run the Christmas Pass store in our days. He'd made a little money and been back home, but the climate and the people drove him crazy and back he came.

"He was at a loose end and as I couldn't find any one else who'd look at the proposition I decided to try to persuade him to come in with me and told him the yarn. He thought it was just bull, but he was willing to take a chance.

"We outfitted right there and fortunately got hold of some ex-Black Watch, who of course were trained. For the first fifty miles or more we had no trouble at all. Then we bumped the same tribe you did. Oh, by the way—you'll see why presently—I happened to tear my left forearm badly with a thorn which began to suppurate a little, so I was wearing my coat instead of the usual shirt sleeves when we arrived there."

"That's where you gave the chief a rifle?"

"Sure I did, darn him!"

"Same *kraal* where the Matakini turned up. Go on."

"We were stronger than you; and Harvey had no nerves and a filthy temper, which I hadn't discovered until too late. He was one of the old pioneers and had no use for natives anyway. After the usual *indaba* we refused to wait for the chief's permission, and, striking camp, announced that if anybody attempted to stop us we would fight. There was the —— of a hubbub, but no one attempted to get in our road.

"That afternoon we made another village, who bolted into the bush; and we occupied the *kraal*. Next morning at daybreak they tried to rush us. It was a pretty scrap. Our Matabele Black Watch fought as they usually do—right up to the limit. In my heart I had begun to curse myself for giving way to Harvey, for these people fought not only with a bravery I didn't expect but with a discipline; and they were well armed, too. Then I didn't know why. —— knows how many hundreds they seemed. We didn't have a chance. They simply overwhelmed us.

"Of course both of us were determined never to be taken alive. To tell the truth, old boy, I was mighty sick. Madder than —— to think that this was the end of the trip without a dog's run for my money.

"They had wiped out most of our men, and our porters had fled and surrendered. You know what happened to them. And we were boxed in the chief's hut, Harvey at one end and I at the other, firing rifles so hot you couldn't touch the barrels.

"Harvey had gotten a bullet in his thigh, but I was untouched save for a scratch on the head through my hat. Then suddenly they ceased fire and disappeared.

"As we couldn't see anybody we too stopped firing. Harvey thought that it was a ruse. So did I. Presently a voice shouted out from somewhere behind a hut asking us to surrender and saying that we would not be killed. Harvey sent a bullet in the direction by way of answer. There was silence after that.

"We fired a few volleys around in all directions just to work 'em up and make 'em put an end to the business. But there was no reply. Not knowing what to make of it, we held an *indaba* together, but couldn't guess what the game was. By the way they had fought I couldn't get the idea that they were scared of us two white men without any assistance.

"I patched up Harvey's wound as well as I could. We had our medicine-chest with us fortunately.

"Then I looked out and around. Not a sign of anybody could I see save a few goats and chickens. I didn't want to leave Harvey alone, but at his insistence that if they got me he could finish off by himself if they rushed him, I went.

"Not a darned soul could I find in the village save the dead; nor did any one fire at me. I couldn't make head nor tail of it. What on earth could have scared 'em off?

"I walked out of the village, which was in fairly thick jungle. There I caught a glimpse of eyes watching me. As nobody fired at me I thought I ought to return the compliment.

"I went back to Harvey, who was as puzzled as I was. Anyway we had scoff, smoked and kept a lookout. Never in all my experience had I known natives or otherwise to act like that; nor had Harvey.

"If he hadn't been wounded we'd have set out on foot. Of course we couldn't take any of our goods, which we had used to make a barricade in the chief's hut. The only thing we could do was to wait and curse. They were of course playing the same game as with you—marking time.

"Next morning—we took watches all night—we heard some one hailing us in English. Imagine my surprize when in answer the Matakini of all people should walk calmly up the village dressed like a native, as he was when you saw him. I recollected him—particularly from the gold bangle on his arm—and I was wondering all the time whether he remembered me. He has the devil's own memory, that son of a gun.

"Two native chiefs with gold bangles on their arms—which excited me some, you bet!—came with him. I happened to be dressing my forearm when they came up. To my astonishment the two chiefs uttered a startled grunt and immediately went down on their knees before me.

" 'Where you get that?' the Matakini demanded, pointing at the bangle on my wounded forearm.

"I guessed instantly that it had some such significance as his own must have. I retorted that that was my business. The Matakini began talking to the two chiefs with him in a dialect I didn't understand, and they appeared to be insisting upon something.

"The Matakini turned and said he wished to speak to me alone. Naturally I refused, saying that Harvey was my partner and asking him who in Hades he was anyway.

"That was the only time I've ever seen the Matakini scared. He glanced again at the bangle on my arm and then at me and spoke some words which I didn't understand. Then said he in English:

" 'I am Tubaal, son of Kain. Who you are?'

"Well, that startled me some! . . . But Harvey didn't get it. I tried to pull my wits together and held out my hand. More shocks, although some I didn't understand. Then the Matakini told me that we could keep all our goods on condition that we came to see the City of Baal. When he said *that* right out loud as it were I nearly threw a fit."

X

"THEN YOU DON'T OWE your safety solely to the Phœnician bangle you found in the ruins?" I asked.

"No," replied Billy. "To the combination. Had it merely been the latter I should never have dreamed of using it, and secondly the Matakini, who didn't want me in at all, would have ignored it. But of course I didn't realize all that until afterward.

"He was as good as his words. We both were given hammocks and all our goods were collected. You can imagine that I was pleased all to pieces when I actually saw the city!

"We were both taken to this house here and comfortably installed as you see. But we weren't allowed to go wandering about—or at least Harvey wasn't; and for many days he couldn't. I doctored him myself, but the wound in the thigh proved troublesome.

"As I told you, Harvey was pig-headed and wouldn't understand why I was treated differently from himself; nor would he see that it was to our mutual advantage that it should be so—a fact which had saved his life as well as mine.

"They took me off to see the elders, several of whom to my astonishment spoke English just as my New York man had said. After they had put me through my paces they had a private *indaba* and decided that I must be considered as a full-blown brother Phœnician. The Matakini didn't like this and wanted to oppose the decision; but he couldn't as he himself was practically a stray dog same as me, although in his case there is a possibility that he is a descendant of the Phœnicians. They certainly were in Malta and Cyprus, for the ruins of their temples are there; and the bangle which he has he says was given him by his mother from the temple of Golga in Cyprus, and moreover it was nearly of the highest degree.

"I was to be given a preceptor and after some instruction was raised from one degree to another. In the mean while, Harvey began to get more cantankerous and couldn't or wouldn't understand why I should be initiated into the cult when they wouldn't have him.

"I had suggested the matter to my preceptor; but his answer was that Harvey never could be as he wasn't one of us Phœnicians either in body or spirit as he put it—meaning the bangle or the other thing. Harvey accused me of going back upon my partnership in not immediately pinching all the gold in the place and getting out, or something equally idiotic. Do what I would I couldn't persuade him that I was playing straight and for our mutual benefit.

"What could I do? He was having just as easy a time as I. We were excellently fed and even whisky and tobacco were obtained for us from Beira. But nothing would suit him.

"Another point was that he wanted to know everything that went on during the initiating and so on. You can understand why I couldn't tell him.

"The position became very awkward and strained. And I, knowing more than he did, was scared that he would break out and cause trouble.

"I explained my scheme over and over again to him: that when I had reached the highest degree I would have more power both in their eyes and in knowledge of the principles operating these weird people; that when the time came I would play for the breaking of this tabu or whatever it was and bring in civilization.

"Maybe I had altered my point of view somewhat from the crude idea of looting to an interest in this extraordinary relic of prehistoric man, and at the same time saw in the end the same result as far as hard cash went. But no; Harvey couldn't see beyond raiding and looting.

"Rationally he was plumb crazy in insisting that we load up with as much gold as we could and make a getaway, and then organize an expedition to come back and take the place. In the first case I was extremely doubtful of any success in escaping. We were closely watched and would have to penetrate through circles of these subordinate tribes, something of the system having been explained to me by my preceptor; secondly Harvey wouldn't realize that to form an expedition to fight a way here and capture the city one would want another chartered company's police.

"One day after arguing for an hour or so and he had had a bellyful of whisky he accused me of shirking the partnership and said he was going to cut a way out for himself whether I liked to come or not. When I protested at the unfairness he said he'd thank me to keep my mouth shut and not betray him to 'these bleeding natives.'

"I lost my temper and said he could do what he pleased, of course; but I warned him that the attempt would end in disaster. That night the fool filled a golden ampulla with gold bangles and things and took my golden mask—I think he was crazed with the sight of so much gold—shot some of the slaves and got away.

"This occurred when I was down below there. When I returned and heard what had happened I naturally thought that as well as committing practical suicide he'd put me in the cart, too. I couldn't help cursing his impetuous idiocy and waited, wondering what was going to happen.

"After the siesta my preceptor and the Matakini came to me and informed me that my friend had escaped from the city but had been shot down by some of the outer brethren, as they called the natives, in accordance with the law; and most politely expressed their regard for me as a deserving, faithful brother.

"That made me feel rather rotten about Harvey, but after all if he had only trusted me that would never have happened. He had in effect brought the whole thing on himself. Don't you think so, Faxy, old man?"

"Yes; I think I rather do from what you tell me, Billy," I replied, recollecting difficulties I had had myself with strange partners on expeditions who developed unforeseen tempers and cranks.

"Well, I'm glad you do think so; for sometimes I've been rather sore with myself, although what else I could have done I don't know. After Harvey went I progressed pretty rapidly and studied the Phœnician lingo as well. Maybe I was a bit biased or blinded by my interest and the progress I was making, for I began to think that the Matakini wasn't such a bad sort after all.

"True, I didn't see much of him. I had begun to get an inside point of view and to realize that I had tumbled across the last of an otherwise extinct race. Man, there's not such a magnificent example of prehistoric life on earth. And for wealth—well, you've seen! They've got to fall some day; and if the game were botched the whole show would fall into the hands of these blessed Portuguese and you can imagine what they'd do with it!

"D'you know, according to their own legends and records—in cuneiform characters I think they are—they came here over two thousand years ago. In the sixth or seventh century B.C. they were sent by Necho, a king of Egypt, and they claim that they were the first to sail right around Africa. Think of it, man; about the time that Sappho and Æsop strutted around.

"This country and upper Rhodesia had about a dozen cities or more like this. The palaces of the Pharaohs and Cleopatra were furnished with gold and ivory by these people. They sailed in galleons from what must have been a Phœnician seaport which was destroyed by the sea—the sand-spit where Beira stands now.

"They had schools and colleges and thousands of slaves, of whom these tribes are the remnants. They had roads and imported horses."

"Horses!" I echoed. "But what about the tsetse fly?"

"Wasn't any tsetse fly centuries ago, man! You recollect the king in the golden helmet? They claim that he is the direct descendant of Inarchos, first king of Argos. He lives in the enormous palace built round the lips of the sunken temple with his wives and practically all the women left who are not the wives of the priests.

"No, he isn't a priest. For some reason the king can not be. He is both sacred and yet a layman. The idea is, I think, that he's supposed to know all things without the trouble of learning 'em."

"But are all the other fellows priests?"

"Sure. They're all that are left. You see, they are forbidden like the San Blas Indians to mate with any other tribe. Somewhere about the time old Columbus discovered the States there was a terrible plague which nearly destroyed the lot. The seaport was wiped out too by the sea.

"In their weakened state wild tribes in the interior rose and they had to gather the remnants of their people in this place, the City of Baal. Their galleys were gone and they seem to have been cut off by some Asiatic upheaval, probably when the Turks took Constantinople—the fall of the Eastern Empire.

"They had no more fresh blood coming in so the race began to die out, which was accelerated by this hellish custom of the sacrifice of the first born. Yet they're as proud as Lucifer.

"At the end of the last century they began sending out messengers to seek their fellows, but they say that none of the true faith now exist. The Matakini is the only one except myself whom they have admitted, and that because of the bangle; and in his case also his origin on the site of the Temple of Golga, which fact, by the way, they sent to corroborate.

"Their one object now is to preserve the race and faith intact to the end. I mean all this is what I found out then.

"The next shock I got was when my preceptor informed me that on being initiated into the mysteries of the thirty-third degree I am expected to marry about a dozen or so of their women. But once I got there I thought I could find a way out of that.

"All the time I hadn't realized how the Matakini was steadily working against me. He's more fanatical than they are.

"They buttered me up until I fell for the idea that I really had won their confidence. To test it I proposed that I should be allowed to go to Beira on the pretext of getting guns and provisions. Oh, yes; the ancients take quite well to modern whisky!

"I had every intention of keeping my oath. Say, have you ever remarked how quaint it is that a brother never or seldom gives the secrets away even if he abandons the order? I had no intention of telling you that night in Beira more than I am doing now.

"Unknown to me, I was watched the whole time; and when I produced that ampulla the agents thought I was playing traitor and 'outed' you and kidnaped me for judgment at the hands of the brethren. I am safe in a way as long as I am here, for they are forbidden to shed the blood of a brother except the first born—and they haven't any now—and before he's initiated.

"That's why again I pretended that I didn't know you in the street. I was scared that if I did they would imagine collusion and kill you outright."

"But what was your plan to get me in, too?"

"You're a brother of the third and I intended to procure you a bangle of the same degree as mine, which would protect you. I felt sure they would adopt you as a Phœnician just as they had done with me.

"When we had passed the thirty-third I reckoned we could move things in the way I had suggested—break the tabu slowly and bring in civilization. That is, I did then; but now—"

"Well, go on."

"When they got me back there was a —— of an *indaba,* and the Matakini gained his point of postponing my thirty-first degree until I had proved my fidelity—darn him—which prevents my discovering the secret rites of the inner temple, to which only those of thirtieth degree onward are admitted, tonight. Until that moment I had had faith—I really had in most of their statements.

"The other day that girl, who is the daughter of my preceptor—one of the crowd whom I'm supposed to marry when I'm initiated—remarked about a splendid stranger she had seen. At first I thought that she meant you. Of course as a woman she knows nothing about the secrets of the cult. But when she mentioned that he was the biggest man she had ever seen I knew that he couldn't be you.

"Yesterday I took a walk toward the aqueduct in a part where I'd never been before, and when passing a walled terrace garden I heard a voice shouting; and, my ——, I'm dead sure it was the voice of Harvey, who they told me had been shot and killed.

"Several facts which I had never noticed all together now, as it were, jumped out at me. The deserters who had disappeared mysteriously, the missing prospectors, the missionary and the Matakini's partner; and the knowledge of the sacrifice of the first born! They haven't had any first born for years. Don't you see they may have adopted a substitute?

"Again, probably the Matakini's pleasant idea was to keep me for a victim instead of a brother. If that's right the Matakini has been a sort of supply agent for the substitute sacrifice. That's what he wanted you and me for when he captured us by the Ruenya!"

"Good Lord!" I exclaimed. "Then *that's* what they've been keeping me for!"

"Sure. Probably like the Incas who used to give the sacrifice a —— of a time for a month and then cut his heart out alive."

XI

AS FAR AS WE COULD MAKE OUT from the evidence Billy's surmise seemed too ghastly true. He had been, as he put it, so up in the air at the conclusion that he had decided to try that night to enter the inner temple, and when I had found him he had been seeking to locate a secret knob which operated a sliding gate which he believed to be there.

The question now was, What could we possibly do to save Harvey if Billy's theory should be right? To attempt an open rescue by going to the house where Harvey was imprisoned was obviously futile.

We sat discussing plans until a slave came with food. Billy hastily hid me in a corner behind a screen of fiber mats woven in colors into crude pictures of gods and symbolical beasts. After I had shared Billy's lunch—ample for two or three and very good—we decided to have a siesta and renew the discussion afterward. In case of accident Billy made me up a couch in a massage-room— they were great on that— which had stone slabs like a Turkish bath. The massage-room adjoined the atrium, which had the usual Roman bath hewn in the solid granite and supplied by the general conduit system.

I was awakened slowly by the sound of voices, and by listening intently through the thick walls decided that the Matakini himself was visiting Billy. He remained for about an hour, and when he had gone Billy came in to me with a grave face.

"I'm more'n ever sure," he broke out, "that that darn little rat is the official sacrifice-hunter."

"What's the matter now? Have they found that elder or the eunuch I killed?"

"No; but they know that Ishtar Iddina is missing, and of course they suspect you. Luckily they seem to think—unless the Matakini was trying to trap me—that you've gotten outside the town. Anyway they don't seem to suspect that you've been down below.

"But the Matakini's showing his hand more; threatening me in an underhand sort of way, hinting that although I'm supposed to be a brother that the brethren are beginning to suspect that I aided you to escape and that if it is proved that I've done so they'll sort of excommunicate me and thus avoid the tabu of taking a brother's life, which leaves one subject to the oath. You know. And until this is proved one way or the other

I am suspended; can't go even to the public show tonight. I'm mighty sure that the Matakini's playing up to get me as one of his darned sacrifices."

"Well, but I'm in the same boat, old man."

"You? Oh, sure. But —— it, man, who's going to get you out of the mess if I'm taken, too?"

"Don't see what on earth you can do, old boy," I objected, "either for me or for Harvey."

Billy gazed at me as if he were bewildered; then he lighted a cigaret and sat on the end of the couch.

"That's right," he admitted at length. "No more do I. What the —— are we to do? ——," he broke out again; "Harvey, and then you! Just as I was teaching 'em to feed out of my hand! Getting the whole darned outfit where I wanted it!"

I stared at him. He looked at me.

"Good Lord, I'm sorry, old man," said he, interpreting my thoughts. "But I believe I'm going a bit buggy in this darned crazy before-Christ world."

He grinned.

"I'd got a bug in my head," he added, "that I could lead 'em straight to decent civilization, I think, or some fool ideas of that sort. Let's cut the idealism and get down to brass tacks. My ——," he added, "that's queer. The finding of Harvey still alive and the theory about the Matakini's sort of shaken me up. All I know is that something's got to happen."

"Look here, old boy," said I when we had been arguing and arriving at nowhere for some time, "the only thing is that we must get down below tonight and see this big show. If there is a sacrifice and that sort of thing and Harvey happens to be the star, we'll have to rescue him if we can. Anyway we can't let those fiends have him. But you say they won't let you down there?"

"So the Matakini said. But I guess we'll get there all the same and hide in the corridor as you did. That's all there is to it."

We discussed the matter further, but could not discover any other practical plan; and moreover we were wholly unable to hazard a guess as to what we could or would be able to do. Food came along about sundown, and then we prepared.

Billy hadn't a gun of any sort. He had had one, but since the Beira episode they had taken it away from him. He took my rifle and I the automatic.

When we were ready Billy remarked that he wondered whether his slaves were watching him, which gave me a mild shock; and I began to realize the effect of so many months in this atmosphere of early Assyria or wherever the Phœnicians originally came from. He went out to investigate and returned with one native whose scared eyes rolled at the sight of me.

"The others are away at the festival," said Billy, "and I guess they left this gentleman to look after me. We'll just tie him up out of harm's way."

We bound and gagged him and left him in the massage-room. As we walked, carrying our masks, I noticed that the drums, reeds and lutes had already begun.

From a road which ran near the house we could hear the hum of people evidently making for the great temple. Fortunately we met no one in the short distance to the copse which was the tabu ground.

"Look," whispered Billy; "my lamps are not lighted. You creep up one side and I will the other. Then flash your torch to see whether any of 'em are there waiting for me. If any one's there we must get him. If one gets away we're done for sure."

Very cautiously we stole up, and when we were on either side we peeked in and I switched the torch at the same moment. In the beam shone the whites of two pairs of eyes in shiny black faces. Two mouths opened in a yell of terror. Dropping our masks, Billy and I sprang after them.

For a moment they were paralyzed by fright at the "demon's eye." I had my hand on an oily shoulder, but it wriggled from my grasp. I heard Billy swear. As I switched on the light I saw two forms racing down the corridor and just beyond the black shadow of a sharp curve, beyond which, I recollected, were steps.

I shut off the torch and ran, hoping that they would be blinded by the glare and fall down the stairs in the sudden darkness. Happily I was right. Either one fouled the other or else they both collided with the angle of the wall, for we arrived at the top in time for the torch to reveal black arms and legs reaching the bottom head foremost.

Billy and I nearly followed suit in our haste to secure them. And when we did we were hard put to it to hold their oiled bodies and keep them from hollering at the same time. In the struggle the torch had fallen on the floor, throwing a useless beam against a wall.

When I had got my fellow half-throttled I grabbed the torch to find out how Billy was getting on. He was just arising from the ground with his robes very much torn; and I noticed that his man did not rise.

"Is he dead?" said I.

"Broke his fool back," answered Billy. "How about your fellow?"

"Better take his legs and we'll take him up outside."

"All right; but we'll have to come back for this fellow in case any of his mates come along."

We did so and left the quick, gagged and tied to a tree, watching over the dead in the little copse.

We found the first chamber already lighted as usual and hurried along to the second, where we decided to hide in the conduit tunnel which I had used before until all the priests had passed through to the temple. The body of the eunuch whose neck I had been compelled to break was still there so we concluded that we had nothing to fear from his discovery.

We talked in whispers as long as we dared, still futilely discussing what we could do. Billy opined that we, or he, should have tried to get in touch with Harvey—if it were Harvey. But it was too late to do anything now.

It was about an hour before the first priest emerged from his corridor. After him the others followed in fairly rapid succession, Billy remarking those on one side and I those on the other to prevent awkward mistakes. All the time we could hear the throb of drums and tang of lutes.

When all had gone we waited about twenty minutes; and then, adjusting the gold masks in case we should meet anybody unforeseen, we marched up the temple corridor. Fortunately the wings of the bull decorating each side of the doorway provided each of us with a good cover.

The king man in the golden helmet and his priests were all in their places and had already begun a weird chant. There were even more lamps and flambeaux, I noticed, about the colossal golden image. Instead of a few hundred chiefs as on the previous evening, the body of the temple from the transept to the public entrance was a mass of natives, men and women, several thousands, upon whose ebony arms only here and there gleamed gold bangles, the relative scarcity of these ornaments indicating that the ordinary public, as it were, were admitted.

Around the aisles between the pillars and the decorated walls paraded the bands of oiled eunuchs swinging golden censers. For quite an hour or more the chanting continued. As the music ceased a tallish man—the high priest, Billy whispered to me—advanced a few paces toward the altar and began another chant in an extremely high and clear tenor which seemed to ring all around the vast temple in the silence.

This continued for about ten minutes. Then as he stopped, the golden bull bellowed and belched fire from his nostrils and every person in the great audience, including priests, eunuchs and the congregation, except the high priest, flung themselves forward upon the ground and groaned lustily in unison.

As the belching and bellowing ceased the moaning stopped. All raised their heads—I noticed the frightened, rolling eyes of those near me—as a singularly sweet voice like a female's seemed to emerge from the throat of the brazen god, singing what appeared to be a lament in verse; for at the end of each stanza the whole body of the priests answered in a bass chorus like a trained choir.

This litany, which continued for some twenty minutes or more, was to my ears pleasing; wild, with a terrible melancholy running through it, reminding me of a shepherd's song I had heard in the Andes which was supposed to be an ancient chant of the Inca priests. Billy said he had never heard it before.

When the god's very beautiful voice ceased the music burst out—a fast, exciting rhythm like a hymn of war. I expected a kind of liturgy, such as they had celebrated before with the host in the pyx; but instead of this, I saw that as the hymn ceased abruptly, the king and priests and the congregation again flung themselves flat.

Save for the breathing of the multitude there was such silence that from away above beneath the bright stars came the faint, harsh squall of a forest bird.

While we were wondering what was going to happen there dashed from each side of the god nude young girls with long hair, who began a wild dance in front of the altar to the clashing of cymbals which they carried in their hands. Evidently it was tabu to look, for not a head moved from the ground. I detected another commotion to one side of the idol. This developed into more women carrying a heavy weight. The sacrifice?

What their movements were we could not see. Suddenly the dancers fled like the ballet in a theater, revealing in the outstretched hands of the bull-god the gross figure of a white man bound and naked.

As in the silence the congregation and priests raised their heads and began to moan, the ground at the base of the idol opened and from the cavity came flames and smoke.

"Good ——," I exclaimed.

Forgetting caution, we stood up to see whether we could recognize Harvey; and as we stared the bull snorted fire again and the hands moved down, allowing the bound body to slide slowly until it fell into the roaring fire.

XII

FOR A FEW moments we both were too startled and horrified to speak. Fortunately everybody was too absorbed in groaning and moaning hysterically to notice us standing in the doorway of the temple corridor. The priests were howling like dervishes to the clangor of the music.

The identity of Harvey had disappeared. Only the facts that the victim had been undoubtedly a white man and that it was too late to rescue him remained.

But what to do? To attempt to shoot up the crowd would quickly be ended by our being torn to pieces by the excited mob.

As we hesitated, the flames ceased, evidently owing to the closure of the trap in front of the god. Billy decided matters by clutching my arm and shouting in my ear.

"The secret door. Keep on your mask. Come on!"

We ran hastily back to the first chamber, and while I held the torch Billy examined the most prominent figure on the bas-relief along the walls. Feverishly he tried to pull, to push and to twist every projection that might be a secret button. Nothing moved.

"I know there's a door in every cavern like this," he remarked, and began upon another figure with no result.

"It's more than probably concealed in the figure of the god," I commented. "Let's dynamite it."

"Dynamite!" he exclaimed scornfully. "Where on earth—"

"I have," said I, producing a stick, a fuse and a few detonators from my pocket. "Here; let's shove it in the brute's nostrils," I added, partly influenced by a childish wish to hurt the god of brutality and secondly because the nostrils were the only cavities. Then as I began to push the stick in as far as I could, Billy shouted—

"It's moving, by ——; it's moving!"

Sure enough, slowly a block of the wall about five feet broad, the edges of which were cunningly hidden by the decoration, began to swing on a pivot. Billy had naturally tried every projection, whereas the secret spring was in one or both of the cavities. Within was darkness, but the torch revealed a corridor with steps descending steeply. Inside we tried to shut the door; but evidently there was another spring within, and we hadn't time to spare to search for it.

After about fifty or sixty steps we reached the level, along which we hurried, still wearing our masks, which would at any rate conceal our identity should we meet any one. We saw a yellow gleam round a curve and approached cautiously. Through the door, the silhouette of which was broken by the wings of the mythological bull, glowing in the light of thousands of oil lamps was what appeared to be a replica of the temple above in solid gold.

Every figure of the hundreds around the walls and columns was clothed in beaten metal. Upon the altar was another idol of the bull-god even more colossal, whose eyes gleamed like some monstrous cat, whose nostrils shot beams of blood, and whose glittering hands, instead of being outstretched for a victim, were posed Buddha-fashion as if in satisfaction upon the knees, just in front of a heap of white objects upon the altar table.

But what puzzled us was that the transept of the temple was covered with long stone altars or daises about two feet from the ground which were already set with hundreds of golden platters and ampullæ; around were low divans, Roman fashion, suggesting a vast banquet. Behind another barricade of gold and ivory the chancel was similarly equipped, but the table and the floor were of beaten gold.

We certainly had not forgotten for what we had come, yet the sight of that temple of gold made us as if stupefied with drunkenness. Billy was the first to recover. He drew my attention to a fact that I had not even noticed.

"Good Lord, there isn't a man here!" he exclaimed.

As we held a whispered consultation there came a burst, dim but distinct, of the wild strains of the other temple. Looking around, we made out in the lofty roof a number of black shafts which were apparently ventilating-tunnels. On the opposite side of the temple were two other corridor-entrances like the one in which we were standing.

We decided to explore. With our guns ready beneath our robes we stalked boldly up the transept, remarking the thickness of the shell-like golden platters. Thence we went across the golden floor of the chancel. As we approached the altar before the bull-god we saw that the heap of white things was composed of human bones, babies' bones such as I had seen the first night before the shrine in the grove.

"Good ——, Billy," I exclaimed, pointing to an adult femur, "Harvey's gone—if he was Harvey!"

"Mighty strange," he commented, examining the bone. "If Harvey was the victim, he was cast into the fire; but you can't burn a body and retain the bones."

The god's eyes, we saw, were great emeralds; and the blood-stained beams of the nostrils were caused by enormous rubies.

"I never knew there were emeralds in Africa—around here, at all events," remarked Billy.

"Or rubies," said I. "But probably they're very ancient; brought them with them from Assyria or wherever they came from."

"Sssh!" Again came the outburst of wild music, which ceased as abruptly.

"This must have some connection with the upper temple," I observed.

"Probably," assented Billy. "Possibly the sound comes down when they open the trap of the furnace. Let's find out."

Around at the back of the great image were three doors, each of which was illuminated. We hesitated which to follow.

"Wait for the next sound of music and follow that," suggested Billy. "That ought to lead somewhere."

The next time it came undoubtedly from the center corridor. I admit myself that as we crept along deeper into the extraordinary bowels of the mountain I thought that, even if we did release Harvey or whoever he was, in the end we should each provide a sacrifice for the great god Baal.

Twenty yards on in the ensuing silence we caught the murmur of voices. Creeping along very cautiously, we came to a cavern brightly lighted, in which were some dozen eunuchs squatting and standing in attitudes of expectation around what appeared to be an enormous bed or divan.

Presently as we watched, wondering what on earth could be happening, a bright red glow in the roof revealed a shaft. Simultaneously we heard a burst of music. A few seconds afterward a dark body fell out of the roof cavity on to the big divan and bounced. As the music was shut off one of the eunuchs seized a tiny black baby and bore it off in his arms.

"Good —— ——!" I ejaculated. "The first born!"

"That fire's a fake!" exclaimed Billy. "They don't burn 'em! *That's* why those bones are white!"

"But if that's so, then Harvey, or whoever he was, isn't dead. We may be in time yet! Let's hold up these fellows and investigate."

"No, no!" urged Billy. "Wait a moment. I think I've got a hunch that each of these eunuchs means one baby; and then we're free."

Billy was right. The rain of babies from a fiery sky continued.

"Look here," said I. "This show is going to last some time. Let's investigate those other corridors."

We returned; and, listening at the left-hand one, we caught the faint, continuous sound of music and chanting; then suddenly the bellow of the god.

We entered, and ten yards down found another shaft, up which ran a spiral staircase carved out of the rock. Billy leading, we began to ascend. The light from the lamp below did not carry far, but above glimmered the faint glow of a single light. As we mounted Billy stopped and under cover of the music whispered:

"There's a priest guy on a kind of platform. I can't make out what he's doing. He's alone, I think."

We proceeded a little farther and could see that the man stood in a small kind of cave scarcely big enough to stand erect in, and appeared to be working at something.

Just then came another bellow and a flash of red.

"I've got it! Next time the bull bellows drop him with your automatic."

We waited. With the flash of red and as the bellow was in full blast I fired. The bellow ended in a snort as the priest crumpled and fell off the platform down the shaft, nearly taking Billy with him. We hurried to the top and found ourselves in a small chamber.

At first we did not realize that we were inside the god's great head until, peering through two of five apertures, we saw the vast mass of natives in the body of the upper temple moaning and howling in the midst of an indescribable saturnalia.

The upper two holes were the eyes, the middle tubes were the nostrils and the lower slit, into which was stuck a cow's horn, the mouth. Upon a slab which acted as a table were some smoldering fagots of resinous wood and a primitive bellows made out of a goatskin, through which evidently the priest had blown fire through the nostrils of the god Baal for the edification of the assemblage.

Looking down the nostrils at a lower elevation than the eyes, we could observe the chancel. The last of a procession of priests was defiling behind the god, and the gold-helmeted king was being carried away in his golden *machilla*. We held a hurried consultation.

"That baby-sacrifice is over," declared Billy, "and now those darned beasts are up to some more deviltry. Let's get down."

"No," said I; "one moment. We're in this time to see it through. Let's dynamite the —— thing. That'll put the fear of God in 'em!"

"By ——, that's the great idea," assented Billy. "Look here, shove a long fuse in so as to give us time to get down and rush that mob of baby-murderers. Then she ought to scare —— out of 'em and generally give 'em something else to think about."

We lost some few minutes finding a convenient spot to place the charge. There was no tool of any sort that we could use to make a hole, so I jammed the stick as hard as I dared in the horn of the mouth and adjusted a fuse timed for about ten minutes. Then, firing her, we scurried down. At the bottom, undiscovered, we found the officiating priest as dead as his own god.

Then, readjusting our masks, we advanced. Passing across the mouth of the entrance at the back of the god was the last of a procession of eunuchs bearing a heavy burden. Taking a chance, we crept after them, seeking cover behind the bulk of the idol.

In the body of the temple were some hundreds of the priests without their masks lolling upon the divans in the Roman manner. Among them circulated the women I had seen dancing on the previous evening.

On the floor of the golden chancel before the golden table lounged thirty-two other priests, also without masks. These were evidently of the highest degree, the thirty-third. At the far end we recognized the Matakini. From somewhere hidden came wild music similar to that in the upper temple.

What the burden was that the eunuchs had been carrying we could not see as they were occupied directly in front of the god, evidently at the altar.

"Say," whispered Billy, "shove another stick in the back of this fellow. Time her about the same. The other will be the cue for us to get out of the light and start something."

This time from the outside it was easier to find a likely spot, for the god was provided with a bull's tail. Tight under that I wedged the charge and fired the fuse, making it an inch shorter than the first one. With a keen eye on my wrist-watch we waited.

"About two minutes to go," I whispered.

Suddenly, almost drowning the changing, came a bellow of rage, and a voice in English poured out a terrible stream of oaths such as I never have heard matched.

"That's Harvey, all right!" whispered Billy, and I swear he chuckled. "Let's peek!"

We crept quietly along the side of the great pedestal. Upon the altar lay the naked form of an enormously fat blond man, and in front of him stood a white-bearded priest chanting as he held aloft a golden knife.

Just as the weapon flashed yellow above the belly my automatic spat. The high priest collapsed. The next instant Billy's rifle cracked. Another priest in the act of rising pitched across the golden table.

"Quick!" yelled Billy. "Hold 'em off while I cut Harvey loose!"

At the first report every priest in the temple was on his feet. Eunuchs and women ran yelling and screaming in every direction. One priest after another sprawled on the golden floor as they rushed, while Billy, seizing the golden knife of sacrifice, hewed Harvey's bonds.

"Back away!" I shouted as I saw that Harvey was free. "She's going!"

Simultaneously with my words came a reverberating roar. The golden walls of the temple seemed to quiver. Priests, women and eunuchs were paralyzed in grotesque attitudes of rage and fear.

"Come on! Come!" I heard Billy yelling at Harvey.

We ran swiftly across to the corridor from which we had entered. Then just as a great clamor broke out the colossal golden god rose bodily forward and as the concussion smote us, crashed upon the golden table, burying the high priest beneath him.

XIII

WITH THE LAST REVERBERATION of the fall of the god came a terrible wail as of one in mortal agony. This was taken up by the remainder of the priests, who one and all threw themselves upon the ground and began to tear their robes and pluck out their beards.

"Come on," said I; "they've forgotten us. Up the corridor there and get out through the open gate."

"Here!" exclaimed Harvey, waddling a few paces to clutch a gleaming eye of the god that had been shot across the chancel. "What about loading up some of these —— trinkets and things?"

"Are you still crazy?" demanded Billy wrathfully. "Shut up and come along or they'll wake up and get after us in a minute."

Piloting Harvey on each side, we ran across the temple right through the yowling women and eunuchs and up the corridor by which we had entered. But at the top we found that the slab of rock had either closed automatically or been shut.

"Blow it up," urged Billy, but I couldn't as I hadn't any more dynamite-sticks.

Frantically he tried to find the secret spring, but the door on the inside was undecorated and presented a bare surface of smooth rock with no cavity of any sort.

"We'll go back," decided Billy, "although we may have to fight our way through. Come on!"

Again Harvey jibbed, grumbling and swearing that we had got him into an adjective mess. He trotted ahead after Billy, panting like a white hippopotamus. In the temple we found priests still wailing and tearing their clothes.

The center of the three doors brought us into the bottom of the fire-trap. Passing through another short corridor, we came into a long, low cavern, undecorated, around the sides of which were a dozen fires or more burning beneath great metal caldrons looking like an enormous kitchen. At the far end was a crowd of terrified eunuchs yammering at what was apparently a closed door.

"We'll never get through that bunch!" exclaimed Billy. "What's that?" A sullen continuous roar began. "Come on back through the temple!"

As we reached the door the roar increased in volume and we saw a flood of water over the floor of the temple already a foot deep in which priests were flopping about, yowling and tearing their hair; others were embracing women, who were weeping, laughing and dancing. As we paused to gaze at this bedlam a shriek drew our attention to a figure dancing on top of the fallen god—the Matakini, who screamed out:

"The Law! The Law! After Baal ees the flood! The Law! The Law!"

"That —— maniac's let loose the aqueduct on us," said Billy.

"The shaft to the other temple," I shouted. "Come, Billy! The fall of the god's driven them insane."

We ran across the temple again. Harvey panted after us, clutching his emerald and clanking with gold.

We passed the body of the dead priest and reached the spiral stairway, which was intact. Mounting, we came out through a hole where had stood the other idol. The upper temple was deserted. The floor was covered with stone platters and ampullæ of wine, most of them overset or broken.

They had been feasting as well as carousing, for scattered about were lumps of white meat. The formation of one attracted my attention. I stopped to pick it up. It was a baby's hand!

Instantly I saw the explanation of the many unaccountable things. They were cannibals! That was why their prisoners were treated so well! Harvey, fat and panting beside me! That was why the child's bones of the great Baal's altar below and of the shrine in the grove were white.

The burning was symbolical of the sacrifice of the first fruit or first born to Baal, of which they ate themselves—the eons-old practise of savage races to obtain by the act, as they imagined, part of the strength and wisdom of the god.

The Phœnicians themselves could no longer afford first born; the religious law had been altered, as usual, to satisfy the demands of expediency. The Matakini had been, as Billy had surmised, the official sacrifice-hunter. That was why in the police days he had wanted both Billy and me; that was where five of the deserters, the prospectors and the missionary had gone!

When we reached the top of the steps of the public entrance we found ourselves in a large courtyard, in the walls of which were several doors profusely decorated. At the far end was an open gate illuminated by golden torches, which led into the open. The streets were deserted.

At Billy's suggestion we went to hunt up the king fellow with our masks on, leaving the naked Harvey decorated with loot to wait for our return. We found the old man with a crowd of women and guards in the hall of an atrium of the palace.

Sternly Billy announced that the temple had been destroyed by the anger of Baal and that to the only two survivors of the sacred priesthood had the god given his confidence and commands. Knowing nothing of the secret rites or even the inner theology and accustomed to obey the priests implicitly, the ancient king Tchelkonos had our wishes carried out without demurring, sending messengers to the native population—who each and all had fled the city, believing that like Sodom and Gomorrah it was about to be destroyed—ordering them to return and await the commands of the mouthpiece—vide Billy and me—of the god. This on the morrow they did.

But when we went back for Harvey he had disappeared. That he had been tempted by his short-sighted craze for more loot to go back into the temple was evident as he had left his booty, emerald as well, in a corner of the courtyard. Whether he had fallen into the water or had been hit on the head we never knew; although weeks later when we had drained the temple dry by blasting the doors open, every one of which the maniac Matakini or one of the priests had closed to insure their own doom, we came upon his fat carcass among the others.

Adventure, September 3, 1921

Buried Gods

THE MOMBASA-KISUMU EXPRESS sneezed and coughed up the steep gradient near the summit of El Bergon. On each of the small platforms of the five coaches were whites, the men in terai hats and shirt sleeves, and the women in lawn.

On the edge of the roof of the second car was seated a young man in a solar helmet and khaki whose clear-cut lips in the clean-shaven face were set aggressively as if he were determined to register in his mind every sight of the trip through a country in which apparently the Bronx Zoo had cut loose. Passing through the dense forest around the Highlands, little was to be seen; yet any moment a glimpse might likely be caught of elephant, a fleeing koodoo or possibly a rhino prepared to dispute the passage of the other armor-clad monster.

As they snorted through a cutting and began to gather way on a short straightaway, there appeared in a clearing in the forest a blue glint in the sun, and a rhythmic panting was heard.

"I say, Beffert," called out a young English official on the platform beneath, "this is Macnamara's place. You'd better get your traps ready. They'll pull up for a moment, and you can hop off."

Dorsay Beffert slung himself down and yanked a Wolsey valise and a grip from the interior. They approached a small siding stacked with timber and slowed up before a sawmill worked by an oil engine beneath a corrugated-iron roof some forty yards away. On higher ground were three shacks nestling against the deep blue of the forest edge.

After hurried good-bys Dorsay clambered down the car-step clutching his guns as the train slowed down, dropped his baggage and jumped off.

The equatorial sun was more than hot. A Wolsey valise packed with blankets is heavy. But the white men working at the mill showed not the slightest interest in the stranger, whom they must have seen alight.

"Well, I guess Macnamara will send a boy along," muttered Dorsay, and set out.

Beneath the iron roof, three white men and several natives manipulated the whirring circular saws in an atmosphere of heat and oil. They looked up at him as he approached. A young man said cheerily—

"Good morning!"

"Good morning," returned Dorsay a little bewilderedly, looking first at a tallish man with drooping mustaches in khaki slacks, and then at the other, a small man in soiled corduroys with a short pipe stuck in the nest of a scrubby beard who looked like a bad-tempered Scotch terrier. Dorsay turned to the most respectable man and said tentatively, "Dr. Macnamara?"

The man jerked his head toward the disreputable little man with the pipe. Dorsay repeated the inquiry. The sharp eyes looked up at him, and he nodded. Slightly annoyed, Dorsay tendered a letter. The doctor glanced at it and thrust it in his pocket with a gesture which did not conceal irritation.

"All right. Look around. Tiffin ten minutes," he growled, and went on pushing a log into the teeth of a saw.

Dorsay hesitated, annoyed and puzzled by the abrupt manner of a man from whom as a doctor and a friend of an uncle he had expected at least common courtesy if not a welcome. He caught the eye of the young man, who winked. Dorsay went over to him, intending to ask for some one to fetch his baggage; but:

"If the fellow's so darned sore about it I'll go back," he thought; but the knowledge that there was not a down train for two days complicated matters.

He glanced again at the doctor, who was working and smoking as if he had never seen or heard of him. The man in the khaki slacks smiled dourly and said—

"Jolly hot work, what?"

Dorsay agreed and began to ask conversational questions. He heard the little doctor suddenly bawl at some one in the native lingo, and, looking around, saw two natives carrying his baggage. Immediately afterward a steam whistle blew; and the doctor, walking across, stopped the engine, put on his coat, and said, "Come along."

"Crazy," Dorsay muttered to himself.

The little man led him in silence across the clearing to the center shack, which was evidently the mess-hut. In the corner was a basin and towels.

"Wash," said the doctor, and stood aside.

While obeying this mandate Dorsay politely tried to break this extraordinary taciturnity, but the replies elicited were a grunted "yes" or "no."

Two Australians who had been working in the forest—a short, dark fellow and a medium-sized, fair man—came in, and they—Dorsay, the doctor and the two whites whom Dorsay had met at the mill—all sat down to lunch. Beyond a few curt sentences to the newcomers about tree-felling the little doctor spoke scarcely a word throughout the meal.

The man with the drooping mustaches—who, Dorsay learned, was the doctor's brother—seemed faintly amused at everything. The meal ended, the doctor strode back to the mill after a curt, "See you at dinner."

To fill up time and to avoid the doctor until he apparently felt fit to receive a guest, Dorsay accepted an invitation to go into the forest to watch the Australians' operations.

"Been here long?" remarked Dorsay conversationally as they walked.

"About two years," said Simpson, the fair man; "but Dorky here, he's an old-timer. Ten years, ain't it?"

"Yes, and a ruddy 'ole it is," grumbled his partner, Dorkin, who had never lost his Sydney accent. "If I could only lie me bloomin' 'ands on a pile me for 'ome and booty."

Dorsay looked at him.

"Queer kind of a man, the doctor, isn't he?" he continued.

"Bit off his nut," said Simpson. "Been here too long. But he's all right to everybody 'cept himself."

"Might make a mint of money outer this outfit, but he won't. Won't answer letters. If anybody wants any timber they have to come or send personally.

"He's known from Uganda to the Coast. Came out here about twenty years ago with Lord Wintercomb as his private doctor and wouldn't go back. He's been right up in the interior. Had a ⸺ of a time. Got a touch of the sun, I reckon; but he's all right."

Up a narrow track in the dense forest they came upon a bunch of natives who hauled the logs down to the mill. Stark naked they were, and as dark as sepia.

"Kavirondo from the Lake," said Simpson. "Black fellows around here—that is, out in the open—won't do a stroke of work. Never would. Masai, y'know. Scrap like ——; them and the Wakikuyu played old Harry for years in the early days."

"Oh, yes; guess I saw some of 'em coming up the line," said Dorsay. "Tall fellows, stark, with yellow ocher and white painted on 'em. Is that one?" he added, indicating a tall native who had suddenly emerged from a wall of undergrowth.

"No; that's Wanderobo, a hunting tribe. They don't seem to have any proper village. Just wander about through the forest."

Dorsay eyed the man interestedly. He seemed a finer specimen than usual of the African; slender, tall, graceful in his carriage and with what appeared a wild, amused smile on his lips which were not very negroid. He stopped to speak to the Australian lumberman.

"Says he's got some good news for the doctor," said Simpson. "Probably spotted some elephant. Not supposed to shoot without a license, but about fifty square miles of this stuff"—he waved a hand at the almost impenetrable jungle—"belongs to him; and he don't care a ——!"

"Oh, Lordy, what luck!" exclaimed Dorsay. "Wonder if he'll take me along?"

"Mebbe—if he happens to feel good and cottons to you. But take my tip; don't ask him. If you do he'll refuse."

As the native talked, Dorsay noticed an oblong tiny packet swinging from the man's neck by a small chain made of steel links.

"Is that a trade chain?" he asked.

"No. A tribe subject to the Masai make 'em and their spears. Beauties, aren't they? I've heard that they are descendants of people who used to make chain mail for the Abyssinians."

"Ask him if he wants to sell it," urged Dorsay. "It's the first like it I've seen."

"He says no," replied Simpson, " 'cos the charm is very powerful."

"What! That dirty, filthy packet thing on the end? Rot. Tell him I'll give him a dollar—I mean five rupees—for it."

"That's no good. He doesn't know what money is. Have to offer trade goods."

"Well— Say, I'm crazy to have that chain. Look here, I'll give him the wrist-watch. Will he know what that is?"

"But it's far too much, man."

"Oh, it isn't up to much. Steel, but she goes well; and she's got a phosphorescent face. That'll amuse him."

While Simpson talked the native eyed the proffered watch, bent and listened to the ticking, grinned, and took off the chain.

"Ask him where he got it."

"Says he took it off an enemy he killed," reported Simpson. "But you mustn't believe everything they tell you."

Amusedly Dorsay left him futilely trying to buckle the watch on his wrist.

"Pouf! It stinks like a skunk!" Dorsay exclaimed as he examined the charm.

"What do they make these charms of?" he inquired, putting it in his pocket.

"Darned if I know," said Simpson.

Dorsay spent the afternoon with the two lumbermen who worked on contract for the doctor so that they did not mind his eccentric methods of doing business. The heat in the jungle was not so intense as Dorsay had imagined it would be, for there was very little moisture; and, being some six thousand feet up in the air, the climate was rare and cool; only the direct rays of the equatorial sun were no less fierce.

Here right on the line of the equator the sun drops almost as suddenly as a shooting star and night comes like a cold hand, making a warm jacket appreciated. At dinner the little doctor was still morosely silent.

After the coffee, when it seemed the custom was for everybody to disperse to his quarters and Dorsay was wondering where he was to sleep, the little man said—

"Come and have a grog, young man."

He led him across to the other shack, which was divided into two compartments, the first a kind of office, and the inner a bedroom in which was roaring a great fire of logs. An extra camp-bed had been made up, on which was Dorsay's valise already opened out.

As silently as before, the doctor produced a bottle and glasses, and, thrusting some Indian cigars before his guest, lounged before the fire and appeared to fall into a reverie. Dorsay sipped his liquor and began to grow uncomfortable in the presence of this mute image.

Not knowing what to do, he began to fidget with the chain and essayed a question regarding native charms. To his surprize the doctor blinked at him in the light of the fire like a terrier on a rug, and, without preamble, launched into a most discursive mood, describing East Africa and his adventures.

Interested in the story, Dorsay forgot the charm until some hours later the doctor, noticing it in his hand, asked him where he had gotten it.

"Yours is probably merely some leaves from a sacred tree—if it's Wanderobo—giving keen sight to the hunter."

The expert's opinion somehow depreciated the value of the purchase in Dorsay's mind; and, prompted by an idea, he tore off the wrapping. The doctor, reading the reaction in his guest's mind, watched him amusedly. Inside the outer filthy rag was a skin covering, and within that was wrapped what appeared to be another piece of rag, fairly clean.

"Good Lord, what is it?" he ejaculated as he smoothed out in the palm of his hand what was evidently a piece of cloth torn from a shirt with dark stains upon it.

"Oh," said the doctor casually, "probably some part of the clothes of some murdered white which they think will give the wearer the power of a white. They think, you know, that whatever belongs to you is part of the soul, and consequently—"

"But there's writing on it—in blood!" exclaimed Dorsay. "Look!"

He spread out the remnant closer to the light of the fire.

"Look! 'Mount Elgon—help—buried—' What's that word? And this?"

"Let me see," said the doctor quietly.

He gazed at the message anew.

"Can't see. Get a light."

He rose, lighted a lamp, and flattened out the rag on the table.

"That's 'Mount Elgon—help—buried' right enough. Now, what's buried? The others are indecipherable."

"What d'you think's buried?" demanded Dorsay.

"Ivory probably. There's much buried ivory all over the country."

"But why should any one—"

"Blood. Nothing else to write with. Possibly dying."

"Can't make it out," persisted Dorsay. " 'Mount Elgon,' " he repeated slowly, " 'help—buried'; something, about 'live' and 'gods'—and written in blood. What on earth can it mean? Where is 'Mount Elgon?' "

"To the northwest about a hundred miles."

"By ——, doctor," Dorsay exclaimed, looking up, "I'm going to find out what it does mean!"

"I shouldn't, young man. It's a dangerous country there. It's not opened up. Several have gone up there, but few ever come back. Probably this fellow was one."

"All the more reason to find out," persisted Dorsay. "Perhaps the ivory, or whatever it is, is still there."

"Possibly, and possibly not," returned the doctor, yawning. "I'm going to turn in. D'you want anything? Another drink? No? Well, good night then."

But half the night Dorsay stared into the flickering fire, clutching the mysterious message in his hand.

II

DORSAY WAS AWAKENED by a boy with the coffee. The chain he found wound about his wrist as if symbolical of his determination not to relinquish the idea evoked by the message in the charm. Through the window the hard stars were paling.

Resentfully he eyed the stocky outline of the doctor pulling on his pants. The doctor grunted some unintelligible greeting and went out. By the time Dorsay had hastily dragged on his clothes and followed into the other room the day had come.

"Good Lord!" he exclaimed. "Snow!"

For the clearing and the shack roofs were gleaming white beneath them as the sun shot above the trees as if hauled rapidly by stage mechanism.

"Hoar-frost every night," snapped the doctor, slopping in a basin. "Let me look at your charm," he added as he threw the water out of the door.

The rays of the mounting sun confirmed the previous night's discovery. The rag was undoubtedly a portion torn from a shirt of striped cotton such as was sold in whites' stores. Evidently the message had been written with some blunt instrument, possibly a piece of stick, and the blood had soaked into the material like ink upon blotting-paper, but the words "Mount Elgon—help—buried—" were readable.

The rest was utterly indecipherable—a mere blob of stains and chunks of congealed blood except for one word which appeared to be "goods" or "gods."

"H'm," grunted the doctor, "some poor fool who doesn't know Africa's greed."

Vaguely startled by such words from the little man, Dorsay stared at him. The bright eyes twinkled like a terrier's at the sight of a bone.

"Come 'long; breakfast."

"But this?" said Dorsay, indicating the bloody message in his hand.

The doctor's black muzzle seemed to grin.

"Make a nice curio for you to take home."

"But, say, d'you really mean you're not going to do anything about it?"

"Pff!" snorted the doctor. "I've got my mill to look after. No time for wildcat schemes. Show you elephant tomorrow."

Dorsay looked at him, conscious of rising anger at what he considered the lack of sporting instinct in Doctor Macnamara.

"Thanks," he said a trifle stiffly, "but I sha'n't have time. I'll take the down train tomorrow, for I'm going after this."

"You don't realize what you're taking on," snapped the doctor.

"Probably," replied Dorsay. "That's what will make it more interesting."

"Probably make another who won't come back, young man."

"Still more interesting," retorted Dorsay.

At breakfast he could not resist showing the message to the others, hoping that some one would volunteer to go along. But the doctor's brother merely smiled amusedly, and the other deprecated the possibility of ever locating the site of the supposed buried ivory.

"Nothing to work on," said Simpson. "My ——, Elgon's as big as Tasmania, and the Turkana won't stand monkeying with. 'Sides, Government won't let you go in."

Dorsay spent the whole day mooning about the shacks and wandering on the verge of the forest. Sometimes he sat in the shade staring at the blood-stained rag as if trying to extract more information, at other times day-dreaming of the tragedy or adventure that lay behind.

He couldn't understand how any man with red blood could refuse such an opportunity. True, he didn't know all the difficulties ahead, but that's where the fun lay, to his thinking. The chief trouble as he saw it was the lack of the native speech. He would have to hire an interpreter. Anyway he would return to the Travelers' Club at Nairobi to see if he couldn't hunt up some one sporting enough to go in with him.

At dinner he might have been accused of sulking. Within, excitement was burning so intensely that he could not discuss the matter in cold blood; resentment, too, paralyzed his tongue. In the evening the doctor, after preparing his guns for the morrow, launched again into his discursive mood—which developed apparently only after sundown—but he did not mention elephant.

Next morning the doctor aroused Dorsay.

"Come on, young man; time to start."

"But there isn't any train until nine-thirty, is there, doctor?" inquired Dorsay.

"H'm. So you're going down then, eh?"

"Sure I am. Haven't I said so? I'm very much obliged for your hospitality, doctor," continued Dorsay stiffly. "And I'm sorry I can't stay on, but— Well, when I've made up my mind I kinder got to go through with it."

"H'm, I see. Obstinate young cub, eh? Same stock as your uncle."

"Sure, I hope I am."

"Good-by and good luck, my boy. If you get through alive come and tell me what you found. Good-by."

After a tight grip of the hand the little doctor was gone. Conscious of a renewed sense of disappointment that the doctor hadn't changed his mind at the last moment, Dorsay lay staring at the embers of the fire, dreaming. Pity too, he thought; for apparently there wasn't another man as good as the little doctor in the whole country who knew as much about natives.

At breakfast Dorkin asked to have a look at the blood message again, and this time evinced more interest than before, poring over it for some time in the full rays of the sun together with his partner, with whom he had evidently been discussing the affair.

"—— queer, that's wot it is," said Dorkin. "But it ain't worth tiking up, Jack. Good luck to yer, mister."

"Thanks," said Dorsay, wondering vaguely why such a decent chap as Simpson seemed should be partners with such a shifty-looking specimen. At 9:45 he boarded the down train, and by the evening he was back in the Travelers' Club.

Macnamara had said the Turkana district, which was nominally British, was not under administration and had scarcely ever been explored, and moreover was forbidden territory to any save Government-organized expeditions. Therefore it behooved him to be careful how he approached any one.

He obtained surveyors' section maps of the country to the south and west of Mount Elgon, which he found to be about ten thousand feet high but with very long slopes. The western side was in the Uganda Protectorate and the eastern and southern in British East Africa, mainly distinguished by the large blank spaces.

He began to hunt about for some old settler from whom he would extract information on which to base the nominal reason for his trip. In the meanwhile he would quietly get together provisions and seek a reliable interpreter. He already had a big-game license, so that there was nothing suspicious in these maneuvers.

Four days after he had been back, a farmer named Ferney, whom he had met before and who had been in the country for some ten years or more, came into town. Dorsay had rather liked him before, and in him he decided to confide. On the veranda after lunch Ferney listened attentively to the little that Dorsay had to relate and interestedly examined the message.

"You say the Wanderobo you bought this from said he took it from an enemy killed in battle? Well, all that sounds pretty plausible. The enemy might have been one of the Turkana or allied tribes. They would make a charm out of this sort of thing.

"But I'm afraid you're on a wild-goose chase, my lad. The fellow who wrote this is probably dead, and what's the use of it? There's no clue at all. Elgon! My ——, you might as well say East Africa and finish with it. If you'll take my advice, forget all about it. Besides the Turkana country is closed by the Government."

"Darn the Government" muttered Dorsay to himself. "All these darn Englishmen seem scared to their eye-teeth of the government."

He retired feeling somewhat damped but nevertheless doggedly determined. He had succeeded in securing a cook, a Mohammedan, a reputable *shikari*, and an interpreter whose villainous face he did not like at all. However there was nothing to be done but to go straight ahead. He had another man in mind whom he determined to try later.

"There must be something to it," he pondered sleepily.

When the light was pouring in at the window he thought he was still dreaming for a familiar voice was saying:

"I say, wake up young man—Beffert!"

Beside his bed stood the little doctor, grinning at him.

"Hullo, doctor," said Dorsay drowsily. "You've come down?"

"Yes, I'm coming in with you if you're still game."

"What! You will! That's great! But why—"

"Oh that ruddy mill bores me," returned the doctor, "so I decided to come on. Anyway," he added, "you'd never get through yourself; and I owe your uncle—"

"Cut that out, please!" exclaimed Dorsay, bridling. "If I can't run—"

"That's all right, my boy. Have it any way you like. Get your bath and we'll talk plans over. You haven't been yapping all over the town I hope?"

The doctor's explanation of why he had changed his mind never was satisfactorily explained—unless it be by his actions before and since; for times out of number had he solemnly declared to the countryside at large that he had given up the trail for good, was now to be depended upon as a practising physician, a farmer, a storekeeper, a lumberman—always with the result that, if some one didn't tempt him back, he took care to tempt himself.

However, under his experienced control the *safari* was quickly got together.

The quickest approach to the Elgon country was to go up to Kisumu on the lake and start from there, but the doctor, who preferred to travel with donkeys as being easier to control and feed than porters, proposed to visit property he had in the northern Wakikuyu country, which was almost on the trail from Nairobi, where the animals could be obtained. Besides a shooting-party at Nairobi going to Kisumu to start for the Eldama Ravine would be open to suspicion, and the Government officials had quite as much dislike for the eccentric doctor as he had for them. Anyway, he said, there was no particular hurry.

The doctor, as leader of the expedition, forbade any elephant-shooting.

However a week out, fate, through the medium of Mahomet, decided that Dorsay's thirst should be slaked. Mahomet, now cook, who had at one time been a syce and seemingly nourished an ambition to be a *shikari*, expressed in constant appeals to be allowed to accompany them upon their hunt for buck. One afternoon in a district where elephant were exceedingly plentiful the doctor and his Wanderobo hunter and Dorsay and the *shikari* set out as usual.

About a mile from camp when they were walking through open forest country about a hundred yards apart there came suddenly the report of a rifle followed by the trumpeting of an elephant near to Dorsay.

Wondering from whom the shot could possibly have come, he ran in the direction. As he rounded a great clump of trees he saw in an open glade fifty feet in front of him a slight figure in khaki fleeing madly just ahead of a charging elephant. Vaguely recollecting instructions, he aimed at the base of the uplifted trunk and fired.

As the great beast swerved aside, trumpeting ferociously, Mahomet had the sense to dart away to the right into thick bush. Standing in the middle of the open glade, the elephant winded Dorsay and charged.

As the brute seemed towering above him, Dorsay fired, realizing to his dismay that he had aimed at the mighty chest instead of the brain through the mouth.

He was seized and dashed to the ground. The elephant appeared to be falling upon him. He felt the contracting of the stomach muscle in horror of the coming impact, and wriggled. The wriggle and his slenderness saved his life, for the tusks passed on either side of his body. Then, possibly thinking that he had slain his enemy, the elephant rose, and picking up the body, cast it into a bush.

Stunned by the fall, Dorsay lay on his back, staring at the treetops. Then, the excitement spurring him, he scrambled to his feet and ran through the bush in time to see his quarry, who was leaning against a tree, sink on to the earth.

His second shot had passed through the joint of the foreleg into the lungs.

III

DORSAY HAD HAD NO BONES actually broken. He escaped with only some severe contusions which forced him to forego the hunt and to travel in a hammock for some days.

On the fourth day he had wanted to walk, but the doctor insisted that he had better rest a while longer. However, the doctor was proved wrong by a rhinoceros, which, charging the caravan, put the porters to flight and revealed to Dorsay that his tree-climbing powers had not in the least been impaired nor his injuries so serious as the doctor said they were.

They were now come to where the broken-forested country gives way to rolling plains which eventually run into the waterless tracts of the Nyasso Nyro.

Here, in the midst of a fairly thickly populated district, was the doctor's farm, as he called it, which, like so many East African farms of the period, consisted merely of virgin bush and grazing-land on which were some of the doctor's cattle in charge of a neighboring chief. For the benefit of Dorsay, El Hakkim—as the natives called the doctor—arranged a dance, and an impressive sight it was with the drums going and some thousand warriors, whose naked bodies gleamed with grease and paint, dancing and screaming as they brandished their spears with blades twice as long as bayonets.

They rested there for three days while the doctor paid off the porters, arranged for the donkeys, and selected a dozen warriors whom to their delight he armed with Martini rifles. However, an unexpected delay was occasioned by the chief wizard who, making magic to consult the oracle, reported that the venture was doomed to disaster. Instantly the dozen warriors recanted.

Dorsay, little used to the native, was naturally rather intolerant, particularly when the doctor insisted upon the gravity of the case inasmuch as they might well have to find soldiers elsewhere.

Talking the matter over that night by the camp-fire, the doctor admitted that he was somewhat puzzled; for, as an old hand at the game, he had not forgotten to tickle the palm of the witch-doctor so that he could suitably propitiate the spirits.

There was to be another *shauri* on the morrow at sunrise. The returning porters were due to leave at the same time, but that did not matter much, as they, at any rate, had the donkeys for transport. Not yet realizing the power of superstition among natives, Dorsay suggested that the doctor use his personal influence with the chief to make the warriors think differently or the wizard alter his interpretation.

"No, my lad," vetoed the doctor. "Nothing in that. The chief is as scared of the witch-doctor as—well, as kings used to be of black magic. Even if he could persuade 'em to come along they would never be any good.

"First time we struck trouble their hearts would stick to their ribs, as they say, and they'd bolt, believing that the awful things the wizard had said were coming true. No, no, leave it to me. The only way out is to try to hold over for a few days and give the oracle a chance to change its mind—with the assistance of sheep or maybe a calf."

"You mean some one trying to get at us through the wizard, eh? But who could be doing that here, doc?"

"Dunno, my lad. Maybe just jealousy, or maybe some superstition about the color of your hair, for instance. Lesser things than that have slaughtered tribes, as the Bible will tell you if you ever read it. If any one wishes to understand the Old Testament let him live in Africa."

In the morning Dorsay awoke about the hour of the monkey. Somewhere far away a jackal was yelping dismally; and close by a night bird screeched harshly at regular intervals. He lay still sleepily formulating the fifty-first theory of the origin of the mysterious message which he wore on the aborigine's chain around his neck.

As he glanced through the tent, remarking that the stars were still brilliant, he noticed the canvas flap move. He remarked vaguely that there was no wind. As his eyes grew accustomed to the light he saw his coat, which was hanging on a camp-chair on the other side of the small tent, disappear.

"What the ——," he began and sat up.

He saw something like an enormous snake wriggling across the floor. As it came beneath the light of the stars he caught the gleam of a black body.

He snatched up his revolver, which he kept beneath his pillow, and dived from under the mosquito-bar. Opposite to his was the doctor's tent; to the right their servants' and *shikaris'*; to the left a *zareba* of branches and saplings.

He prowled around the encampment but nothing moved. Beginning to doubt whether he had really seen a man or whether he had dreamed it, he returned to the tent. Undoubtedly his coat was gone. Money, he supposed, the thief was after. There had been some thousand rupees in paper, a check-book and some loose cartridges. But the loss of his coat was annoying, in spite of the fact that he, of course, had a spare one. Naturally he related his experience to the doctor at breakfast. The doctor expressed surprize as the Wakikuyu are not very notorious thieves, and concluded that the thief had probably been one of the porters.

After a prolonged *indaba* the doctor contrived to arrange that they should stop for five days until a new quarter of the moon was due, when the wizard would again consult the oracle.

"By the way," the doctor said that night when, as usual before the camp-fire, he was in a loquacious mood, "I've good news for you, my lad. Talking with Yanganga, I very gently pumped him about the Turkana and tribes around there. Of course these people call 'em *shenzi*—savages, you know—and he says that they say they have a white god who is, of course, invulnerable and all that. He is, it seems, the spirit of the Elgon Mountain."

"Oh Lordy!" exclaimed Dorsay delightedly. "Then there is some truth in it, you think?"

"Very weird things are possible in Mother Africa, my son. As a matter of fact, these people here are jealous and think that the Turkana are trying to imitate them, for they too had once a white king. What? Oh, yes, I knew him. As a matter of fact, I made him king. He deserted from a ship in Mombasa and—Mahomet! Boy! Whisky—soda! *Upesi!*"

Older and inured to native ways, the doctor was less impatient than Dorsay. However, they now filled in time with shooting. Dorsay to his delight bagged two elephants and the doctor three; for here they were practically out of touch with the administration, in a district where usually the little man was accustomed to doing as he pleased.

On the fifth day and all night a dance was held in honor of the full moon, and the wizard, after casting his spells, declared that the times were propitious for the start— thanks possibly to the present of a calf. The chosen twelve were in excellent spirits.

Next day the donkeys were loaded up and the caravan started. After twenty-four hours' march the going became uninteresting, for they entered upon a tongue of the stony, waterless desert stretching up from the Nyasso Nyro. The doctor figured on striking the confines of the Turkana country on the sixth day out, traveling fairly hard.

In order to lessen the strain of the passage on man and beast, the doctor decided to make extra marches by night, profiting by the light of the moon; so that, instead of the usual five days to cross the strip of desert, they reached the country where there was sweet water, scrub and a few trees, on the night of the third day. Here they were to halt for twenty-four hours to give the animals time to recuperate and get a square feed.

Toiling for hours every day in the powerful rays of the equatorial sun across an expanse of dazzling white was both tiresome and trying.

The plan proposed by the doctor was that when they reached the first of the Turkana villages where they would have to sue the chief Yamba for permission to enter the country and generally be fumigated in the native way against white men's evil spirits, they would pose as traders wishing to traverse the country peaceably.

As the blood-stained message had failed to give them any hint of the locality, they would work up toward the mountain and judiciously attempt through their own men to discover the whereabouts of the reputed white king who, the doctor thought, would prove to be the writer of the message; or at any rate one who could aid them. Direct question to the natives would seal their lips for good, if it didn't lead to active and instant hostility.

The moon rose that night toward nine o'clock.

The order of march was to leave about nine and march until four or five and camp again for the day, as the animals could make better going in the comparative cool of the night. After that, since they would be getting into an inhabited country, this would be inadvisable lest they provoke an attack by the natives, who might suppose them to be evil spirits of the night.

They had been under way about two hours. In the lead was the Wanderobo hunter upon whom devolved the duty of selecting the path through the purple and silver of the night.

Following him came Dorsay and the doctor and six of the warriors, their long-bladed spears like white flames in the moonlight. Behind the donkeys, tail to tail, trudged as patiently as only a burro can. In the rear came Mahomet and the personal servants and the remainder of the Wakikuyu men.

As the Wanderobo turned down a shallow *donga*, he suddenly dropped on to his knees with his head to the earth.

"Down! Down! Quick!" whispered the doctor, imitating him.

As he obeyed, Dorsay saw that the Wakikuyu were already flat on the ground.

Doubling back on the trail, the Wanderobo ran like a monkey on all fours. Dorsay heard the doctor swear as the men whispered.

For a while Dorsay's untrained ears failed to note anything other than the usual murmuring of the *veld*. Then, just as the doctor spoke, he caught the faint but unmistakable thud of galloping hoofs.

As the doctor was speaking rapidly in the dialect, Dorsay's momentary bewilderment at the idea of horses in central Africa was solved by the recollection of a story of the doctor's in which it appeared that the Abyssinians and Somalis in mountainous country, who had and could keep horses, were in the habit of raiding south to the confines of the Wakikuyu and Turkana country, for ivory and slaves.

Just as some of the men, in obedience to the doctor's orders, were hustling the donkeys into a herd, came the sound of hoofs striking stones, and the figures of mounted men in what looked like Arab robes broke from a sparse clump of trees silhouetted against the sky.

"Quick!" exclaimed the doctor, throwing himself out flat with his rifle. "Shoot for all you're worth."

As Dorsay followed his example the doctor's rifle spoke, and there began erratic firing from the Wakikuyu behind them and down the trail, answered by a wild yell.

Dorsay saw three men, one of whom he thought was his bag, tumble off their animals; then a crowd of some twenty were upon them. He was conscious at the same moment of a figure with wild eyes and hair brandishing a spear, looming above him, and of a donkey braying like a Scotch lament over the uproar of shots and yells.

He fired with his revolver and saw the fellow throw up his hands and pitch forward.

The pony swerved violently in full career. A frightened, or wounded, donkey crashed in between them, his loaded panniers knocking him down. As he rose on his knees to get up, slightly stunned, a gun crashed and then a loud yell from the doctor rang in his ears.

Simultaneously arms seized him from behind and he was swung bodily across a saddle-bow. The rifle was wrenched from his grasp.

The concussion had nearly knocked the wind out of him. His long legs were helplessly kicking the air, and he felt the man leaning heavily over his body on to the neck, crushing his stomach on the withers of the horse as it galloped. He gripped a bare leg with his left hand and tried to heave, but he could not get a purchase.

Then, pointing the revolver into the flanks of the horse, he fired.

Instead of dropping the beast bounded convulsively and galloped the faster. The second time the hammer clicked, for it was the last cartridge in the chamber. The plunge of the horse had either startled or nearly unseated the rider, freeing Dorsay's spine for a moment, which gave him opportunity to wriggle round for a hold.

Dropping the useless revolver, he managed to grab an arm and hauled himself up into an embrace of the fellow's neck, preventing the use of either gun or sword by the grip on the shoulders. Both Dorsay's hands were too busily occupied to permit his reaching for his other revolver.

The Somali was both wiry and powerful. For some two minutes, while the horse raced madly on, Dorsay fought desperately to throw him, but the fellow had either twisted his bare right foot under the stirrup-strap, or cord, or had got a purchase of resistance by sticking a leg in the stirrup.

Suddenly the beast dived on to its nose, throwing both of them. They fell on a patch of long grass. But Dorsay had not relaxed his hold. The fellow wriggled and squirmed like a wildcat. Then, deprived by Dorsay's hug of the use of his arms and the sword—to which he still clung—he bit the other's ear. Maddened by the sharp and excruciating pain, Dorsay let go and crashed his fist into the bronze face. He saw the blood spurt, but at the same time the man wriggled from his left arm's grasp.

For one moment as he got free his back was turned. Dorsay released his hold altogether and leaped on to the shoulders, caught the chin in his cupped hands and jerked with all his might. The snap and collapse were almost simultaneous.

Bloody and hot, Dorsay sat in the moonlight beside a dead horse shot through the lower lobe of the heart and a Somali with a broken neck, listening to the twittering murmur of Central Africa.

IV

DORSAY'S FIRST INSTINCT was to listen for sounds of conflict, but, save for the shrilling of a near-by cricket, all was still. He couldn't be far away, he reckoned—not more than a mile at the most. The country around was lightly timbered but enough to prevent one seeing very far. His ear was lacerated and smarted, but otherwise he was uninjured.

The best way to get back to the scene of the fight and pick up the doctor was to follow the spoor of the horse. He rose and had a look at the Somali, who lay in a crumpled heap on his side with his sword like a streak of quicksilver a few feet away.

He pulled the torn robes over the body and began to hunt for the spoor, wondering what had happened to the doctor. Either, he mused, the Somalis must have been beaten off immediately after that first rush or they had taken the caravan.

Although the soil was soft and sandy the long grass made the hoof-marks difficult to follow, and in the moonlight the sheen of the grass after the passage of a heavy body was almost indistinguishable. Then, on a piece of stony ground, he lost the trail.

He began to cast about in circles, trying to pick it up again, but the fear that if he wandered too far away he might lose it altogether decided him to wait until morning.

He sat down beside a big boulder near a tree. He still had a revolver and a belt full of cartridges and also the Somali's sword. Where he had lost the rifle he could not recollect. He reckoned that, if the caravan had beaten off the raiders, the doctor would surely camp right where he was.

The night was warm. The moon was like a gigantic arc lamp. A bird some way off kept screaming harshly. Presently, as he sat semi-dozing with the loaded revolver on his knees, a slight sound startled him.

In the open glade in front of him appeared the form of a big buck with the twisted horns flat upon his withers; behind him was the herd in full gallop. Again came the noise like a strangled cough which had startled him, and on their heels came swift gray shapes. They looked like wolves but as none are in Africa, Dorsay knew that they must be wild dogs.

The procession passed within a hundred feet of him as if across a film screen.

About an hour later jackals began to yelp not far away. Then above them rose a weird howl ending in a sound like a hoarse scream. The jackals and a hyena had found the two dead bodies.

The air grew fresher as the moon sank. When the foreglare of the sun was crimsoning distant Mount Elgon, Dorsay was up and began to hunt about for the trail, which after some difficulty he found, but only to lose it again a few hundred yards farther on. He adopted the same method of casting in circles, but this time he failed to pick it up. Possibly he had reached the point, he reflected, where he had shot the horse and the beast had darted off at right angles. If that were so he would not be so far away from the scene of the attack as he had reckoned.

He decided to fire three shots in rapid succession, trusting that the doctor would hear and understand—that is, if he were free. The alternative seemed no pleasant situation.

After firing, he climbed a small tree and waited on the lookout. Within twenty minutes he caught the glint of a spear. Presently he saw some half-dozen natives spread out in hunting fashion, evidently searching.

"Thank the Lord," he thought, "the doctor's all right. These must have been some of our Wakikuyu friends."

Then he made out that one was driving a donkey.

"Now, that's mighty thoughtful of the little man," commented Dorsay. "But what on earth did he send him loaded for?"

He slid down the tree to meet them. As soon as they saw him they promptly dropped into the grass.

"Now, what the—" began Dorsay, and then he realized that they must be strangers who were scared of him. "Now, what am I to do? I suppose if I don't look out they'll skewer me on general principles.

"Hi!" he shouted, using one of the few Kiswahili words he had already picked up, "*Njema! Njema!* (Good! Good!)"

Immediately a voice cried back at him from out of the grass. Of course he couldn't understand a word, but taking a chance he yelled:

"*Indio! Njema!* (Yes! Good!)"

Six figures rose out of the grass within a spear's throw of him.

"Good Lord," he thought, "they could have had me sure enough. They must have come through the grass like greased snakes.

"*Hodi? Njema?* Huh?" he inquired, grinning and holding out his left hand.

The six jabbered at him simultaneously. He shook his head.

"No sabee?" Tapping his chest, he added:

"Friend, *njema*, huh? El Hakkim"—and pantomimed to represent one looking around for something.

He pointed to the donkey, repeating the doctor's native name, and then touched himself.

"Mine. Sabee?" They stared. He began to imitate a donkey braying and continued tapping his chest. A scared expression flitted across the leader's face, and he tightened his grip on his spear suggestively. Then the donkey lifted up his muzzle and began to bray.

Dorsay stopped the performance, thinking correctly that the natives might suppose he was mad. One pointed toward the distant Elgon and beckoned him to follow. He reflected swiftly. They were too close for him to bring them down before one got home with a spear—that is, unless they bolted at the first shot. But supposing he were rid of them, what could he do? If the doctor had by any mischance been captured or wiped out, he would quickly starve to death in the wilderness unless he could find a village. There did not seem much option, so he grinned pleasantly and gestured, saying—"Lead on, Macduff!"

Macduff, the tallest of the group, each of whom wore six square inches more clothing than the Wakikuyu, led on, and the others, rounding up the donkey, brought up the rear jabbering busily. Once he tried to get them to understand that he was thirsty, but they merely pointed ahead.

As he had no hat he took off his coat and wrapped it around his head as some protection against the equatorial sun. The six hunters—who, Dorsay learned later, while on the trail of some game had been forced to hide from the Somali party and had heard the fight but had not dared approach—led him on for three hours, when they came to an encampment of some fifty men, a small hunting-raiding party of the Turkana of which Dorsay at the time could not know.

It was difficult to determine which created more excitement, the donkey or the white man. They were both conducted inside the *zareba*. Dorsay was made to sit in the shade of a grass lean-to and given water while some of the leaders gathered about him discussing vociferously, and others began to unload the donkey.

At last one fellow with a tuft of gray wool, who seemed to be a chief, tried to interview him. Dorsay did his best to make the native understand that he was anxious to know the doctor's fate, and, to make it plain that if the doctor had escaped, he wished to rejoin him; but this was too complicated for sign language.

Eventually, as neither could get any of the information he wanted, the chief drew the other men away, and in the middle of the *zareba* began a lengthy debate regarding the fate, Dorsay supposed, of himself.

Noticing some of them bearing the contents of the donkey's pack, which happened to be one which bore his own clothes and also the terai hat, Dorsay got up and went over. Immediately he approached they formed a circle, jabbering at him excitedly. He pantomimed the lack of a hat, but they had no intention of giving anything up.

"Unless I want to fight the gang for it," he concluded, "I guess I'd better be good."

The result of the *shauri* was evident. Apparently he was of such importance that the hunting-party was to be abandoned, for they began to prepare for the trail.

Two hours after noon they broke camp. Dorsay, to his intense disgust, was compelled to march as before with his coat over his head in lieu of the terai hat, which, save for the six inches of skin, constituted the chief's sole dress, except that, in the lobe of his ear, in the place of the usual copper rings, was stuck Dorsay's safety-razor.

Several others had taken spare shirts and bound the arms round the waist apron fashion. One young man proudly strutted along in a pair of riding-breeches tied around his neck.

Whether they associated these belongings with him personally, Dorsay could not guess. He had naturally decided not to give up his remaining gun in any circumstances. But they did not attempt to deprive him of it for a reason unknown to Dorsay, who, of course, could have no conception then of a belief that any article actually belonging to a man is impregnated with his being, and therefore that it is mighty dangerous to monkey with a white man's demons—a consistent enough argument if you grant all the premises which the native accepts as indisputable facts.

On the trail he noticed that the very slight baggage, such as food, cooking-gourds, mats, and small tree-cutting adzes, were carried by men who evidently were slaves from another tribe. An hour before sundown they came in fairly thick bush to a water-hole.

The slaves set to work immediately to cut saplings and make a *zareba* and prepare food; but the hunters merely lolled in the shade, elegantly snuffing and discussing the captive.

Fortunately for Dorsay some of them, less lazy than the others, went out and returned with a couple of buck, and the chief graciously sent the white man a hunk of meat.

The situation which began to try his temper was slightly mitigated by a sense of humor, for when the blankets were divided between the chief and his cronies one man solemnly rolled himself up in the mosquito net and another in the canvas Wolsey valise.

Dorsay reasoned that the time had not yet come to kick; any attempt to hold them up he was sure—and was right—would have led to a sticky end. He endeavored to recall all that the little doctor had told him regarding the value of patience in dealing with the native. However, the extreme need of sleep soothed him more than anything else; and, stretched out by the communal fire with the revolver tucked inside his shirt for safety, he slumbered until the dawn.

They marched for another two days.

On the morning of the third he saw signs of cultivation, and passed bunches of cattle and several small villages. Mount Elgon now appreciably closer, seemed less imposing because the slopes are very long.

The morning march was longer than usual. It was near to noon when, in the blazing heat in a rolling, lightly timbered country, they came upon native *shambas*, the size of which suggested a big village. Soon hordes of men, women and children came trooping along the paths from all sides to stare solemnly at a perspiring white man marching with a coat over his head.

The village, Dorsay noticed, was stockaded, whereas the smaller ones had not been; evidently the place of the chief, Tamba.

Inside the barrier were irregular streets of huts with odd chickens, with open beaks, roosting in the shade, and skinny goats dozing. He almost cried out in relief when he saw, seated beside one who was evidently a chief, beneath the shelter which is the village clubhouse, a white man. A wild hope that he would prove to be the doctor died, for the fellow was too big.

Then as he bent beneath the low roof, he exclaimed in astonishment.

The man was Dorkin, the Australian lumberman.

V

"GOOD LORD!" EJACULATED DORSAY in astonishment. "What on earth are you doing here?"

"Fort it wus yew," commented Dorkin. "Where's the dotty little doctor?"

"That's what I want to know," returned Dorsay anxiously. "A Somali party raided us and carried me off, and then these fellows picked me up. Don't they know whether our caravan was wiped out or not?"

"Nope. They come in 'ere and tells the old man they'd captured a white man. I wondered if it was yew, knowing as yew'd be along this w'y."

"Look here," remarked Dorsay, who was still standing, "can't you get me a chair or something?"

"Ain't no more. But you'd better powwow with this black fella 'ere."

He indicated the chief in the chair beside him, a fairly big, corpulent man with a big-bore cartridge stuck through an ear.

"But that's it! I can't speak a word."

Dorsay looked about him, naturally uncomfortable at the idea of sitting on the ground when a native was in a chair, and squatted on the floor.

"If you'll interpret I should like to ask him about sending out to find the doctor."

Dorkin grinned with his broken teeth.

"Yew gotter ruddy cheek!"

"I have?" demanded Dorsay. "How?"

"Only meant this 'ere black fella thinks 'e's a big bug," said Dorkin after a moment's hesitation. "Go on. Wot djer want?"

"Well, tell him that our caravan was attacked and I was carried off. I killed the man, but lost my way and his people found me.

"Tell him I want him to send back to the place near where they found me, and see if the doctor is still there; if not, to find out whether the caravan was wiped out, and if not to follow up the trail and tell the doctor where I am."

"Want a —— of a lot, doncher?"

"Why, what do you mean?"

"Wotjer going to pay 'im wiv?"

"Oh, we'll pay him as soon as he fetches the caravan here."

"But if there ain't no caravan?"

"Oh, well, I can buy—"

He hesitated, recollecting the stolen coat with the thousand rupees in the pocket.

"You know me. I suppose you'll sell me some goods?"

Dorkin looked at him and grinned again.

"Orl right, chummie; don't you worry."

He turned to the chief, who with the crowd of natives had watched every gesture and expression during the conversation.

"O son of Bafala," began Dorkin, "this white man was the servant of El Hakkim, the doctor, who, he tells me, hath been taken as a slave by the Somalis. At the beginning of the fight he ran away, so that your people found him wandering with his heart still stuck fast to his ribs. As he belongs to an inferior tribe I will keep him unless"—he looked at Dorsay interestedly, watching him, and smiled—"unless the son of Bafala wishes to trade for something for which he knows my belly yearns?"

"O Broken Teeth," replied the old chief without a vestige of expression on his features, "indeed thy hands are large (generous) but such is not sweet in the eyes of the people who would commune each with his neighbor, saying, 'Is it then that whites are also gods and slaves?' "

"Orl right, old top," retorted Dorkin, "have it yer own w'y. If yer knew as much abart whites as I dew yew wouldn't fink they wus gawds!"

"What does he say?" interrupted Dorsay.

" 'Is nibs ses 'e'll send back some men and do wot yer want, but 'e wants a price."

"Oh, that doesn't matter," said Dorsay relievedly, "as long as he finds out what's happened to Macnamara. Say, there's another thing. In the fight I lost my helmet, as you see, but these fellows found one of our donkeys which had my kit.

"See the fellow with my safety-razor stuck in his ear? He's wearing my terai hat. He can keep the razor. Guess I'll have to grow a beard anyway."

Dorkin burst into a guffaw and told the chief that he wished to go to his camp and teach the white slave what he had to do.

"That's orl right, chummie," he said to Dorsay; " 'e'll send it along ter me ternight—"

Rather annoyed at having to walk with the coat over his head, Dorsay followed Dorkin through the village and to his camp, which was pitched just outside. He suspected, of course, that the blood-stained message had brought Dorkin on the same quest as the doctor and himself. Well, thought Dorsay, he had a perfect right to do so. He hadn't been bound to secrecy.

"It was my own fault for having shown it to him."

Yet it was annoying, although in his recent plight it didn't seem to matter if there were forty others chasing after the same will-o'-the-wisp.

"By the way," he remarked as they approached the camp outside the village, "where's your partner, Simpson?"

"Oh, 'im?" replied Dorkin with a note of contempt. " 'E's still 'auling lumber. 'E ain't no sport, 'e ain't."

As Dorsay was wondering what might be Dorkin's definition of a "sport," he continued:

" 'E's a regular 'new chum,' that's wot 'e is. I been at the gime too long ter monkey rahnd wiv the like o' 'im."

"I suppose," said Dorsay a bit stiffly, "you've come after the same thing as we have—although you said it wasn't worth the game when I showed you the message?"

"Wot d'yew fink! I want ter tawk to yer abaht that. Come in and sit dahn, will yer?"

They had reached his camp, consisting of a green tent and an old military bell tent for his men. As they sat in camp chairs, Dorkin remarked suddenly—

"Yew ain't got any guns, 'ave yer?"

"No," replied Dorsay mendaciously, pulling his coat over the bulge of the revolver beneath his shirt. "Why?"

"Nuffin. I fort p'raps yer wanted one."

He shouted to one of his men to bring food, lighted a cigar, and turned to Dorsay.

"I s'y, mister, wot d'yew reckon to do?"

"Wait until these people here bring news as to whether the doctor is still alive or not."

"An' if 'e ain't?"

"I don't know," said Dorsay slowly. "Go back, I guess, and organize another expedition—to rescue the doctor if he was captured, and to avenge him if he's killed."

" 'Ow yer going ter do that?"

"Why, surely— As I said, you'll surely give me credit enough in goods to get back."

"Ain't yer got no brass?"

"Well, I haven't on me," admitted Dorsay. "Naturally I carried some with me; but some son-of-a-gun stole my coat with the cash 'way back at Yananga's."

"Go on!" said Dorkin, and grinned. "When do yer want ter go?"

"As soon as these people bring whatever information they can find. How long do you reckon that ought to be?"

"Ow, I'll 'ave an answer fer yer in four d'ys. 'Ave yer still got that bit o' bloody rag on yer?"

"Why, yes," said Dorsay, touching the chain about his neck.

"Gaw lumme!" ejaculated Dorkin. "I never fort o' that! I s'y, let me 'ave a look."

Dorsay detached the chain and unrolled the message. Dorkin snatched and opened.

At that moment one of the village natives approached with a basket of food for sale. Dorkin instantly closed his fist over the rag and swore at him, telling him to go to the other tent where his men were.

"Don't do ter let these swine see too much," he added to Dorsay, who was wondering at the outburst. "See 'ere," he continued. "Yew're going after the doctor, ain't yer? Well, yew give me this rag and I'll give yer enough ter get back."

"But that's no good," said Dorsay. "I mean it doesn't give any help to find the spot or the man who wrote the message. Why do you want it? You know all there is in it?"

"That's orl right. Let me 'ave it?"

Dorsay looked at him.

"Crafty eyes," he thought. "Now, what's behind all this? Has he deciphered something which has escaped me or what? No," he replied aloud. "I'll give you a check—or an order on Nairobi if you like."

"Fat lot o' good that is to me 'ere."

"Tell me what you want it for then."

"Me?" he said indignantly. "Not much! Jus' sorter want ter 'ave it wiv me—fer luck."

"So do I," retorted Dorsay, smiling. "No. I'm sorry, but can't let you have it."

"Oh, yew won't, won't yer?" said Dorkin with an ugly look. "We'll see abaht that."

Deliberately he placed the message in his pocket. "Why fer two pins I'll mike them niggers give yer ——"

"Good ——!" interrupted Dorsay, and stared at the boy bearing the food, who was wearing a khaki jacket. "That's my coat!"

He stared for a second at Dorkin, who was grinning at him insolently.

"Why," he said slowly, "you must have put that man on to steal my coat, to get that message. Is that it? I see."

"Yew ain't getting cross, I 'ope," demanded Dorkin with a grin.

"I'm liable to," retorted Dorsay gravely.

"Go on!" he said decisively.

"As soon as the doctor had left the mill," continued Dorsay, "you sneaked off and tried to steal a march on us! You're a thief!"

"Look 'ere, yew mind 'oo yer talking to," blustered Dorkin, who wore his gun in the hip pocket, rising from his chair.

"You put your hands on that gun and—"

Dorsay leaped and struck. Dorkin went backward over the table. As the native servant fled, he came up again like a cat and made a rush, cursing furiously. Dorsay met him with a left, which was partially countered. Dorkin got him with a right on the temple.

A half-hook from Dorsay's right on the jaw jolted him badly, and a left swiftly following brought curses and blood. He ducked, jumped around the fallen table, came again, feinted and succeeded in reaching Dorsay's jaw, which tumbled him on to the bed in back of the tent.

Dorkin drew the gun as Dorsay was on his knees on the bed. Instinctively he jerked the dirty pillow at the man's head. The bullet seared his hip as he sprang from the bed on top of Dorkin.

The two clinched. Dorsay gripped his arm so that he could not aim. Two bullets went into the ground. With a wrench Dorsay managed to twist Dorkin's wrist until he dropped the revolver; then, breaking, Dorsay leaped back and put the whole of his might into one right punch for the jaw. Dorkin went backward over the canvas washstand and lay still.

From a distance came cries and shouts, but, without the tent, not a native was to be seen. Dorsay stepped over and recovered the message from the man's pocket. Then picking up the revolver Dorkin had dropped, he put Dorkin's terai hat on his own head.

Dorkin took the count and a bit more. As he raised himself on his elbow and saw Dorsay, he scrambled to his feet, bent on continuing the fight. He faced the gun and stopped bewilderedly, not realizing that he had been knocked out.

"You sit down and try to behave," advised Dorsay quietly.

A torrent of language answered him.

"Now quit that. D'you want me to punch you again?"

Dorkin informed him foully that there were several different sorts of white-livered curs. Some of the epithets brought a flush to the young man's face. Dorkin saw it and persevered. Dorsay was well aware of the difficulties of his position and what game Dorkin was playing; but finally a certain reference was insupportable.

"See here, Dorkin," he said with apparent difficulty in speaking, "you've been whipped and you know it, but if you don't understand this I'll surely smash you with my bare hands until you yelp. D'you get me?"

The answer was unprintable.

"Just you walk in front of me to the back of the tent. Your gun's in here on the bed. Now get!"

As Dorsay threw off his coat and Dorkin's terai hat—fortunately the sun was very low—Dorkin obeyed, cursing but game. Dorsay had intended to fight at the rear of the tent, which would shelter them from the village. He noticed two woolly heads peeping out of the bell tent as he walked.

As he turned and threw the revolver on to the bed Dorkin wheeled about like a cat, rushed and planted one blow behind the ear. This treacherous attack maddened Dorsay. He sprang around, and, seizing the man by the waist, lifted him bodily and threw him.

"Now, you swine, come on!"

Although Dorkin undoubtedly knew how to fight, the contortion of his face reassured Dorsay. This time Dorkin did not rush. He held off for a second or two to recover his breath; but could not, after his kind, avoid wasting more in language. But the hesitation showed that he had at last realized that he was up against no tenderfoot. Dorsay was taller, but his adversary was stockily built and could give him a stone in weight.

Dorkin came prancing up with lowered head and his two fists slightly moving, more like a wrestler than a boxer.

Dorsay leaped, and, using his slightly longer reach, got within Dorkin's guard and smashed him on the nose. Dorkin replied with a nasty kidney punch followed by a whirlwind of body blows, leaped away, and, when Dorsay followed up, clinched.

By an effort Dorsay raised him off his feet again, but failed to throw him. But as he came down he managed to get Dorkin's head into chancery and smashed the face cruelly, intent upon punishing him.

Dorkin retorted with short drives at his kidneys, which made him gasp. As he released him and succeeded in getting clear, Dorkin, covered with blood and spitting teeth, rushed, desperately flailing blows regardless of what further punishment he took.

In the first onslaught Dorsay had received some telling blows on face, head and body, and fought for a chance to put Dorkin out again, knowing well that the man would kill him if he got the chance.

For a few seconds Dorkin's attack was so furious that Dorsay began to doubt how long he could hold him off. Then suddenly Dorkin broke away. Dorsay saw that he was groggy.

"If you've had enough—" he began, dropping his hands.

"I'll kill you, you ——," spluttered Dorkin, and rushed.

Dorsay had just time to get home with his left, and Dorkin dropped and lay still.

Then Dorsay became aware that around him, forming a large ring, was a crowd of squatting natives, who had watched with curious eyes this strange form of a white man's fight. Dorsay signaled to the boy who was still wearing the stolen jacket to help carry his master.

As Dorsay filled the wash-basin the natives crowded around the door, eager not to miss one action. With the cold water on his face the Australian came to and peered through one eye.

" 'Struth," he spluttered through his bloody mouth, "yer licked me, then?"

"I did," said Dorsay shortly.

"You ain't no new chum," Dorkin went on, "for you've licked an ex-welterw'ight of Haustralia. A fair knockaht too, —— me ef it warn't."

"Say," said Dorsay anxiously, "you're not wanting any more, are you?"

The bloody mouth contorted, apparently in a grin. "Crikey, not for me, mite."

He extended his hand.

"Yew done me fair."

Dorsay took the hand, and his heart warmed toward him thinking—

"Maybe he is a crook, but he's a darned good sport enough to take a licking."

VI

AFTER THAT EPISODE Dorkin appeared to have decided to be reasonable. He called for his servant, and with a grin returned to Dorsay the stolen coat as the delayed meal was brought in.

"All's fair in love and war, y'know," he said sheepishly, and to Dorsay's surprize produced the thousand rupees from his own wallet. " 'Ope yer ain't looking fer a comeback, are yer?"

"We'll cut that out," retorted Dorsay, "and anyway now you're kind enough to return me my own property, perhaps you'll sell me some goods?"

"Dunno as I mightn't," admitted Dorkin. " 'Ere, I'll tell yer wot I'll do. Yew can 'ave enough for grub and trade-goods and I'll get the bloomin' chief ter tike yer back on the trile ter see if yer can't pick up the dotty little doctor. 'Ow'll that suit? W'ite, I call it."

Dorsay reflected. What to do without an interpreter he did not know. The suggestion seemed good, for with the protection of the chief's people he might discover from the last camp pretty well what had happened, and at the worst he could continue on to the friendly Wakikuyu people, who were friends of the doctor, and so to Nairobi where he could begin over again.

He regarded Dorkin once more. Although Dorkin certainly was a rough-neck he appeared to bear no malice and, thought Dorsay, he would be more than pleased to get rid of him, as long as he was not continuing on the search for the supposed ivory cache.

"That's a bet then; but you're goin' to play straight this time, Dorkin?"

A stream of oaths attested to his sincerity.

"Yer know," he added, "I wus a ruddy fool, I wus. Abaht that there dirty rag, y'know. Sorter got it in me 'ead that it 'ud bring me luck. Course, it ain't no good cep' fer wot it says, and I know that orl right. Then I finks yew're a sorter new chum. But, oh my, I s'y!" he grinned affably. "Yew're a wonder, yew are!"

"Yes," agreed Dorsay. "I couldn't understand why you seemed to put such a value on it anyway."

"Oh, I'm like that, I am. Once I gits a hidea in me 'ead, carn't sorter git it aht. Arsk Simpson. 'E alms says I'm wooden-'eaded. But there, we're chums nah."

He dived into his "scoff-box" for a bottle of whisky to prove the statement, and afterward began seriously to gather the goods which would be necessary for Dorsay.

"Carn't give yer a tent," he said; "but, 'ere"—handing out a water-proof sheet—"yer kin mike one o' that till yer git back."

In the afternoon Dorsay sent up, demanding an interview with the chief, Yamba; but a refusal came back, making an appointment for the following morning.

When twilight came Dorsay began to grow a little uneasy, wondering whether he had better lie awake all night revolver in hand; and later, noticing Dorkin taking some quinine, he wondered whether the Australian had a medicine-case containing opium or any sleeping-powders or poison. But evidently Dorkin had not, for, upon a casual inquiry for some Warburg's tincture, Dorkin swore he had forgotten to bring any.

However, to make sure, Dorsay used his coat as a pillow, although Dorkin, roughly solicitous, made him up a bed on the floor on the other side of the tent.

After dinner Dorkin became garrulous with whisky.

"Rummy, ain't it," he said once, "me and yew trying ter kill each other off, and 'ere we are a-sittin' as chummy as never was!"

Dorsay agreed dryly that it was, and became astonished when shortly afterward Dorkin lapsed into a semi-maudlin state, insisting upon telling a sentimental story about his old mother who was waiting in Sydney for her darling son to return.

"That's wot mide me do it!" he wailed. "I'm as tender-'earted as a kiddie, I am. Wouldn't 'urt a fly, gorlumme."

Dorsay grew suspicious. He pretended to doze off, although he had great difficulty in not doing so, for he badly needed a sleep.

For half an hour Dorkin rambled on—

"Yew awike? Ain't sleeping, are yer?"

At last he put out the candle and sank back with a prodigious sigh.

Faintly conscious that a drum up in the village was beating, Dorsay started awake at the creak of the camp-bed. After a slight interval came another creak. But Dorsay noticed that the regular breathing, as of a sleeper, ceased at each creak. As he felt for his gun he caught the faintest gleam from the tent-flap of light on steel.

Holding the gun in one hand, he rose in one motion, dragging the blankets with him, and leaped straight upon the head of the bed, pinioning the man's arm and smothering his head, from which came an oath.

"If you struggle, I'll put a hole through you," warned Dorsay.

"I ain't doin' nothin'," came the muffled voice. "Wot's the matter wiv yer?"

Having heard the light thud of the revolver on the floor, between the bed and the tent-wall, Dorsay released him, and pressing the muzzle against his middle, ordered him to light a match.

"Look 'ere, wot're yer plying at?" began Dorkin indignantly. " 'Ad a nightmare or somefing? Ain't we chums nah?"

For answer Dorsay retrieved his revolver.

"This time I keep it until we part," said he sharply, "and you'll either consent to let me tie you up or you'll sit right there till morning."

Dorkin swore and blustered, but finally, sneering, said he supposed he might as well. Dorsay tied him well, and with the two revolvers and Dorkin's rifle beneath the blankets went peacefully to sleep.

The difficulty of realizing that the springs of action in other people are not necessarily the same motives as one's own is well known to psychologists, and this fact faintly dawned upon Dorsay as they made their way to the village for the interview with the chief.

He began to doubt whether he had not after all made an error in the night; allowed his jumpy nerves to imagine the creaking of the bed and the thud of the falling revolver. Perhaps the latter had just naturally slid off the bed or from under the pillow.

As men of Dorkin's caliber were new to him, Dorsay found it impossible not to credit him with some sense of fair play; also, he very badly wanted to believe, for his own sake, inasmuch as his position was so very much the worse if that were so. Without even sufficient knowledge of the language to ask his way, and little idea at all of the lay of the country, for Dorkin had not supplied him with a map, he was in pretty bad case.

The more he pondered the matter the more he persuaded himself that Dorkin, at any rate, would play the game in interpreting, for the sake of getting him away.

They found the chief Yamba with his elders under the shade of the council club-house.

After the preliminary greetings of native etiquette had been passed and the usual fencing around the actual subject in hand, Dorkin, pointing to Dorsay, began a long harangue, listened to with great attention by the assembled chiefs. Dorsay, wondering what it was all about, noticed that the chief Yamba—he with the big-bore cartridge stuck through his ear—regarded him with the masked curiosity of the native.

After some crude rhetoric, complimenting the chiefs, and principally himself, Dorkin was saying:

"And as for this white man here who is no true brother of mine but an outcast, one driven from his own tribe, disgraced before his people, I deliver him back into thine hands as thou dost desire, O Black Elephant, son of Bafala. By reason of the water which floweth from my heart (pity) have I bestowed upon him a few inconsiderable trifles, which, at thy will, are thine. Let not his magic stick with five voices cause thy heart to stick to thy ribs, for truly are they so bewitched that they will be like the spittle of a jealous woman.

"And so as it seemeth good unto thee, take him away and make him a slave unto thy gods or take his body to make good medicine. For this do I ask of thee but one thing, O great chief; that I may trade peaceably among thy people as thou hast already granted me, and moreover that I be free to wander where I list, seeking to harm none and friendly with thy people of the mountains."

"What have you said?" inquired Dorsay anxiously, as the corpulent chief solemnly regarded the man who wore his safety-razor for an ear-piece and a shriveled old man wearing three black feathers.

"Don't yew worry abaht it," returned Dorkin. "I've been tellin' 'im orf proper. 'E's got to tike yew dahn to where they fahnd yer and find that there bloomin' camp jus' as yew says, see?"

"And then?"

"If yer carn't find yer dotty doctor, they'll set yer over on the Nairobi road."

"Is that true, Dorkin?"

"See me wet!" exclaimed Dorkin, eloquently, spitting on his fingers and wiping them across his throat. "See me dry! Cut me froat if I tell a lie! Swelp me!"

"H'm! Well, what have I got to do now?"

"Yew go along wif them fellas when I beggar orf, and they'll show yer the road."

"As Broken Teeth hath said, so shall it be," returned Yamba, the chief. "He shall be free to trade, as we have sworn, throughout our country, even to the mountains where no ivory is—"

"That's where the bloomin' stuff is!" muttered Dorkin. "Wot-O!"

"And with the inferior white man shall we do that which shall seem good unto us."

"As long as yer keeps 'im busy for a month or two I don't give a —— if yer cuts his bloomin' liver aht," mumbled Dorkin.

"What did you say?" asked Dorsay.

"Nuffin'! Jigger bitin' me."

He rose, holding out his hand.

"Good luck, ole top. 'Ope yer git 'ome orl right. Sorry we didn't seem ter 'it it off."

"If only," said Dorsay, accepting the hand diffidently, "if only I could talk the lingo! By ——," he added suddenly, suspicious of the man's grin, "if you've put me in, I'll come back and get you."

"Don't lose yer 'air, sonny," jeered Dorkin; and, turning on his heel, he walked back to his camp, leaving Dorsay with his few trade-goods and blankets.

"Is there truth in the son of Bangala that it was this Golden Teeth here who overthrew Broken Teeth?" inquired Yamba of the shriveled sorcerer.

"Aye, truly. He is the greater man, and in him is more strength. Let him be chosen."

"Be it so," assented the chief.

"But," protested Tanka, he of the safety-razor earring, "three gods be stronger than two, as is well known. Let Broken Teeth also be of the sacred band."

"Thou hast the truth by the ears," returned Yamba. "Is that not so, O great Mangu?"

"Thou hast spoken," said the old man.

"Come and feed as thou wilt," invited Tanka of Dorsay, "and we will make ready."

Although Dorsay could not comprehend a word, he understood the gesture of invitation; and obeyed.

VII

As DORSAY FOLLOWED the man to a hut allotted to him, where he found the goods Dorkin had "sold" him, he experienced, in spite of the bad character which Dorkin had manifested, a distinct regret at leaving him—even turned on the threshold to watch the retreating figure.

There had always been a hope, if a knock-kneed one, that the fellow was interpreting correctly, and the imperative desire that such should be the case was almost as strengthening as a leg-iron.

As he squatted on his haunches with his arms around his knees in the shade of the hut, watching and listening vainly to the chatter of the natives, he became the more depressed, wondering what had really happened to the little doctor, trying to decide whether Dorkin had played him false.

Without any means of communication with the natives, what chance had he? They might, for all he knew to the contrary, be taking him away to massacre, or Heaven knew what. The idea of death suggested the mysterious message written on the charm. Perhaps he, too, was doomed to a similar fate, whatever that was.

He pondered for a long while, trying to discover what motive had caused Dorkin to attempt theft and murder for the sake of the charm. But the more he mused the more puzzled he became. Perhaps after all the man had told the truth when he had confessed, or pretended to confess, that he had got a crazy idea in his head about "the bloody rag." He had certainly seemed more or less mad, and he was such a liar that one couldn't believe a word he said.

When the sun was about half-way down the western course his former friend, Tanka, who wore the safety-razor, came up and spoke volubly. From his gestures and the presence of some slaves, who proceeded to load themselves with his goods, he gathered they were about to start.

As they left the village he saw the tail of Dorkin's *safari* disappearing over a slight rise in the direction of Mount Elgon. The sight gave another tug at his heart.

"Lead on, Gillette," said he cheerily, and fell in behind the waiting Tanka.

As he had never had any experience of the trail, he had little notion from which direction he had arrived in the village, or what general course he had traveled in company with the doctor. He retained a vague impression that the sun had set more or less ahead of them every evening. Now, it seemed, they were to continue in the same direction, parallel to Mount Elgon.

The more he pondered on the question the less certain he became, after the fashion of one lost in the desert. At length he decided to object and try to draw conclusions from the man's demeanor. Then what he thought was a brilliant idea struck him. Surely they would understand the word *hakkim*—doctor. He stopped and called—

"Hey, you—Gillette!"

Tanka, the chief with the safety-razor in his ear, turned about as if he really knew his name. Dorsay pointed down the trail they were following, and made a vigorous negative sign, and then, indicating the south, said repeatedly—

"*Hakkim, hakkim.* Savee? *Hakkim.*"

Gillette appeared to be very much interested. The slight expression of bewilderment which he permitted on the mask of his face faded, and he smiled amiably as if he understood perfectly. He repeated a statement several times in which Dorsay thought he distinguished the same word, *hakkim.*

Half-persuaded that the man comprehended, he pointed down the trail again, saying interrogatively—

"*Hakkim?*" and then, pointing south—"which, eh?"

"*Hakkim,*" repeated Gillette decidedly, gesturing down the trail to the west.

They marched on through some forest country until half an hour before sundown, when they came upon a small village. As before he was given a hut, and very courteously a mess of native food was sent to him. But he had enough of that to last a lifetime.

Then he discovered that Dorkin had omitted to put a can-opener with the provisions. However, after half an hour's hard work he succeeded in opening a portion and scraping out some beef.

The following day they were off at dawn, and except for a short rest at noon marched all day through dense forest, winding and turning until Dorsay had lost all sense of direction. For three more days the route was continued, never leaving fairly dense forest save for small glades which did not give the inexperienced Dorsay much chance to orientate.

On the fourth day he began to become fidgety and nervous, for he reckoned that by now they should be approaching the camp where the Somalis had attacked them.

He could not recollect such continuous thick timber on the journey from that spot; yet that, he argued, did not necessarily mean they were not making in that direction. There might very well be many other trails. But the observation made him more uneasy, and he noticed that the undergrowth was growing less dense and the ground more rocky. Several times he expostulated, pointing and saying—

"*Hakkim*?" But each time Gillette talked amiably and repeated the word as if he quite understood what was meant.

That evening they camped in the open in a *zareba* which the slaves made. During the night he was very much conscious of cold, and at dawn when he sat up he remarked with a shock that the blanket was stiff and the grass white with hoar-frost.

"My Lordy!" he muttered, rubbing his blue hands. "This is like the climate at the doctor's place, El Bergon."

He stared blankly at the group of natives squatting around their fire and added—

"Good Heavens, we must be half-way up Mount Elgon!"

The inference startled him. He had been deceived. They had been traveling in the opposite direction from the last camp of the doctor, where Dorkin had promised they should guide him? Even, instead of traveling west parallel to the mountain, as he had once suspected, evidently they had, under cover of the forest, made straight north for the mountain.

Why, why had he trusted the word of that blackguard? He had known that he was a shameless liar—should have known that he had been lying all the time. Where were his captors leading him?

He started to his feet in momentary panic, his hand upon his revolver. He was determined to be understood and obeyed.

Then he paused. What could he do? He could not communicate one word. Flourishing a gun wouldn't do any good; might scare them into reprisals.

And again, how was he to know where the doctor was? Perhaps he might be around. Perhaps, after all, they were conducting him to the doctor, who would not have stopped in camp forever.

Doubt and the realization of his impotence made him wish to cry or swear with rage; he didn't care which. Soberly he decided that the best thing to do was to wait and see what was going to happen.

With his faculties of observation sharpened by anxiety, he remarked that the sun rose above the forest at twenty past six. Allowing for the fact that they were very nearly on the equator he estimated from the approximate height of the trees that they must be on the northeastern slope of the mountain. As they started on the trail again, he demanded perfunctorily of Gillette—

"*Hakkim?*"

In the eyes of Tanka seemed to lurk a subtle sense of amusement as he politely repeated the word.

"Good Lord," reflected Dorsay with misgiving, "I wonder whether he does understand, or whether he thinks the word is some sort of magic or a white man's greeting? Heaven knows the way these minds work."

For lack of any other feasible plan, he followed docilely. Half an hour farther on they passed an abandoned *zareba*, by the dead fire of which Dorsay caught the gleam of an empty sardine-can. The sight cheered him. Perhaps the doctor had passed. Anyway a white man had camped there.

The aspect of the country changed.

The forest thinned; granite boulders and outcroppings of rock streaked with quartz peeped above the sparse grass. Soon they were traversing open rolling downs. Ahead of them was a series of ragged escarpments and the blue of the mountain summits beyond.

At this sight Dorsay had another strong instinct to rebel. But the recollection of the sardine-can and the inability to formulate any feasible plan of action suppressed the desire. Instead of resting as usual the *safari* continued on through the heat.

About four he saw light smoke amid hummocky rocks. Presently they came to a village, a small one, but stockaded. As they conducted him to a hut he looked around vainly for signs of a white man.

Toward sundown a drum began to beat, and after dark he saw the flicker of many fires somewhere in the center of the village and heard the natives chanting. He pondered for a while, and then decided to investigate.

The village about him he found deserted. He made toward the light and sound. He could distinguish dimly in the night the silhouettes of men, forms prancing against the orange of fires.

Within a few more spaces he came up against a heavy palisade of ivory tusks. In spite of the danger and the uncertainty of his fate the thrill of treasure smote him lightly. Dorkin, he reflected, evidently had known what he had been talking about. Then a new idea struck him. Could the writer of the message be imprisoned here? Was this the "buried goods"?

The doctor had said that it would probably turn out to be ivory. Yet these tusks could scarcely be said to be buried. But the man, where was he? And "goods" or "gods," what had that meant?

In the center of the enclosure he saw a solitary tree with great boughs, having either falling branches like willows or creepers reaching the ground, forming a canopy within which he could discern, dimly seated upon a stool, the form of a man whom he knew to be Tanka by the glint of the fire on his safety-razor earring. Around and about the fires in the front circled and capered three men with three feathers stuck in the wool of each head.

Around the three witch-doctors, one of whom he recognized by the peculiar tufts of hair upon his face as the man who had been present at the *shauri* with the supreme chief, Yamba, were the villagers and the members of the *safari* grouped upon their haunches, grunting in chorus. Dorsay watched interestedly.

The three performers suddenly dropped flat upon their stomachs, facing the lone tree as simultaneously the drums ceased. A silence of several moments was broken only by the bleat of a kid. As Dorsay was wondering what the interruption portended, he observed that the eldest of the three was squirming forward toward something which had been placed, presumedly by Tanka, within the tree, upon the ground.

Mangu, the head witch-doctor, seized and raised the object in his hands.

Dorsay caught the glint of light on metal, and then with a thrill recognized by the shape of the brass cylinder a compass which had belonged to the little doctor. But his first conclusion that Macnamara must be somewhere around was dissipated by the reflection that perhaps they might have got it from his body or from the Somalis.

Evidently by the movement of the needle upon the disk it was taken by the savages to be alive, for, gingerly placing the compass in the full light of the nearest fire, the three crouched around it, and, pointing fingers, shouted something which inspired the crowd with awe.

During another silence the three men bent over the small cylinder as if consulting an oracle. Then, one, peering close above the glass, suddenly sprang to his feet and pointed in the direction in which Dorsay was standing outside the palisade. Instantly half the squatting natives beyond the fires leaped up and, rushing to the gate, raced around the ivory fence toward him.

As he faced the advancing throng, rather uncertain what he should do, they set up a terrific howl at the sight of him, echoed triumphantly by the three doctors, who immediately began cavorting around the compass, which they evidently believed had revealed the presence of the stranger. With his hand inside his shirt upon the revolver, Dorsay, knowing not what else to do, suffered them to lead him around the palisade and into the enclosure.

As he advanced toward the tree, to his astonishment the three witch-doctors ceased their howling and in unison with Tanka, who had remained seated within the canopy of the tree, threw themselves flat upon their faces before him. Bewildered at this maneuver he half turned to find that he was the only individual within the enclosure who was erect upon his feet.

"Good Lordy," thought he with a thrill of relief, "they must take the doctor's compass for some kind of an oracle which they think has pointed me out as a god or something. I wonder if the doc is somewhere around. Almost feel as if I could sense him. Perhaps, after all, he's fixed this business to get me free."

He gazed around, half expecting to see his deliverer walking out of the shadows. Looking down at the prostrate forms about him and buoyed by expectant hope, Dorsay almost laughed at the ridiculous figure that he felt he cut. But save for the persistent bleating of the kid, which had lost its dam, above the low grunting of the natives, nothing happened.

Suddenly Tanka, his quaint earring gleaming in the light, leaped up, screeching.

Instantly the drums began to beat wildly and everybody scrambled up. Darting forward, the three doctors snatched up three blazing brands from the nearest fire. Tanka, moving swiftly to Dorsay's side, shouted wildly: "*Hakkim! Hakkim!*" And pointed to the three magicians, who stood as if expecting him to do something.

"*Hakkim!*" repeated Dorsay exultingly.

Mangu led the way toward the entrance of the palisade. Tanka again excitedly shouted after them: "*Hakkim! Hakkim!*" mixed up with other words which Dorsay did not understand.

"Wants me to follow," interpreted Dorsay to himself and, excited by hope, obeyed.

The whole gang, whooping and screeching, followed as far as the stockade of the village. Then across the bare, rocky ground beneath the rising half-moon, went the strange procession.

The three witch-doctors pranced in the van, screeching and capering, their torches lighting the fair man's face as he followed, searching the darkness eagerly for signs of some white man's camp. The grave Tanka brought up the rear. Behind them Dorsay could hear the wild chant of the village people and feel the throb of the drums upon his ear-drums.

"Where the mischief can the camp be here?" he demanded of himself, remarking that the ground was growing steeper every yard. Then he noticed that the lower stars were suddenly shut off, and made out the dense gloom of an escarpment in front.

The next moment the torches gleamed upon the light blue of gneiss rock. The three doctors were screaming their chant and dancing with as much gusto as ever. Dorsay hesitated. Tanka, his eyes gleaming with ferocity or excitement, Dorsay did not know which, loomed beside him, whispering ferociously: "*Hakkim! Hakkim!*" and pointing ahead.

Once more Dorsay found comfort in the word.

"I suppose it's all right," he muttered, and walked on to find himself before a fairly large natural door of a cave in the blank wall of rock, into which without hesitation the three doctors pranced. Above them, by the light of the brands, Dorsay saw that the cave was enormous, the yellow light gleaming fantastically on great stalactites and stalagmites.

As he entered, the thrum of the village drums and the chanting was cut off. He followed a dozen yards or more, mazed by the profusion of bizarre effects. The three doctors had cavorted on ahead, seemingly too lost in frenzy to recall his presence at all. Leaping high in the air at every step, their screeching voices hit the roof and came back in a dozen different echoes until the place seemed alive with ghostly screams, and their black bodies and feathers in the flickering lights were like gnomes dodging among the pinnacles of rock. It occurred to him that the doctor surely could not live in a cave. Again he halted.

"Say!" exclaimed Dorsay, prompted by a suspicion that all was not right, as his hand clutched at his revolver. "I'm not going any farther."

He wheeled. But Tanka was not behind him. Simultaneously the three doctors ceased screeching and the torches were extinguished. For a few seconds he stood, merely conscious of red lights flitting across the retina of his eyes. The silence and darkness seemed like a flashing blow.

"My God, I'm trapped!" he exclaimed aloud, as the truth struck him.

He listened intently. Hearing a stone rattle, he fired in the direction. The flash and the reverberations blinded and stunned him. He rushed forward angrily. A blow nearly felled him. He put out a hand and touched jagged rock, and, placing his fingers on his face, felt sticky warmth. The appalling suddenness of the change mazed him.

He stood stock still with the revolver clutched in one hand. He grabbed his pocket in a panic lest no matches were left. They rattled reassuringly. But there were not many. Cautiously he struck one, and, holding it in his cupped hand, peered around. The tiny flame was nearly swamped by the depth of the darkness; faintly it lighted a portion of the glistening stalagmite upon which he had bumped his head.

Which way was the cave door? In turning he had lost his bearings. He listened. The silence seemed as dense as the rock about him. He lighted another match, moved, and stopped. No use looking for the door with a light.

He stamped out the match and waited until he thought his eyes were focused to the darkness. Sticking the revolver in his pocket, he began to feel his way slowly. Several times, growing panicky, he lighted a match, only to find trunks of stalagmites which appeared like a forest. He had no idea which way he was going, yet he could not bear to stay still long.

At last—after half an hour or so, he reckoned—while pausing to strain his eyes in the blackness and to listen intently, he thought he saw a glimmer that was lighter than the cave darkness. Not daring to light another match for fear of losing the direction, he blundered on slowly.

Within twenty steps he was sure that he was not mistaken, and in ten more he felt the cooler air of the open. The door seemed to be the same, judging by the size and shape, as that by which he had entered. Then he noticed that he could not see the stars.

There seemed to be a wall in front of him. He looked up. There was a circle of stars as at the top of a shaft.

As he fumbled for the match-box he started at the shuffle of a foot. A voice close beside him giggled shrilly. He wheeled, conscious of goose-flesh, as he hurriedly struck a match.

In the circle of dim light the wild eyes of a white man were peering idiotically at him from out of a shaggy mass of white hair.

Dorsay's nervous fingers dropped the match.

"He, he, he, he!" giggled the man in the gloom.

VIII

THE UNEXPECTED VISION, following upon the experience in the caves of stalactites, paralyzed Dorsay's faculties. He could merely stare without realizing that the dim figure in the dark was in the realm of reality. The giggling ceased.

He was conscious of hard breathing, the call of some bird a long way off, and the distant thrum of drums. Possibly a few seconds later, although it seemed to him many minutes, his mind started to work again; he realized that the man was not a ghost or a figment of the mind, but an indubitable white man, and he was aware that the fellow stank, a sour acrid smell. He said quietly—

"Who are you, sir?"

The answer was an appalling shriek, and as he involuntarily stepped back a pace he felt the wind of the man's arms. The next instant he had disappeared. Dorsay gazed around, wondering how the creature had so quickly vanished; then conscious of the cave-mouth immediately behind him, sidestepped so that he had his back against solid rock.

He was more nervous and shaken by the uncanny apparition than he had been when he had found himself trapped in the cave of stalagmites.

Holding the revolver in his hand, he tried to pierce the intense gloom of what had appeared to be the bottom of a shaft. In one direction he could make out some mass that seemed lighter than the rock, but too large to be human or animal. Of the stranger he could not distinguish any sign.

"Say, are you there?" he called softly, not wishing to startle the man.

At the third call a gentle giggle came from out the darkness, but from which direction he could not determine. The sound made him shudder.

"Good Lord, he must be mad!" he exclaimed aloud; and again as if in wild assent floated the giggle.

He looked up at the sapphire disc seemingly perforated with holes of brilliant light. The throb of the drums was rhythmic and unceasing. He realized that instead of finding the door by which he had entered he had stumbled into some new kind of a trap which seemed to be the bottom of a shaft or volcanic blow-out—where probably, he reflected, they had intended that he should be.

But the white man? Was he the man who had written the mysterious message in blood on a piece of torn shirt?

There was no doubt that the fellow was mad now. A renewed slither of a bare foot on rock drew him about swiftly.

"Say, you!" he shouted. "I'm a white man."

The loud tones flew back at him in echo, mingling with another soft giggle.

"Don't do that!" he said sharply.

The answer was a shriek, which was echoed in a dozen muffled responses, revealing that the man was within the cave.

"My voice seems to irritate him," reflected Dorsay. "Better keep quiet till dawn."

He wondered what the time was, but decided not to light a match lest the flame excite the stranger. Holding the gun in his right hand, he began to edge along the wall of rock, feeling with his left. The wall was seemingly circular.

A few yards away he stumbled over something on the floor which rattled.

"He, he, he!" came the giggle from the other side of him.

"Go away or I'll shoot!" exclaimed Dorsay, startled at what he thought for a moment was another maniac.

"I'll shoot!" returned the mocking single echo, followed by a wild screech thrown back in turn.

Came the slither of bare feet on rock, and all was quiet again. Dorsay sank down cautiously on to his haunches, deciding not to move until he could see. Squatting with his back against the rock, he tried to puzzle out where he could be and what was about to happen. If this creature was the man who had written the message he must since have gone mad. Why?

The possibilities suggested were not pleasant. If this man had never succeeded in escaping, how could he expect to? But was there more than one man? What did the natives intend? Why should they imprison a white man in the bottom of a hole until he went mad? What did they gain? Was this the god the little doctor had spoken of, whom the Turkana were reputed to have? But a mad god—in a hole, kept in a pit like a bear?

He recollected the story of the man who had been king or god of the Wakikuyu, but he had been practically free, living like a great chief among them. Macnamara had told him that he could have no idea of the practises of which savages were capable, of the strange rites which their fantastic beliefs caused them to carry out.

The night was chilly, but Dorsay felt colder still within. Imagination began to suggest dreadful manners in which this wreck of a white had become insane.

"Not that," he muttered, tightening his grip on the haft of his gun.

Yet one couldn't— Perhaps the other fellow—

A soft giggle nearer to him seemed to pinch the valves of his heart.

"All right," he said soothingly, and stopped to clear his throat. "That's all right."

The man whined like a dog.

"Oh, ——," muttered Dorsay, stirring uneasily, "I shall go crazy before dawn if he goes on like that."

He looked up anxiously at the stars. A faint glow was staining one side; then he saw by the hue that it was caused by the half-moon mounting toward the zenith.

"I've got to hold myself together," he told himself sternly. "The day will come some time, and then I can see what I'm doing. Anyway things always look more awful in the night."

He sat on, gripping his nails into his palm occasionally at the frequent terrible sounds murmuring in the darkness.

As the horned moon sailed above the tunnel top he gazed eagerly about in the lesser darkness. The dull mass which he had noticed before, as lighter than the surroundings, glimmered brighter until he made out vaguely a stack of elephant tusks. That, he thought, must be the "buried" ivory or "goods" referred to in the message. The whereabouts of the madman he could not discover, and dared not investigate for fear of exciting him.

Slowly the light faded again, and the stars grew brilliant as the moon passed over the far lip.

Throughout the night the distant drums throbbed continuously. His legs and arms grew stiff with cold and the rigid position; for, every time he moved or coughed the other occupant made terrible whines—or giggled, which was worse. Time seemed to have stopped, but at length the pallor of the old moon was warmed by the flush of sunrise.

His eyes strained eagerly to follow the light, slowly percolating like milk poured into rum, but not until the rim was stained crimson by the sunrise could he distinguish objects clearly. There was no sign of the other occupant, whom he had not heard for some time. The prison he saw to be the bottom of a volcanic shaft, about fifty feet across.

The walls were as perpendicular as a lamp glass. The things he had stumbled upon during the night, which had rattled, were, he saw, the bones of a sheep or a goat.

He rose and walked cautiously across to the great stack of ivory, which contained a thousand tusks at least, worth over a quarter of a million dollars. But he was too occupied with his position to be much excited at the moment.

He stopped cautiously at the edge and looked around. Through the cave door, and the only one, by which he had entered, the white stalactites and stalagmites gleamed in the growing light, suggesting the top and bottom jagged teeth of some terrible beast with its mouth open. Besides refuse and many pieces of broken native calabash blackened by fire, there was nothing on the smooth surface of the shaft bottom.

He continued on around the corner of the stack and stopped. Lying asleep on the hard floor within a crude hut made out of some of the tusks, was the white stranger. Dorsay tiptoed toward him and peered down at him.

The body was that of a big man. The shoulder-blades stuck through the remnant of a striped cotton hunting-shirt like the hips of an old cab-horse. The hair and beard were long, matted and snow white. One claw-like hand, protruding beyond the head, revealed long nails.

In the corner of the primitive shelter was a rifle with the barrel yellow with rust. A jack-knife, broken near the haft, was in another corner, peeping from behind a pile of blackened calabash. Asleep, the face of the man looked peaceful and untroubled.

Rather from the fear of witnessing the lunacy leap into the eyes than from any other consideration, Dorsay withdrew silently. For a moment he stood like a caged bird staring upward at the small circle of paling blue sky above him. He placed one hand over his brow for a moment as if the sight were too painful or brilliant.

He glanced again around the empty floor and at the teeth-staring cave. The re-checking, as it were, of the situation seemed like a heavy burden. He sat down and held his head in his hands and concentrated to marshal all the facts he had as yet observed.

Evidently the other prisoner had either been lowered into the trap or had been lured the same way as he had been. That was evident. The walls were quite twenty-five feet high and utterly unscalable.

Through the door into the cave and out by the way he had come in lay the only hope of escape. Yet why hadn't this poor soul, he asked himself, been able to find that way out? That he hadn't arrived crazy was revealed by the fact that he had been intelligent enough to tear off a bit, or several bits for all he knew, of his striped shirt and somehow heave them out of the shaft—probably by tying them to pieces of broken calabash, surmised Dorsay.

He wondered how long ago that had been. He had no means of even guessing, and the principal could not tell him now. Surely he must have been there for a very long time. One didn't go crazy in a few weeks. Yet—

He jumped to his feet muttering:

"It's no use sitting here. I've just got to find a way out."

He gave another glance to reassure himself that the other was still sleeping, and then made for the cave door.

"Cave can't be very big," he added to himself. "Ought to be mighty easy to find the glow of daylight through the other door."

He made straight ahead, keeping the door behind him; went on until the forest of stalactites and stalagmites shut it out. Then he peered in all directions, but no sign of a glow could he distinguish.

He struck a few of his remaining matches and continued on, telling himself that the reason why the other man had failed was because he had not had light to carry him far enough; he would succeed and come back to rescue the poor soul. The sense of desperation in the depth of his mind prevented him from thinking beyond that open door to the wide world.

Every two matches he stopped, peered, waited to focus his eyes, blundered on, and lighted another. He had meant to use only half the matches in case— The half was gone, and more. Seven remained. But there was no sign of a light.

He sat down in the dark, trying to determine to return.

"Good Lord!" he exclaimed aloud, and a dozen whispers came back to him mockingly.

He searched after and found the thought which had been startled away— Why had he decided to seek straight ahead? He must have already gone farther than he had come during the night. Why, perhaps the missing entrance was to the left—within perhaps a few feet of the tunnel mouth! How foolish!

He rose with renewed hope. Or the right? Ah! Or the left front? Or the right front? Or perhaps there was a passage through which he had blundered in the dark? Or possibly the cave mouth was blocked with stone or some sort of door? Possibilities dashed about in his brain like disturbed bats in an old tower.

"Oh, God!"

" 'Od! 'Od! 'Od!"

He clenched his teeth and began again. His feet hit something which tinkled familiarly. He struck the last but one match. He saw the skeleton of a man who had evidently died in the dark, crouched against a stalagmite; already the shoulders were partially coated with the preserving calcium carbonate; beside him was an old-fashioned gun rusty and white.

Dorsay blundered on, doggedly feeling his way. . . . Distinctly he could make out sunlight, blessed sunlight. He shouted, in spite of the weird echoes, and ran.

The sun was right over the tunnel shaft; and, sitting in the warmth, was the lunatic gnawing a bone like an animal.

Dorsay sat down in the sun feeling slightly sick and giddy, yet glad of the heat after the damp of the cave. The man continued gnawing his bone, which Dorsay noticed he had taken from an overset calabash near him, which had contained bits of a half-cooked goat.

But where had the food come from? Evidently it had been lowered from the shaft mouth by the fiber cord attached.

The sight stirred natural hunger and thirst. In the bright sun the man seemed just a poor witless soul who, as Dorsay approached, giggled ingratiatingly. Naively unconscious in his plight of any civilized tricks, Dorsay tore off a piece of meat and bone and began to chew hungrily. The other prisoner grinned and wriggled like a friendly dog.

Watching him as he ate, Dorsay realized that the ghastly shrieks and giggles during the night had had no malicious intent, but were the amicable gambols of a pup. Perhaps somewhere in the blighted man's subconscious mind he recognized Dorsay as a fellow white and wished to express his pleasure in primitive fashion. But the idea depressed Dorsay; for dimly he saw what he too might become some day.

As soon as he had finished eating his bone the fellow scrambled over to a fresh spot in the retreating sun-rays, curled up, and went to sleep.

Dorsay, vainly attempting to work out a solution, sat sadly watching the curve of yellow sunshine mount the eastern side of the tunnel. Try as he would he could not find a feasible method of escape; not even the wildest project.

He eyed the cord by which the food-gourd had been lowered, but the plaited fiber was far too fragile to bear a man's weight even if he could succeed in attaching it to something that would catch on the rim of the tunnel. He had five cartridges in his revolver and twelve in his pocket; the rifle-cartridges still in his belt were, of course, useless. He decided to use nine of the former for as many days, at sunset, in the wild hope that the doctor might be near at hand.

He had visions of lying in wait until the savages came to lower the food, and trying to drop one. But what good would that do should he be successful? That wouldn't help him to get out. He seemed doomed either to die of despair or become insane and live the life of a captive bear.

The other prisoner was still sleeping and continued to do so all the afternoon. Dorsay almost felt violently angry with the man because he had lost his reason and could therefore not give him any information or even the companionship which he craved.

He began to pace up and down the pit like one of the bears he had imagined. At last, feeling thirsty, he went inside the ghostly cave to drink from a pool, when an idea that already he was a primitive animal thrusting his snout into the water, sent him back to retain some of his human dignity with the aid of a broken calabash.

In the cooling of the twilight, for in the bottom of the pit the light lingered longer than the tropical dawning on the surface, the lunatic awoke. Dorsay was squatted in a corner by the stack of ivory.

He noticed that the man looked around expectantly. On seeing him, he giggled, and, shambling across, sat down close to him like a lost cat seeking protection. Yet the friendly action in this creature, with only the resemblance of a human being, made Dorsay shudder.

As soon as dark had fallen the fellow became restless, and, prowling about, began those ghastly giggles and shrieks, seemingly engaged in a monstrous game of hide and seek. A vision of himself, mowing and giggling, joining every night in this horrific play, sent Dorsay pacing to and fro in the darkness unable to tear his eyes from regarding the brilliant stars above.

There were no drums. He passed the night in slow pacing to and fro, feeling as if he was an officer of the watch on the Flying Dutchman, knowing he was doomed never to reach port.

Dorsay was rather astonished at the way in which he became accustomed to the giggling and shrieking of his companion, occupied in a world of primitive imagination, the mystery of which only a child could understand. The practical reason for playing at night and sleeping during the day was manifest to his calmer mind: in the chilly air one required exercise, lacking any method of making a fire or preserving natural heat.

About an hour after the rim of the tunnel had been stained crimson by the unseen sun a calabash containing goat-flesh, two chickens, and a gourd with milk warm from the cow was lowered. But the sight of the food cheered him.

Even his useless project of "dropping one" would have been impossible; for they did not reveal as much as a head, pushing the gourd over the rim most cautiously. Evidently the natives did not trust their gods, if such they were, although they fed them well.

The morning he spent anxiously watching for the first ray of sunlight to reach the bottom of the pit. His "pal," as he termed the lunatic with a faint smile, revealing the heart of the man in adversity, slept as usual, and he followed suit.

Many days and nights passed as like each other as cigars in a box. He refused to count them—on the same principle that any man who spent his time solely counting the number of possible days to his life would probably become insane, or as a philosophic smoker on a desert island would refuse to calculate how many smokes remained in the one box saved from the wreck.

Rather to his astonishment the fate of the little doctor appeared to have become a dematerialized memory, as indeed had many other facts of life—his mother, probably in Bar Harbor at this time of the year; a married sister, whom he had thought he cared for more than any other in the world, at Salem, N.C.; a lawyer brother in New York; and others. In spite of his will to the contrary concrete facts of life loomed as large as a pyramid in a desert: anxiety that the calabash of food would appear on the skyline; when the first ray of yellow heat would reach a tactile distance; when it would vanish too far up the wall to reach. . . . He was conscious, too, that he had grown older; that if ever he escaped he would be a man, no longer merely a careless boy bent on seeing something of the world.

But usually he dodged these reflections; deliberately he tried to shut his mind to the future, for a good reason. His attitude was summed up or symbolized by a habit of sitting with clenched jaws regarding the amiable imbecilities of the other man while he repeated as if it were an incantation:

"I've got to hold out. Never become like that. I can do it. I will—"

Illimitable days and nights were broken one afternoon when the curve of the sun was a man's height above the pit bottom. Dorsay was seated against the wall on the spot where the last ray had disappeared, contemplating the charm, the message written in blood by his pal, who was sleeping in the ivory hut, pondering vaguely upon the strange chance that had caused him to buy that insignificant talisman which had led him into such a dismal plight, when a muffled yell, followed by gnome-like echoes, caused him to stare alarmedly at the cave mouth.

From the ghostly gleaming teeth of the fantastic dragon was erupted the form of Dorkin, bloody-faced and streaming oaths like the disheveled victim of some violent encounter.

IX

DORSAY IMAGINED that he was dreaming. The man stood there blinking in the comparative glare with one hand to his brow, his squat shoulders humped, glaring around the pit bottom like a bull emerging into an arena. He did not see Dorsay, and his eyes were fixed greedily on the great stack of tusks.

An oath ripped from his lips, shattering Dorsay's sense of illusion. Dorsay was conscious of resentment at the intrusion of this person. He rose. Dorkin heard him and wheeled about, drawing up his gun. Then he stopped and stared.

"Blimey!" he ejaculated. "Yew!"

"Yes, I'm here," answered Dorsay, and, rather surprized at the futility of the question, added—"What do you want?"

Dorkin scowled and looked suspiciously around. He seemed puzzled and uneasy.

"Wot d'jew want?" he demanded truculently. " 'Ow did yer git 'ere, heh?"

"How did you get here?" returned Dorsay, more conscious of practical affairs.

"Me? Why, I came 'ere after the splosh," said Dorkin with a grin, glancing at the ivory. "Wot djer fink?— Thort yew wus 'ome by now."

Then he suddenly sidestepped to get the solid wall behind him instead of the cave mouth. Dorsay noticed the maneuver, and remarked the swift movements of the furtive eyes.

"The cave!" he muttered to himself. "But how did you get in here?" persisted Dorsay. "Don't you know where you are?"

"Course I do! But 'ow in —— did yew git 'ere? That's wot I want ter know. See?"

They both had remained standing antagonistically. Dorsay glanced apprehensively—he did not know why—at the ivory hut where the lunatic was lying asleep.

"Well," said Dorsay patiently with a slight laugh, "I was foolish enough to walk here—apparently as you have done."

"Wot djer mean? 'Ow long yew been 'ere?"

"I don't want to know," returned Dorsay in a low voice.

Dorkin moved a pace sidewise watching stealthily.

"Wot djer mean?"

"Exactly what I said," said Dorsay with a sigh. "I don't want to know how long I've been here. Neither will you soon."

Again Dorkin glanced hurriedly about, as if suspicious of some kind of a trap in the words. Then he regarded Dorsay cunningly.

"Balmy," he rapped out. "That's what yew are!"

"Not yet. Not yet. Thank God!"

The tone of the voice puzzled Dorkin. He wiped the back of his hand across his beard, which was bloody, and took a step forward irritably.

" 'Oo 're gittin' at?"

"No one."

Dorsay sank down in his favorite place by the wall, as if he were both tired and bored.

"You're a liar and a thief, Dorkin, and a would-be murderer—if you're not already, for all I know—but I wouldn't wish this fate on you even if you did—"

"Wot the —— djer mean?"

Dorkin glanced swiftly at the mouth of the cave as if fearful of something behind him, and, dragging the gun, strode across and bent over Dorsay menacingly.

"Look 'ere, none o' yer lip! Wot djer mean?"

"I mean," said Dorsay, slowly and tiredly, watching the mounting curve of sunlight on the circular wall, "that you've fallen into a trap, and that you'll never get out. As far as I understand, from what the doctor told me, these natives think we're kind of gods.

Anyway we're fed and kept here like bears in a pit, and here you'll stop until—until—Oh, I don't want to think about *that*."

The information percolated slowly into Dorkin's mind. He straightened up. The small eyes blinked. Some knowledge of native ways and legends corroborated Dorsay's statement of the position.

"Garn!" he exploded suddenly. "Scared, that's wot yew are! 'Ow djer get 'ere? From that there cave?"

Dorsay nodded.

"Well, wot's ter stop yer gittin' aht the sime wy, heh? Garn, ye're orf yer crumpet!"

"If you mean I'm crazy already," returned Dorsay, "you're wrong. Nor do I intend to be, but *you* will very soon, Dorkin, just the same as that other poor soul."

Dorkin started, and glanced around.

"Wot!" he exclaimed. " 'Nother feller? Were? Black feller? . . . Oh, my—"

At that moment, like a lazy cat, the white-haired lunatic emerged from his hut, and, seeing the stranger, stood and giggled.

At the motion of Dorkin's gun the maniac leaped swiftly and disappeared through the cave mouth, from which echoed a dozen muffled echoes of a derisive shriek.

"Gor," muttered Dorkin, " 'e's orf 'is nut."

"I told you he was," reminded Dorsay.

Dorkin looked at Dorsay and back at the cave mouth swiftly. The half-raised rifle quivered slightly.

"Leave that gun alone," continued Dorsay equably. "He's perfectly harmless."

"But 'e's balmy," spluttered Dorkin.

"Am I to shoot you as soon as you go crazy?" demanded Dorsay tetchily.

"Me? Crazy! Wot djer gittin' at? I ain't crazy. I—"

He stopped, glanced suspiciously at the cave mouth and then at the stack of ivory. He looked at Dorsay slowly.

"Gor!" he said, pawed his eyes with the back of his hand and fell to staring at the tusks.

Dorsay watched his pose and the tense strain of the eyes:

"He's had an awful fright and he's trying to bluff," he observed to himself, without interest. "Got lost in the cave, I guess."

Slowly Dorkin tore his eyes away from the half a million dollars, gazed at Dorsay as if unable to believe that he were really there, and sat down suddenly with the rifle across his knees. He opened his lips to speak and then, glancing nervously at the cave mouth, snapped—

"W'ere's 'e gawn?"

"Don't know."

"Carnt 'e git aht?"

"I've told you."

A broken snicker was followed by a shriek and muffled echoes.

"Oh, gor!" exclaimed Dorkin, starting. "Wot's 'e do that fer?"

"He's mad, I told you."

"Lumme."

A scared expression came into Dorkin's eyes.

" 'Re yew mad, too?"

"Not yet."

"Crikey, can't stand this."

Dorkin scrambled to his feet hurriedly, looked toward the cave mouth, hesitated, and then, bending over Dorsay, whispered—

"D'yer fink 'e saw somefing?"

"What did you see?" queried Dorsay with some interest.

"Me? I—I— Is it true wot yer tole me abaht not gittin' aw'y?"

"Unfortunately, yes."

"Gawd's truf?"

"Unfortunately, yes."

"But they tole me the stuff wus in 'ere."

"Well, it is, isn't it?"

"They tole me I could 'ave it."

There was a resentful whimper in the voice like a deceived child's.

"Well, there it is."

"I got bloomin' eyes, ain't I?" retorted Dorkin savagely.

"H'm. Who brought you here, anyway?"

"Some of me own men." Dorkin scowled at the recollection and burst out: "Darned scuts, never can trust a ruddy nigger. That Yamakala—me head man—'e told me 'e got the tip stright from Mangu, the witch-doctor bloke, that the stuff was 'ere. Brought me las' night afore the moon rose. Then when I wus 'arf wy 'e turned and bolted, the mangy swine. Afore I cud let 'im 'ave one, too. In wiv that there streak o' guts ter get me *safari*."

"Why didn't you go back after him?"

"Arter 'im?"

Dorkin seemed about to choke with indignation.

" 'Ow cud I w'en there wasn't no more light than in the backyard o' ——?"

He paused to shoot a glance at the cave mouth.

"Never see a plice like that afore. Ruddy hawful. But I come on. Tikes somefin' ter stop me."

"So you've been in there since last night?"

"Yus, the ruddy 'ole. But I'll git 'im, mark me."

"Why don't you?"

"Heh?"

He bent lower over Dorsay, as if he had suddenly recollected something he had forgotten.

"But yew s'y as we carn't git aht?"

"That's right," answered Dorsay, noticing the "we."

"Garn," exploded Dorkin with sudden energy. "It ain't true. Oh, haw, there 'e is agine!"

The lunatic had come out of the cave silently and was watching them. Dorsay beckoned to him. He came trotting across with the cringing eyes of a cur fixed on the stranger, and, sidling beside Dorsay, cuddled to him.

This time Dorkin watched him with the awe of the ignorant for the insane. He straightened up, glanced at Dorsay, and bellowed, as if wild with rage:

"Yew're a bloomin' pair of balmies, that's wot yew are. I'm orf."

He strode toward the cave mouth. On the threshold he stopped to stare at the ivory, walked across and around it, evidently measuring the quantity. Then he turned and shouted:

"Comin' back for this lot, I am, and don't yer ferget it, yer pair of balmies! So long!"

And, turning, he plunged resolutely into the fangs of the ghostly cave.

"I wonder what he's angry with us for?" commented Dorsay aloud, and looked at his pal, who began to snicker softly.

The curve of sunlight shrank up the gorge, blazed upon the eastern rim and disappeared. In the cool the madman awoke and began his nightly game with the shadows and the people of his disordered mind.

Dorsay, who had dozed too, resumed his usual promenade. Although he wondered what had happened to Dorkin the incident seemed very unreal. If there was any definite emotion it was a hope that he wouldn't come back, would escape, anything rather than insist upon dragging him back to terrible reality.

He looked up at the disk of perforated sky. There was no moon now, and the stars were frostily brilliant. The giggles and yells of the madman had become normal to him. When he was fairly warm he would crouch in the hut of ivory and doze for a while until the chill awoke him and then recommence the perpetual promenade. Sometimes the lunatic would fall in beside him and follow like a dog, until, tiring, he would scamper off upon his own mysterious errands.

During one of these moments that Dorkin reappeared, Dorsay heard a groaning curse as he stumbled out of the cave. He didn't see his two fellow prisoners, and cried out—

"Oh, my ——, they've gawn!"

"No they haven't," answered Dorsay, and wanted to laugh; yet he dared not because the madman giggled; but he heard Dorkin's words—

"Oh, thank Gawd!"

Dorkin came toward him eagerly. The lunatic turned a giggle into a shriek, and, darting past him, disappeared into the cave. Dorkin made a gulping noise and collided with Dorsay, who noticed that he was trembling as with an ague. He clutched him by the arm.

"Is it truf?" he whispered hoarsely. "We carn't git aht?"

"I told you so."

"Yus, but—but—"

He seized Dorsay's arm again.

"I fort I'd never git aht o' that ruddy cave. Never git aht. Oh, ——, it's hawful."

"Yes; it's worse than this, isn't it?"

"Oh, ——, I—I. Look 'ere, I ain't been right wiv yew. I know it. But yew won't leave me, will yer? Swear yer won't? I carn't stand it."

"I'm not likely to—unfortunately. Say, you'll have to pull yourself together, Dorkin, else you'll—"

"Wot's the good? Wot's the ——'s the good?"

He flung himself away and subsided into a corner growling—

"If I git 'old of 'im, ——!"

Dorsay continued pacing, trying not to give way to the thoughts which Dorkin's entry excited in teeming clouds. Dorkin remained crouched against the rock, alternately swearing and groaning. The lunatic, for some reason, kept quiet, gibbering occasionally just within the cave mouth. At last the stars paled. Dorsay noticed that Dorkin had not got his rifle.

"Probably lost it in the cave. So much the better," he thought, "for he'll get ugly sooner or later."

When the madman came scampering past him to reach the ivory hut, Dorkin scowled.

"Better have a sleep, Dorkin," advised Dorsay on his way to the hut. "We're fed about eight."

Dorkin mumbled unintelligently. Later Dorsay was awakened by revolver-shots. He started up with his mind in a blaze of hope. He saw Dorkin standing in the middle of the pit bottom, jumping with rage and firing wildly above the gourd of food as it was being lowered.

"It's no use doing that," he called out as the lunatic in a frenzy of fear dashed past him into the cave.

Dorkin wheeled about, and with an oath threatened to "put one" in him if he didn't "hold his jaw." At that moment the madman shrieked. Dorkin fired into the cave mouth.

The act infuriated Dorsay. He shouted and rushed at Dorkin. The small eyes were gleaming with mad rage. As Dorkin fired, Dorsay leaped.

The bullet clipped his ear.

This excuse for action seemed to release something in him that had long been tugging for freedom—something which was already loosed in the other man. He grabbed at Dorkin's wrist with one hand and smashed into his face with the other. Dorkin jabbed him in the ribs and brought up his knee at the same time. Dorsay, hurt, gripped the other's neck and, savagely winding a leg around Dorkin's, threw him. The revolver clattered on the rocky floor.

Maddened by pain and disgust and the tearing of the man's teeth, Dorsay exerted every ounce of strength and skill, knowing, more than he had in the previous fight, that the man had become a more dangerous killer through sheer terror.

Once, as Dorkin in a heave managed to get atop of him and had his hand upon his windpipe, Dorsay saw, as through a cloud, the form of the lunatic, dancing and giggling about them.

Vainly Dorsay tried to twist the wrist of the hand whose fingers were around his throat. Abandoning the attempt, he managed to seize Dorkin's other wrist, and, twining his leg between his adversary's, contrived to half-throw him on to his side. Then, swiftly grasping one ankle, by a desperate effort of his spine and body he secured the right leg in a lock. At the first jerk the knee-cap cracked with the strain. Dorkin released his strangling grip.

For several moments, to get his breath, Dorsay held him. Then, changing to an arm-lock, he climbed on top of him.

"See here, Dorkin," he said thickly, "you've got to do what you're told. Understand that?"

"I wasn't doin' nuffin," pretended Dorkin sulkily, "till that there ruddy idjit larfed at me, and then you—"

"That'll do!"

Dorsay slid off his opponent's body and seized the revolver.

"Now get up!"

Dorkin obeyed, glancing malevolently at the lunatic, who was standing by the cave mouth ready to seek refuge. Dorsay, ashamed and half-frightened by the animal fury that had possessed him, and partially conscious that he should have killed the killer, stalked over to the food-basket and curtly handed a share to Dorkin. Then, taking the rest, he walked to the cave mouth and called softly to the lunatic. Sitting together, with the revolvers in Dorsay's pockets, Dorsay and the witless one ate their food, while Dorkin sulkily chewed by the edge of the stack of ivory tusks.

Throughout the day Dorkin refused to speak and remained squatting sullenly by himself, growling and scowling at the lunatic. Realizing that Dorkin would probably try to recover his revolver and that he could not keep awake always, Dorsay, when going into the cave to drink, hid both Dorkin's weapon and his own.

In the warmth of the middle day and afternoon he slept as usual with the lunatic huddled beside him. When he awakened he knew that Dorkin had tried his pockets for the guns. Dorkin grinned spitefully, said he would "do for" the "gigglin' idjit" and began a systematic search, first among the tusks. When he failed to find the guns he grew vicious, swore continually, and threatened. Once he bawled out with a hysterical note—

"If it wasn't fer yew, yer ——, I wouldn't be in this 'ole; —— yew and yer dotty doctor."

But watching Dorkin and protecting the lunatic began to tell on Dorsay. He became more nervous, and the continual strain wore down his morale. He grew to hope that some end would come. Then Dorkin developed other symptoms. He would awake screaming and make sudden savage rushes after the witless one. When Dorsay interfered he would retreat, muttering and gibbering unintelligibly.

Every day he would persist in sitting and dozing in the short sun-rays without a hat or covering. Dorsay warned him, but received snarling curses.

"He won't last long," Dorsay commented that night, "and then he'll try to kill us both. I ought to shoot him," he added, as a statement of cold fact.

A few days afterward Dorsay was awakened by a scream, felt a heavy body fall upon him and savage hands about his throttle. He knew what was happening and fought desperately. He had scarcely any chance; for Dorkin, taking him when he was asleep had secured a strangle-hold. He writhed and kicked, but Dorkin had pinioned one arm with a thigh and rendered his legs useless by straddling his stomach. Dorkin's thumbs and fingers sank deeper. Dorsay felt his tongue swelling, his lungs bursting, and the pain was like scorching iron pincers in his throat.

Then suddenly came a feeling of concussion. The fingers relaxed, and his aggressor rolled over helplessly. Dorsay sat up, choking and pawing up at his lacerated throat. Through bloodshot eyes he saw mistily that Dorkin was lying still with blood flowing from his skull, and beside him was the lunatic, staring bewilderedly at him. He grew vaguely aware that the dreadful light had gone out of those eyes, as the man placed his hand to his white hair and whispered slowly—

"Who—are—you?"

X

"WHO AM I?"

Dorsay repeated the words mechanically.

"Why—"

"And who did that?"

The man pointed to the corpse of Dorkin, the head of which was almost split in two from a blow from a small tusk, lying weltering in blood.

"Who did—"

Dorsay stared, still holding his throat. Then he realized the fact that a blow, or the excitement, had restored the man's reason.

"Why you must— But don't you recollect anything? Don't you remember me?"

"You?"

The man passed his hand across his eyes bewilderedly.

"Never saw you before, my dear chap. Er—who are you, and how did you come here—and this?"

"Well, my name is Dorsay Beffert. I'm an American. Those savages brought me here where I found you. This fellow came some days ago. He was a trader after this ivory. I knew him. He tried to shoot you—"

"Shoot *me*?"

"Yes; but that's days ago. A while ago he tried to strangle me, and you must have felled him with that small tusk there. But don't you recollect anything at all?"

"Nothing," responded the man incredulously. "The last I remember was— Oh, my God, I got lost in the cave, I think, and—and—I can't remember."

He held his head with both hands as if trying to recall the past."

"Who are you?" interposed Dorsay.

"I? I'm Geoffrey Constable. These natives tricked me in here— Oh, I don't know. Last year, I suppose. I don't know. What month is it?"

"Probably July—as far as I know. When did you come here?

"March, nineteen-three."

"Nineteen-three! Good Lord, this is nineteen-six!"

Geoffrey Constable stared at Dorsay.

"Three years!" he repeated dully. "Three years! My ——!"

His eyes wandered around the circular wall of their prison and rested at length on the corpse of Dorkin.

"Did I kill this man? Why?"

"Because he tried to kill me in my sleep. You saved my life."

"I did? Why did he want to kill you? I mean," he added, "what's the use of killing—anything—here?"

"Quite so," assented Dorsay soothingly. "But he did. He was going a little crazy. Couldn't stand it, I guess. He was a rough-neck anyway."

"Rough-neck?"

"Yes; bad-man."

"Oh."

Constable gazed at Dorsay musingly.

"Of course you haven't been long here yet, have you? H'm. I suppose I must have become—er—unbalanced. Was I?"

"Yes—slightly. I mean you didn't—didn't seem to recognize me—I mean as a white man," added Dorsay embarrassedly.

"Oh, really?"

Constable pointed suddenly to the curve of sunlight about seven feet up the wall.

"I remember that. See that ridge? Well, it's twenty-four minutes past three o'clock. I had a watch—at first. By Jove!"

He turned with interest, clutched his wrist, and then began feeling the remnants of his pants where his pockets had been. "I wonder what I've done with it?"

He twiddled meditatively with his long white beard.

"By gad," he remarked, "rather nice of you to turn up."

He laughed—sanely.

"Although rough luck, I must say. Haven't any scissors, have you? My hair seems rather long, what? And my beard—"

Pulling the ragged ends, he glanced down, and started violently.

"My ——, it's white!"

Dorsay did not reply.

"Is that true?" he demanded. "Or am I—?"

"No. It's true—and your hair."

"And it used to be black!"

His eyes filled with tears. Dorsay looked away. Constable rose to his feet, and began examining his clothes.

"Good ——! Good ——! I remember," he muttered. "I tore up bits of my shirt and threw them over the crater in a piece of calabash. Oh my ——, how long was that ago!"

"Yes, I know," responded Dorsay. "I found one. That's what brought me here."

"Brought you here? What, to rescue me? That was sporting!"

He smiled and held out his hand.

"Thanks, Mr. —er—?"

"Beffert."

"Mr. Beffert. But where? How?"

"I found it on a native as a charm, and then I came along with a doctor friend of mine, Macnamara—"

"Mac! What! Mac?"

"Yes; do you know him?"

"Where is he?"

"I wish I knew."

Oblivious, in this excitement, of the weltering corpse of him who had been the unconscious cause of restoring Constable's reason, they talked on for some half an hour or more. Constable, it appeared, had come down from the Sudan, and among the Turkana had been trapped as Dorsay and Dorkin had been.

When he had arrived there had been another white, a Scotchman, McCullough, a dour soul, said Constable, who would never talk and had one day disappeared. Constable had never known whether he had died or had escaped. Dorsay thought of the skeleton he had stumbled upon in the cave.

They buried the remains of Dorkin, or rather carried them as far into the cave as they could. They could do no more.

In the society of this man who had endured so much until his brain had given way, Dorsay's desire to live, and courage to think, revived. He would watch Constable sometimes with a kind of awe, recollecting the giggling "thing" which had cringed and cowered for protection. The more he saw of Constable the better he realized how the man had withstood two or three years of solitary confinement in such environment; for as an experienced hunter and explorer he had a fund of mental life and a courage that nothing appeared to be able to daunt.

Days melted into each other. Constable so drew Dorsay's attention from the concrete present by stories of exploration and a philosophic presentation of life, founded on his experiences in many lands, that he almost forgot their sorry plight and began to draw, as many a prisoner has done before, a queer pleasure from the effortless life of a caged animal, relieved of the daily struggle for existence.

At length, while pacing in the dark of a moonless night, there came to them a sound that quickened the action of their hearts, yet which was stoppered by a clutching fear of illusion.

"Did you hear that?" whispered Constable as the two stood stock still in the well of their prison, staring incredulously at the perforated disk of the sky.

"Beff-ert! Are you there?" came a familiar voice from above before Dorsay could reply.

"Yes, yes! Oh, my ——!" shouted Dorsay, hoarsely, almost stifled with emotion and clutching at Constable's arm. "Is that you, doctor?"

"Sssh!" came back warningly, and the faint outline of an arm waved broke the rim of the crater against the frosty stars. "Are you all right?"

"Yes, thank God. But ——"

"Alone?"

"No, no. There's a friend of yours here. Geoffrey Constable—"

"What!"

"Hullo, Mac!" chimed in Constable quietly. "How are you? Jolly glad to see you— or rather"—he laughed softly—"jolly glad to hear you!"

"Well, I'm ——!" floated gently the voice of the little doctor. "Where the deuce did you pop up from? But, ssh! No time now. Listen. I'll throw you a rope and you'll have to swarm up."

"Right-o! But half a moment. Anybody with you?"

"A couple of my men and a donkey," returned Macnamara. "We'll have to break round the mountain for Uganda. Look out!"

Again an arm broke the rim line and a fiber rope wriggled against the stars, the end of which hit the perpendicular sides of the shaft with a smack.

"You go first," said Dorsay.

"No. But wait," returned Constable. "I say, Mac, better cover our tracks, hadn't we? We'll rig up a body here to look like one of us asleep so that they won't smell a rat tomorrow morning, what?"

"Good idea, old man," assented the doctor. "Give us a longer start. But all the same they won't follow farther than the lower slopes for fear of the mountain devil."

"Right-o! Come on, young-feller-me-lad," added Constable to Dorsay. "We'll have to lug your dead friend out. It's a nasty job, but he'll sleep just as well here as inside the cave, poor soul."

XI

BY DAWN THE LITTLE EXPEDITION had gained the northern elbow of the mountain and was hidden by the mist which often dwells around the summit of Mount Elgon.

The going was rough and cold in their slight tropical clothes, particularly for Constable, but they plugged on steadily, warming up in the heat of the rising sun, until about noon, when, reasonably safe from any pursuit, if the natives had discovered their flight, they halted in sight of the plain of Busoga, covered in swamp and forest, beneath them.

"No," replied the doctor as they sat around the camp-fire, in answer to a long-deferred question regarding the upshot of the Somali's attack. "They wiped out about half my men and got away with three of them and two donkeys."

"And one perfectly good American," interrupted Dorsay, smiling. "Don't forget that."

"I didn't," asserted the little doctor, grinning like a Scotch terrier. "At first I thought the darned American had kicked the bucket. Anyway I followed up your trail and found your dead friend and the horse. Horse spoor easy enough; but your trail was difficult.

"However, we eventually found the spot where you had met several natives and my donkey. I arrived at Yamba's only a few hours after you and Dorkin had left. Of course, I hadn't the remotest notion who he was. The old man swore you had left together, but I knew he was lying.

"They tried to put me off for some time, and then suddenly came round and offered to lead me straight to you. I smelt a rat. I came to a village not far from the sacred one where they led you out into the trap, and then refused to budge. I suspected something was in the wind, but couldn't make out exactly what.

"Through my men and overhearing one of their *shauris* I knew that you were near, and that some witch-doctor business was on. I tried to buy the local man, but he tried to double-cross me. By the way, did you see anything of a compass?"

"Surely I did," assented Dorsay, and related the circumstances.

"Well, I managed to get Mangu," continued the doctor, "the old fellow and chief of the witch-doctors, to come to see me, and kidded him that this was an extra special piece of magic which would reveal the man whom the gods had appointed and all that sort of thing. Sheer bluff, of course, because I had only a ghost of a notion what I was talking about—guesswork; but I wasn't far wrong.

"You had rotten luck. About four to one against the needle hitting right on you. If it hadn't, it might not have saved you altogether, but at any rate it would have delayed matters.

"Well, that night I heard the caterwauling and guessed that something had gone wrong. I darn't barge in, but had to sit quiet and watch."

"Then things began to get uncomfortable. A lot of monkey work was going on around. Mangu came later and wanted to lead me straight to my white friend, you or Dorkin. I refused. They would have simply trapped me as well.

"I tried to find out where you were from the local man. Not a bad sort. Wanted like the deuce to have the cattle I offered, but the spirits of his ancestors, and you people in the hole there, scared him stiff.

"However, I learned by piecing together scraps and what not, something of the system, and guessed pretty accurately what had happened. As you probably know, Connie, they mess up the concrete with the abstract; kings same thing as gods in their eyes, you know. But from the little they had seen and heard in those days and since, they knew that the whites were more powerful with their guns and what not than the blacks.

"Then some enterprising witch-doctor must have said, 'Let's have white gods, and so we'll be stronger than any other tribe.' Logical enough; but premises somewhat rocky, what?"

"Yes, I had heard of the system up north and came along to find out all about it. I did," said Constable dryly.

The two ex-gods laughed, feeling that now they could afford to do so.

"Well, to get along with the yarn," continued the little doctor, "I started working on that basis. While I was thinking things out Mangu and company began to get ugly. Evidently they wanted to get me safely planted.

"Well, matters got to such a pitch that I saw I couldn't get out to make up a relief expedition as I had half thought of, and that it was up to me to save my own skin to get yours out, young man."

"Very nice of you, doctor."

"H'm," grinned the doctor. "I tell you frankly there was a time when I thought that it was about time to check up accounts for Gabriel and cussed myself for a fool for ever allowing you to kid me into such a mess at my age. Well, they got so jolly nasty, generally, that I had to think up something or chuck up the sponge.

"Then my local pal began to get scared of Mangu, and I saw that I couldn't trust him any longer. I saw too that I had to do something to settle matters, and above all to get Mangu and the head witch-doctors out of the light before I would stand a sporting chance of getting near you or of saving myself. Then one night I heard the drums going and thought that it was for my funeral—it must have been about the time of Dorkin's introduction to the cave, from what you say.

"Suddenly I recalled the message written on the charm that had lured us into the untidy mess. I knew very well that any part of a god is sacred. That's why they had made a charm out of your shirt, Connie. I hadn't got a striped shirt, but I tore up a piece of *bafta* and faked the blood writing.

"It worked like magic. They were scared to death of me. Let me do pretty well what I liked. I cussed myself for a prince of fools for not having thought of it before."

"Good Lordy!" exclaimed Dorsay. "Dorkin must have known something of that. That's why he tried to steal my charm and tried to murder me for it! If I had only known!"

"I don't know so much," demurred Constable. "Had he known, why didn't he fake it as you did, Mac?"

"Too darned stupid, I guess," put in Dorsay.

"Probably, from what I know of him," agreed the doctor.

"Say, doc," continued Dorsay, "what does '*hakkim*' mean?"

"In Kiswahili Arabic it means doctor. Why?"

"Oh, that's what I thought and kept on asking Gillette—the guy with my safety razor in his ear—for you by that name. That's how they got me into the cave. He pointed and kept saying, '*hakkim, hakkim,*' and I fell for it, thinking he meant you."

"Oh, but that's not Turkana lingo. Probably he didn't understand a word. But you must always remember that a native is particularly sensitive to suggestion. He regards a white—usually—as a superior being; is scared; and therefore anxious to please.

"You'll remark the same thing in a peasant. If you say, 'This is so,' he'll possibly reply, 'Oh, yes, sir!' On the other hand if you say, 'This isn't so,' he'll as well say, 'Oh, no, sir!'

"But in your case, Gillette, as you call him, was probably kidding you—anything to get you into the cave and the trap."

"That's what I thought—afterward."

"Evidently that's their game with each one," commented Constable. "They promised to show me this god—and I bit! Naturally I never suspected that I was intended for part of the menagerie."

"Yes, they are not such bad psychologists. Roughly speaking, these witch-doctors know human weaknesses and play them for all they're worth. That's their trade after all."

"Plenty of white witch-doctors, too, who make a good living!" added Constable with a laugh.

"You bet," assented the doctor, grinning, "otherwise most politicians would be out of a job, what? Well, after I got that magic going they left me alone, gave me permission to go where I liked through the country and all that sort of thing, you know. But I daren't begin any real attempt to rescue you until Mangu, et al., had gone home.

"They might be nice to me with what they thought was your shirt-tail in my hands, Connie, but I didn't think they'd stand for monkeying with their gods, what? Well, after that all I could do was to sit tight and wait my chance.

"I think Mangu got jolly wild over the charm business, for it deprived him of an extra god; but he couldn't get over the authenticity, as it were, of the sacred relic. Finally he got peeved and went home cussing. Then my local friend became more friendly and I found out where you were.

"A few days ago most of the village went on a hunting-raiding expedition and I seized my chance. That's all."

The three white men sat for a while in silence, staring at the glowing end of a log, occasionally throwing a handful of twigs upon the coals to keep them alight. The air was sharp and cold, and the vastness of the African night seemed to press them closer to the blaze.

The orange glow, lighting up their faces, betrayed three curiously different expressions.

Dorsay, though smug and content with having passed through an experience that would keep the home folks thrilled for years to come, looked like a happy tramp, with his stubby growth of beard, and an old, weather-beaten pipe stuck between his sun-cracked lips.

Constable, with gray patriarchal beard spread over his broad, bony chest, was dreaming terrible dreams. His sunken eyes seemed to look back with increasing horror on the years he had spent in the frightful pit.

Only the little doctor was alert. His small eyes twinkled restlessly, darting frequently at the haggard countenance of his old friend.

"Constable," he said abruptly, "why didn't you try to get out?"

"Get out?" broke in Dorsay. "It was impossible!"

"Impossible," Constable echoed dully, not having quite grasped the significance of the doctor's words.

"That's rot," insisted the doctor impatiently. "There were lots of ways—ladder of ivory—make a bit of string to guide you through the tunnel—"

"Oh, oh, I see!" exclaimed Constable sharply as his reawakened brain grasped the query.

Then in a puzzled tone:

"But I did. You must have seen. I was always planning something."

His face became animated, and his eyes sparkled.

"As soon as I fully realized they had me imprisoned—for life—I set to work to get out. I made tools with my belt-buckle and the nails from my shoes—and I built a ladder of ivory, with the longest, heaviest tusks at the base. It took me over a year; but I did it, and half the time my hands were so raw I could suck the blood from them.

"I spent a full week shifting my ladder into position. When I reached the top—it was shaky and flimsy as straw—my hand came about four feet from the rim of the pit. Of course, I should have gone down again and worked some more. But I'd used up my last scrap of metal. I was desperate. So near the top—I must have gone a bit crazy to be free. I jumped for it.

"The added pressure of that spring snapped the ivory under me. I went crashing all the way down to the bottom. I broke some bones and lost a lot of blood—and must have lain there for two or three days—"

"Didn't the niggers ever know?" exclaimed Dorsay.

"No. They never looked down. Afraid of accidents, I suppose. Afterward I made a shelter of the ivory."

The Englishman paused, and drew a shaking hand slowly across his forehead.

"Next thing I did," he continued with a rush, "was to try to explore the cave systematically. I saved the fat from the goats' meat and made a candle with a wick from the threads of my shirt. Then a cloudburst came and my last few matches were dissolved in mud, leaving only some useless phosphorus."

"Good Lordy!" exclaimed Dorsay. "I should think you *would* have gone crazy!"

The Englishman looked fixedly at Dorsay for a moment.

"A couple of times, young fellow, I thought I was—"

"Yes, yes," said the little doctor impatiently; "get on."

"Well," continued Constable, "I preserved the mud and phosphorus in a bit of hollow ivory. Then I raveled my shirt and what remained of my socks and underwear, and spun a long cord with the thread.

"With this I began to trace my way out through the labyrinth. Whenever I came to a doubtful point I'd pick out a bit of stone and smear it with phosphorus; so I left glowing points behind me.

"There's something ruddy awful in groping through a slimy tunnel, black as ———. Not a sound but the infernal drip-drip-drip of the water from the tips of the stalactites. Once in a while I'd barge into a stalactite, and it would collapse with a splash and a sound like the soft wheeze of a river animal.

"There was a little comfort in looking back at the glowing spots of phosphorus; so as I went on I smeared the rocks more and more thickly.

"I had just smudged some on a small round stone like a large volcanic pebble, and had continued on for a few steps, when suddenly I felt absolutely sick. The cord in my hand had parted!

"Water must have soaked through the flimsy thread, and it broke at the first strain. My only hope then was to follow the points of phosphorus immediately, and get back before the glow faded away. By this time I was jumpy and scared—nothing but a bundle of nerves anyway, you know.

"I turned quickly, and began blundering my way back, my heart beating a hundred to the minute.

"And the first thing I saw in the dead blackness in front of me was a skull in a ball of pale flame, with black, empty eyes and gaping mouth grinning at me.

"Of course, it was only the round stone I had smeared with phosphorus. But the shock was too sudden for me to grasp that then. I must have yelled and—and gone a bit—eh—balmy—because I haven't the foggiest notion what happened next until young Beffert here caught me smashing the Australian—the next day—I think it was."

His voice trailed off, and his eyes remained fixed dully on the coals. His hands stole almost furtively up to the matted beard. Then he scrambled widely to his feet.

"Good ———!" he cried. "It's true, then! It's true!"

His companions looked up, startled and silent. For a moment they could think of nothing to say. Then the tenseness passed from Geoffrey Constable's face.

He faced the darkness with a reckless light blazing in his eyes, and shook his fist in the direction of the Turkana village.

"All right," he cried. "Six years I've given you! But you'll pay—you'll pay—fifty thousand blinking quid!—a fortune in ivory! Gentlemen, it's ready for us whenever we want to collect. Are you with me?"

And the young American and the grizzled little doctor jumped to their feet with yells of enthusiasm that rang through the night, and stilled—for a moment—the wild, threatening voices of Africa.

Adventure, June 20, 1922

Gifts of Diamonds

FOREWORD

A WRITER'S MAIL-BAG is usually supposed to contain rejection slips and bills, varied by way of breaking the monotony, by a check. But one morning, in 19—, among the aforesaid classical contents was a registered package which I naturally took to be a returned manuscript or a bundle of proofs. Then I observed that the parcel had been readdressed and bore the stamps of the British Central Africa Protectorate. Wondering who on earth could have sent me anything from Blantyre, where I had never been, I cut the string and discovered on the top of a bundle of manuscripts a letter. The manuscripts were fairly difficult to decipher from age and exposure. I have no need of explanation. I have merely arranged them in the most intelligible order.

Office of the District Commissioner.

Masapani, B.C.A.

February 15, 1921.

Sir:—I have come into possession of certain papers addressed to you and herewith enclosed.

My duty as sub-commissioner took me into the country of the Makanga on the Portuguese border, a district which has but lately come under practical administration. The case had to do with a particularly malignant outbreak of witchcraft. During the course of my investigations I learned that the defendant, a local chief, had a notorious reputation as a witch-doctor on account of some extremely powerful fetish which he possessed. I ruled that the fetish in question should be brought into court, which was accordingly done. It proved to be a rusty dispatch case of the ordinary kind, upon which was faintly discernible the initials B.W.H.

Although I made every possible effort I was unable to discover in what circumstances the box, which the natives ignorantly considered a fetish, had come into the man's possession.

Upon forcing the lock I discovered the aforesaid papers addressed to you. I may state that in my official capacity I have read them, and that in order to avoid unnecessary porterage and freight I have not deemed it necessary to send the box, which is of no intrinsic value.

I have the honor to be, sir,   Your obedient servant, etc.

Written in pencil, around the margin of a page of one of my own short stories—scarcely decipherable:

Monomatapa's, March 23, 1912.

My dear old boy:—I guess you will be more than considerably surprized to hear from me! Lots of cocktails must have flowed down your throat since last we raised our elbows in company. Since then the most banal (?) things have happened and the strangest. Of course I've never forgotten you nor our trip Barotse way, and particularly lately— But if ever you get this it is due to the chance of my coming across this yarn of yours in a magazine sent in the last mail—mor'n a year ago—I bumped against Harry Martin of all people in Quilimane. But he was too —— wise. Haven't got time to explain. You'll see. By the row they're making I guess it's "Time, gentlemen, please!" —— nasty medicine. Feel sick in the belly like a kid going ——. But they'll pay. Love, dear old pal.—

Bran.

Scribbled in large letters across print:

—— *Sake Don't Fall For This. Enough Fool Adventurers?*

Written in ink and indelible pencil in a canvas-covered note-book:

Feb. 28.—I've surely never dreamed of writing a kind of an autobiography, but as I've read the two magazines and the three newspapers from cover to cover at least twenty times including the ads, and the job will keep me from thinking, which is neither healthy nor amusing just now, I am going to do so. At any rate I'm in good company—as you'll see. If it ever reaches civilization it may serve for a yarn to warn other fool adventurers from chasing will-o'-the-wisps of fortune.

Yet I guess it won't; for we of the breed blessed or cursed with a mania to wander the four corners of the earth wishing there were five, will never listen to reason like the fellow who hiked up the Andes and down again, just because some fool had told him it couldn't be done. I guess this is my fifth corner. Reminds me of some nursery riddle—when you get in, you can't get out. What is it? I suppose I'd better start in the ancient manner of chroniclers by giving some account of myself. So here goes!

I'm five-feet-eleven in my bare toes, fairly husky, ginger-haired, and I was born and raised in Bawston, U.S.A., although I don't pronounce it like that and only mention the fact when I'm drunk. My father came of an old family, never worked and yet seemed to be respectable as far as I ever knew him. This doesn't seem right somehow, but I've read something like it in an old book and anyway, Charles, you can put on the trimmings.

I escaped when I was about seventeen with an accent, some Latin, less Greek and fixed ideas on pirates and explorers—they seemed to be the same to me. Since then I've gotten rid of all of 'em except the pirate and the explorer. However, I only got as far as New York. I hadn't known then that pirates herded in towns and as I was rather crude on exploring I had to be rescued.

Dad seemed more bored than angry, and after mother had quit weeping, I was packed off West to learn to be a man. I was a diligent student for quite a while until I got tired of alkali dust and the deplorable lack of bad-men. Then I continued West until I hit Frisco. "Two Years before the Mast," it was I think started an awful craving to "round the Horn." Dad seemed to think well of the proposition. Some unknown gentlemen in Frisco got the money and I the trip round the Horn.

By the time I had arrived in Shanghai I was prejudiced in my estimate of the writer of that book. There I got into an argument with a fellow who didn't like my face. I'm not crazy about it myself. Describe it, Charles, and be as merciful as you can. Anyway, he went to hospital and I to jail, from which delectable abode I was rescued by the American consul. Somehow or other I'm always being rescued. But there's nothing doing this time I guess—

I read this over yesterday and swore I'd quit. I'm not a writer anyway. But I'll have a shot to go through with it as I reckon it does me good.

It's awful hot today and the mosquitoes are already busy, even though it's only about four. There's a thrumming of those guitar things from the women's quarters and young slave girls—dandy figures, like young antelopes—are bringing water through the compound from the river.

After the Shanghai affair, the consul—a solemn fool with no soul—wanted to ship me back to the States like a returned empty, but nothing for me. I borrowed some money from him, giving him a check on Dad and skipped. I turned up in Colombo where of course I put up at the Galle Face, and went broke. Darned nice boys that bunch were. Fellow took me up to his plantation and made me so comfy I might have stopped there till now. ——, don't I sometimes wish I had! He was a white man, Jimmy Fergusson. I hope he's going strong and wonder whether he recollects the night the Tamil coolies ran amuck and old Tindley fell in the lake with a knife-cut through his pants?

Heard from Dad up in the hills. He was mighty peeved; seemed to have figured out that I ought to have become Emperor of China by this time, just because I was his son, bless him! But he was a sport. Sent some money as usual and a hint that when I was prepared to quit fooling he'd be pleased to see me, but not until then. He came from the South and by all accounts overheard when he was spinning yarns about the North and South with old Judge Blenkinsopp from Georgia, when mother wasn't there and I wasn't supposed to be listening, he had been a wild blade himself. I can recollect—guess I must have been about nine or ten—the dad sprawling his legs in a chair and pulling his long mustaches with his "By ——, yessir," "By ——, no sir," and deciding with much pride, that he was a pirate!

Singabulu turned up with an order from the Monomatapa that I was to walk about the compound for the people to see. Like —— I did. They're outside now, moaning and groaning their heads off, and there they can darn well stop until—

But I'm writing this to keep my mind occupied.

Well to go on. After Colombo I went back to China just in time to get mixed up in the Boxer rising. Then I had the idea of going back home by way of Europe, but got tempted and fell for a Thibetan expedition through meeting Sir Alfred Trent. The dad helped me again. The outfit ended by getting shut up in a Buddhist monastery in the Gobi where they proposed to make a one-night show of us for the benefit of the faithful. The British Indian Government cussed like blazes and had to send an expedition to dig us out.

Two years later I got back to Calcutta to hear of dad's death. That shook me up badly. It appeared from letters from sis that he'd dropped every darn cent—or pretty near—speculating. Anyway I'd have to work for my living.

That did me a mighty lot of good—I mean having to work for a spell. About that time I got a romantic bug in my head that I'd retrieve the family fortunes. You see the mater and sis had practically been sold up and weren't having at all a good time and as I seemed to be the only he-male around it seemed up to me.

With what little cash I had left I went off to South Africa, intending to find a second De Beers, arguing optimistically that if there was one there must be another. I was right, but it took me many years to find this place and now— I've got one pretty nigh as big as the Kohinoor right here in my pocket in a Bull bag, but I guess it'll stop there as far as I can see, and over there in a calabash—

I spent a couple of years around the Kalahari and the Vaal and learned lots of useful things, but I didn't get any nearer mending the family exchequer. Then came the Barotse expedition with you, Charles, and although luck wasn't with us, we didn't have a bad time, did we? I've got the scar of that pot leg on my ribs still. After you went to Europe and there was nothing doing in the company promotion business, I tried East Africa, still chasing stones.

I did find a likely pipe down German East, but couldn't do anything for I was too busy keeping a whole skin. I eventually got back as far as fifty miles from Nairobi, carrying a rifle with no cartridges and the clothes I stood up in—or rather lay down in, for I got kinder tired and went to sleep under a bush where a police-patrol hunting Nandi found me in time. Rescued again, you see! I never had any luck!

After that for a spell I really did have to work for a living—by work I mean for another fellow. Didn't like it at all. Since the Kalahari failure I had never written home. What was the good anyway? I couldn't do anything. They'd hear fast enough from me when— Well, it's mostly that way with our bunch, isn't it?

It was at Nairobi that I met Tom Perrinkle. He'd been all over Egypt, Arabia and the Lord knows where and lately he'd quit a surveyor's job on the rail-head and took me along for a prospecting-hunting trip. The hunting was fine, but the other was a dud. Tom was a white man right through and crazy. But what he didn't know about mining wasn't worth the trouble and he taught me heaps.

He left me there to make for Johannesburg via Delagoa Bay. He wanted me to go, but I'd had enough of the south. I didn't feel I had any luck there. You know the feeling. Finally I got a job on the rail through him. I tinkered and cussed for a year or more with no chance of getting out of the rut, and I was mighty sorry before I was through that I hadn't accepted Tom's offer.

Then I started up in Uganda with the few bucks I'd saved—yessir, I surely did save—transport running and trading. Worked it up some and six months later when I was so right up to the neck with the monotony of it—it would have taken twenty years to clean up enough to put the family right anyway—I got a fair offer. I dealt and cleared out. Where to go I didn't know.

A chance conversation in the hotel at Mombasa and the fact that a down-coast boat was in decided me to go south as far as Quilimane and see what was doing. No sooner had I landed on the mole than the first man I ran into was Harry Martin, whom you'll remember in Bulawayo. He's married—pretty little Portuguese girl—got fat in spite of the heat, and is running a saloon, hotel, ship-chandlers, and seems to have a finger in half a dozen outfits there.

In the evening when we were sitting on the *piazza* yarning, and I was fishing for news of any mining or other likely venture, he asked whether by chance I knew Tom

Perrinkle.

"Sure," said I.

"Thought so by your thatch," said he.

And then he told me that Tom had passed through some eighteen months or more before; he'd gotten a notion, said Harry, to go prospecting up to the northwest, toward the border of German East, where the country had never been touched by a white. He wanted Harry to go along, but he was married and all that and too fat to have any romance. Anyway, off went Tom. Then six months later Harry got a letter by runner telling what he called the craziest yarn he'd ever set eyes on. Tom reckoned he was on the road to find a second Kimberley. Of course this made me sit up and take notice.

"Where is he?" I asked excitedly.

"Kingdom Come probably, old son," returned Harry in his heavy, funny-man style. "He wanted me to go in with him. I don't think! Those days are past for me. Anyway, he wanted a lot of gear sent up and I sent it, and that's the last I've heard of him from that day to this."

"Oh, my ——!" I groaned. "If only I'd have come down with him!"

When I pestered him for details, he grunted, and clambering out of his chair, fetched a packet.

"Read the crazy loon's nonsense for yourself, only if you'll take my advice you'll let it be."

Sitting under the light from the window, with a Portuguese wailing a love-song to a guitar somewhere around, I read this letter:

Kalambwi's Kraal.

My dear Martin:

You're a lazy sinner, loving too much the flesh-pots of Egypt. Only to the righteous and the energetic are the true rewards of virtue! Hasten, thou sluggard and gird up thy loins, pick up thy staff and follow in my footsteps, while the way is yet open! Tell your charming wife that indeed she shall have diamonds far too large for her coral ears and for a pendant a cluster that shall strike blind the eyes of the envious as a too little reward for granting you leave of absence!

To reduce to vile terms of commerce and barter understandable to your ears coarsened by much trafficking with the wily Portuguese and the simple native, I can not descend farther than to invite you to become co-director in a claim that's going to make old man Eckstein, Rhodes, Beit and that common crowd look like lousy beggars on the steps of Our Lady of Sorrows in the Plaza.

I am trying to hunt up something that will put some ginger into your carcass, you unbelieving son of Satan, for I shall want some one to help me support fat Midas. I shall be so —— rich that I shan't have a soul in the world with whom I can possibly be on speaking terms!

Proofs, foul heretic? All right. I've got them here in my hand. Suppose I've got to tell you everything, else there won't be an earthly chance of moving you. Here they are.

Well, first of all, the whole thing happened as a direct reward of my well-known virtue and interest in matters not of this world and all that sort of thing. A week ago I ran into an Arab from Zanzibar just near here. A nice old man, Tippoo Tib style, making the works of Allah beautiful throughout the land and so pious that he doesn't have to be able to read in order to quote the Koran backwards and forwards—for which much praise to said Allah.

Well, we did a bit of trade and afterward over coffee—where do these swine get their coffee? I'll swear it was real mocha, but I was too interested to ask. Afterward, over said coffee, we became engrossed in dispute as the fathers would say. I found his theology differed something exceedingly to that current in Arabia and Egypt; it seemed to be a special brand of his own. I'm big guns on Islamic law, which probably you never guessed. The dispute waxed mighty and I, not having a Koran on me, defied him to show reason, cause or justice according to the sacred words of Mohammed.

The gray-bearded sinner, only too willing to confound the heretic, fumbled somewhere around his fat belly and dragged forth a small book with a filthy worn cover, with odds and ends of charms attached, as they have in some parts. Solemnly opening the book on his knees he appeared to quote a passage of a sura confirming his contention. I told him that I could read Arabic and begged him to permit me to see the passage which I maintained was garbled out of all semblance to the original. Triumphantly he handed the book to me with one henna nail on a paragraph written in—now what d'you think?—French!

Had I not had the habit of the Arab manner I should have given a yell of derisive laughter, but for the sake of curiosity to know what it was, thinking at first that it was perhaps a translation in French, I pretended to consult the alleged oracle of divine wisdom written in such a crabbed tiny hand that one might forgive a man who couldn't read a word in any language, for thinking that it might be Arabic, Sanskrit or Chinese.

I wonder he didn't hear my brain machinery start off with a whirr. I squeezed some sense out of that paragraph and a few others and did a hundred yards mental sprint in less than ten seconds. I pulled a face and told him I was forced to admit that he was right. He was tickled to death—but not so much as I was.

I made pretty remarks about that wonderful copy of the Koran and various observations regarding the antiquity of the text and begged permission to look over it. Turning to the end casually I had all I could do not to start an Irish jig and kiss the wily old sinner at the same time. After fossicking around as much as I dared, I returned the book, remarking that I wished that I had such a splendid copy. I duly noted how he rose to the bait by the faint gleam in his watery eyes.

I hung around making love to old Mahmud Ali for a week and more before I struck. Then saying that I was going on *safari*, I casually asked to see the wonderful book once more, dallied about, admiring the filthy cover and the charms, and said half laughing that I'd rather like to have it, and how much did he want for it. Of course he said it wasn't for sale. But I knew better. Is there anything an Arab has, except his wives, that isn't for sale? But it took me three more days and cost me three loads of goods, but— Oh, had he known what he'd been carrying around for —— knows how many years! He swore he'd had it since a young man and had taken it from a slave who had had it as a fetish. Quite likely the old boy wasn't lying for once.

I know, oh romantic one, you're fuming in the heat and wanting to know what it was anyway! Ah, ha ha! and also cube-root ho! ho! The body of the "Koran" was the diary of a Frenchman. First part uninteresting; ordinary fossicking about and what not.

But, about half-way through there's an entry at Tete where he had met a Jesuit who had told him a yarn that had made him so excited that most of it I couldn't read.

The next entry, two days later, he had sobered down, and gave facts. It appeared that the Jesuit had been talking about the early martyrdom and all that of their order in Africa and in the course of the narrative had mentioned the first Jesuits who had penetrated into the interior by the river Cuamba. These three had managed to get into the "middle of Africa" according to him, had established a station there more or less and then had been strangled by the Monomatapa.

Gonçalo da Silveria was the name of the leader and they had managed to get out reports to their superior in Chindé, who duly sent it on to the then governor-general of Portuguese East Africa, which was at that time under the vice royalty of Portuguese India, at Cochin, the Dom Affonso Gonzalvo d'Alboquerque the son of the Grande Affonso.

This had happened in 1561. More than two hundred years later along came Dom Francisco Jose Maria de Laçerada e Almeida—about 1797—as local governor. He was an energetic blighter apparently, Portuguese or no, and conceived the idea of establishing a chain of stations right across the continent from Portuguese East Africa to Angola on the Portuguese West.

Before starting on this trip he had naturally read up the archives and came across the account of the three murdered Jesuits and their report to the governor, in which it was incidentally mentioned that when building their hut on the ground which the Monomatapa had given them, they had found some whitey-green pebbles and had noticed the peculiar color of the ground, a kind of yellow-bluey clay, they described it. Oh, oh, to think of it, the sweet innocents!

They didn't know, but Gonçalo, the old dear, imagined that they might be diamonds and begged leave to send two as big as a pigeon's egg as samples, which, if they so proved worthy, be given, one to His Excellence and the other as an offering for his preservation in Africa to the Blessed Lady of Sorrows in Sofala. Makes one positively ill, old man!

What became of the specimens as big as pigeons' eggs, history doth not relate; probably stuck in somebody's podgy fingers on the way. Well, all this was given *in extenso* for that dear old Mathurin le Coq had laboriously copied—evidently translated—from a copy which the Jesuit had made from the original in Cochin. This was sewn up in that wonderful Koran!

Now, you rotten unbeliever! More? All right!

Well, Dom Francisco Jose Maria de Laçerada e Almeida was a merry soul and evidently thought that a Pride of Africa would look well in his august sovereign's hatband and bring him considerable preferment as well as those stones which might go to grace his own manly beauty and purse. His letters to a friend in Quilimane were unearthed by our friend the Jesuit and revealed several interesting items.

The chief is that his excellency the Dom after traveling up the Zambesi beyond Tete, their most westward station, arrived at a river running north—the Shire—where he did a little private exploring, cunning old ——!

One letter says that they had come out upon a lake—Nyassa obviously—and were following it. The last letter from him states that they have left the lake for the east and have been marching for fifteen days; he is in great hopes of reaching the

Kraal of the Monomatapa, with the help of the Virgin, the site of the murder of the three holy martyrs on the morrow. He's great on religious concern for the Christian reburial of the bodies—as if he actually could have expected to find their two-hundred-year-old bones—and then complains bitterly of ill health and much fever, and adds inconsequently that he had the day before obtained a round pebble from one of his servants, who had picked it up in the dry river-bed where they are encamped and which he is sure is undoubtedly a diamond.

After that he disappears. The only trace of his fate can be found in the archives which states that Dom Francisco and all the rest of it, died of fever in Central Africa in 1798.

Isn't that enough to stir your sluggish blood, you great ox?

Well, it was enough for our friend, Mathurin le Coq. He seems a pious sort of ——, for he attributes the find to the direct act of God acting presumably through the Jesuit. Anyway he started getting things together immediately. He doesn't say exactly whether the Jesuit was in on the venture, too, but it sounds like it from the help the priest gave him.

Well, the rest of his diary is a brusk account of the trip, direction, approximate mileage, tribes encountered, scraps; a map—pretty crude, it's true—is pasted in the book as well. Yes, and the stones are there all right! He describes the ground as "sewn with stones as thickly as the altar of Notre Dame de Paris," which tells where he came from!

The last few entries are concerned with his arrival at the Monomatapas, who "received him very well" giving rich presents of ivory and who he comments, had not the faintest idea of the value of the pebbles scattered about the dry river-bed near the kraal. Seems a pretty big kraal, by the way, and the country around densely populated. What price labor, old dear?

The very last entry is written in a fever-shaken fist and reports sickness. Quite possibly the poor —— went under as Dom Thingummy seems to have done. Still they didn't know as much about malaria as we do now and it can't be worse than the coast anyway.

Now, if you don't think this is good enough and twice more, I do! Are you coming? If you don't—well you shan't play in my palace yard!

But seriously, man, up sticks and come along. Lord knows there's enough for a squadron of Rhodeses. On a trip like this one wants a good partner, one who's acclimated and knows Kiswahili and a bit of the lingo. If you won't, of course you won't and that's all. But I'm —— sorry if I can't shift you. You're just the man who would fit in. —— marriage! There, I can't help it, but that's what to my mind always ruins a man. If it wasn't for that charming little girl of yours you'd come running, —— you. A real good sport is hard to find. I'll wait here until your runner returns.

I had a red-haired young blighter with me up East and wanted to bring him along, but the silly ass wouldn't come. He'd suit splendidly but I can't waste the time to get him down.

By the way, I'm enclosing a list of gear I want and a draft on da Gama. Shove it off quickly. If you should come in, we'll double the order and fix up your own outfit.

By-by, you unbelieving heathen.

Tom Perrinkle.

P.S. Double that cigar order. The Lord knows when I'll get a chance to renew it.

Imagine the effect on me, old man! The dream of dreams, and one of the best in the world waiting to welcome me there! Besides, hadn't old Tom asked for me? How I cursed the fool hunch that had headed me off! You bet I didn't waste two seconds in deciding. At last, I thought, I can go home and do the prodigal son stunt in style and provide the fatted calf my own little self. I even wrote a letter to the mater and sis, I was so up in the air about it. I'm sorry I did so now.

Of course, old Harry grunted and croaked like a dismal married raven about not having heard from Tom for all that while. "———," said I, "why, you boob, he's too busy digging up Kohinoors to write!" As I was a bit shy on the outfit for a venture like that, he butted in handsomely in goods.

Thinking things over, and I did nothing else all day and three-quarters of the sweaty nights, I was fully alive to the benefit of having a good partner. I was certain that if I could locate one, Tom wouldn't kick at all, for as he had said, "there's enough for a squadron of Rhodeses!" But as far as Harry knew at the moment there wasn't a likely man he'd trust farther than he could throw him, in Quilimane.

I determined to see it through alone and, moreover, to travel straight for Kalambwi's kraal—Harry found me a boy to take me—and pick up Tom's trail. Without the Frenchman's map—and Tom hadn't remarked where he had started from—there was no use in following up the Zambesi and Shire on the Dom's trail.

Of course it took more than a few days to get together the *safari* and besides I had to wait for a few things to be sent up from Delagoa. On the Sunday following who should turn up but Jack Wheeler from British East, where he'd been some four years. He seemed a good sport, was a good shot, and spoke Kiswahili. I didn't know much of him—just casually in Nairobi, but I knew that you had known him in the police in Rhodesia, and Harry as well. He was looking for a job. Harry suggested it, I liked the cut of him, and I thought it was a God-given chance.

Harry had a great big dog—Lord knows what breed, cross between a mastiff and a wolf he looked—which he told me I could have as he was too much of a handful with women around. If I filled him up with arsenic, said he, we might get him through the fly belt and maybe he'd live. Wheeler looked at the beast and remarked that he'd be a nuisance on the trip if he was savage. I laughed and said casually, "Oh, don't be an old woman! I'll break him in."

The next day Wheeler turned up with a young yellow beast about as big as a collie, and asked politely enough whether I'd mind his bringing the dog along.

"Sure," said I, "if one don't get through maybe the other will and they'll always be mighty useful as camp dogs. Maybe we can train 'em for buck hunting."

So it was Kopman and Oompie came along. We fixed matters up and on the second of February, 1912, we started out from Quilimane.

Night, old man, I'm going to quit for my wrist aches like ———. They're busy with the drums tonight. Sometimes they get on my nerves.

Last night I had a fit of the blues, regular southern ones, if you know what I mean. Wanted to lift my head and howl wolf fashion, just the same I've seen a darky do way down Louisiana way. Then I got mad; talked to myself as a fellow does alone. If I only knew what's happened to Tom and the others. That's the thing that drives me crazy—

Just fed, and like an animal, which I seem likely to become, I feel better. I'll go on with the yarn and forget things maybe.

Well, we got clear of the Qua Qua River and hummed along fine. I was mighty pleased that Wheeler could sling the bat, as you Britishers say. He seemed a great kid and we'd sit yapping about what we'd do with the dough we were so sure to clean up. I told about Tom, what a great fellow he was, and the times we'd had, and swapped the usual camp-fire yarns.

Wheeler's dog would lie at his feet and proved a friendly beast, but Kopman was as Harry had described him, a devil dog. He'd growl even when I fed him and the first time we had the inevitable difference of opinion I had to tie him up and thrash him with a sjambok, with a gun in my left hand in case he broke loose, for he'd have surely had me. After more than several arguments he took it into his savage head that I was boss, but the nearest he'd ever get to being pally was to sit beside me and show his fangs as I patted his great skull. He wouldn't have anything to do with anybody else and treated Oompie as some kind of no-account stiff who had somehow wandered into camp.

Five days out we were well into the lion belt and had to tie the dogs up at night. At the scent down-wind or the roar, Oompie would crouch and whimper, but Kopman would stare savagely into the night and growl steadily. Harry had said he was reported to have tackled and killed a hyena on his own. I was scared lest he'd make a break and go for the nearest lion and get his back broken for his trouble.

The next night we were camped by a small river and had built a *zareba*, for the boys were jumpy about the lions. About eight we were sitting by the fire listening to a fellow roaring about half a mile away and the continuous growl of Kopman, when suddenly Wheeler grabbed for his rifle lying against a camp chair and I noticed Kopman's mane standing erect. Listening, we heard close to the *zareba* fence the low *wough* of a lion.

"That beggar means mischief," said Wheeler. "Let's go after him."

"Don't shoot except for a sure shot," I warned, as I took my rifle and shouted to my headman, Gambazi, to get a brand from the fire.

"Lie down, you fool."

I was swearing at Kopman, who was straining on his chain pegged to the ground, when I heard a shout and Wheeler fired. Then came a scream and a hubbub and I saw in the gleam of the fire a tawny mass dragging away a native. I leaped over a camp chair and running, fired for the shoulder. As I jerked at the magazine, the beast rose at me. I turned to dodge, tripped over a calabash, and came down on my face in the fire. I was conscious of a growling noise and a grunt, yells from my boys and a shot as I scrambled through the embers and out the other side.

When I rose I saw the lion on the ground and Kopman with his fangs buried in the wind-pipe. Expecting to see one blow of the terrified paw rip the dog open I raised my rifle, but heard Wheeler shouting: "All right! Got him!"

Kopman, breaking his chain, had charged the beast as he was turning to grab me, and almost simultaneously, Wheeler, not six yards away, had fired, getting him behind the left ear. I had to lambaste Kopman with a pole to make him let go the dead beast and then he wanted to turn on me. The boy had been badly mauled in the thigh and I found that my shirt sleeve had been ripped and that I was bleeding from a flesh wound in the shoulder-blade. Rescued once more, you see.

"Thanks," said I to Wheeler, as we returned to our fire, "you and Kopman sure saved me some trouble."

"Kopman!" he answered with a laugh. "Why I had to fire —— quick to save you both!"

I glanced at him, not liking the tone and the way he had said it, and felt, too, a bit humiliated. Of course I didn't take any notice, merely thinking afterward that he hadn't got much tact. From that moment he seemed to take a violent dislike to Kopman. Why, I couldn't understand as the brute wasn't his anyway.

One evening, after we had gotten out of the lion belt and Kopman was loose, I heard him growl and came out from the tent to see Wheeler with a block of wood in his hand as if about to heave it at the dog, who was lying crouched for a spring with bare fangs. As I called to the dog to lie down, Wheeler turned away. I said to him quietly:

"Say, old man, I wish you'd leave the dog alone. He didn't try to go for you, did he?"

"Oh, he's a swine," retorted Wheeler, as he walked to the tent. "Best thing you can do with him is to put a bullet in his head."

I stared at him for a moment wondering at the evident viciousness of the tone, and then, thinking: "Oh, he's got a touch of malaria! Forget it." For fellows do get cranky, you know, with a temperature.

Well, we went along quietly after that outwardly, although there was an irritation rising underneath. Wheeler, to my disgust, began to sulk and if there's one thing I hate, it is that. I'd rather have a man who flares up and spits out his grievance than one who hugs it to himself all the time. He marched alone, swearing at Oompie if the beast got anywhere near to Kopman, would answer in monosyllables and generally looked so glum and depressing that I longed to kick him. I seriously thought about sending him back, but I couldn't find any valid excuse and it was rather late for that.

The trail up to Kalambwi's wasn't very interesting; very little game and a lot of thin timber uninhabited and not much water. We did it in ten days, not bad going, for the men were pretty well loaded up, as I had taken as few as I could. There I had reckoned to get another crowd to go on with, as I thought it probable that Tom had done.

But on the first interview with the old man I found that there was going to be a lot of bother. Tom, it appeared, hadn't taken any men from there, or Kalambwi said he hadn't; anyway, they seemed to have a rooted objection to traveling northwest and to carrying loads at all.

However, they weren't much good, being fairly poor specimens hereabout. I decided to do my best to persuade my Quilimane men to come on with me and started negotiations right away. Of course, knowing or guessing that I was in a hole, they promptly started asking fantastic prices. However, after many *shauris*, I secured half of them and persuaded four bold lads from Kalambwi's to take a chance, which only necessitated leaving a couple of loads behind.

On the second day, who should turn up but Mahmud Ali, the fellow from whom Tom had gotten the wonderful Koran. I saw his caravan coming in as I was going to the *kraal* for a *shauri* with the chief, guessed who he was and wondered who the young Arab was with him. When I got back I found them both, and he turned out to be the Mahmud's son, Hafid ben Ali. During the palaver I carefully kept away from dangerous ground, merely inquiring whether he had met Tom, who was a friend of mine, and had heard what had happened to him.

Mahmud replied that he hadn't seen or heard of him for a year or more, when he had left from this same *kraal*, going prospecting to the northeast. To forestall the inevitable question of our destination, I volunteered the information that we were going to follow Tom's route. Mahmud thought that there was little likelihood of pay stuff there, and we went on talking about other things.

After they had gone, I said to Wheeler, for I hadn't foreseen the wild chance that had brought Mahmud there as we were passing—

"Say, don't forget if they come over rubbering round to keep up the yarn about our following Tom's trail to the northeast."

"Why?" demanded Wheeler, in his obstinate way. "What's the use of that?"

"Why, this fellow is the very man from whom Tom got the Koran with the Frenchman's diary in it and the other papers. Didn't you tumble when he came over? Naturally he'd be mighty sore if he knew."

"No," replied Wheeler, who seemed genuinely surprized. "Never entered my head."

The next day I had to go over for more talkee-talkee and when I got back there were the two Arabs again. As I walked into camp I saw by the expression on Wheeler's face that something was up. He was jabbering away excitedly and examining something lying on the camp table.

"Look, man, look at this!" he exclaimed, as I was exchanging the usual salutations with the two Arabs, and strewed over the table were about a dozen or more small gold nuggets. "This fellow's found an alluvial bed somewhere near the headwaters of the Lurio. I vote we go there!"

I made a pretense of looking at the samples, wondering why an Arab should go out of his way to put an easy fortune in our hands for nothing, and immediately became suspicious. I thanked him for the hint, talked vaguely about the place, the kind of ground and technical things. As soon as they were gone, Wheeler turned on me excitedly.

"Look here, I'm for going after that! That's pretty certain, but this diamond outfit— who knows whether there's anything in it at all."

"Aren't you fool-proof yet?" I retorted. "D'you think that Arab is going to shove a fortune in your pocket for nothing? Wild horses wouldn't drag the secret out of him if he had located such a find! Good Lord, you are simple!"

"Simple or not," he returned angrily, "I can see as straight as most, and if anything's more simple-minded than making a wild goose chase on the crazy hopes of your friend Perrinkle—whom you haven't even seen or heard of since he started out—I'd like to know it. Why, you haven't even seen a sample or any —— thing, and here this fellow has something to show at any rate. Harry Martin wasn't such an ass as to swallow the bait as you did."

"Why did you come then?"

"Because I wanted a job and —— well had to."

"Thanks," said I, dryly, "but if you feel like that about it you'd better go along with your Arab friend."

At that he went up in the air.

"All right, I will," said he, "if you'll let me have the goods and guns."

"I can't possibly do that," I retorted. "It isn't reasonable. You agreed to take a job with me, and it was mighty fair. You get your wages, win or lose, and twenty-five per cent of all findings. What you've got to holler about on that I don't know."

"Bah!" he snarled, turning away, "you knew that —— well when you said that."

He went off sulking and I felt mighty sore. "Bright kind of pard," thought I, "for a trip like this," and wished to —— I'd tried it out on my own, as Tom had done. The rest of the two days before I could get away he spent most of the time in the Arab's camp fiddling about with the gold nuggets, which seemed to have turned his head.

After dinner on the evening before we were due to leave, Wheeler, who was staring sulkily at the fire, smoking, said grumpily—

"You won't reconsider going round by the Lurio to look up that place, Harvie?"

"Can't you see it's impossible?" I retorted, a bit sharply perhaps, for I was getting riled with his sulky business. "I started out on this and I'm going to see it through."

He scowled and kicked a log irritably, but didn't say a word. I fell to wondering dismally what was going to be the end of it; for I felt that it couldn't go on indefinitely. I studied him furtively, there in the dim light of the fire, speculating as to what was the real cause of his filthy temper—just sheer cussedness, I reckoned, a kind of kink some folks are born with—yet he'd seemed such a sporting kid way back in Quilimane. But then that's always the way. You never know a man until you're out of civilization.

Next morning, as we were striking camp, and the men were squabbling over their loads, he suddenly grumbled something about saying a word of good-by and stalked over to the Arab's camp.

"Lord!" I reflected, as I watched him going, "how I wish he'd stay there!"

And he was so long in showing up that I had begun to think that he had deserted at the last moment. Then, just as I had decided not to wait any longer, but to give the order to march, a shot rang out, followed by commotion in the Arab's camp.

"Of all the crazy boobs!" I muttered, as I hastened over. "What idiocy has he done now?"

By the time I got there I found him at the entrance of their *zareba*, in the middle of an excited group of natives, with Mahmud and his son jabbering their heads off.

"What the ——'s the matter now?" I demanded in English, as I came up.

"Caught one of these —— little rats trying to steal the bolt of my gun, and let him have it."

"What! You've shot one?"

"No," he snapped. "Missed!"

"But how the mischief could he steal—"

"Left my gun outside the tent while I was talking to Mahmud here. He's cutting up nasty about the swine."

I joined in the debate then. We adjourned to the tent and wasted three hours with the two of them. Mahmud appeared to be absurdly angry over the three drops of blood the fool Wheeler had drawn from a Somali's forearm. In the end I had to pay two blankets by way of compensation. All very annoying and irritating and moreover, Wheeler, in his insane way, seemed to think that he was the injured party, and I was hard put to it to keep the peace, for the fool could easily have landed us in a serious scrap had he killed the boy. What the man had wanted to steal a bolt for I couldn't comprehend, although for a Somali, to whom stealing is second nature, it was feasible.

The presence of a white man in this part of the world was so rare that it was a time-mark in native life—therefore I had little difficulty, in this thickly populated district, in tracing Tom's movements of a year and a half ago, usually finding at each village some one to act as guide to, or to tell me the name of the next.

For the first few days out Wheeler seemed to have forgotten the craze for gold and also his resentment against me, for he had got rid of his fit of the sulks and talked camp-fire chatter at night as he had used to do. Even at Kopman he would good-naturedly make faces and swear that he ought to be kept in a cage.

Except in a more or less permanent camp we had shared the same tent in order to avoid the nuisance of pitching and striking every night and Kopman slept on the outside of my camp-bed and Oompie on the outside of Wheeler's. On the night of the fifth day out I got up about four-thirty, and went outside, and as usual Kopman followed me. Oompie, who was not so well-trained, followed. I was looking at the half moon above the trees and wondering vaguely what had happened to Tom when I heard Wheeler shouting irritably:

"Oompie! Oompie! Come here, blast you!"

A few feet from me the dog was standing investigating a bush. Again came Wheeler's voice. Suddenly he darted through the tent door, shouting almost shrill with rage:

"By ——! I'll shoot that ruddy beast!"

I saw the gleam of the barrel of his revolver. A swift pang of rage sent me in a leap toward him.

"Don't be a fool," I commanded him, standing between him and the dog. "You're crazy, man!"

"I'll shoot that blasted beast of yours, too, for two pins. It's his fault, I'll shoot him, by ——!"

"What's the matter with you?" I demanded. "Naturally my dog followed me and Oompie came after him. Don't fool with that gun, and go to bed."

I walked past him calling to Kopman. I heard a quick step and Wheeler sprang after me. In the light of the hurricane lamp hung to the center pole I saw his eyes glaring insanely.

"By the living ——!" he shouted. "I'll put a bullet through you!"

My gun was under my pillow, but I turned and looked at him as he pointed his gun at me.

"You're a fool, Wheeler," I said quietly. "Go to bed and don't be childish!"

Then I turned my back and rolled on to my bed, sliding my hand on to my own gun as I did so. I heard his breath coming fast. As I turned, ready to shoot, I saw him throw his revolver on to the bed and sit down suddenly. Then I pulled up my blankets and rolled in. Two minutes afterward I heard him sobbing.

"Good Lord," I thought, startled and kind of scared, "the fellow must be going crazy." Listening to a big man weep like a kid is one of the most horrible things I've ever heard.

Next morning I felt very much warmer toward him and half expected him to hold out his hand and say, "Sorry, I made a fool of myself," or something. But no, never a word. He avoided my eyes and rapidly developed a fresh fit of the sulks. That made me so mad that I began to have regrets that I hadn't taken the legitimate opportunity to shoot him when he pulled on me; also an active hatred of the man began to work, a combination of disgust and contempt.

A couple of days later, when we were halted for a spell on the top of a ridge, I was staring down the trail. To my astonishment I noticed another caravan coming along. At the first moment I had a wild hope that it might be Tom, but obviously he wouldn't be following me up. I didn't say anything to Wheeler, as I wasn't in the humor, and let the caravan go on. Presently the stranger emerged from a bit of scrub into the open again. I counted about thirty porters and then in the bright sun distinguished the robes of several Arabs or Somalis.

"Good Lord," I thought, "it must be Mahmud—and following me!"

It wasn't very likely that another Arab party would be on my trail. I drew back and went on pondering suspiciously upon what it could mean.

Sure enough, at that evening's camp, which happened to be a water-hole without any village near, the caravan toiled in, and at the tail was Hafid ben Ali, Mahmud Ali's son. Mighty queer, I thought, and waited.

I feel very tired. Malaria coming on, I think. Couldn't resist looking at my bag of stones, and thinking what it would mean to the mater and sis. What had happened to them, what were they doing— Good ——, we could pretty nigh buy up Georgia. I've thought myself nearly crazy trying to find a way out. Force is obviously impossible and these ——. But, oh, what's the use? The other fellows— You'll see. Perhaps. Well, if you don't, your literary executor, if you have such a creature, will. All a question of time. And for me, too, I guess. But in the mean time I've got to stick to my job. Really does me good. Kind of feel as if I were having a chat with you, old man.

I recollect I was mighty sick that night. I mean when Hafid ben Ali turned up. The very first thing I noticed was that no sooner had the caravan arrived than Wheeler looked cheerful. I hated myself for it at the time, but just naturally I became suspicious. What was this Arab camping on my trail for? To me there seemed only one answer. Wheeler must have talked. Thought I, the son-of-a-gun will come nosing over here in half an hour. I'd better get it over and know what I'm doing at any rate.

"Say here, Wheeler," I said. "Frankly I'll be almighty glad if we have a straight talk."

"We've had several, haven't we?" he retorted.

"Not on your life! Now, what's this Arab doing skulking jackal style behind us?"

"I don't know."

"Well, I do. You must have talked. Is that right?"

"Talked! Haven't said a word!"

"Maybe not directly," said I. "Now look here, play the game. Did you or did you not tell him that we were out for Tom's find?"

"You told him yourself that we were going to follow Tom's trail," retorted Wheeler. "Maybe he wants to find Perrinkle to get that Koran back!"

"Ah!" I exclaimed, "then if he knows about the Koran he knows what's inside it. You must have told him."

"I've never said a word about the Koran. I may have said something about his crazy idea of finding diamonds as big as rocks."

"When?"

"Oh, before you barged in that first day. Wasn't my fault. How was I to know that he was the fellow? I've never said a word since."

"Of course, you —— fool! That's why the next day he came along with that fool yarn about the placer up the Lurio way, and you wanted to fall for it. Why, man, he knows Tom is no fool. If he could have tricked us into going northeast, he'd have been free to follow this trail same as we're doing. Oh, my ——!"

"But he's got a perfect right to follow the same trail as we have and—"

"Oh, ——!" I snapped, turning away, "he's got a perfect right to go to ——, and you, too!"

I was mad. The man was that dangerous combination, half knave and half fool, the type most difficult to counter because you never know which is going to turn up, the fool or the knave.

However, Hafid didn't turn up, and I requested Wheeler to stay in camp, an order at which he scowled but obeyed.

The most irritating part was that of course the Arab had a right to follow on my trail—thanks to that idiot's wagging tongue. I couldn't order him away and neither by the look of his outfit was there any sense in working up a fight. I wished that I knew exactly how much the Arab did know. The most dangerous thing that I could see was that he might bribe or scare my men into deserting me.

All I could do was to keep my eyes skinned and trust nothing to Wheeler's romantic vision. At each camp I forbade any stranger to enter the *zareba*, but about the only one I could trust on that score was Kopman and I took pains to let everybody know that the dog was loose at night.

You can imagine what it was in a situation like that. I confess I began to be suspicious that Wheeler had made a secret bargain with the Arabs and that the row over the man who had tried to steal the rifle bolt was a frame-up to put me off the scent, but since then I don't think that was so; pretty sure it wasn't. But when your nerves get worked up, your judgment's apt to stray, and, anyway, many a man has gone to the chair on less evidence than that.

For a week we plugged along almost without incident. Sometimes Ali would camp near, at others he wouldn't turn up; but never did he make an attempt to call on us. All the time I was trying to work out a scheme to throw him off the scent; even considered going back on my tracks to see if he'd leave me, and then make a detour. But there were two things against that—one was that my provisions and ammunition weren't unlimited, and the porters might kick; and, secondly, he was just as capable, if not more so, of following up Tom's trail.

About two days after that, I think it was, Wheeler brought matters to a crisis. We had both been out shooting for the pot in different directions. When I came back he was sitting by the fire. There was something wrong I could see by his attitude. I noticed that his dog Oompie was not there and as I came up, said pleasantly—

"Hello, where's Oompie?"

He raised his head, glared at me, and rising to his feet, snarled—

"Shot the swine—and it's about time I did the same for you!"

"Say, here," said I, firing up, "you'd better take back those words."

"I won't. But I tell you what I will do. Take that rifle of yours and I'll take mine, and we'll fight it out at a hundred yards. Whoever comes off takes the kitty."

" 'Re you crazy?"

"I'm not. But I'm fed up with you and your —— dog as well. You never liked me, and, by ——, I've no time for you. Things can't go on like this. You called me an old woman. No man'll do that!"

"Called you—called you—what?" I stammered, flabbergasted by the idiotic accusation.

"An old woman—back there in Quilimane—you've called me a fool a hundred times."

I stared at him, simply unable to grasp right off what on earth he was driving at. I thought for a second that he had gone insane, but he didn't look it—not more than usual.

"Old woman!" I repeated inanely.

The repetition seemed to infuriate him the more.

"That's what you said before and by ——, you'll pay for it now. Come on, you cur!"

He reached for his rifle lying against a camp-chair. Then it dawned on me that he was serious. I leaped and kicked the gun he was reaching for and stepped on it.

"Say, here, Wheeler," said I, "this is about the worst thing we could do with natives around, but you insist on it, and, by —— you'll get it. It's not a rifle you'll have but your hands."

And with that I threw my own rifle from me and smacked him across the face.

He was game all right, the more's the pity. He came for me like a wounded leopard. But I guess I've been in a few more rougher rough-and-tumbles than he had, and I was real mad. I realized, too, that I'd got to smash him badly or else he wouldn't know who was boss. I did. At the finish, because he insisted upon it, I was compelled to put him out.

I hated the whole performance, with the natives standing around watching. I'd have given anything to have avoided it, but— While he was recovering, I again indulged in idiotic hopes. Now, thought I, we've had it out, we'll be real pals.

No, sir. What he did, as soon as he was fit, was to come up and say:

"Look here, Harvie, will you accept that challenge with the rifles or not? One hundred yards to the death."

"You crazy boy," said I, more or less good-humoredly. "Haven't you had enough?"

"Will you, or not?"

"Sure I won't."

"You're frightened," he began.

"Say," I interrupted, "if you want another hiding, you'll get it and quickly."

"That isn't the point. You licked me, I'll admit, but I can't stop with you after—"

"Go to blazes!" I snapped, disgustedly.

"I'll not. I'll join the Arab over there rather than stay with you."

"Join who the —— you please," I retorted, turning on my heel, "only get out of my camp!"

He did too—within twenty minutes—merely taking blankets and rifle. As I saw him going I very nearly ran after him, wanting to cry, "Come back, and don't be an idiot," but I knew that it would have been of no use. And anyway I hadn't forgotten his wanton murder of his dog. One thing he had said had been true—that we couldn't have gone on like it. Of course the effect on the camp was bad. The natives couldn't understand either the fight between the two whites or the one going over to the Arab camp. In the evening I recollected that several weeks' wages were due to Wheeler, and with a few other things I could spare, sent them over to him. I thought he might refuse, but he didn't. My boy came back and said that the *bwana*, who was in the tent feeding with the Arab, had taken them without a word. Although I really regretted the affair, I did feel more comfortable that night. Kind of peaceful without that sulky face mooning about, liable to blow up at any moment sort of feeling. A possibility I thought of but dismissed, as I didn't reckon he was yellow anyway, was that he might plot with the Arab to get me out of the way.

Next morning, when I broke camp, to my astonishment there was no sign of Hafid and my late partner moving. Probably, I reflected, that silly young fool's so haughty that he just can't bear to march within sight of me, or possibly he's come to his senses and realizes what a fool he's made of himself.

We were now coming to the end of the thickly populated district, and from the reports of the natives, faced a long trek through an uninhabited region, fairly dry and with no game. That night, Wheeler and Hafid didn't show up, so I had the local chief to myself. I heard that Tom had passed through this very village and found a man who would show me the trail for a day's march.

I tried to get him or another to come along as guide, but again came that reluctance, more pronounced, to traveling in that direction. Having noticed this before, I had throughout kept my men as much as possible away from contact with the local people, knowing too well that some superstition was often quite enough to start a panic of desertion.

Somehow I detected myself seeking an excuse to stop over a day to see whether Wheeler, on coming up, would make an overture, for the longer I thought about it, the less I liked the idea of a white in company with an Arab, particularly a hotheaded fool type such as Wheeler.

However, I marched only a couple of hours later than usual next morning, having seen no signs of the other caravan. That day I noted the mean direction of the trail, for all native paths wander almost around the compass. I found it to be north northwest by west and on that course I determined to stick.

That night I kept my ears open, and as I had half-feared, detected an uneasiness among the porters grouped about their fire, where was the local guide, due to return to his village on the morrow. I remained awake the whole of that night to keep an eye upon them. Even then, when daylight came, there were the four Kalambwi men missing, and the local native as well, in spite of the fact that he hadn't yet been paid. I sent my headman and a few whom I thought I could trust, to beat around in the long grass and scrub; but they only succeeded in bringing back one, who confessed that the guide had told him that the people on the other side were wicked and that the country was bewitched.

I herded 'em all together and gave 'em a lecture, a combination of threats and alleged proofs that my white medicine was stronger than anything that these wild people could possibly have. The Quilimane boys, being a little more sophisticated and impressed by the doings of the whites, with the aid of many presents promised their allegiance if they stuck it through. As they were all pretty well loaded up, and particularly as I needed to make good time, I had to abandon some more loads. However, I had some consolation in the hope that the panic would spread among the Kalambwi men who were with the Arab.

For five more days we made good going, seeing nothing at all except the interminable light timber-scrub, no game and scarcely a bird. The last village had reported variously upon the distance to the inhabited country, some saying six days and others twenty. Throughout I hadn't seen a sign of the Arab's *safari*, which almost made me wonder whether he had given up the chase. Naturally I often speculated as to how Wheeler was getting along with his new partner and what sort of terms he had made with him. Yet I couldn't help but feel relieved that he had gone.

The following day, I think it was, I noticed that Kopman was doomed—the fly had gotten him, in spite of Harry's arsenic preventative. The staring coat and a slight discharge from the nostrils were sure symptoms. I pumped some more arsenic into him—when I had him bound and chained—but that would only hold him together, I knew, until the first rains or he got wet.

That same night we were camped in a slight clump of trees by a dry river-bed, from which water was obtainable by digging. I hadn't bothered to put up the tent and had my bed under a big thorn-tree. I dropped off to sleep earlier than usual, and waking from some sort of a dream, saw above me the enormous fangs of a monstrous jaw, shadowed by the moon on my mosquito net. For a moment I was paralyzed with terror. Then I recognized Kopman standing on the bed with his forepaws, yawning. I laughed at the fright I had had and patted him, at which he growled in his friendly manner.

After lying awake for some time, pondering about things, I heard him growling slightly again. But then he always grumbled if a boy moved to throw another log on the fire. I quieted him and dropped off to sleep. The next thing I knew was Kopman's bass roar mixed up with a shriek.

I scrambled out of bed, revolver in hand, and saw that the dog had some one down a few yards away. Yelling for my boy, I seized Kopman by the collar and with trouble dragged him away with his chops covered in blood. Just as I was thinking that the beast had made a fearful mistake, I caught in the moonlight the gleam of a dagger and the contour of the face of the man, a Somali, whose throat had been entirely torn out.

From whom he was a messenger I had no shadow of doubt. I knew also that, although I hadn't seen him since the village, Hafid ben Ali must be camping somewhere upon my trail.

Naturally my thoughts turned to Wheeler—yet I was sure that he hadn't had any hand in such a dastardly attempt at murder. Then another idea flew into my head. If this Arab was so determined to remove me, why should he not be equally anxious to get rid of Wheeler?

The time was twenty minutes to four. The moon was due to set about five. Taking Kopman with me, my rifle and revolver, I set out on the back trail, determined to see Wheeler and demand explanations from the Arab. But as I reviewed the situation, I saw that I couldn't do anything. Probably Wheeler wouldn't know anything about the matter; the Arab would merely swear that the Somali didn't belong to him and I couldn't prove it. However, I walked on steadily until daylight, with never a sign of the Arab camp. The country was flat, with light timber and scrub, so that he might be camped within half a mile. On the other hand, he might be two days behind me and had sent on this murderer so that he'd be well out of the way in case the attempt failed. I swore and went back.

Feel more cheerful to-day and had a better night. I think scratching away at this all day is a relief. Lord, I'd give weight for weight in stones for tobacco! Old Singabulu came in this morning for a long chat; think he means well and would help me if he could. But do what I can I can't get any information out of him—just says nothing or starts talking about something else. He's very curious to know the manners and customs of whites in their own country, Somewhat difficult to explain for want of objects to liken things to. Appears the Monomatapa is getting better. Nothing was the matter I guess but overeating. Wish there would be and then I may get a chance—

Well, after the Somali episode I made my head-boy take it in turns with me to stand watch at night, four hours each. The more I worried about Wheeler, the more I thought I ought to halt for a day; yet there was always the uncertainty of water ahead. I slugged along for another three days and then quite suddenly came upon a native path and signs of long abandoned fields, and then upon a small river, with permanent pools of water even in the dry season.

I camped there for thirty-six hours, to give the porters a needed rest, but Wheeler and Hafid did not show up. The day I spent in fossicking in that river-bed, but nothing promising did I find. The next morning I saw smoke and within an hour we were approaching a village, which I saw at a glance belonged to a different tribe from the Kalambwi, for it was heavily stockaded and placed in a strategic point on a bend of the river.

Our coming seemed quite unexpected, for the women working in some outlying fields of *rupoko*, immediately set up the shrilling which is the sign of the approach of strangers, and took to the bush. Immediately, inside the village began a commotion. A drum began to tap out a message. In the customary manner I halted my *safari* and advanced with my head-boy carrying my stool behind me.

A hubbub arose as they saw us, and through the narrow gate stalked a tallish warrior, wearing a trade shirt, and armed with a spear and a Martini rifle. The fellow's carriage and build reminded me of the Zulu. At ten yards from me he halted and held up a hand, crying a greeting. I replied in the customary way, and after a short parley, he led me into the *kraal* and to the club-house in the center, about which were clustered some fifty warriors and many women. Seated on a mat was the chief, a wrinkled old fellow, evidently of great age.

The *shauri* proved most satisfactory, the chief expressing his pleasure at seeing a white man, offered me a hut, and intimated gently, that all strangers were expected to go straight to pay their respects to the Monomatapa—which was nothing out of the ordinary. I made him a few presents and then pitched my camp near the *kraal*. Scarcely had my men got busy than food and chickens' eggs, milk and calabashes of *rupoko* began to arrive on the heads of the women.

"Fine," I thought, as I smoked my pipe that night, feeling more than a trifle excited.

"Seems a hospitable guy and sure I'll be glad to see the Monomatapa, as according to those papers of our French friend, that's where the stones are."

I wondered, too, whether Tom had come through this village or had struck the country at another point, but I, for policy's sake, didn't dare ask until the morrow.

The first shock I got in the morning. Intending to stay there that day, I had taken the luxury of having my coffee in bed. While I was drinking it, I heard a terrific discussion going on outside. I called my boy, Gambazi, and asked what was on. He said he didn't know and would go and inquire. However, I slipped out myself to my table. I saw Gambazi talking to them and then they all turned and came in a body to me. Their headman calmly announced that they didn't wish to go any further. I asked why, but they immediately began to prevaricate, maintaining that the agreement had been as far as the next inhabited country. They were right; that had been the arrangement. I replied that they would have to wait until I had had a *shauri* with the chief about getting fresh men, and they went off grumbling.

However, much to my delight, the chief made no trouble at all about it, promising me as many men as I liked to take me to the capital. I asked him casually about Tom, but he said that he had never before had a white man at this particular village.

I went back to camp in great spirits and paid off my porters cheerfully. Lordy, I thought, if it's going to be as easy as this, probably Tom's just cleaned up what he wanted, sent a letter to Harry which never reached him, and went on to Nyassa and out that way home.

Wheeler and Hafid didn't show up that evening, and I began to wonder what could have happened to them. Possibly all their Kalambwi men had deserted, as had mine, and they had had to go back. That was quite feasible. Perhaps, too, that was the main motive of the attempt at murder—to stop me getting such a long start at all costs.

I had told the chief that I wished to start the next morning, and sure enough, with the sun came the number of porters required. They were not, I noticed, of the same tribe as the warriors, probably slaves, which would account for the Kalambwi's mens' terror of the Vealanga, as they called themselves.

The change in the country was abrupt. The timber grew thicker, a park-like country, open grass glades and thick clumps of big trees; and the population grew denser at every mile, mostly small villages but all close together, surrounded with fields, and swarming with life. At each village I was well received by the headman and always offered a hut, which I invariably refused on account of the usual inhabitants.

After the second day I noticed that the villages were no longer stockaded; only, I reckoned, the frontier ones, revealing, for a native tribe, some powerful government which eliminated any inter-tribal warfare so common in Africa.

For four days we followed the depression of the river and for two days more were traveling over undulating open country in which was much cattle, the small native kind, of course. Once, I recollect, when drinking some warm milk straight from the cow, which I'm crazy about, I felt as if I were a bird of bad omen. For they seemed a peaceful, happy people and I knew well what would happen immediately if these new diamond fields were known to the white world. I partially decided then and there that when I had had my fill, I would never reveal the place to anybody. Some one else would discover it in time anyway.

Then we struck the river again or rather I think another one, into which the other flows. It was bigger and had a slight flow of water as well as the deep permanent pools. This river I am sure must flow into Lake Nyassa. Three days later, after passing through a denser population than ever, we arrived at the *kraal* of the Monomatapa. As Le Coq had, according to Tom, hinted in his diary, it was mighty big for this part of the world; contains, I reckon, fully two thousand huts, spread around the king's enclosure in the center.

I gathered from the warrior who had been my guide that I would be expected to occupy a large hut which, as was the custom of the king, was kept for the use of foreign guests. Fearing to wound his royal susceptibilities I accepted this time. Among the streets of huts, well-constructed somewhat after the beehive Zulu style, I noticed several oblong ones, speaking of Arab influence, belonging to notables.

The royal compound, containing, as I afterward found out, some four hundred huts and houses, was perched on a slight butte dominating the town, and the walls were of heavy stakes with fire-hardened spikes. As, with my rifle under my arm, Kopman at my heels, and Gambazi following with my stool at the van of my little *safari*, we passed through the gate, roughly fashioned of hippopotamus tusks bound with fiber and copper wire, into the compound, and whom should I see, sitting in the shade of a hut than Hafid ben Ali.

"The swine!" I thought. "He must have made a detour by forced marches and gotten around and before me."

I walked straight up to him, with my gun handy, and greeted him curtly. He responded very civilly. Then I demanded:

"Where is the white man who was with you?"

"As Allah is great!" he returned quietly, meeting my eyes steadily, "he hath been taken by a lion the fourth night after he left thee."

A lion! I hadn't seen a trace of a lion in the whole country since the Qua Qua river valley on the coast. Yet what could I do? I daren't call him a liar and shoot him out of hand. Apart from the fact that I hadn't any proof, such an act here would have entailed trouble instantly. I turned on my heel and walked on without a word. "Poor ———," I thought, "he certainly paid mighty heavily for his crack-brained temper."

Dreaming about you, old man, last night. Seemed we were in New York having a high time on the Madison roof, and all of a sudden Singubulu and Kopman walked in. Nobody seemed at all surprized, and then somehow, as in dreams, you disappeared, and sitting there all dolled up, was the Monomatapa. I've been looking over Le Coq and Murchison's diaries again. Does me good somehow to know we aren't alone. Gregarious animal, man, eh?

The guest chamber turned out to be quite a decent hut, with a compound to itself. Even was there a charpoy—bed frame made of crossed reims—for Gambazi to sling my blankets on. "Sure!" thought I, "this fellow's no piker!" It was well that I had some considerable Oriental training, for a fellow has to have a well-developed streak of patience in dealing with such folk, and to sit there for the three days demanded by the infernal etiquette—pinched from the Arabs by the way—while there was a young Kimberley, as I imagined, sitting on its hams around the corner, yipping for me, and not show a ruffled hair of anxiety, took some doing.

The first annoyance was that I had to stop in my own abode like a prisoner, not being allowed to wander even around the town until the Lord of Water Elephants—Monomatapa—had duly given me leave. All the time, too, I was tortured by wondering what that darned murdering Arab was up to. Of course I speculated a lot about Tom, but I was fairly satisfied that he had long ago cleared out with a nice load.

An old man with a gray mossy tuft of beard, called Singubulu, who was master of ceremonies I afterward discovered, looked after me, superintending the women who brought food, chickens and so on, and politely asking my wishes, none of which could be granted, except relating to such food as they had.

On the first and second nights, there was a —— of a hubbub going on around me in the king's quarters; drums going and some kind of stringed instruments, and the usual howling and chanting, which was, Singubulu informed me, the last of the marriage celebrations of one of the Monomatapa's numerous sons.

In the afternoon, I saw from my open door, Hafid ben Ali passing, evidently going up for an audience. He saw me all right though he pretended not to. Anyway, I can sleep peacefully, for with Kopman by my bedside, he's not likely to try to pull off any more murder.

It occurred to me that he couldn't possibly have arrived very long before me, so I wondered why he, too, wasn't in a guest house. I asked Singubulu and learned that an Arab is not treated like a white man. The idea rather flattered my vanity and I thought that I would probably be able to do more with the Monomatapa than he could.

On the morning of the fourth day, old Singubulu routed me out at sunrise to go see the king's minister or *katikiro*, as he is called in Uganda. Inside the great compound are other enclosures, one within the other. I was led to the second from the interior one, in which I could remark the largest house I had yet seen in the town, oblong in shape, which I reckoned must be the royal residence.

The minister I found seated on a carved wooden stool beneath a large tree, surrounded by quite two hundred chiefs and courtiers I supposed, mostly dressed in skins and feathers. He was a huge, powerful man, in the prime of life, inclined to a belly, very black and more negroid than the men about him. He was wearing a dirty white robe and a filthy fez cap and on his large wrists were bangles of iv—

Singubulu interrupted me. After a long palaver about nothing, he wanted to know whether I would let him have a small piece of my hair. I couldn't see any harm in giving it to him. Then I suddenly thought that I ought to make him pay for it by giving me some information. I told him that if he'd tell me what had become of Wheeler and the others, he could shave my head if he liked. Nothing doing, although the temptation was big I could see. All this took about two hours of *shauri*. However I've found something that he dearly wants. The utter inability to get anything out of them, the torturing uncertainty gave me an awful fit of depression again. I shall be mighty glad when—well, when I do know something at any rate.

Well, the first minister accepted my presents and my statement that I had come to visit his country with a grunt and a sniffing cough. He has some kind of asthmatical affliction. I went on with the usual preamble of compliments and the rest of it. In return, he explained to me very earnestly, backed by grunts from his warriors, what an extremely important person he is, ruler over uncounted men from his sacred person to the sea, but that he was delighted to have a white man, of whom he had heard so much, come to visit him.

Of course I was burning to start negotiations for permission to explore the river-bed, but etiquette and custom forbade any such attempt at a first interview. However, I presently mentioned that I had had a friend who had set out to visit him some twenty moons ago, to which he replied that he had never seen him.

This gave me a shock. What! I thought, Tom never got here. What could have happened to him? Perhaps, after all, this wasn't the right place—and my heart sank. Yet possibly he had turned aside and gone off somewhere else, although that wasn't like him in the least. Maybe he had fallen sick and—

But I daren't reveal any surprize and turned the topic to a mild request for permission to see the town, to which I was given a grunted assent.

After I had taken leave I was followed by a man carrying a tusk of ivory and a calabash. I couldn't think what the calabash could contain and dared not look until I was alone in my guest chamber.

Honest to ——, at first I thought I had gone insane and then I nearly swooned—for there were seven stones as big as pigeon's eggs, diamonds beyond question!

Man, have you ever held in your hands a fortune beyond your wildest dreams? Not a possibility but an actual fact—indisputable. As I sat there on the bed, holding those seven dull pebbles, such ordinary looking pebbles to the lay eye, that a man would have kicked them aside. I think I became hysterical. My imagination went crazy. I saw the mater and sis with a palace on Fifth Avenue and a place at Bar Harbor, the old family estates in Georgia brought back, regardless of price.

I was the owner of a thousand-ton full-rigged yacht with auxiliary steam, to continue wandering about the earth. If I'd had a girl I should have probably suffocated her in diamond pendants as big as walnuts. I know that I laughed so much that Kopman growled at me.

What insatiable greed a man has! It never even occurred to me to be content with that handful of kings' ransoms. I steadily set in to get more drunk on the possibilities that the river-bed would yield. How to wait until the morrow for the interview with the king I didn't know. I recollected, of course, all the most favorable extracts in Tom's letter of the Jesuits' reports, the diamonds as big as pigeons' eggs! And holy smoke, wasn't it true?

What had happened to Tom disturbed me little in my orgy of greed. I took it for granted that as he hadn't been here at all, as the minister of Monomatapa had said, that he had foolishly gone off on some other venture. Never mind, he could have fifty per cent, of what I got for having put me on to this Solomon's treasure.

I laughed again at the naiveté of this black potentate, giving away enough wealth to buy his own kingdom several times over. Seemed a shame in a way, like taking candy from a child, or worse, as this child didn't even know that it was candy at all.

I thought of poor Wheeler, too, and called him a fool again in my intoxication, for having been so childishly silly as to quarrel with me. Lord, hadn't I used the restraint of a saint? Hadn't he provoked me beyond endurance? Darn shame, the poor kid! Anyway, I'd see that his folks, if I could find them, should have what would have been his share.

Oh, what a pig man is! Immediately, I confess, I began to hedge; for I saw that if I went fifty with Tom and twenty-five per cent to Wheeler's folk, only twenty-five would remain to me and that seemed mighty unfair. Solemnly I reduced Tom's share to twenty-five and Wheeler's to ten, and all this on the supposition that I was going to dig at least a sackful of diamonds, as big as the ones I had in the calabash, from the river.

On the top of that came another panic. What was that swine of an Arab doing? Had the Monomatapa given him such a present? Singubulu's statement that Arabs were not treated as whites comforted me. But I had visions of the fellow down on the river, busy with pick and shovel and sluice; could see his excited eyes, as he picked out the great pebbles.

Well, with such idiotic dreams I tortured myself all through that sleepless night. Morning came and with it I had to fight to keep the glitter of greed out of my eyes. Not to miss any melodramatic act, to keep up the native ignorance of value, I scattered the diamonds in a corner by the overturned calabash, as if they weren't worth looking at a second time.

Singubulu nearly drove me crazy by not turning up until nigh ten o'clock. I swear I was sick with anxiety and excitement. After the usual maddening preliminaries, he mentioned that on the morrow I could perhaps be able to see the Monomatapa himself. I think that I considered myself the greatest diplomat the world had ever seen when I retorted that there was no hurry, perhaps the day after would suit His Majesty better.

Oh, the torture! However, I was free to wander around the village and suggested that he should accompany me. As soon as he had assented I was stricken with fear for my diamonds lying scattered on the floor. Some one might steal them! Hafid ben Ali might have the nerve to call and lift them, of course. Yet I couldn't gather them up and put them in my pockets before Singubulu. After an agonizing moment I solved the problem by tying Kopman in the same corner, adding what I conceived to be a master stroke by kicking the pebbles behind him.

On the whole of that stroll through the town I was just aching to edge toward the river just for the sake even of a glance to see what it looked like; but I knew that I was only permitted to walk within the confines of the walls or small fence which ran round the outskirts. As we passed the street by which I had entered, I noticed that the house where I had spoken to Hafid ben Ali was deserted. The deuce, thought I, with a pang, he's busy hard at work down in the river-bed, and refrained from asking Singubulu for fear of allying myself in their minds with the Arab's ambitions.

However, I did manage to see the river from one portion of the town built on a slight cliff, and was rewarded merely by the sight of a deep pool of water, where the only thing I could see was a couple of hippo asleep in the shallows opposite.

Throughout the walk I was naturally regarded with considerable curiosity by the women and children, although the few warriors and notables I encountered evidently deemed it beneath their dignity to be astonished or to show any interest. As we passed along the palisade of stakes I noticed, stuck on the spikes over a door made of the tusks of the hippopotamus, some half a dozen human heads. As I drew near, I was surprized by the amount of hair for a negro, and then gave a gasp of surprize, for they were the heads of Hafid ben Ali and his men!

For a moment the ghastly objects gave me a shock, and I couldn't resist asking Singubulu what he had done to be so honored.

"He is an Arab!" replied Singubulu, simply.

Thank the Lord they don't treat Arabs as white men, I reflected, recollecting Singubulu's information, but all the same I walked home to my hut in a much quieter mood.

Been down with a dose of fever for six days. Luckily I still have quinine—although don't quite see what it matters anyway. Singubulu wanted me to have some herb concoction the natives use and I took it. Don't know what it is but it surely makes you sweat some. Feel rather shaky and despondent in consequence.

Sitting in the guest-hut, after meeting the heads of Hafid ben Ali and his men, I grew kind of reflective for a bit. If Hafid had murdered Wheeler, as I suspected, he had surely been revenged. I tried to figure out the whyfor of it, but couldn't find any satisfactory conclusion except that the Arabs might have wiped out a bunch of this tribe at some time or other, and they had continued a death feud against them. But then if that had been the case, Hafid would have known and not strolled up with such a small *safari.* Another alternative was that the slaughter had been committed at the whim of a savage despot. The fact made me recollect the strangulation of the three Jesuits in 1561. I became still more reflective.

Yet the prospect of vast wealth, nay, vast wealth lying actually in your two hands, is a powerful tonic, and I began to grow optimistic before nightfall. 1561 was a long, long time ago, and in those days whites were not so uncomfortably close. Nowadays, even such an independent chief would surely think twice before outraging a white, and as Singubulu had said, they treated white men differently.

A horrid suspicion that perhaps Tom had been murdered was soon eliminated by what seemed an obvious fact; if they had been murdering anybody lately, their skulls would surely still be on the stakes of the enclosure, for by such I knew the Africans put much store and prestige. After all that wasn't enough to spoil my sleep, and now there was no fear of a Somali trying to knife me, and Hafid wasn't digging my diamonds, which was some comfort anyway.

The next morning I went for a stroll on my own around the village. Nobody molested me, and as before seemed to avoid looking at me. I noticed that every time I appeared near an outlet from the village, there were several armed warriors within a few yards. Might have been coincidence, but I was mighty sure it wasn't. I couldn't refrain from some morbid curiosity from passing by the royal gate which was festooned with heads. They were just stuck roughly on each spike, which was black with clotted blood, and as I looked I started, for the second on the left bore a startling resemblance to the Somali whom Kopman had killed. Of course it couldn't have been that man, but might probably have been a brother.

The following morning, Singubulu turned up and informed me that the Monomatapa would receive me in "grand audience." I didn't quite make out what he meant by the phrase, and he explained that that meant "in the Sacred House upon the hill," which I took to mean the big hut I had remarked within the innermost enclosure. Then he hinted that it was not etiquette to carry arms with me. I didn't like that, you bet— particularly with the recollection of Hafid and company's heads decorating the gate through which I would pass.

I pretended to acquiesce and slipped my revolver in my shirt, and as I had already locked up my stones in my steel box, to which I tied Kopman, I announced that I was ready. Singubulu conducted me up through the compound as far as the same enclosure where I had been before, which was as far as I could see empty, except for the huts and houses. Then, leading to the right, he urged me into a large hut, which was hung with charms of various kinds.

I jibbed, demanding to know whether the Monomatapa was inside. Singubulu replied that he wasn't, but that before seeing him within the Sacred House on the hill, I would have to be disenchanted. Now I didn't know very much about native superstitions, but I had run against the frequent one of the devils that are supposed to be attached to whites and strangers generally, and usually even before entering a country they will have some sort of a ceremony, either squirting some mess on you or killing a cock and burying it or something of that sort, so that I wasn't very much surprized, thinking that it was the ordinary nonsense.

Inside the hut was very dark, foul, and full of an acrid smell from a fire in the center, around which I could dimly make out the forms of some dozen men, dressed up in feathers on their heads, evidently witch-doctors, who were chanting in a scarcely audible voice. I was made to sit down on a mat right in the draft of the smoke, which made my eyes smart and caught my throat. Singubulu, squatting beside me, whispered to my dismay that I must open my shirt so that a magic potion might be rubbed on my throat. I thought of my gun and contracted my belly muscles as I obeyed, to let it slip as far down as possible.

The door was shut and we were almost in darkness, save for the glow of the fire. They went on chanting for some time, with me I coughing and wiping my eyes. Suddenly a figure arose and began to yell incantations. Some one threw some stuff on the fire, which crackled and emitted clouds of bitter smoke which stung my eyes and brought on a furious fit of coughing.

Then I felt something hot and sticky thrust upon my wind-pipe. More smoke poured in my face. I felt suffocating, but tried hard to stick it out. The fumes died down and I made out the vague figures around the fire chanting their heads off. And how they stank! I don't know how much longer it was, but I know I was conscious of the fleas getting busy before Singubulu whispered to me to rise. Then, as I gladly did so, I clutched at my shirt. My revolver was gone!

It was only by a great effort of control that I didn't begin hitting out right and left, but I instantly knew the futility of such a course. The man who'd taken the gun would be out of that dark hole like a cat if he wasn't already. I swore to myself and stalked out without a word, knowing that my only chance was to pretend that I didn't know.

As I stood blinking in the glare, Singubulu urged me toward the next gate. I obeyed, trying swiftly to work out what the game could be. Evidently, I argued, it couldn't be that they wanted to murder me, for they could have done that a dozen times. Seemed to me that the thief had been either some enterprising witch-doctor, who had taken the opportunity to get a good bang-stick with six voices, or else it was a regular polite way of protecting royalty.

The next gate was practically the same as the first, but with higher and heavier stakes. Inside that I passed between two quite large houses, oblong, and apparently built of sun-dried bricks, each having a large and long veranda. Some fifty yards beyond were two big trees, between which we walked, and came upon a magnificent fence composed of elephant tusks with their points turned inward to my surprise, as usually they were employed the other way as a protection against storming. Immediately outside this gate, constructed, only more elaborately, of hippopotamus tusks, was a tiny oblong hut, but three feet high, with doors of tusks, too.

As I passed through I admit I glanced about uncomfortably to see whether there were any more decorations in the form of skulls. But there was none, to my relief. Within, and standing alone, in a space some thirty yards in diameter, which was the crown of the butte, was a large hut with ivory doors, the exact replica of the tiny one without, which I then recognized as the devil-house, provided on the principle that if you don't entertain his satanic majesty he will come into your own house, the inference being that the said devil is fortunately so stupid that he doesn't know the difference between a real house and a doll's.

To my surprize, the place seemed deserted. Singubulu led the way toward the large hut. I followed and entered, expecting to see the Monomatapa seated within, probably with some of the doctors or nobles.

The interior was very dark. As I blinked, a scuffle of feet caused me to wheel and rush out of the door in time to see Singubulu bolt through the gate like a rabbit into its hole. Suspecting treachery and on the impulse keenly aware that now I was unarmed, I raced after him.

On the threshold of that gate in the ivory palisade I was brought up by young women standing with their long-bladed spears presented like a solid phalanx of Roman soldiery.

As far as I recollect, I stood and stared like an idiot at those women. Young they were, all of them; muscular and well-made; nude, save for jackal-skins from the waist, and their woolly hair was dressed into a cone. At first I couldn't grasp the fact—I mean that they were women balled me up entirely. Their spears were long and ugly and they evidently meant business. As I stepped back to reconsider, a drum broke out just below and a screaming yell, followed by a continuous chant. The women stood there, six of them, like statues.

I looked around at the ivory fence and then I understood why all the points were turned inward. To vault over them was impossible; to climb them would be some job, and meanwhile you could be speared as easily as sticking a fork in a pie.

I walked boldly up to the entrance again and made as if to walk through. Instantly the three women leaders jabbed within an inch of my body. I suppose we are so biased by our point of view that I could scarcely understand that they would injure me; for they were women. But that workmanlike stab reassured me on that point. I stepped back and quickly. Then I realized why the revolver had been stolen. I walked slowly around the enclosure of ivory tusks, with the points turned inward, and as I did so I noticed that two of the armed Amazons accompanied me on the other side of the fence. There was no other outlet. I was trapped. But why? For what?

I sat down in the shade of the hut veranda and stared perplexedly at the one entrance. Just without, three of the women squatted on their haunches, half-balancing on the haft of their spears. I tried to solve the mystery of what was intended but could not arrive at any satisfactory solution. The first thought had been that they were going to hack off my head as they had done Hafid's and his men's, but then I had seen him going up from his house in the village only a few hours before his execution. Yet there was time for that, I recollected uneasily, for the sun was high.

When something really dangerous threatens, sometimes you feel curiously calm; almost indifferent. I did then. I had an illusion that I was thinking things over very quietly. Women, I kept on repeating. But why women soldiers? Were they going to cut off my head that afternoon or not? That was the most pressing question. Unarmed, what could I do? I blamed myself bitterly for consenting to leave my rifle behind and allowing my gun to be stolen. But then, had I had it, I reflected, they would have probably knocked me on the head or speared me right away.

Then said I, what am I going to do? Obviously stop where I was. Women or no, I wouldn't have a dog's chance of passing through those savage females unarmed. The drumming and chanting was still going on. To celebrate my capture, I supposed. I looked vaguely at the hut, which seemed well constructed and to be kept in good repair. I got up and walked around it and found another door on the other side. From there you could see the roofs of the whole town, the fields, the deep pool of the river, and the forest beyond. Glancing down I noted another darned female figure squatting outside the ivory fence, watching me through the interstices.

I walked inside the hut. The interior was large and lofty. On the floor were native woven grass mats. As my eyes became accustomed to the shade, I remarked a number of objects around the walls. Then I started. Among them I had first recognised my own steel dispatch box and suit-case, and upon it the calabash containing my seven stones! Beside these things was every article of mine, with the exception of my rifles. They must have speared Kopman as soon as I had left. I sat down on my own trunk, bewildered, trying to solve the puzzle. Staring round I got another shock.

Alongside the wall was a long steel uniform case, much battered, that I knew well; I scarcely had need to glance at the half-erased initials T.P. to know that it had belonged to Tom. The panic of fear that seized me at the sight was confirmed as I saw beyond his helmet, khaki breeches and leggings and all his clothes, down even to his darned socks. In a swift glance I noticed that his were not the only things. The hut was like a lost property office.

My hands were trembling as I opened Tom's box where, on the top, as if hastily thrown in, I found his diary, which seizing, I almost ran out on to the veranda to read.

Here I interpolate that part of Tom Perrinkle's diary, dating from his departure from Kalambwi's *kraal*:

Feb. 15.

Martin's runner came in today. The blighter won't come along as I thought. —— his eyes. Dear old Mahmud left three days ago. I was torn between laughing and apologising when he went, for he's quite a sportsman in his way. I almost suspected that he'd spotted something when he happened to ask whether I had found the copy—of the Koran— interesting. Of course I said, "Yes," bless his heart. Still he'd do me for every cent I had, had he half a chance, but all the same I suppose I'll send him a decent commission out of what I find. Tried to get a few extra boys from Kalambwi, but the old scoundrel hummed and haa'd and finally promised, but none turned up. Says he will send for some, but I won't wait as I can get along fairly well without them. Extraordinary sunset, green, purple and gold, unusual in dry season.

Feb. 21.

Belt of Kalambwi's people finishes here. Reports say anything from seven to twenty days to people of the Monomatapa, who they say is wicked, which on closer investigation appears to mean given to slave-raiding. Going carefully through Le Coq's diary I see that he quotes some one as saying that the Monomatapa once ruled as far south as the Cuamba, the Zambezi evidently. From his description of their physique and customs, they seem to be an offshoot of the Zulu; possibly an earlier immigration than the Angoni and the Matabele. Interesting. Been studying his crude map. He came up on the Dom's trail, but I think that I can't be far wrong in calculation and must certainly strike his trail if not the Monomatapa people, who can't even now be so small that you couldn't hit 'em.

Feb. 25.

Beastly going; monotonous scrub and ragged timber; very bad water. Porters getting fed up. So would I be if I didn't know there was something at the end. If it turns out trumps and a quarter as good as Le Coq makes out I'll have more than enough to fit out the South American trip. If it isn't, I think I'll chuck up Africa all the same—for a while anyhow. But still I feel in my bones that there will be something there; enough to run home; have some hunting and give Kitty a surprize. Quaint how a man can't leave a woman alone! She certainly didn't play cricket with me, but yet I'd—oh Lord, probably if I met her I'd be cured: would see she's got old or something. Still I'd take the risk. What a —— fool a man is! And what bosh a man writes—in Africa!

Feb. 27.

Scrub giving more to timber. Tempted to spend a day fossicking in what looked like auriferous reef. Looks like striking a river soon. Porters fairly done in and I have driven 'em a bit not knowing how long this patch would last. Still the beggars have done more than this in their lives. My favorite pipe got plugged and that —— fool of a Martin forgot to include cleaners. Haven't got any wire so I'll have to try grass which always breaks. —— business.

Feb. 28.

Came on old plantations three hours after sunrise and very soon struck a *kraal* fortified; noticed that type of warrior corroborates my Zulu theory. Formation of spear and battle-ax confirms. Chief young and rather cheeky, but apparently obliging. Speaks a curious Makalange dialect but with most obvious traces of the Zulu click in it. Have a distinct class of slaves evidently recruited from surrounding tribes and using a distinct dialect in consequence. There's a *spruit* here but typically waterless, save for pools in dry season but no signs of likely blue or yellow ground. Sewn with granite outcrops and ordinary quartz which hold up the water for the pools. Forgot to note that this is undoubtedly the people of the Monomatapa.

Chief gave me amusing lecture, recounting that the Monomatapa was ruler over uncounted warriors from his sacred person to the Cuamba and the sea, and contemptuously asked me how many soldiers my king had. Bless his little heart, it will be a sad day for him when he finds out, and if what Le Coq says is true I'm afraid it will be jolly soon. However, he promised the extra porters required and they turned up on time, too. That confounded pipe blocked again. —— Martin!

March 2.

Soil rich and fertile here, heavier growth of trees; thickly populated. This is undoubtedly the district as described by Le Coq. Much agriculture and cattle but observe all work done by slaves, the warrior class and their women neither working nor apparently intermarrying with the subject race. Slight promises of auriferous outcrops here but no time to prospect, and besides don't wish yet to let them have an idea that I'm after minerals. One hopeful sign is that they all deny having seen a white, which probably means that none have been here since Le Coq's time, and anyway he came in from the lake, following the Dom's trail.

March 13.

Monomatapa's *kraal*. Arrived on the tenth day. Biggest *kraal* I've ever seen among the Bantu; population must be somewhere about twenty thousand, counting women and slaves. Very hospitable. Have guest-house well made and kept. Old man, one Singubulu, detailed to look after me; kind of master of ceremonies, I presume, after the Baganda model. Town built on bend of river, which must flow into Lake Nyassa. Running water and deep pools, although I have as yet only glimpsed it from the town. Can't say it looks promising, but there may be pans near by which Le Coq described as sewn with stones like the altar of Notre Dame de Paris. Good for his shade may he be correct! Must have been hard luck to peg out of fever just as the Dom did apparently. Doesn't appear a particularly malarial country either.

March 18.

Saw the Monomatapa's headman today. Big brute of a fellow, looks almost pure Zulu; much more so than the Angoni. Gave him the usual presents and never had such a shock in my life for in return he gave me a tusk of ivory and a calabash containing seven almost flawless stones and each one as big as a walnut—each one a small fortune. No fuss about it at all. Apparently haven't the slightest idea of the value. I examined them cursorily and asked if he had more like them to trade and was told that I could have as many as I liked. Don't understand it. Seems uncanny. If they have no value to them, why should they give them as presents? Some white must have taught them that white men like them. Le Coq? That might be a feasible explanation. Sitting here in the guest-hut I feel almost scared—new for me—at having fortune thrust into my hands in this effortless manner. Good job I'm not superstitious.

March 20.

The mystery of the diamonds is explained. I'm a prisoner, but apparently kept for some *ju-ju* practise, whether cannibalism or not I can't find out.

It began two days after my visit to the prime minister. During the night my revolver was stolen. The following morning Singubulu came to take me to see the Monomatapa himself, but I was not allowed to go armed and couldn't possibly conceal a rifle. They put me through the usual witch-doctor disenchanting and led me to a lone hut within a palisade of ivory tusks and suddenly left me alone. On trying to get out I was met by a guard of Amazons, who I learn from Murchison—cold-blooded brute—are the king's official wives and sacred. This is the way that Le Coq went out unless he died of fever before they got him here, and the other man Murchison as well as the Dom, for in this *ju-ju* house are all their effects apparently on the customary principle as applied to kings and sacred bodies generally that all their belongings are possessed by powerful magic. True, none of their or my guns are here, but they may combine, as they often do, common sense with religion, and keep them in a special house. I have no weapon of any sort except a hunting-knife but am fashioning a kind of dagger out of a hippo tooth, of which the doors are made. The fate of the Jesuits haunts me.

March 21.

The drums have started in full blast. I think Murchison's speculations are right, for this is the end of the second quarter of the moon and tomorrow night will be the full of the Autumnal equinox. I have made every attempt to get away but those beastly women are there night and day. It's a —— way to go out. Wish I hadn't read Murchison's diary, which makes me feel more uncomfortable than ever. Well, I've warmed both hands before the fire of life, as some one said—was it Fielding?—but I'm —— if I'm ready to depart—not *à la* Jesuit anyway. If worse comes to the worst, I suppose I'll contribute these notes to this strange library of the dead.

(written hurriedly in pencil)

March 22.

Screaming, yelling, howling! They're coming. *Vale!*

(Brandon Harvie's diary continued)

Guess any man would feel bad when he hears of his best pal's death and receives a death sentence at the same time. I sat for a long time with that worn little book in my hand, staring out into the dancing heat upon the river.

What I thought, I don't know; seemed stupefied. Kind of suffocating feeling as if you were enclosed in a small box, yes already, or in a coffin. Yet how had he died? *À la* Jesuit? That was not by any means sure. Fighting? How would I die? The date I knew was about March tenth, eleven or twelve more days to live.

I was disturbed by a woman's voice calling from the entrance. Some calabashes had been placed just within the gate and she bade me eat. Eat! Ugh!

I fell to thinking again. The drums were still throbbing away. But somehow my brain wouldn't work. I could see flutters of pictures of the murder of Tom and then ourselves. But the other man of whom Tom had written? I went inside, found another steel uniform case and in it carefully packed besides books of notes, one bound in vellum marked, Diary. "Sir John Pratte Murchison," which I took out on to the veranda.

(Extracts from diary of Murchison)

May 15.

Ujiji—Heard most interesting account from Major Albrecht the political officer here. Appears genuine and a splendid case of totemism, the hippopotamus being the symbol; also of the most complete system of divine autocracy of which I have ever heard. The Monomatapa, Lord of Water Elephants, derived from the totem, as the ruler is styled, once entered into office, is said to disappear from mortal ken inasmuch as he becomes a hippopotamus who lives in a sacred pool by the river, and yet possesses some hundred official wives, who are soldiers, and whose duty it is to guard the sacred dwelling. The inconsistency of the account is very typical of the native mind.

It is said that at a special feast, at the Autumnal equinox, the king is seen by his subjects, seated on his throne in the palace and is actually a hippopotamus talking in the tongue of man. Of course there must be some jugglery about this on the part of the priests.

Albrecht informs me that by repute, centuries ago, this Monomatapa ruled over an enormous kingdom extending from as far north as here and as far south as the Zambesi, but that now it has dwindled by the incursions of the whites to a relatively small area in Portuguese East Africa. It is supposed to be situated about Lat: 12, Long: 35. No white had yet visited this extraordinary relic. Whether the people are exogamous as totemic tribes usually are, Albrecht had no reliable information. This extremely interesting account he obtained from a chief in one of the most southern districts in their territory.

I have fully determined to visit this strange monarch. In any case it will not interfere greatly with my schedule, for I can return either across Lake Nyassa or round the north end and so on to Bangweolo. The opportunity is certainly irresistible. Albrecht will loan me a boat as far as the southern end of Tanganyika.

Bagaka. June 10.

Evidently this Monomatapa has an unsavory reputation, as I find it utterly impossible to obtain canoes here to land my expedition on the eastern shore of Lake Nyassa within five days' paddle, such as I have estimated to be about Lat: 12. Probably this is due to fear of being taken as slaves. No doubt this undiscovered tribe, who are still independent of the Portuguese, retain their old-time customs in the matter of slavery and other practises. This will indeed make them far more interesting, giving one a rare opportunity of studying the native uninfluenced by civilization.

June 17.

Have been here a week. Excessively annoying, but at last have discovered a way to avoid the land journey by buying the canoes outright. I can at all events depend upon the Wanyamwezi not to be influenced by the local natives, for they have both respect for their German masters and a stronger belief in the what they call magic of the white man. The rock formation here is curious. Paleozoic—

June 20.

Another three days wasted. Quite irritating. Even my Wanyamwezi, in whom I had such faith, proved restless. They protested at first that they couldn't paddle but as they come from the lake-shore district I knew this to be an impudent lie. However, after much bother and giving of extravagant presents and promises of more largesse, they have consented. My six Sudanese askaris and personal servants fortunately are impervious to the ideas of these savages, as they so amusingly call them. We start tomorrow morning.

It suddenly occurred to me today that I may better have gone to Bangeolo first, and then across to Nyassa, as then I should arrive at about time to witness the feast at the Autumnal equinox. I am rather annoyed with myself for this flagrant stupidity, as the fête must be most interesting indeed.

Kavabi's, Lake Nyassa, June 28.

We have been paddling six days, camping at night on the foreshore. Today we arrived at this village. Instead of, as I had imagined from the alarming reports that my boys brought me, finding a hostile people, they appear very friendly indeed.

Unfortunately no one in the village speaks Kiswahili and I am compelled to use Mohammed and I suspect that he is very much at sea with this dialect. The Wanyamwezi understand perfectly, but to have two interpreters is excessively annoying. However, there is no help for it. The chief *via* Malinko and Mohammed corroborates the report that as yet no white has visited Monomatapa. He is very polite, places a hut at my disposal and even offers to provide canoes and paddlers. This is most unusual—

My rebellious Wanyamwezi have come in a body and asked me to accept this offer as soon as they learned of it from their fellows, and request that they may be allowed to wait for me at Bagaka's at the head of the lake, maintaining that these people will be glad to paddle me back. Am disgusted with their cowardice. But as the chief, Kavabi, is willing so to do, I have accepted their suggestion. Even then they had the impertinence to demand the promised presents! I can not persuade or buy my Wanyamwezi assistant interpreter to come. He will not leave his brothers. Most irritating.

They are quite a well-made people, the men stalwart and the women very pleasing, particularly the young. Extremely black; far more so than the natives farther north. They have as I suspect an inferior race in bondage; are smaller and less stockily built. As far as I can gather through this irritating double interpretation they do not intermarry. Other questions regarding exogamy I shall leave until I am at the Monomatapa's where probably I will find some one who can speak Kiswahili.

July 10.

Traveled by river all the way to within a few miles of the Monomatapa's although a great number of rapids necessitated much porterage. Just below the town the river spread out into a vast lake, a dry pan at this time of the year, full of pebbles, lying on and embedded in a bluey clay— On the washouts I noticed, too, a curious bluish green serpentinous rock— The village is very large and contains— Very hospitable. Keep a guest-hut. In this case it is really commodious and fairly clean. My men quartered in the compound.

Have to wait three days, the prescribed time, according to etiquette. One, Singubulu, a man about forty I should imagine, is detailed to look after me. Have tried to get details of customs out of him but he seems very obtuse and it is very hard and exhausting work through Mohammed, who really is an irritating fool. No one here speaks Kiswahili. I shall stay long enough to learn something of the language.

July 13.

Just been to visit the prime minister, a young and powerful negro. Gave him the usual presents. I had understood from Mohammed that I was to see the Monomatapa, but I presume the idiot misunderstood. However, this young man promised that I should within a day or two. On leaving, he gave as presents a huge ivory tusk and a calabash. I have just been examining the contents of that calabash. There are seven pebbles, mostly in the form of an octahedron, about two inches in diameter. Although I am not sure I really believe they are diamonds. Really will be most interesting if they should prove to be, and if so, apparently the natives have no idea of the value. Yet why should they give them to me? More possibly connected with some idea of magic.

Have never known Mohammed so irritatingly stupid. He says he has overheard men talking and that they intend to murder him. I said I supposed he meant "us." But no, he insisted "himself" only. He has muddled things again or else he has suddenly acquired a gift of tongues. But he is nearly insane with fright. I am going for a walk alone around the village.

July 17.

The most extraordinarily interesting thing has happened. Mohammed was right. He is dead, and all my men. I am a prisoner.

On my walk I noticed that armed men kept constantly near me although nobody seemed to have enough curiosity to stare. As I was returning along the palisade around the king's compound, I saw eight heads upon the spikes, and as I approached to my indignant astonishment, I recognized them as those of Mohammed, my personal servant, a Somali, and the six askaris. They were so freshly murdered that the blood dripped upon my walking-stick as I stood by them.

I looked around angrily, but beyond some few women about their domestic business and children, there was nobody; that is, within sight. Furious with this cold-blooded treachery, I hastened to my hut where I was lodged, to find it completely sacked; not an article remained. Now fortunately although I have a service revolver, I never carry it, always finding that a gun excites opposition and that a walking-stick, as Livingstone considered, was invariably sufficient. However, not having the divine confidence of that great missionary, I carry an automatic in my trouser pocket in case of unforeseen violence. I was glad of that now.

Just as I was turning to seek some one in authority, the man Singubulu came along. I asked him sharply in Kiswahili what was the meaning of the outrage. Evidently he didn't understand a word but he pointed up the hill to the king's quarters. I assented vigorously, understanding that he meant me to appeal to the king or the minister. Still very angry, for apparently they meant no ill toward me, I permitted him to lead me. We passed through two enclosures, one within the other, and stopped at the door of a large hut with a low roof. He beckoned me to enter. Thinking that the king or the minister was there, I did so.

A pungent smoke caught me by the throat as I stooped. Around a fire were some eight men chanting softly, and as I stood peering through the gloom, wondering what was intended, the man Singubulu spoke to me, pointing upward as if meaning something higher and then into the pot.

I understood immediately, for knowing the very familiar custom of disenchantment, I interpreted it evidently meant that I was to see the mysterious Monomatapa himself—for of course I didn't believe him to be a hippopotamus.

So I assented and they placed some hot resinous compound on my throat. I was still very angry indeed, but knew well that I could not enforce my indignation upon them except through their chief. Therefore I followed again, walking-stick in hand, as Singubulu urged me up the hill. The next enclosure was composed of many houses, well built. Then we came to a marvelous stockade, composed of ivory tusks. In the center was a solitary house. This I took to be the *sanctum sanctorum* of the Monomatapa, and confess that in spite of the serious matter in hand I was really thrilled. I walked in, expecting to see I knew not what— The hut, save for native mats, and, to my astonishment, my own kit, was absolutely empty.

I turned. The man, Singubulu, had disappeared. I walked out. The compound was also empty. I stood and pondered what was to happen. Then I saw standing in the one entrance women armed with spears. Dear me, I recollect reflecting, they must be the Amazons guarding the sacred—what? I stopped, for there was nothing in the enclosure except—myself.

I was sacred; obviously they were there to guard me. I walked down to the gate slowly. Immediately six of them presented their long spears at me—young women, too. I spoke to them, but they did not understand. I smiled. And they smiled back. I made as if to pass through them but they thrust forward their spears in a most dangerous manner. I still had my automatic in my pocket, but they were women, and such strapping wenches! Besides no one seems to wish to harm me. I couldn't bring back the murdered men. I had an idea, a most interesting idea. I walked back thoughtfully to the hut—

July 20.

Besides my own effects I have discovered the habits of three monks, Jesuits, their underclothes, rosaries and crucifixes. The material is in such a state that they must be very old indeed, possibly centuries. They are evidently regarded as fetishes, which corroborates my theory.

After much reflection I have decided that either they consider me some form of a god and will endeavor to keep me here for life on the principle that where the god is they will benefit by his power, or they may have some system of annual sacrifice connected with the idea of the dying god who is resurrected in the Spring, but this does not seem so likely here in the tropics, where there is so little difference in the climate. On the other hand, the sacrifice may be one derived from that in remote ages and as recorded in South America and other parts of Africa, of killing the god and burying his members in various parts of the kingdom in order that the crops may be reinvigorated.

The motive for the slaughter of Mohammed and the Somalis I can not conceive. Does not appear to have any relation to a religious rite. Possibly the Arabs have been their raiders in times past. However, as this is July, and the Autumnal equinox is somewhere from the 21st to the 25th of March, I shall have some seven months or more in which to study the subject.

Singubulu has made advances and on the assurance that I will not attack him with my stick, appears to wish to be friendly. I shall endeavor to see this curious ceremony unless my actual life is threatened, when with the aid of my automatic, I shall do my utmost to escape. More I can not do. But first of all I must use every effort to master this dialect. I am to be well fed apparently and as, fortunately, I do not smoke,

I shall want for little. I sincerely hope that I may be spared to obtain some details of anthropological value.

(Continuation of Brandon Harvie)

I read, as far as that and then I stopped—for the time. That fellow surely had some nerve the way he took it. I sat on for a long time, I guess, just browsing on what I'd taken in and trying to figure it out. Automatic or no, I reflected afterward it hadn't done him much good, although he might have had the poor satisfaction of taking some of them with him. After all, what could he have done? He couldn't fight his way with a gun through a whole tribe, not like this mob at any rate. And, Lord, he had seven months to wait and think about it. Just as he studied the lingo and tried to pump old Singubulu for secrets to pass the time, so am I writing you this. If you get one, you get the other. His gun made me think of Tom's ivory dagger. Didn't seem much use about making one, yet—I don't know. I'm with Tom. I'd rather go out scrapping than sheep fashion.

Queer how Le Coq's Koran got away from here for all his other gear's here. But it ends, as Tom said, on a remark about fever and before he'd gotten caught in this monkey trap. Guess it must have been stolen before.

Afterward I went back and finished Murchison's diary. Just as he reckoned he'd do, he did. He'd learned the dialect mighty quick and as you'll see, it's full of legends and stuff about superstitions, right to the end. Doesn't scarcely say a word about worrying over it. Great stuff his farewell: "Good-by! Tomorrow I'll be a dead god or a man alive!"

March 25.

Nothing has happened yet. Wheeler *wasn't* killed by a lion. I heard his voice when they were yelling their heads off and I thought they were coming for me. They're still yelling and the drums are going like mad.

April 10.

I've been ill. Nervous breakdown, I reckon. I was all worked up to face whatever was going to happen and nothing happened, and I think the shock—seems funny— knocked me off my balance, or maybe malaria at the same time. But I *did* hear Wheeler's voice. That was before I got sick, when they were yelling, and I was expecting them to make a rush for me. The performance was in the next courtyard below me. I distinctly heard Wheeler's shout in English, "God help me, I'll—" and the sentence ended in a shriek. Then there were three more screams and the last one sounded muffled as if a sack or something had been thrown over his head. It was Wheeler's voice, of that I'm dead sure.

They kept up the drums and yelling for two more days every hour of which I expected them to rush for me. The strain made me ill; I couldn't eat and sat there with the ivory dagger in my hand bracing my muscles at every howl until I ached from head to foot. Then I kind of petered out, as far as I can make out, for I have only vague recollections of Singubulu around me and of his making me swallow some concoctions. I still feel groggy and jumpy. But I can't figure out what is going to happen, why they didn't come for me as they seem to have done with Tom and the other fellows. They must have massacred Wheeler somehow. If only I knew.

January 13, 1913.

I haven't been able to look at this diary for nearly twelve months. I wonder whether you will ever see it, Charles, whether this library of the dead will be added to by other fellows? Sometimes I feel hopeful—even of looking you up and spinning the yarn personally. Who knows? But that's only sometimes. I'm feeling particularly good just now, and that's why I've got the pluck to write again. After that jolt last year when poor Wheeler went out and I went a bit off my rocker, the very sight of this made me—yes, I'll tell the truth, made me want to blub like a kid.

I'd better explain, I guess, in case I shan't have the chance to. But I musn't think about that—

After I pulled myself together last year I wasted a lot of time cussing and prowling about my yard here like a bear in the zoo. I wouldn't or couldn't eat, got mighty thin until even old Singubulu got worried about it. Made me think that they were cannibals. Then, following Murchison's plan, I started in to learn the lingo thoroughly and also to read his diary, Tom's and Le Coq's, with the hope of getting a tip of some sort. Lordy, I read 'em over and over until I pretty nearly knew 'em by heart, but I couldn't seem to strike any idea that might prove useful. I'd get pessimistic and ask myself why I should be able to figure out a way when the Murchison fellow couldn't, who was a much cleverer guy than I am, and knew heaps more about the native.

Then one afternoon in the rainy season when I had the blues, staring dismally at the Amazons' outfit next door, I got a real brain wave. I had been gloomily trying to work out how they had killed poor Wheeler and recalled his oath and then the strangled scream. That word "strangled" recalled part of the story of the old Jesuits who, the record stated, had been strangled in 1561 and then instantly I got up and hunted in Murchison's diary again for a passage about native superstitions in which he had said something about them never spilling the blood of a chief or a god, which accounted for the method adopted by the Monomatapa.

Still that didn't seem to get me much for-rarder. Then browsing over the passage again I came across another entry about native superstitions in which he went on to say that "usually these victims representing the gods are so sacred that no man or woman's eye may rest upon them, nor their sacrifice be performed except by the holy priests." Farther on he says that among the Bawemba—whoever they are—upon the death of the god depended the safety of the tribe. "Should indeed," he remarks, "such an unprecedented accident occur as the escape of the representative god then would the sky fall upon the ground, the cattle would be destroyed, the crop fail, and ruin and desolation descend upon the people."

Linking all this together I got the great idea. For it seemed to me, as evidently I was reckoned a god or the representative of a god, that could I get out of the sacred enclosure none except the priests or Amazons would dare to touch me; in fact, would bolt for their lives.

I chewed on that idea for weeks and the more I picked up the lingo, the more I could get out of Singubulu—not that he told, but by piecing together scraps—and I got my wits sharpened some. I decided that there was something in it, at any rate a sporting chance and my only one. But the trouble was how to get outside the sacred enclosure, at least, if not the village?

The idea warmed me up more than a lot, believe me. Among other wild schemes to get out of the trap I had thought of the obvious one of tunneling beneath the ivory palisade, but had abandoned that, thinking that they would surely get me, if not in the village, in the countryside. Now I reconsidered it and made a careful examination of the butte. Fortunately it wasn't hard rock, but shale with veins of soft sandstone. The ivory knife poor Tom had made would serve as a tool. It would be a mighty tough job, but I reckoned I had until next March to do it.

Another point was how to prevent old Singubulu poking his nose in, for I dare only attempt it in the hut where I could hide the earth and stuff from the hole. My only solution to that was to pretend to be an eccentric god and refuse to have him in my hut.

My wits began to work like a greased wheel. I thought up a scheme to interest him in white magic, told him that I was about to carry out big medicine in the hut, and that nobody would be allowed to enter, for if they did the magic would be killed and the person injured. He quite got that, kind of appealed to him I think; and he seemed to have more respect for me, on the principle, I suppose, as Murchison suggests, that the more powerful the god, the more prosperous in war and peace the people.

Well, that's my little hope, old man, and I've been working like a son-of-a-gun every night—after trying Singubulu out for a week—ever since. I thanked my stars for those veins of sandstone, otherwise I'd have had no means of shoring the tunnel shaft. Some —— of a job and my hands are rags. I've got the tunnel now, I calculate, some thirty feet beyond the nearest Amazon hut, and as they always at night patrol or rather squat close alongside the ivory fence, I reckon I can snake out of that enclosure without being spotted. In the village at night no one budges an inch for fear of spirits. The Amazons, Singubulu tells me, have extra special charms and are holy anyway. I've got to be a lively spirit that night! Once out, if my theory is O.K., I follow the river, pinch the first canoe way below the rapids, and make for Lake Nyassa along the route Murchison came up.

Writing this bucks me a —— of a lot. Feel as if I'm drinking cocktails with you again, old man! I'm taking the seven diamonds with me, but I guess my greed's a bit cured, for I'm not for stopping to hunt in the river-bed for the sackfuls I was after!

Still already I've an idea to hunt you up and we'll both start a real expedition to come back here and rescue the dead man's library besides the trimmings!

February 22.

I'm through! Tonight there's no moon and I make the attempt about nine when they've most gone to bed. The diamonds are in my pocket and I have still the worn ivory dagger. Everything else I'll have to leave. I've tried to bluff old Singubulu that for reasons of magic I mustn't eat or drink for three days and that no one must enter the compound. He seems very impressed and if he falls for it, it will give me an extra chance to get away some distance down-river. *Au revoir*, old man! Feel bucked at the idea of doing something anyway.

(End of Brandon Harvie's diary)

I met Brandon Harvie's sister in hospital garb in Paris in 1917. When I inquired for dear old Bran, she replied gravely:

"Don't you know? He fell in his first action with the Foreign Legion last year."

The Frontier, March 1925

WHITE MAGIC

IN A SQUARE GRASS-THATCHED HUT, the mud walls of which were decorated with photographs and pages from illustrated journals, four troopers of the British South African Police sat at a deal table playing cards. Large tin mugs of tepid tea stood at each man's left hand beside the small heap of kaffir beans used as chips.

"Call," droned a fat-faced fellow with drooping, fair mustache. "Too mooch!" he grunted, as his opponent spread out tens over sixes.

"Vy you call?" whined the winner, grabbing the pot with swarthy, hairy hands as the Dutchman carelessly showed a pair of aces. *Nom de Dieu*, ven I haf somet'ing nobody vant to bet!"

"Aw, quit it!" admonished Tug Wilson, stretching muscular, naked arms over his head. "Neither of you two stiffs could bluff a flea into an extra hop. Oh, darn these flies!" He slapped an ear close-set above a straight jaw.

"The only thing the matter with this country," he orated, lifting the tip of each card as he dealt, "is that since Munojumbo quit business it's duller than a Bible class. Police!" he scoffed. "I've been in the darned outfit two years and the only thing I've arrested is a glandered mule. Sure, I'll raise you, Pete. Rest cure for neurasthenics and highbrows, I'll tell the world!"

"Awa' ma laddies!" said a voice behind him. A tall, dour sergeant stood blocking the glare of the hot sun without.

"Patrol. You're on the roster for duty. Saddle up!"

"Why, whatever would be the matter, Sergeant?" demanded Tug, mimicking the Scotch accent. "Is it a dog gone mad and bitten himself? It's the ambulance you'll be wanting, Ah'm thinkin'."

"It is not," retorted Sergeant Crawford solemnly. "Matanga's dead and they'd be burning alive the auld wife for witchcraft. Shake a leg noo. It's an express call from the Native Commissioner and we'll ha' to ride for it. For the de'ils will be burning the lass this nicht wi' the moon."

In ten minutes the men had on their boots and khaki tunics, rolled blankets and patrol cans, slipped on bandoliers; and, taking their saddles from the trees by each cot, were trooping to the stables.

"Give us the details, Jock," said Pete Titton, a long narrow slab of John Bull, as the party rode out of camp with a section of the Black Watch in the rear.

"No details," said Sergeant Crawford. "We've just got to stop the show, and if they try to blather arrest the son, Zuloki. There's a lad I've no liking for. He's a long time been hankering after daddy's breeks, I'm thinking, and ower young to remember the last basting they got."

"And I guess the old woman's his mother," put in Tug. "She'll be jealous of the younger wives and ambitious for her son. Mother love stuff. We'll just arrest 'em both for murder in the first degree."

"We canna do that, laddie," retorted the sergeant. "There's no proof."

"But that's what we've got to find, isn't it?"

"No. Orders are to stop the burning. No charge of murder. There'll be no time for scoff," the sergeant added, glancing at the sun. "Moon rises at eight."

"Better leave the Black Watch to follow on then," suggested Tug. "I can spiel enough to make 'em understand."

By sundown the police could hear the throb of drums, and it was obvious that they could not reach the chief's *kraal* at a walking pace before moon-rise, so leaving orders with the sergeant of the Black Watch, they cantered on.

The native path wound along valleys between boulder-jumbled *kopjes* now coming upon an open *vlei*, and then leading through open bush and parklike clumps of trees. Tug Wilson, by general consent the best tracker in the troop, led the way. Occasionally came the swishing of a startled herd of buck racing off, the call of a night bird, and ever the throbbing of the drums. Presently to these sounds was added a faint chanting.

"Quite on the cards we may have a scrap after all," said Pete to the sergeant as they slowed up to make the passage of a swamp.

"Maybe," assented Crawford. "Anyhow we'll pull up at da Gomez's winkel and see if he can put us up to anything. He's a canny lad, and should know the latest."

The milk of the rising moon was already swamping the stars before they came in sight of the *kraal*, a large one of over a thousand huts straddling as usual on the slopes of a boulder-strewn *kopje*.

Da Gomez was a Portuguese, a reputed former army doctor, a seemingly inoffensive little person usually as mum as a clam about his own affairs. He had evidently heard the patrol, or had been expecting them, for the door of his store opened and against the light of the paraffin swing lamp stood the dwarf-like figure of the owner.

"Goot evening, shentlemen!" said he as the five reined up before the low corrugated iron veranda roof. "Gom and haf a drink, Sergeant."

"No, no. In a hurry," said Crawford. "We're over here to stop yon witch burning. Know anything aboot it?"

"I haf heard," said da Gomez. "Eet ees tomorrow night, yes?"

"Tomorrow night nothing," put in Tug. "Can't you hear the yowling now?"

"Dey make der—vot you gall—beggining, yes? Dey tell me dat, yes?"

"The Commissioner says it's tonight," returned Crawford slowly, "and I'm not taking any chances, man."

"But yes, gom and haf a drink. All—yes?"

"Good night! Come on, laddies!"

"If that bird don't watch his step," said Tug as they cantered away, "he'll sure ruin himself with those drinks."

In the center of the village, where, as customarily, was a large open space and the men's club house, fires glowed. About them the forms of half nude natives swayed from shadow to glow like tiny gnomes, and the high treble of the tribal singer and the hungry bass grunt of the mob in response floated on the night air with sinister clarity. The moon was already silhouetting odd trees and humped rocks upon the summit as the patrol scrambled up to the outskirts of the village unnoticed.

If the natives had any thoughts of interference from the whites, they had forgotten them in the excitement, for not a soul was on guard; everybody, even babes, apparently, being massed in the village square worked themselves into a proper state of hysteria to enjoy the sacrificial rites.

In the center a huge fire of dry saplings and logs was burning fiercely. Around it danced the warriors, led by Zuloki, the new chief, who was capering higher and screaming louder than any other man. Behind, forming an outer ring, the women swayed and shuffled, moaning to the throb of the drums and Kaffir pianos.

As Tug and the sergeant charged knee to knee through the irregular lanes formed by huts and boulders, the former spotted a commotion to the right, near the club house.

"There she goes!" he yelled, and swerved Crawford's mount toward a pack of screeching women who were struggling through the ranks of the howling warriors, bearing a figure in their midst.

"Quick, mon!" shouted Crawford, perceiving Tug's object was to separate the hideous gang from the main body of the warriors.

But Tug was too late, for as his horse bowled over the first two of the warriors, the shrieking hags cast their burden into the flames.

Tug rammed home the spurs, scattering warriors and women, and put the horse at the fire. In the third bound the beast felt the heat of the flames, swerved and leaped sideways.

With a smothered curse Tug slid out of the saddle almost into the fire, and, revolver in left hand, grabbed the feet of the screeching victim and dragged her out.

"Quick," yelled Crawford, grasping the situation. "To him, lads!"

Spurring his animal through the excited mob Crawford reached Tug, whose horse had plunged away riderless.

"Up, man, up!" he shouted.

But Tug thrust the quivering body onto Crawford's saddle bow.

"Git; I'll follow!" he cried, and sprang to the next man, Pete; swung up behind him, and together they charged back through the milling mob into the darkness of the *veld*.

All this had happened in a few seconds before the startled natives, doped with hysteria, could grasp its meaning. For several moments only a few realized that whites were among them; the others, uninterrupted by the horses, kept up their frantic howling and capering; even the drums were still throbbing.

"Where to, Sergeant?" shouted Tug as the double-burdened horse pounded alongside.

"Da Gomez. He's a bit o' a doc, they say, and by the way she's squealing, maybe this puir body will need a bit o' tending."

Behind them the drums had ceased. A pandemonium of screams, yells, and howls devoid of any rhythm was in full blast; and against the glow of the fire demoniac gnomes rushed hither and thither, like a disturbed ant's nest.

Da Gomez rushed excitedly onto the veranda as the cavalcade drew up.

"Vot der matter? Vot der matter?" he demanded. "You no stop dem, yes?"

"We stopped 'em all right," responded Tug, "and got the old lady. She's a handmade job for you, I guess!"

"Here she is, Gomez," said Crawford from the saddle. "Help me down with her. I'll get you to doctor her a wee. She needs it, the puir body."

But instead of taking the quivering and now whimpering bundle of skinny limbs, da Gomez stared gaping.

"Here, get out of the daylight!" snapped Pete, and brushing the little man aside he dumped the old negress on the counter of the store beneath the lamp.

She proved to be burned slightly here and there and her hair was singed off; but examination showed no serious injury. Da Gomez seemed too bewildered, or reluctant, to approach until Crawford shoved him forward.

"Do yer job, man, and lively!" the sergeant said sharply. "What's the matter with ye, any hoo?" Then as da Gomez seemed to recover his wits the sergeant turned round and sent Huykers on the back trail to bring up the Black Watch to the store. "Yon black de'ils'll make no fuss the nicht, I'm thinking," he remarked. "Its dark and they'll ha' to have a grand *indaba* first to find out what did happen. So we'll camp here."

"Vot you do in morning, *Senhor* Sergeant?" da Gomez inquired.

"Arrest Zuloki," retorted Jock curtly.

" 'Rest Zuloki!" Da Gomez's pop-eyes goggled. He seemed scared.

"Sure thing," said Tug, eyeing him. "He's the chief, ain't he?"

"Ye needn't have any fear your trade'll be ruined, da Gomez," soothed Crawford, thinking the man was frightened about the attitude of the natives to whites after the arrest. "Noo, how aboot the whuskey ye're so free with?"

The Black Watch, twenty in number, arrived and camped in front of the store. The pandemonium in the village died down about midnight, but the fire glowed all night; and in the glow sat the elders holding the *indaba* prophesied by the sergeant.

II

AT THE MEETING OF DAWN and moonlight the five whites mounted and with the Black Watch in the rear rode across to the village. Their coming was signalled as soon as they started and immediately the great *kraal* began to hum like a beehive in swarm.

To the east of the dancing square, amid the rocks and boulders, was the cattle *kraal*—and the old chief Matanga had been comparatively wealthy in cattle—but there was no sign of small boys dragging away the thorn bushes which blocked the entrance; an ominous symptom signifying usually that the people were in a warlike mood.

"It's that loon, Zuloki," grumbled Crawford. "He's of a mind to be cheeky."

However, as they neared the *kraal* no active hostile demonstration was made. The sergeant of the Black Watch, Takaki, was ordered ahead to demand that Zuloki come forth to make an *indaba*. The giant Angoni, of Zulu origin, strode blithely forward, grinning in hopeful anticipation of a refusal.

"Ho! Zuloki, son of the Black Elephant!" bawled Takaki in the customary formula, "advance and make *indaba* with thy masters, the white men. Ho! Come!"

From the mass of warriors armed with spears—although the police knew that many muskets were hidden in the crowd, also—Zuloki, a slender young buck as black as a stove, clad in a store shirt with many copper and brass bangles, stepped out as haughtily as the Angoni. Advancing within twenty yards of the sergeant he saluted and squatted, gravely followed by a group of elders who formed a half circle about him.

"Ask him," instructed the sergeant, who had no working knowledge of the dialect, "why he permitted the burning of the old woman, which he knows is forbidden?"

"It is the custom of my fathers and the ancient law of my people," retorted Zuloki, insolently, yet with utterly expressionless eyes.

"It is forbidden by the whites, your masters," translated Takaki freely. "Hath the wine of the palm entered thy head that thou hast become mad?"

"Tell the *umlungu*," retorted Zuloki, knowing this use of the word meaning "white man" instead of "chief" was an insult, "that a tree that hath grown for a thousand moons may not be pulled down even by an elephant."

"Eh!" grunted the elders in approval.

"Darned nerve," commented Tug, who could follow the words. "But he's nobody's fool, that kid."

"The white man is stronger than elephants, fiercer than lions, swifter than leopards!" responded the giant Angoni. "These are his words: that thou, Zuloki, come with them to render count of thy deeds to the master."

"Nay," Zuloki refused, "that may not be. This woman made magic against my father. Was it not so, my brethren?"

"Eh! Eh!"

"Therefore, as the law says, must she die lest his ghost be angry and destroy us."

"Then tell him," ordered Crawford, "that I shall arrest him now."

"Nay," responded Zuloki confidently. "That may not be, for I am the chief in my father's place."

"He who touches the body of the Black Elephant dies," spoke up a wizened old man clad in masses of beads, shells, and amulets, and wearing the rim of a cast off helmet, who sat next to Zuloki.

"Arrest him, Takaki," commanded the sergeant.

"He dies who touches him!" warned the old man again.

"Who is the old man?" inquired Crawford as Takaki hesitated.

"The witch-doctor, master." The giant Angoni's spine seemed suddenly to have melted. "They say he is very powerful, master. He knows."

"Nonsense," snapped the sergeant. "Arrest them both."

Still Takaki, born of the greatest fighting race in Africa, he who would have charged a whole regiment single handed and died laughing, hesitated; his eyes even began to roll.

"Damnation, man," exploded Crawford. "D'you hear what I said?"

"Yes, *Inkoos*."

Takaki's right hand shot up in the ancient royal salute of the Zulus.

"Bayete!" he exclaimed; then advanced slowly—they could not see his eyes.

Zuloki remained as still as one of the boulders about him.

"Rise, O Zuloki!" the big Angoni commanded sternly, standing above him.

Zuloki did not bat an eyelid.

Slowly, the big black sergeant reached down.

"I arrest you!" he said.

Simultaneously as the hand touched the arm of Zuloki, the witch-doctor pointed his finger in the black's face.

"Tabu," he cried clearly.

Zuloki remained immobile, seeming scarcely to breathe. The Angoni was seen to start upward, to gasp. His whole body writhed in an intense, violent convulsion, sagged at the knees and pitched forward on its face.

"*Ough*," rose a murmur of admiration from the massed ranks of the warriors behind.

For a few moments none of the whites could realize what had happened. Zuloki still sat motionless, not even condescending to glance at the prone figure beside him.

Oaths burst from the whites almost simultaneously. Tug and Crawford threw themselves from their horses and ran forward revolver in hand. Not a native moved.

Tug was the first to reach the group. He seized and turned over Takaki.

"Dead!" he muttered incredulously, looking up as Crawford reached him.

"Ah'll fix th' hound o' hell," bellowed the sergeant furiously, and pointing his revolver at Zuloki's head—the eyes of the native never blinked—he seized him roughly by the arm.

"Get oop, ye black!"

Again the witch-doctor's hand shot out. "Tabu!" he menaced.

The sergeant gasped. Zuloki sank back upon his haunches, imperturbable; as the revolver went off in the air, the white man swayed, writhed, sagged and collapsed even as the black sergeant had done.

"*Ough!*" came the same subdued grunt from the natives, and a shriller note of superstitious terror from the goggle-eyed Black Watch.

III

UTTERLY CONFOUNDED, tug stood staring at the form of his commander, who lay crumpled up, one arm doubled under him, the other sticking out in a grotesque gesture. Time stood still. Everything seemed to be hushed, waiting, listening.

Then he realized that Jock was dead. But how? It was incredible. He had seen distinctly that the witch-doctor had not actually touched the sergeant. The sinister black finger had merely pointed into Jock's face, almost, but not quite touching him between the eyes as he had stooped to drag the chief to his feet. Besides, even if the wizard had touched the men, no man can kill by pointing, or even touching.

Despite his white training and scorn of superstition, a horrid cold feeling crept beneath his skin. Takaki, the black sergeant, must have known that he was going to his death, hence the "Bayete" salute.

Impossible? Yet it had been done; twice.

As Tug's brain began to function again, the first impulse was to shoot both chief and witch-doctor, and order the Black Watch to help wipe out the *kraal* to avenge his murdered comrade. But reason vetoed the natural instinct; such an act would inevitably bring about a general rising entailing the massacre of many whites scattered about the countryside; also he was sworn to uphold the law; was indeed its representative.

"I'll get you yet, you black swine!" he suddenly exploded, and pointing the revolver at Zuloki's head, bade him in the dialect to stand up or he would kill him. Tug was standing on the side farthest from the witch-doctor. Zuloki palpably hesitated.

"He touched thee not," Tug heard the witch-doctor whisper.

Then the chief rose.

"And you!"

The wizened wizard rose with more alacrity.

"Cover them with your rifles, boys!" commanded Tug, who as senior trooper was in charge, "and keep 'em covered. At the slightest attempt to escape or turn, shoot. But make 'em walk ahead, and for God's sake don't touch the beasts," he added hurriedly.

IV

MROVO STATION had not long been established and most of the buildings had wattle and daub wall. No regular jail had as yet been built. When Tug had made a verbal report to the commanding officer, who scoffed at the alleged magical powers of the witch-doctor and was violently angry at the death of his sergeant, the prisoners were handcuffed and chained to the center pole of the forage hut, and a white guard mounted lest the Black Watch might be influenced by native superstition.

"Anyway," said Tug to his buddies as they went off to eat, "that cans the sacred stuff. It's some stunt of the witch-doctor's; but just what, I can't get."

"Perhaps," suggested Huykers, "dey would haf taken a chance if deir own peoples were looking, hein?"

"Yep, something in that maybe," admitted Tug. "Say, Dubois, did you see clearly what happened?"

"Yes, I tink I see. He raise 'is arm and say dat vord and—poof! Yock 'e fall! Der black sergeant I could not see because 'is back vas to me."

"M'm. Neither of you fellows saw something that flashed?"

"Flashed? No. Vot was it like?"

"Just a tiny spark—like a spark plug contact? No? Don't know myself whether I saw it or not. I was knocked all of a heap. Must have been mistaken."

"You must have," agreed Pete. "For that's rot. Can't work up a theory of a nigger using a battery, and anyhow he'd have to carry some powerful battery to kill a man so quick."

"Guess you're right, son. That wouldn't hold even with a cub reporter," Tug admitted. "But I'll get that black murderer if the law don't. Poor old Jock," he sighed. "Well, hoof it, you fellows. The Old Man will be waiting in the orderly room with Bertie for official evidence. But by golly," Tug added, rising, "I've got a hunch that that guy with the bone regalia killed the old chief Matanga, and he and Zuloki framed it on the old woman and split the loot. I'll put that up to the skipper."

They collected their prisoners and marched them up to the orderly room, the first building in mud bricks as yet constructed, where, beside the C.O., was the Native Commissioner, Berthold, known as Bertie, a Colonial from Natal who spoke the dialect.

But the official interrogation elicited nothing new. Both prisoners denied that they had slain their chief; and the intended victim of the suttee, to the astonishment of all, asserted that her witchcraft had slain her husband, a deed calculated to gain the chiefdom for her son, just as Jock had guessed. She seemed very proud of the crime.

Then Zuloki and the witch-doctor, to their utter indifference, were formally indicted on the charges of murder and attempted murder for trial at the Salisbury Assizes, and the woman charged with murder on her own statement. Tug, with another sergeant, nineteen white troopers and a company of the Black Watch, was detailed to leave at daybreak to bring in some of the *indunas* as witnesses.

That afternoon they buried with military honors the remains of Sergeant Jock Crawford.

Later as the men were returning from "stables" passing the forage store, they heard a chant in progress.

"Myking magic!" said a Cockney called Jukes with a derisive laugh. "We'll all be dead in the morning, see if we ain't."

"Aw, quit it!" snapped Tug irritably. "If you'd seen the show you wouldn't be so darned fresh about it."

"Oo-er!" mocked trooper Jukes. " 'Ow much will yer bet they vanish in thin hair termorrow? Bottle o' *dop*? I'm gyme. Garn, yer ain't a sport. Any'ow, Hi'm on guard ternight so yer 'ave a cinch ter win."

"Some smart Alec, aren't you?" responded Tug feebly, for he was deeply cut by the sudden end of the dour Scotch sergeant.

All that evening, for hours, from the prisoners' hut continued the wailing chant.

"I wish that old fool of a guard would make those rats stop that racket," growled Pete, who had already turned in.

"Got nerves?" inquired Tug. "Me, too, ole son."

The chant continued, maddening in its persistent monotony after taps. Once they heard one of the guards bang the butt of his rifle against the mud wall.

"*Didimalla! Didimalla!* Shut up!" he shouted. But the chant went on.

The next thing that Tug knew was the blare of the reveille. On the last bugle note came a sudden shout followed by voices talking angrily. Tug dragged on his pants and rushed out.

The first thing he noticed was that the cone roof of the forage hut had sagged in strangely. He ran up.

Lying on the ground close to the wall of the prison hut and directly beneath the window were two bodies, one fallen across the other, Troopers Jukes and Mason.

Again Tug felt that chilly sensation, despite himself. He stared incredulously.

"They've gone, the swine!" he heard someone explaining to a new arrival. "The old man must have slipped his handcuffs and found a saw, for he's cut through the center pole—look at it!—and killed these two chaps, God only knows how!"

Beneath the window was another hole in the mud wall through which the murderers had made their escape. Evidently Mason had been killed first, and then Jukes had fallen into some kind of a trap when he came to see what was wrong.

But again—how had the guards been slain?

There was no visible mark upon the body of either man.

Significantly, both rifles and bandoliers had gone, too.

"There's only one answer to this," shouted Tug in a mad rage, voicing the feelings of all, "and that's go get 'em—the whole boiling, damn 'em!"

V

BOOTS AND SADDLES!

Half an hour later the troop was lined up. Only three-fifths were mounted, the others having lost their animals by the prevalent horsesickness. Formed up behind them were the Black Watch, laggards running from their quarters buckling on their accoutrements.

Presently came the skipper, scowling savagely.

"Who the devil was the benighted fool who handcuffed those prisoners?" he barked.

"I did, sir," spoke up Tug.

"Hadn't you got the horse sense to see that the fellow couldn't slip his hands?"

"No, sir. He must have used grease anyway, probably from the other's wool. And besides I manacled them by the legs as well."

"Where in thunder did he get a saw?"

"Must have been left behind by accident, sir."

"Armory's the place for tools. Which of you men left it there? Come, speak up quick!"

"I—I dunno, sir," stuttered a smallish man, the mess cook, "but perhaps I did. I was a-sawing up some boxes there, sir, to make shelves for the mess hut, sir, and maybe I forgot it. I'm sorry, sir."

"Sorry be damned! You've cost two men's lives. Sergeant-major, put that man under arrest."

"Notice he don't ask who killed Jukes and Mason," mumbled the reputed wag of the troop to another man, "maybe he's gone and forgotten it!"

But no one smiled.

"Wonder what he thinks he's going to do?" queried Tug of Pete, his riding half section. "If he tries to wipe their eyes he'll start a rebellion sure. Not that I'm kicking, boy!"

"Well," commented sober Pete, "with those leg irons they can't have got far by now."

As soon as they were out of camp came an order to deploy in skirmish order, the Black Watch in the center and the mounted whites on the flanks, with the hope of rounding up the escaped prisoners before they reached their village.

"Pah!" snorted Tug at this wily manoeuver. "Might as well try to catch a mosquito in the dark! Why don't he gallop right through and put a cordon round the village and pinch the elders before they know what's hit 'em?"

As he maliciously predicted, no sign of the fugitives was found; but fully half an hour before their arrival they heard the drums getting busy—their approach had been signalled. It seemed incredible that two shackled men had made the distance before them, yet the natives might have sent the hag ahead, or gone by short cuts only known to the natives.

On entering the valley in which the *kraal* was situated Captain Vickers ordered column formation. He consulted much with Berthold, but seemed very undecided what course to pursue. Finally he led the troop up and through the village to the great square. A few old hags and sore-eyed pickannies peered indifferently from neighboring huts while the machine-gun team unloaded their mule.

"Looks bad!" muttered the skipper. "What d'you think, Berthold?"

"M'm, m'm," mumbled Berthold whose wits always seemed rusty, "I'll try to get in touch with them and hold an *indaba*."

"I should burn the *kraal*, sir," suggested the sergeant-major, who was half Boer. "Teach 'em a lesson, sir, y'know."

"Can't do that," objected the Native Commissioner. "Isn't legal."

"Damn the law!" retorted Captain Vickers, pulling furiously at his mustaches. "The swine have murdered three of my men."

"Couldn't possibly sanction," mumbled Berthold, who as the civil power had command, as far as native affairs were concerned, until martial law was proclaimed. "They're all up around in the *kopjes*."

"Well, get 'em down, sir, get 'em down!" snapped Captain Vickers disgustedly.

Berthold sent off one of his messenger police boys into the *kopjes*.

"If they won't come in," he added lamely, "I'll have to report the matter to the Chief Native Commissioner."

"And the C.N.C. will write across Pioneer Street, to the Deputy Assistant Acting Secretary of the Governor who will write back to you for further information, and you'll write back, and he'll write to the boiled shirt flunky of the C.N.C., who'll forget it for a week because there's a ladies' tennis tournament on; and then he'll write to old Byron at Zintos, who'll talk bosh to Munojumbo, and then about a hundred years hence we'll hear that the culprits have unfortunately fled across the Portuguese border—and between the lot of you, you'll have spilled about as much bloody ink as there was red blood in my men's veins, sir!"

"Can't do anything else," mumbled Berthold rather unhappily as the skipper, fuming, flung himself out of the saddle and ordered the grinning troop to dismount and go easy.

"Sorry, Berthold," he added a moment afterward as the N.C. still sat like a melancholy pelican on his horse. "Not your fault, of course. Come and sit in the shade."

"I think," said Berthold slowly, "that we might be justified in confiscating their cattle if the two prisoners are not given up."

"Ah!" exclaimed the skipper, "that's something, anyhow. Ought to bring 'em to their senses and down here pretty quick. And the cattle are all down by the store in a bunch."

He gave the order for ten men to ride off and round them up and the others to off saddle.

"That's the whichaway!" concurred Tug with delight. "I said ole Buffalo Bill's a regular fellow!"

Scarcely had they heard the distant whoops of the round-up than they saw a tiny figure rush out of the store gesticulating excitedly. A long conversation ensued between one of the police and da Gomez—at least on the latter's side. Finally the trooper wheeled about and came galloping back to the village. He rode straight for the skipper.

"Yon lad," he reported, "says as t' cattle belong to him, sir."

"What's that?" exploded Captain Vickers.

"Yes, sir." The trooper held out a document. "Says as Matanga, t'auld chief sold 'em and here's t' papers."

The document was a regular bill of sale, signed with a wobbly cross with the words 'Matanga his mark,' and witnessed by Charles Dawson, a missionary who had a station some fifteen miles away.

"Dawson!" snorted Captain Vickers, and on general principles added, "Damn these missionaries."

On its face the document was perfectly valid.

"Bring that man over here," ordered the skipper after a short consultation with Berthold. "Think it's genuine, Berthold?"

"Looks it," said the Native Commissioner. "Although it does seem queer that a chief sells *all* his cattle. Do you know the signature?"

"Not from Adam's."

The men filed off to water the horses and when they came back da Gomez was there, spluttering excitedly.

"No, no, *Senhor Capitan*, you cannot take my cattle! Eet ees not my fault. Day vas bought for goots. T'ree year I trade—only for cattle; and I pay heem look after for me. Soon I begin large farm. Yes, *senhor*. Dat ees goot beel of sale. My friend Meester Dawson he vitnesses, yes, *Senhor Capitan*."

"Now look here, da Gomez," said Berthold, "you're hand in glove with these people. What do you know about this affair? How were those men killed? You hear them talk all the time."

"I not know netting, *senhor*. Vot, you tink dey tell me, a viteman? Ha! Ha! No, nevaire a native. I hear talk, yes. Dey say it was weetchcraft of der doctor. I do not know."

He looked like an excited baboon as the sweat rolled down his hairy face and his hands pawed the hot air.

"Damn you and Dawson, too," grumbled the skipper. "You may go."

Stalemate—that's all there was to it. Unless the signature was proved a forgery the police could not touch the cattle; besides, there was no object in doing so, for the natives would merely laugh. That they would come in from the bush not even Berthold really thought. However, Captain Vickers dispatched a man to Dawson's to corroborate da Gomez's statements.

Meanwhile Tug had been lying on his back in the shade of a hut, unmindful of native fleas, listening and thinking hard.

"Say, Pete," he commented at length, "I've got a hunch that that bill of sale's a frame-up. Bertie's right. It just ain't natural for a chief to sell all his cattle. Why, man, he'd have a stack of goods to fill twenty huts. There's seven or eight hundred head there. It just gets my goat to see a darn gang of blacks put it over on a white. Why, here we are sitting around like a bunch of pelicans in a Louisiana swamp—and three of us gone west. To hell with this palaver; I'm going to fix something with some pep in it." Tug grinned maliciously and made straight for Captain Vickers, who was sitting on his saddle beneath a tree smoking and talking to Berthold.

"May I speak to you a moment, sir?"

Captain Vickers looked up and scowled.

"Oh, you're the damn fool who helped us into this mess, eh?"

"Yes," responded Tug placidly, "I guess I'm that same damn fool."

"What d'you want?"

Tug spoke quickly and to the point for possibly five minutes. The skipper forgot to put his pipe in his mouth.

"M'm. Not bad. What d'you think, Berthold?"

"Jolly risky."

"M'm." The skipper eyed Tug reflectively. "But if you can't get 'em out?"

"I'll guarantee they'll come out or else they'll never come out," returned Tug oracularly.

"Can you speak the dialect? Oh, you can, eh?" The skipper couldn't, although he had been ten years in the same country. "Well, you may do it on your own responsibility. Berthold's a witness. We'll be here in case you need help."

"No, sir. If the troops stay nearby there'll be nothing doing. The blacks won't come near the village."

"The man's right," assented the Native Commissioner.

"M'm. Well, all right." Captain Vickers held out his hand. "Good luck, my man!"

Tug looked at the hand, smiled, took it, and drawled, "Thanks, ole top!"

VI

HALF AN HOUR LATER, after driving back the inquisitive women and children by a nominal search of the huts, the skipper gave the word to march and the police column withdrew, leaving two troopers with emergency rations and water armed with two revolvers each, hidden in the granary adjacent to the chief's principal hut.

Lying well back in the darkness, covered nearly to the neck in *rupoko*—a kind of millet seed—they listened for the last *clop* of a hoof in the rocky ascent. Some time elapsed before they caught the shrill chattering of women, who evidently had come timidly to find out what damage the whites had done, and who now expressed their astonishment in clucks and clicks that nothing had been touched.

An hour of sweaty, suffocating darkness passed before the two men heard what they had been waiting for: first, a distant bugle call signifying that the column was out of sight of the village; second, the high-pitched voice of a woman speaking to someone at a distance. By the phosphorescent dial on Tug's wrist-watch it was just six o'clock, a quarter of an hour to sunset in these latitudes. Almost immediately afterward rolled the bass notes of a man's voice. The natives were returning to the village in a swarm, jabbering excitedly.

Cautiously the two troopers crawled nearer the entrance, which looked at an angle upon the chief's house, an oblong building after the white man's fashion with higher walls, a window and a high doorway. Behind the light fence which surrounded this hut they could hear the chief's wives chattering as they prepared their lord's evening meal; but Tug could not distinguish, so alike are native voices to a white ear, whether or no the old lady who had been rescued from the burning was there.

Suddenly against the orange and green of the short sunset appeared the slender figure of Zuloki and the bent one of Takini, the witch-doctor; neither wore handcuffs nor leg irons.

"How did they do it?" whispered Pete. "Natives don't have files."

As if in answer, immediately behind walked the baboon-like figure of da Gomez.

"Little rat!" muttered Tug. "He's sure been hiding 'em up in the store all the time, I'll bet a wad."

"Let's rush 'em now," suggested Pete impatiently. "We can hold 'em up and shoot if they try to rush us. Which they wouldn't dare."

"No, no, Pete. I'm out to get the goods on 'em and clear up that mystery business. And maybe they'd play that same trick on us—whatever it was. They've done it three times, and I'm going to find out the how of it. Gomez is in this for sure, and at present we've got nothing on him."

The three suspects were followed at intervals by half a dozen elders into the chief's hut, to which food was brought by the women.

From the granary Tug could not catch anything save the murmur of talk, but as soon as night was wholly come he began a belly-crawl across the compound; leaving Pete, who couldn't understand the dialect, to cover him. He succeeded in reaching the back of the hut unobserved, despite the protest of some roosting fowls.

At the moment, Zuloki was demanding in an angry voice that da Gomez should fulfill some promise, that they should be supplied with more of something previously mentioned; and da Gomez was replying that it was impossible, and that the promise had been made for the next moon. The argument continued for some time between the two in the rambling native fashion, but the listener could not get a clue as to the object desired.

Then da Gomez, as if exasperated, suddenly announced that he would take his cattle and go. Sneeringly, Zuloki asked if he were going to get the other *umlungus* to drive them for him? The Portuguese retorted that he had made his trade and wanted no more; that anyway Zuloki had no more cattle to trade.

"Nay, I have now my father's cattle," responded Zuloki. "Are they not sweet, too, in the mouth of the white man? Eh! but all whites are thieves. The Great Elephant hath many more cattle hungered for by thee. Are these not white words, O Sinuzi?"

"They are white words, O Zuloki," responded the man addressed. Evidently from the reply he was the emissary of Munojumbo, the paramount chief. "But the Black One is angered with thee in that thou hast raised the wrath of the whites ere the time was yet ripe to strike." Tug started slightly. "None but a foolish boy would have held the burning, knowing that the whites would send their soldiers to take thee. Eh!"

" 'Twas the law of our ancestors," returned Zuloki sulkily.

"Who art thou to throw the words of the Black One over thy shoulder? Even so wouldst thou shoot at a bird and scare the buck? Couldst not await the word? Most wroth is he that thou shouldst have slain the three white soldiers and the black one by thy magic, for what shall madden a dog more than being bitten? Eh!"

" 'Twas Takini, not I," objected the boy.

"Even so, art thou not chief? And thou, Takini, art bidden to the Presence to make manifest thy powers before him."

" 'Tis past the time of the moon," excused the witch-doctor.

But Tug, not waiting for more, wriggled back as swiftly as he dared; and touching Pete on the leg, led him into the recesses of the granary.

"Pete, old-timer," he told him, "it's mighty serious. We're just on the edge of a general rebellion. That's what made Zuloki so fresh. That little Portuguese rat has been running arms, I'm dead sure. That's what his possession of the cattle means. The herd isn't all his, by the way; so that bill of sale's a fake to gain time. Seems old Matanga wouldn't deal; wanted to remain loyal apparently. I figure that's why they put him away. Now the kid's got a swollen head and has nearly busted the show by the burning and killing, and the big chief's after his scalp. Gomez is scared stiff knowing that instead of waiting till next moon, when all the harvest is in, they'll start right away. Now he hasn't got time to get clear. Now, whether they break out now or within a few days they'll surely raise hell for a time. You must make a break, right away, before the moon rises. Tell the skipper and get him to wireless headquarters. Then the big boss can have all the principal chiefs seized right away—Munojumbo in particular. Tell him he's all right."

"But you, Tug?"

"Me? I'm going to get these fellows—before they get me, anyway. But that don't count, man. Think of the hundreds of women and children, and what'll happen if we don't go through with it."

"That's right, but—"

"But nothing. Say, I'm dead sure they'll be having an *indaba* presently. Probably without drums, so's not to attract attention. Then you make a break for it. If you get caught I'll hear your shots and try to get the message through myself."

"No," decided Pete. "I'll go now before the moon."

"Right! And say, Pete, try to get old Buffalo Bill to snap into it and have the boys around this *kraal* at daybreak? Good luck, old boy."

Their hands met in the dark.

"*Hambe gahle*, go carefully!" returned Pete.

"Bet your life, boy," said Tug as his friend disappeared.

The discussion within the chief's hut had become more excited. Da Gomez was demanding that his cattle should be driven on the morrow to the Portuguese border twenty miles away, but significantly his words were utterly ignored. In the little man's voice was the hysteria of panic; volubly he was reproaching Zuloki with broken faith, fatuously asking what they would have done without his aid. He talked until he was out of breath. Then Zuloki inquired of the emissary from Munojumbo when the word would go forth.

That, said the man coldly, will be told at the official *indaba*, as is the custom.

"If thou wilt do even as I have asked thee, then indeed shalt thou depart with that which is thine," said the witch-doctor to da Gomez.

"That I cannot do," returned da Gomez frantically, "for I have no more, and to get some would eat up many moons even as it did in the beginning."

"Thou hast heard the words of the chief? Then am I no longer thy friend."

The effect of that simple speech was to bring from the little man a spate of words to which none made reply. His voice gradually faded into a whimpering.

Save for the noisy eating of the company there was silence. Then suddenly Zuloki said something sharply which Tug could not catch. Followed a stifled screech and the sound of scuffling.

Tug's hand fell on his revolver butt and he crouched. More movements and the low mutters of men; then some one began talking as if nothing had happened.

Came da Gomez's voice crying a native proverb.

"O Takini, he who breaketh his word breaketh his spear."

Tug slumped to earth again, musing. Glad they haven't killed the little rat, he thought. May be useful if I can get hold of him. Evidently the witch-doctor needs something badly which da Gomez can't supply any longer. What can it be? Arms? That would be more in Zuloki's line. Something to do with the magic stunt? But even then I can't see what, for the darned witch-doctor never touched either of them. H'm. I'll have to watch that moon.

The natives within went on talking in low tones so that he could only catch a word here and there. A sound of men stirring came from all about the village; they were beginning to assemble for the *indaba*. Presently the east showed the first smother of the moon. Tug was hoping that they would leave the Portuguese alone, in the hut, but just then Zuloki raised his voice and a young warrior appeared who was told to guard the prisoner. The others rose and stalked away.

Tug listened. Da Gomez was speaking in a low voice to the guard; from one or two words Tug caught, he gathered that he was fatuously trying to bribe him.

"If I can make that bird squeal he'll be worth something," decided Tug, and began to crawl swiftly round the western side of the hut, the chatter from the assembling warriors on the square helping to cover the sound of his movements.

Lying flat, revolver in hand, he peered into the denser shadows of the hut. The only light was the faint glow of half-dead embers, and the stars visible through a window on the eastern side. Da Gomez was still pleading with the guard, which helped to distract the latter's attention, and served to locate both.

On second thought Tug pushed his revolver back into the holster. There must be no shooting; this was a job for hands. He crouched ready, hoping that da Gomez would become more excited, but instead he began to despair and his voice fell to a whimper. Just then came a flurry of chatter from the square and a woman called to another. Slipping inside, Tug inadvertently kicked a calabash.

He heard a guttural exclamation, but quite naturally the guard looked in the doorway for an intruder. He advanced until he stood against the stars, a tall lithe savage, the spear gleaming liquidly.

As tug rose cautiously the native ear detected the creak of clothes. Just as Tug's fist shot out, timed for a knockout on the jaw, he turned. The blow missed.

As the mouth opened and the spear arm drew back, Tug leaped and had him by the throat, turning the shout into a choked squawk, as simultaneously he kicked the man's legs from beneath him to prevent him from using the spear.

They crashed to the floor. Tug dared not let go of the fellow's windpipe; knew that his only chance was to throttle him. But the savage, oiled and painted, was wiry and powerful as a piece of oiled wire hawser.

At first he tried to stab with the spear, but fortunately he had grasped the haft too far up for such close-quarter work. Then dropping it, he used his hands, tearing at Tug's arms and at the same time struggling madly to get his knees under his opponent's belly. Once he almost succeeded and nearly threw Tug off.

The savage was making an infernal row with his nose, and Tug heard da Gomez cry out in the dialect, for in the darkness of the hut he could not have seen that the attacker was a white man.

"Shut up!" gasped Tug at him.

The efforts of the young warrior were getting appreciably weaker, and Tug dug in his thumbs with the strength of desperation. Suddenly the man stopped lacerating his bare arms and tore madly at his face, seeking his eyes, which Tug protected by pressing his face against the negro's oily wool. Beyond tearing out some hair and wounding his scalp, the man was too far gone now to do much damage; and as Tug increased the pressure again the body went limp. But Tug held on a few minutes more to make sure. Then, panting, bloody, and sweaty, he released the warrior.

By the protruding tongue and upturned eyes the savage seemed dead, but to take no risks Tug gagged him with a strip of his own loin cloth.

"Who are you?" whimpered da Gomez, who against the lesser darkness of the door had discovered him for a white man.

"I'm Tug Wilson of C Troop. You know me all right," Tug told him, going over to where the little man lay in the western corner.

"You came to rescue me?"

"Like hell I did!" growled Tug. "Now listen here. I'm going to ask questions. You're going to answer 'em, and if you start lying you'll stop where you are. Get me?"

"*Si, senhor*, but—"

"But nothing. I'm talking—and don't talk so darned loud. You've been running arms?"

"*Senhor*, I—"

"That's enough. I know."

"No, *senhor*, I—I nevaire bring guns into der country."

"I know you have. But how did you fix it?"

"I nevaire bring der guns, *senhor*. Dey go fetch 'em in der Portuguese country."

"I get you. You mean you've brought 'em as far as the border and these fellows have been slipping over in bunches and bringing 'em in themselves."

"*Si, senhor*, but I nevaire—"

"Never nothing! Anyway, it was a cute stunt. Since when has this been going on?"

"Only two years, *senhor*. I—"

"Only two years! Sacred snakes! They must have enough guns to fix an army corps. No wonder they're so fresh! Anyway that's that. Now, just what was the witch-doctor so sore about—what was it you can't get for him?"

"You heard."

"Sure I heard." Da Gomez was silent. "Now, quit trying to think up something. Was it anything to do with the magic killing stunt?"

"I no understan', *senhor*."

"Yes, you do. Now stir up that think-tank."

As the slightest jingle of beads caught his ears, Tug slipped across into the darker corner of the hut. Into the square beam of moonlight shining through the window entered Takini, the witch-doctor. His mind evidently intent upon the prisoner in the corner, he did not notice the corpse of the guard until he stepped on a hand.

He grunted and sank upon his haunches over the body. As Tug leaped, almost seeing the cry of alarm in the man's throat, his foot slipped upon some discarded food and he sprawled forward on his hands.

The witch-doctor jerked away his head just as Tug, lifting himself on one hand, thrust out the other to grasp the ancient's throat.

In that position, with his fingers within an inch of the wizard's neck, he was arrested by the glare of terror in the eyes revealed clearly by the bright African moonlight, and as he looked the witch-doctor gasped and toppled over—even as his victims had done.

VII

TUG WAS TOO AMAZED to move, simply staring at the huddled form of the witch-doctor. Dead he was as canned salmon.

As Tug, still incredulous, turned over the body it dawned upon him that his hand had been thrust out within an inch of the wrinkled chest as the witch-doctor had turned his head, which was exactly the same gesture that the wizard himself had used in the two murders.

There was no trickery about it, then? Was it magic or had the wizard slain by suggestion? Tug had heard of the lethal effect of suggestion used by witch-doctors the world over upon gullible brethren who, condemned by them with suitable flummery, would in nine cases out of ten obligingly die of sheer fright, much to the prestige of the craft. Yet the latter couldn't have been so, for although the black sergeant might conceivably have been susceptible it was utterly impossible that superstition or suggestion should have killed hard-headed Jock.

Yet how had it been done? Here within a few minutes he had killed the expert himself by nothing more than the repetition of the same gesture!

Again Tug gazed at the upturned face in the moonlight, the glassy eyes staring in terror, frozen by sudden death, scarcely able to believe his senses.

Outside the murmur of voices indicated that the *indaba* was still in progress. Why had the witch-doctor stolen back alone to see the prisoner?

"Eet ees magic, as I tell the *senhor*," came da Gomez's sibilant whisper.

In the intensity of the last few moments, Tug had forgotten the presence of the little Portuguese.

"Bosh!" retorted Tug. "He—he just died—heart disease, I guess. Anyway, he was old."

"Vot you do now, *senhor*?" Somehow da Gomez's voice seemed cheerful, as if a great anxiety had been lifted. "You make me loose, please?"

Tug hesitated, the back of his mind still occupied with the mystery.

"I think you'll do very well as you are until you get to Salisbury."

"Sal'sbury! You take me Sal'sbury?"

The first word was almost a scream of terror; the rest a savage sneer. He seemed suddenly to have realized Tug's object.

"Sure, my son, that's right where you're going along with Mr. Zuloki, too."

"How you take Zuloki?" demanded da Gomez.

"That's my business, I guess."

"S'pose I shout, yes?" threatened da Gomez.

"It'll be your last shout on this little earth."

Da Gomez remained silent, pondering.

"Hell, that was mighty careless of me," muttered Tug on a sudden, scratching himself, for the hut was infested with vermin. He stepped forward and dragged the two bodies onto the raised platform, which, covered with mats and blankets, formed the chief's bed. Then he stopped by the door and peeked out. From the square the continuous murmur of voices reassured him.

"*Senhor!*"

"Well?"

"Will make loose my arms, please? Dey hurt mooch and I cannot run way, *senhor*."

"That's so," agreed Tug. "No sense in torturing you, I guess."

He dragged the little man into the beam of moonlight. They surely had trussed him good and plenty. With a knife, Tug cut his arm bonds.

"Oooch!" exclaimed da Gomez gratefully. "Tank you, *senhor*!"

Slowly he began working his arms and shoulders propped up against the wall. A flurry of chatter without distracted Tug's attention. As he went back to the door da Gomez made a sudden sound like a curse in his own tongue. Tug sat down just within the threshold to watch. Once he turned his head to look at his prisoner. He hadn't attempted to move, and was pulling a hand stiffly out of an inside pocket.

"*Senhor!* Will you come, please?"

"What for?"

"I want to show you someting."

"Well, show it!"

"You no can see dere."

"Yes, I can."

"No, *senhor*, please!"

"What on earth is it?"

"I show you. Come!"

Tug watched him suspiciously. There was a peculiar excited eager look in the goggly eyes.

"That'll keep."

"No, no, *senhor*," persisted the little man. "*Senhor*, I do know how dat weetch-doctor he do magic kill."

"Oh you do, do you? Why didn't you find that out before?"

"I was frightened, *senhor*."

"Don't doubt it. But why can you now?"

" 'Cos I tink better tell all."

Tug eyed him.

"All right. You keep it for Salisbury."

He turned his head away to peek out again, thinking. What was the guy after, he wondered. Some treachery, surely. When the chief comes along he'll probably bawl and give me away; hoping to get his cattle back that way. Guess I'd better tie him up, and gag him as well.

Tug rose and strode over to the Portuguese.

"Vot you do?"

"Never mind what I'm going to do."

Just as Tug bent over him to pick up the native rawhide with which he had been bound, da Gomez's eyes shifted as a poor boxer's will, to the point of attack on his chest.

Thinking he had a knife, Tug struck swiftly with his open palm, a defensive chopping blow, simultaneously throwing his body sideways.

As his hand met da Gomez's, he saw a tiny flash in the moon rays. Something terribly powerful seemed to stab him within the nose and the throat.

He gasped; and his lungs seemed on fire.

VIII

TUG WAS AWARE OF A CURIOUS OBJECT shaped like a tombstone which towered before his eyes in the moonlight. Then he was conscious of a burning pain in the chest and that his mouth was as dry as a stone. For several moments he could not imagine what this strange object could be. Then driven by the terrible thirst he stirred—to find that he had been lying crumpled up on the floor and that the "tombstone" was one of da Gomez's boots.

A drink from the water bottle refreshed him and started his fuddled wits working. Da Gomez was still sitting propped against the wall, but with his head on one side. Tug thought he was dead until he detected faint, spasmodic efforts at breathing.

Picking up reality where he had been forced to drop it, Tug glanced toward the door, whence came still the reassuring chatter of the *indaba*.

What had happened? He recollected the same tiny flash which he had thought he had seen when Jock Crawford had been killed by the witch-doctor. He rose to his knees and peered at the semi-conscious Portuguese. One hand was lying palm up. On the tip of the index finger was a spot of blood, and as he looked something glittered—a tiny piece of glass embedded in the flesh.

Glass? Tug glanced at the floor. More splinters glittered, very thin, fragile glass, and among them was a globular fragment.

As he stared at them something of the truth dawned. The splinters on the floor and on da Gomez's finger were fragments of a glass capsule which had contained a very powerful volatile poison. By the chance of striking da Gomez's hand and simultaneously throwing his body aside, he had escaped the full force of the fumes; and da Gomez, too, must have only partially inhaled them.

Now he could see the whole trick. The hand was thrust forward to crush the fragile capsule directly beneath the victim's nose. Probably the operator at the time carefully held his own breath. This was what the witch-doctor had been so urgently demanding, and which da Gomez could not supply. As for the former's death, the knowledge of the deadly effects of the gesture from a white man's hand—which he might have mistaken for da Gomez's—had killed him by sheer fright.

In an access of fury at the contemptible deed, Tug furiously shook da Gomez's shoulder. The little man opened his eyes, gulped, made an inarticulate noise and grasped his throat.

"Here, you louse!" said Tug and thrust the water bottle at him.

He drank, grimacing painfully, and sighed.

"Now see here," continued Tug ferociously, "where did you get that darned dope from?"

Da Gomez, apparently still only half conscious, goggled at the fragment of capsule on Tug's finger.

"Speak quick or I'll blow your brains out now!"

"I—I make 'em," stuttered da Gomez.

"What is it? How?"

"Cyanide mercury. Make hot in tube. Catch gas," said da Gomez, with a certain pride as of a man speaking of his life work. "I no just soldier doctor. One time—Oporto—I am great doctor. Da Gomez not my name."

"I get you," said Tug slowly. "Guess you left your home town for your neighbor's health! What put you up to this trick?"

"Weetch-doctor he want something kill no man know how. But I no make for heem use for white—only for black man."

"And I guess he paid well?"

"He geef mooch cattle, yes. Why not? You tink I want stop his damn country all my life, *senhor*? I, great doctor? No."

"Well," returned Tug, "I kinder guess you're liable to now."

The goggle eyes stared at him and then slowly the shoulders shrugged.

"I make meestake, *senhor*," he said. "I haf lost."

Tug drank more water, for his lungs and throat felt as if they had been scorched. Just as he handed the bottle to the prisoner a low ululation came from a long distance off among the *kopjes*.

Tug started to his feet and ran to the door. The cry was a native warning, and now in high-pitched tenor the message was coming from *kopje* to *kopje*. The response in the village was immediate. Cries and shouts rang out from the square as the *indaba* broke up. Women were shouting and a general commotion began throughout the village. Zuloki's voice rang out in high penetrating tones of alarm, which told Tug that the police were surrounding the *kraal*.

Men were running in all directions to get their arms before the flight into the hills; for the Mashona are not given to stand-up fights, preferring a sudden rush, a swift massacre, and away. Tug was suddenly worried lest Zuloki might escape him by sending a warrior for his arms instead of coming himself. But just as Tug was hesitating whether to go gunning after the chief, he saw him racing with lithe strides for his compound.

"The police have the village surrounded," Tug told da Gomez. "If you cry out when the chief comes I'll plug you sure."

Then an idea struck him, and he grinned. Jerking the body of the dead witch-doctor from the chief's bed he stuck it full in the moonlight.

"There, that'll take the sand out of him!" he muttered.

Then Tug stood in the dark end of the hut. Ten seconds later entered the chief.

"*Ehh!*"

He had stopped in his tracks staring dumbfoundedly at the corpse of the witch-doctor.

Tug stepped out from the shadow, a revolver in each hand.

"I arrest thee, O Zuloki. Thy magic is dead!"

The youth turned startled eyes on the trooper.

"The magic of the white is stronger than thine," continued Tug impressively. "Thou art my prisoner. Sit thee beside the other."

As if the death of the magical taker of life had chased his wits away, Zuloki meekly obeyed, staring at the upturned glassy eyes of Takini, the witch-doctor.

GLOSSARY

aborigine: A member of the indigenous people of a region.

Afrikaans: The South African Dutch language.

Angoni: A warlike people who migrated from the **Natal** into the area of **British Central Africa**.

Alexander, Boyd (1873-1910): British Army officer who explored the Lake Chad area as part of a three-year expedition.

alluvial: Of loose soil formed by flowing water.

arsenic: A poisonous metallic element; used as a disease treatment before the introduction of antibiotics.

askari (Swahili): Soldier; armed guard.

assize: A court session.

auriferous: Containing gold.

Baal: The name of a god in some ancient Middle Eastern civilizations, including Phoenicia. Sometimes depicted as a bull.

B.S.A.P.: British South Africa Police.

Baganda: The people of Buganda, a kingdom on the northwest side of Lake Victoria.

Bantu: The predominant linguistic group of sub-Saharan Africa; includes **Swahili**.

bayete (Ndebele): Hail; a salutation for a king.

Berbers: Non-Arabic tribes common to northern Africa; formerly an ethnic group, now a linguistic group.

Black Watch: Native police.

black-water: Blackwater fever; a severe form of malaria characterized by kidney damage which results in dark red or black urine.

Boer War: Common name for The Second Boer War (1899-1902); conflict between the British Empire and the **Boers**.

Boer: A South African of Dutch extraction.

Boxer rising: The Boxer Rebellion; a Chinese nationalist uprising in 1900.

bwana (Swahili): Master; great man; a respectful form of address.

calabash: A gourd; a hollowed-out fruit used as a container.

charpoy: Bed frame.

cheroot: A cigar with square-cut, untapered ends.

da Gama, Vasco: 15th Century Portuguese explorer who established a sea route from Europe to India (1497-98).

darga: Mud.

De Beers: Company founded by **Cecil Rhodes** to mine the diamond deposits discovered at **Kimberley**, South Africa.

dekko (British slang): A look or glance.

Dinkas: Tall, pastoral people of Sudan.

donga (Zulu, Sindebele): An eroded ravine; a dry watercourse.

dop: Cape brandy.

doss-house: A cheap lodging house; flophouse.

Eckstein, Rhodes, Beit: **Cecil Rhodes** and others of the so-called Randlords who controlled the early years of diamond and gold mining in South Africa.

exogamy: The tradition of marrying outside the tribe.

Flamen Dialis: In ancient Rome, the high priest of Jupiter.

Galle Face: A luxury hotel in Colombo, **Ceylon**; built in 1864.

gneiss: A banded rock, similar to granite.

Great Zimbawbwe: A set of ruins in Southern **Rhodesia**; modern spelling: Zimbabwe.

heliograph: A device for sending telegraphic messages using reflected sunlight.

indaba (Nguni Bantu, South Africa): A native conference.

induna (Nguni Bantu, South Africa): Chief or general.

Inkosi (Sindebele): An address conveying honor, as for a king.

Jack in the Green: A participant in a May Day parade who wears a foliage covering.

ju-ju (West Africa): an object with supposed supernatural powers used as a charm.

Kaffir (Dutch): A black person; considered offensive.

katikiro (Swahili): King's minister.

Kavirondo: A people situated in British East Africa.

kier: Hut.

Kiswahili: **Swahili**.

Kitchener, Lord: Commander of the British forces during the **Boer War**.

Kohinoor: A large and legendary diamond discovered in India; now part of the British Crown Jewels.

koodoo: Kudu; an African antelope.

kopje (Afrikaans): A small hill rising up from the African *veld*.

kraal (Afrikaans): A native village; an enclosure for cattle.

kufa: Dead.

Livingstone, David (1813-1873): A Scottish missionary who explored the interior of Africa in the mid-19th Century.

machilla: A hammock carried by natives.

malaria: A disease, spread by insects, which causes chills, fever, and sweating; potentially fatal if not treated.

manzi muti: Medicine water.

Masai: A pastoral people of **British East Africa**.

Mashona Rebellion: Native uprising against the British in Southern **Rhodesia** (1896).

Matabele: An offshoot of the **Zulus**.

matakini: A flea of the tropics, also called a chigger, jigger, or chigoe, which embeds itself in the skin, especially of the feet.

Messageries: The Compagnie des Messageries Maritime; a French company whose liners linked the colonies.

Moabites: Inhabitants of ancient Moab, a region east of the dead sea in present-day

Jordan.

Moloch (Hebrew): The god Baal; the sacred bull.

mompara: Idiot.

Monomatapa: A 15th century kingdom in the vicinity of the Zambezi River.

Nandi: A pastoral people of **British East Africa**.

Ndebele: A Tribe of Southern **Rhodesia**.

pagazi (Swahili): Porters.

placer: **Alluvial** deposits containing valuable minerals.

quinine: A bitter alkaloid used in the treatment of **malaria**.

R.G.S.: Royal Geographical Society.

Rebellion of '96: **Mashona Rebellion**.

Rhodes, Cecil (1853-1902): British South African; co-founder of **De Beers** diamond mining; colonizer of **Rhodesia**.

rupoko: Millet seed.

Russo-Jap War: Armed conflict between Russia and Japan (1904-05).

safari (Swahili): An expedition for hunting or exploration.

shauri (Swahili): Consultation; deliberation.

shenzi (Swahili): Uncivilized; barbarous; uncouth.

shikari (Persian): A big-game hunter.

Sindebele: Language of the **Ndebele** people.

sjambok (Malay): A heavy whip; a common term in South Africa.

spruit (Afrikaans): A small stream.

sura: A section of the Koran.

suttee: The Hindu practice of a widow cremating herself on her husband's funeral pyre.

Swahili: A **Bantu** language spoken widely in East Africa.

syce: A stableman.

Tamil: A people of southern India and northern **Ceylon**.

terai: A wide-brimmed felt hat.

thimblerigger: A shell-game operator.

tiffin: A midday meal.

Tippoo Tib (1837-1905): Nickname of Hamed bin Muhammed el Murjebi, prominent Afro-Arab ivory and slave-trader who ruled the eastern Congo in the late 19th Century; variant spellings include Tippu Tip.

Turkana: A tribe of East Africa; nomadic herdsmen.

umlungu: White man.

veld (Afrikaans): The open country of southern Africa; grazing land.

vlei (Afrikaans): A shallow depression that collects water; wetland.

Wakikuyu: Belonging to the Kikuyu tribe of **British East Africa**.

Wanyamwezi: Belonging to the Nyamwezi tribe of **British East Africa**.

Wanderobo: Hunter-gatherers of **British East Africa**.

zareba: An enclosure of stakes protecting a campsite.
Zulu: A **Bantu**-people of South Africa, predominately **Natal**.

PLACE NAMES

Albert Lakes: Lake Albert and the other lakes of Africa's Great Lakes region.

Atlas Mountains: A system of ranges in northwest Africa.

Bangweulu: A lake in Northern **Rhodesia**; also spelled Bangweolo.

Barotse: A kingdom of central Africa; in the area of Northern **Rhodesia**.

Beira: An ocean city in central **Portuguese East Africa**.

Blantyre: A city of southern **Nyassa**.

British Central Africa Protectorate: The area of present-day Malawi from 1891-1907.

British East Africa: British territories covering Kenya, Uganda, and Tanganyika.

Bulawayo: A city of southwestern Southern **Rhodesia**.

Busoga: A kingdom on the north rim of Lake Victoria.

Ceylon: An island-nation off the southeastern tip of India; renamed Sri Lanka (1952).

Cochin: A coastal region of southwestern India; renamed Kochi (1996).

Colombo: The capital city of **Ceylon**.

Cuamba River: The **Zambezi River**.

Delagoa Bay: An inlet of the Indian Ocean in southern **Portuguese East Africa**.

Djibouti: A port city on the Gulf of Aden.

Durban: A major South African seaport on the Indian Ocean.

Elandsfontein Junction: A town in northeast South Africa; renamed Germiston (1903).

Eldama Rivine: An area northeast of Lake Victoria.

German East Africa: A German protectorate (1885-WWI) covering Tanganyika, Rwanda, and Burundi.

Inyadiri River: A river of northeastern **Rhodesia** between **Mrewa** and **Mutoko's**; also Nyadiri.

Inyanga: A town in eastern Southern **Rhodesia**; also Nyanga.

Johannesburg: A major city in South Africa.

Kalahari: A large desert in southwest Africa.

Kimberley: A South African city where a large deposit of diamonds were discovered.

Kisumu: A city on the northeast rim of Lake Victoria.

Lake Nyassa: A narrow lake, about 310 miles long, on the eastern borders of **German East Africa** and **Portuguese East Africa**.

Lurio River: A river in **Portuguese East Africa** that runs west-to-east, emptying into the Indian Ocean.

Manzini: A town in central **Swaziland**.

Mashonaland: A region in Southern **Rhodesia**.

Mombasa: Chief seaport of **British East Africa**.

Mount Elgon: An extinct volcano on the Kenya-Uganda border.

Mrewa: A town in northeastern Southern **Rhodesia**.

Mutoko: A town in northeastern Southern **Rhodesia**; also spelled Mtoko, or Mutoko's (for the Mashona king it's named for).

Nairobi: Capital city of **British East Africa**.

Natal: A province of South Africa; formerly a British colony.

nyassa: Lake; also spelled nyasa.

Nyassa: A British protectorate of southeast Africa. Nyasaland from 1907-64. Gained independence as Malawi (1964).

Oporto: A city in northwest Portugal.

Port Said: An Egyptian port at the north entrance to the Suez Canal.

Portuguese East Africa: Mozambique.

Portuguese West Africa: Angola.

Pretoria: A city of South Africa, capital since 1910.

Quilimane: A port city in **Portuguese East Africa**.

Rhodesia: British colony settled by **Cecil Rhodes**. The area formerly consisted of Southern Rhodesia (renamed Zimbabwe, 1980) and Northern Rhodesia (renamed Zambia, 1964).

Ruenya River: A river in northeastern Southern **Rhodesia**.

Salisbury: Capital city of Southern **Rhodesia**. Renamed Harare (1982).

Shire River: A river in **Nyassa** and **Portuguese East Africa**.

Sofala: Major port in **Portuguese East Africa**.

Swaziland: A landlocked country within South Africa.

Tete: A city in northern **Portuguese East Africa**.

Ujiji: A town in **German East Africa** on the shores of Lake Tanganyika.

Umtali: A city in Southern **Rhodesia**; renamed Mutare (1982).

Vaal: Transvaal, a region of northeast South Africa.

Zambezi River: A long river originating in **Portuguese West Africa** and emptying into the Indian Ocean in **Portuguese East Africa**; also called the **Cuamba River**.

Zanzibar: Zanzibar Island, a British protectorate off the coast of **German East Africa**.

OFF-TRAIL PUBLICATIONS
Specializing in the era of American pulp fiction

THE WEIRD DETECTIVE ADVENTURES OF WADE HAMMOND
By Paul Chadwick
Volume 1: 10 stories, 180 pages, $18
Volume 2: 10 stories, 172 pages, $18
Volume 3: 10 stories, 202 pages, $18
Volume 4: 9 stories, 232 pages, $18

> *The Wade Hammond stories complete in four volumes. In these chilling adventures, all from the classic 1930's pulps,* Detective-Dragnet *and* Ten Detective Aces, *freelance investigator Wade Hammond battles a series of weird enemies. Some of the best of '30s pulp fiction.*

DOCTOR COFFIN: The Living Dead Man
By Perley Poore Sheehan • Introduction by John Wooley
8 novelettes, 178 pages, $16

> *Weird stories from* Thrilling Detective, *1932-33. A former character actor who faked his own death, Doctor Coffin runs a string of mortuaries by night and fights crime at night. One of the strangest detective series.*

SUPER-DETECTIVE FLIP BOOK: Two Complete Novels
From the pulp *Super-Detective*:
"Legion of Robots" (November 1940) by Victor Rousseau • Introduction by John McMahan •• "Murder's Migrants" (March 1943) by Robert Leslie Bellem and W.T. Ballard • Introduction by John Wooley
2 short novels, 174 pages, $18

> Super-Detective *started as a Doc Savage-like adventure pulp, then changed format to hardboiled detective. The* Flip Book *features a novel from each of the two phases with intros exploring the historical background. Exciting!*

PULPWOOD DAYS: Volume 1: Editors You Want To Know
Edited by John Locke • 180 pages, $16

*Numerous articles from the writers' magazines by and about pulp editors, with ample biographical profiles. Editors include: Frank E. Blackwell (*Detective Story, Western Story*), Ray Palmer (*Amazing Stories, Fantastic Adventures*), Edwin Baird (*Weird Tales, Detective Tales*), and many more.*

GANG PULP
Edited by John Locke • 19 stories, 294 pages, $24

Hardboiled stories of the criminal underworld from the first year (1929-30) of the gang pulps: Gangster Stories, Racketeer Stories, *etc. These violent tales came under immediate censorship pressure; the history is explored in an in-depth essay. "A remarkable work of popular-culture scholarship"—*MYSTERY SCENE, *Fall 2008.*

THE GANGLAND SAGAS OF BIG NOSE SERRANO
Volume 1: Dames, Dice and the Devil
Volume 2: Horses, Hoboes and Heroes
Volume 3: Hell's Gangster
By Anatole Feldman • Introductions by Will Murray
Each: 4 novels • **Volumes 1-2**: 266 pages, $20 • **Volume 3**: 224 pages, $18

The complete Big Nose Serrano novels from Gangster Stories, Greater Gangster Stories, *and* The Gang Magazine, *1930-35. Feldman was the best of the gang pulp authors, and Big Nose was his most inspired creation, the berserking king of Chicago gangsters.*

CITY OF NUMBERED MEN: The Best of Prison Stories
Introduction by John Locke
12 stories, 278 pages, $20

> *During Prohibition, famed publisher Harold Hersey turned America's
> disintegrating prison system into the hardboiled* Prison Stories *(1930-
> 31). Included are stories from all six issues of this ultra-rare pulp, the
> startling history of* Prison Stories, *complete cover gallery, and "Har-
> old Hersey: Tales of an Ink-Stained Wretch," the first comprehensive
> biography of pulp publishing's most colorful character.*

THE MAGICIAN DETECTIVE: And Other Weird Mysteries
By Fulton Oursler
Introduction by John Locke
7 stories, 210 pages, $18

> *Fulton Oursler was one of the great editors of his time, ruling over the
> Macfadden publishing empire for two decades. But stage magic was
> his first love, and, in his heart, he remained a conjurer in a black cape
> and top hat. In this collection of early fiction, Oursler's bewitching
> imagination takes flight in tales of magic, murder and mesmerizing
> mystery. Also featured is an in-depth exploration of the astonishing
> career of Fulton Oursler.*

GHOST STORIES: The Magazine and Its Makers
Edited by John Locke
Vol 1: 19 stories, 256 pages, $24 • **Vol 2**: 15 stories, 272 pages, $24

> *Macfadden's* Ghost Stories *(1926-31) presented haunted tales in every
> exciting arena: the Western Front, gangland, aviation, the Klondike,
> the circus, etc. The personnel behind* Ghost Stories *were a fascinating
> group: poets and scholars, war heroes and war correspondents,
> adventurers and Bohemians; a few became prolific pulpsters; a
> few became bestselling authors. And a few led haunted lives. Vol 1
> includes the history of* Ghost Stories, *bios of every editor, and every
> Vol 1 author. Vol 2 includes bios of every Vol 2 author, every cover
> artist, and a gallery of all 64* Ghost Stories *covers.*

www.ingramcontent.com/pod-product-compliance
Lightning Source LLC
Chambersburg PA
CBHW030409020726
47493CB00003B/997